M. Charles de Mazade

The Life of Count Cavour

M. Charles de Mazade

The Life of Count Cavour

ISBN/EAN: 9783337419240

Printed in Europe, USA, Canada, Australia, Japan

Cover: Foto ©Raphael Reischuk / pixelio.de

More available books at **www.hansebooks.com**

THE
LIFE OF COUNT CAVOUR.

FROM THE FRENCH

OF

M. CHARLES DE MAZADE.

London:

CHAPMAN & HALL, 193, PICCADILLY.

1877.

PREFACE.

THIS book is composed of the public records of a memorable history, together with less known documents, which I owe to treasured private communications and some personal knowledge of the facts. It is devoted to a man who will ever be ranked as one of the rarest of human kind; for in him there was the union of strength, suavity, passion, suppleness, boldness, and prudence, and he succeeded in all that he undertook.

It may be said with truth that Count Cavour was among the most illustrious of the favourites of fortune in our century. He was not one of those chance favourites whom a happy accident, interest at court, or the winning of popularity, launches to a fleeting renown; but he was of the few that, being privileged to deserve success by the exercise of a consummate skill, leave their names inscribed upon imperishable works.

His mission was fulfilled within the space of ten years— less than the cycle of Tacitus. These ten years sufficed for him to realise a dream of nationality that seemed beyond realisation, and more particularly at the beginning of his parliamentary life; to raise up his country, and to become himself the greatest of Italians, among the foremost of the political men of all time, European in influence, glory, and genius.

It would be writing with levity to say that he was happy, even in his premature end, in escaping, as he did, through an opportune and sudden death, the perplexities of his task. If ever there was a man who needed not to fear to live, and who knew how to precombine and prearrange all for the attainment of a special object, and then to assure his success by guarding himself against the reverses of fortune and the risk of unforeseen events, it was he. Better than any other he knew the right moment when to adventure and to stop, so as always to remain master of the crisis he brought to a head or unwound so daringly, in which none but he was able to preserve a perfect serenity of mind.

Those who knew him, who were mixed up with his labours—and there is one among them, M. Nigra, whose name friendship permits me to write beside that of his first instructor in public affairs—have not forgotten the ready resource, the simple ease, the correctness of judgment in midst of the gravest situations and the keenest contests, displayed by Cavour. He overcame everything. He had arrived at that point when he no longer feared to be unequal to the final trials; he felt

sure of completing that which he had begun, and more ;
for since his death Italy has been sustained by his breath,
and whatever has been done, has only been the completion of projects left behind by him, and animating
his mind up to his last moments.

There is in the life of such a man a profound attraction for those who love the spectacle of a nature marvellously gifted to grapple with events.   It has, moreover, at the present time, almost a direct and practical
interest ; for, apart from the lively remembrance I have
retained of Count Cavour, I must confess that one of my
objects, when I wrote this book in the *Revue des Deux
Mondes,* arose from a desire to bring before those who
may stand in need of the example, this striking image of
a man who knew how to be a great Liberal as well as a
downright head of the Government.   It is what I would
term the moral lesson of this work.   If the aforesaid
moral is made sufficiently prominent, it may not perhaps
be inopportune at a time when, if care be not taken,
party spirit will disturb and confound everything, from
the simplest ideas of Liberalism to the most elementary
conditions of Government.

The signal superiority of Count Cavour consists in
his having been a real Liberal, in the strongest and
fullest acceptation of the word.   The liberty in which he
believed, both from instinct and reason, was to him no
empty formula, nor was it an engine of destruction, or an
implement of war against the Church or the State ; it

was a regular system of public guarantees, impartially
applied and patiently worked out, as free from subterfuge as from violence.   In the working of institutions,
even in the boldest undertakings, he carried a mind free
alike from revolutionary prejudice and timid scruples.
Confidence was a part of his nature, and, granting
whatsoever was due to liberty, he was still, and above all,
the man made to govern.   Let me explain.

Premier of a parliamentary State, he was compelled
to secure to himself a majority ; he required it, for
he understood that, to use his own expression, " there
is no governing on needles' points ; " but the majority
he needed was 'of his creating ; he knew how to direct
and guide it ; he did not abandon it to its own inexperience, its doubts and phantasies ; he thought for it,
and at the right moment ; he did not shrink from the
responsibility of taking a desperate initiative.   When he
debated within himself on the advisability of an alliance
with France and England in the Crimea ; when he ven-
tured to propose to his little Piedmont such works as
economical reform, or the boring of a tunnel through
Mont Cenis, he proved that he had no intention of
allowing the reins of Government to slacken and grow
weak in his grasp.   However deferential his attitude
before public opinion and the Chambers, he knew how to
outshoot and make a way for them.

I admit that he leaned upon a solid and popular
monarchy, and in this he gathered strength ; he was

supported by a king who was a pattern of patriotic and constitutional sovereignty; he was assisted by fellow-workers, such as La Marmora, in the reconstruction of an army. But it was Cavour who obtained the money wherewith to do it, as well as the opportunities of making use of it; adding to the fecundity of his contrivances and the certainty of his combinations an indomitable power in willing and executing. Had he awaited the good pleasure of parties in all his resolutions, he would have waited long; and on more than one occasion he ran great risks, in concert with La Marmora, to carry out military undertakings which have subsequently been the saving of Piedmont in the hour of danger. He did not hesitate to pledge himself, convinced that the affairs of a nation were only placed in his hands for guidance and judicious direction, even under a parliamentary *régime*; and thus he knew how to unite in the fullest measure the spirit of government with the spirit of Liberalism; thus it was that he was more than an eminent man in power, he was a living and working policy, and, after having recast a little country, he created a new nation.

Another name, that of one who may take rank as a competitor in the arena of political conflicts, naturally rises to the mind at the present time. It is now difficult to speak of Count Cavour without being reminded of the Prussian minister who has been enabled to perform in Germany what the Piedmontese minister achieved in Italy. Events are interlinked ; men follow but do not always resemble one another. I have no desire to undervalue the German chancellor ; coming from a Frenchman this would be childish and unworthy. In Prince Bismarck we have good reason to see an enemy, and we do not combat him with idle disparagements. All we can say is, that if Count Cavour and Prince Bismarck appear to have a similar fortune, at least till now, in analogous undertakings, they differ in genius, character, and mode of proceeding, as widely as Italy differs from Germany.

Several private letters written by Prince Bismarck in the course of his career have been published within the last few years ; and they unveil a strangely complex nature ; they reveal the whole man. A man assuredly of powerful originality, impetuous, crabbed, abrupt, and familiar ; of feudal stamp, a Teuton by temperament and education ; mixing confidential communications as to his capacities as a drinker, and the effects of moonlight on the banks of the Rhine, with visions of grandeur and power ; a Mephistophelean politician and diplomatist, despising diplomatic and parliamentary formulas ; impatient for action at all cost, *ferro et igne*, and defining himself with the air of a ruffled giant, from a heap of violent contradictions, in his disturbing and discomposed figure of conqueror.

That is not the portrait of Count Cavour, whom his contemporaries knew and saw at his work. Doubtless,

Prince Bismarck is a great German. Count Cavour was rather, and in the broad humane sense, a great man. He, too, had strength of will and genius, but with perfect cordiality and a very taking charm. Prince Bismarck began by showing himself independent of his parliament, and even in some degree ridiculing it; he provoked the conflict and defied " rebellious " majorities; and if he ended in overruling the Chambers, it was by making his power and success a necessity to his country. Count Cavour worked always with the aid of public opinion and of parliament on his side. What he had been aided by liberty in accomplishing, he leaned on liberty to consolidate, with no despotic impatience, no persecution of beliefs.

And, furthermore, if Prince Bismarck has been a German Cavour, it cannot be said that Cavour was ever an Italian Bismarck. The Piedmontese minister copied no model; he was the first on this field; and what makes his greatness is, that in an unprecedented enterprise, even in success, he has left behind him an example of forethought, judgment, and moderation worthy to be studied universally where politics is still a business.

Had Cavour been solely a great Italian, he would by right have belonged to his fellow-countrymen; and who has better revived his image than my excellent friend Massari, writing with tender fidelity and veneration his volume of recollections, *Il conte di Cavour, Ricordi* *biografici?* *   Such as he was, Cavour belongs not only to Italy, but to the world; and it has struck me that in writing this great life, in showing how a man was able to raise up a fallen nation by genius and policy, it would be a work of service to the conquered, and not without a lesson for the conquerors.

March 2, 1877.

---

* Count Cavour has been the subject of much literary work, both in and out of Italy. It is my duty to mention, besides the substantial literary study by S. Massari, the attractive work by M. de la Rive: *Le Comte de Cavour, récits et souvenirs*, and a very interesting preface, with which S. Artom has headed a collection of Cavour's principal speeches, translated into French. It is, however, only an abridgment of the large collection of *Cavour's Speeches* (12 vols.), published by order of the Chamber of Deputies. I should also mention the *Historia documentata della diplomazia europea in Italia*, by S. Nicomede Bianchi, now in the Record Office at Turin, as being instructive as to contemporaneous history. Many other works might be cited.

CONTENTS.

CHAPTER III.

PARLIAMENTARY REIGN OF CAVOUR—PREPARATIONS FOR WAR.

CHAPTER IV.

THE WAR OF 1859—CAVOUR AND THE PEACE OF VILLAFRANCA.

CHAPTER V.

The Italian Crisis after Villafranca—Cavour and the Cession of Savoy.

PAGE

CHAPTER VI.

Cavour and the Unity of Italy—Rome and Naples.

CHAPTER VII.

The Final Victory of a Policy—Death and Legacy of Cavour.

LIFE OF COUNT CAVOUR.

CHAPTER I.

THE YOUTH OF CAVOUR—PIEDMONT AND ITALY AFTER THE DEFEAT.

A Liberal Conservative—Origin and Antecedents of Cavour—His Family—
His Education and Military Life—A young Piedmontese *Citoyen*—
Agricultor's Life at Leri—Journeys in Switzerland, in France, and in
England—Piedmont and Italy under Charles Albert—Cavour's first
political Ideas—Events preliminary to 1848—Cavour a Journalist—The
constitutional Order of Things at Turin—First War in Lombardy—
Revolutionary Agitations—Battle of Novara—Piedmont after the Defeat—
Communism at Genoa—D'Azeglio's Ministry and the Conclusion of Peace—
The *Standard* and Liberal Institutions—The Beginning of Retribution—
Cavour in Parliament and in the Ministry—Piedmont and the 2nd of
December—The Two Policies—The *Connubio*—Political Development of
Cavour.

I.

ONE of the most extraordinary revolutions of the century has made Italy a constituted nation, and has raised her on a level with the Powers of the world. This can hardly be called a resurrection; Italy, seeing her as she has emerged from contemporary events, in no way resembles what she has ever been before; the sky illumining her, the seas into which she dips on every side, and the many traditions of those twenty brilliant cities which are now joined together in national unity— these are all that she has in common with the past. Modern Italy is a new creation; a work prepared by history, no doubt, but one also which is the combined result of policy, of circumstances, high daring, and profound astuteness.

Now that this work is completed, we regard it as natural and simple; it has become so intimately allied with the general order of things, that we can hardly imagine the successive reactions and upheavings which would be required to destroy it. Only five-and-twenty years ago it seemed an impossibility, so many conditions and events did it presuppose that could not even be reasonably conceived as realisable.

To establish it as a reality, the agents have been European revolutions, changes in the balance of power and of national equilibrium, and wars unexpected, though sagaciously planned; these, together with diplomatic dramas, the disappearance of local sovereignties, and a complete transformation of that which struck the mind as the most immovable of institutions—the temporal power of the Pope. It needed, too, that there should be at the foot of the Alps a small but disciplined and devoted people, of exemplary courage, and at the head of these people a prince made popular by his patriotic sentiments, it may be by an ambition in his blood; and in the councils of this prince and this people, one of those great ministers, who seem to have been created for the most complicated as well as the most perilous of enterprises.

To enter upon a public career at so critical a period, as 1848, and boldly to take in hand the affairs of his country immediately after a national disaster, which threatened to be for a long time irremediable; and in a condition of internal revolution full of uncertainty, to go through all the difficulties of reorganisation amidst the shiftings of European policy, without wavering or a moment's deviation in making everything concur in one aim; to conspire openly for ten years—in the noblest of causes it is true, but in one the triumph of which could realise itself only at the cost of almost impossible changes; and to succeed in gathering to his side alliances and sympathies, I might almost say the force of facts; then suddenly to disappear when the work has reached a point where the past appears as a dream—such was the destiny of Count Cavour.

What Italy would have been without him—what she would still be—one can no longer conceive; it is through him that she has become what she now is; she has become developed, disciplined, and concrete in despite of all her divisions; Italy has become a new power, and she has found in that little Piedmont the frame-work ready-made of a living nationality; and this work of energy, perseverance, suppleness, and profound combinations, is one of the most complete and instructive lessons in the art of governing.

It teaches how a country, overwhelmed by defeat, can be raised again, and how a parliamentary system and established liberty may contribute to carry out a national idea; it shows us how this policy, patiently and strenuously followed under a patriotic inspiration, can frustrate those fatal concurrencies of reaction and revolution which endanger the justest of causes. And, finally, it demonstrates what a Liberal Conservative is, who tempers his genius to identify himself with his country and his time ;—supple in turning all to his purposes, even his adversaries or the unforeseen, while concealing the depth of his calculations under the most equable air ;—knowing how to prepare and command events by the power of a penetrating and unerring reason, and by a constantly inventive boldness in the execution of new and ever-enlarging designs.

One day, towards the autumn of 1850, on the eve of entering for the first time into office as a simple Minister of Commerce, journeying through the provinces of Piedmont, Cavour stopped at Stresa, on the borders of Lago Maggiore, at the house of Rosmini the philosopher, where he met Manzoni. These eminent men conversed on the future destiny of Italy from the top of the villa Bolongaro, keeping their eyes fixed upon the opposite shore, which was then, and seemed likely long to remain, a part of the Austrian dominions. Manzoni, in the simplicity of his soul, did not cease to hope ; Rosmini smiled sadly at this poet's dreams, but Cavour rubbed his hands—it was even at that time a peculiar habit with him—and repeated with persuasive liveliness : " We will do something."

The man who thus lightly disposed of the future was still young and full of life, having lately tried his maiden steel in the revolutionary turmoil of 1848—one who carried with him into the whirlwind of public affairs a clear mind, great strength of will, the most liberal of natures, and a disposition every way fitted for action. He was not a revolutionist meditating the renewal of conspiracies when he spoke of "doing something;" he was, on the contrary, the man of all men the most politic, having in him at once the solidity of the old Piedmontese race without any of its prejudices; and he had, moreover, the patriotic and liberal sap of the later generations, without having ever been a conspirator.

His good fortune consisted in his coming at the right moment, and being prepared by his birth and his education, as well as by his temperament, to meet the chances which might befall him. He was born at Turin, on August 1, 1810, in one of those periods when indeed no one would have said or thought that he who had then received breath would one day, for the benefit of princes then discrowned or banished, revive that name of Italy, with which the whimsical caprice of a glorious despot embroidered a fiction of nationality. He was the second son of the Marquis Michael Benso di Cavour, the last of one of those ancient Piedmontese houses issuing from the little republic of Chieri, called the Republic of the SEVEN B's, because of seven families having lived there which had all made their way in the world: the Bensi, the Balbi, the Balbiani, the Biscaretti, the Buschetti, the Bertoni, the Broglie, destined to figure in another land.* By his paternal grandfather Camillo Cavour was

---

* I recall, as a further characteristic trait of those who love to follow out the genealogies, that the first founder of the house appears to be a personage of the name of Hubert, who comes from Saxony with Frederic Barbarossa. This Hubert, on his return from a pilgrimage to the Holy Land, espouses, at Chieri, the heiress of the Bensi, of whom he takes the name, and at the same time he obtains several fiefs, amongst which is the estate of Santena, where now the last descendant of the race reposes. The title of Marquis of Cavour

linked with Savoy and the amiable race of St. François de Sales; Geneva claimed him on his mother's side, a de Sellon; and he was drawn to France by many relations—by the two sisters of his mother, who were married, one to the Duc de Clermont-Tonnerre, a personage of distinction at the court of the Restoration, the other to the Baron d'Auzers, a gentleman of Auvergne, who, after having been a functionary of the empire beyond the Alps, settled at Turin.

It was in this varied, though very united, social centre, which often met either at Turin or at Geneva, and in this wholesome and strengthening atmosphere, that Camillo Cavour was bred and born: as a child, robust, enjoying his life, sparkling, and bringing happiness to all about him; a young man of a most liberal spirit, prompt and open, with a mind seizing and understanding everything.

Cavour was among the youngest of a generation that, after the Restoration of 1815, and when still oppressed by prolonged reactions, began, in the heavy

dates only from the last century; it was given by King Charles Emmanuel III., in recompense for military services to Michael Antonio Benso, lord of Santena, and lieutenant-general. The Castle of Cavour, situated on the summit of a rock, in the province of Pignerol, is no more than a ruin since Catinat destroyed it in 1691. One day Cavour was asked how it chanced that his armorial bearings were headed by a German motto, "Gott will Recht." "It is supposed," answered he, "that my family originated in Saxony, and that a pilgrim of my name came to Piedmont in 1080. Hence the shells that you see in my coat-of-arms, and the motto which ornaments them. Do you believe this?"—"No." "Neither do I;" and he burst into laughter. Cavour always entertained the broadest and most liberal notions in all that pertains to titles, external dignities, honorary distinctions, but without using any affectation, or ever condescending to flatter base democratic instincts. He was naturally familiar and simple; with his good-humoured frankness he possessed also a well-bred ease, and a sense of personal dignity, which it was well not to offend.

darkness of absolutist reigns, to ripen for the ultimate freedom of Italy.

In 1815, when the tragic warfare which swept away the French Empire had made Piedmont independent, he was only five years of age. At the age of ten he was admitted to the Military Academy, the school of the young nobility, and soon obtained the position of page in the household of the Prince di Carignano—the future Charles Albert—where at once the impetuous vivacity of his natural temper burst out in revolt against this gilded servitude.

At eighteen he was the most brilliant and amiable of sub-lieutenants of engineers, leading a light-minded soldier's life at Vintimille, Turin, and Genoa—especially at Genoa, in which he found the freedom and the attractions of a city of business and pleasure.

In his twenty-second year he had already sent in his resignation, after having undergone the disgrace of a sort of exile at a small station in the Alps, for having uttered a few risky words, which were merely a cry of generous emotion and sympathy, hailing the French Revolution of 1830.

Reduced, for his sole pastime, to play at *tarok* with the contractors for the building of the fort of Bard, his place of exile, and menaced with being always suspected at headquarters, he had resigned himself to be no more than an " obscure citizen of Piedmont," as he termed himself, a son of good family stopped on the threshold of a brilliant career. But this " obscure citizen of Piedmont," this young man whom a breath of liberty come from France had set quivering—this retired officer of twenty-two—was of the order of those who reach the goal by all roads, and who do not allow themselves to be discouraged, or even irritated, by a misunderstanding or a disgrace.

Thus exiled from a soldier's life, on the morrow he was brisk and resolute; he combined the study of agricultural affairs with the enjoyment of the pleasures of the world and a course of travel, taking with him into this larger sphere an inexhaustible store of activity, together with those precociously fixed ideas of liberty and patriotism which gave rise to his utterance that "in his youthful dreams he already saw himself Prime Minister of the Kingdom of Italy;" which also made him write to his aunt, Madame de Sellon, after the "decisive step" of his resignation: "Do not imagine that all I have suffered—morally, be it understood—has in any way abated my love for the views which I previously entertained. These ideas form a part of my existence. I shall profess, teach, and uphold them as long as I have a breath of life." Already we see the whole man in the resigning officer of 1832, and in the rebellious youth of the beginning of the reign—that of Charles Albert—a reign destined to conclude with a national explosion, but which for the moment remained under the hand of Austria and the Jesuits.

II.

Three things contributed to the development and expansion of this happy nature, while giving it the impress of originality. It is evident that Cavour always felt the influence of the family life which had been his first education. He gathered from it that which forms the man and the character. He had become morally developed in a centre where habits of affection and companionship tempered all differences in political and even in religious views ; for if in Turin that society of the Cavours, Auzers, Clermont-Tonnerres was profoundly attached to traditions of supremacy, both religious and monarchical, at Geneva, the Comte de Sellon, a Protestant and a Liberal, kept faithful allegiance to all that was lofty in the ideas of the eighteenth century, and of the French Revolution.

Divided between these family influences, Camillo Cavour was able to reconcile them in his liberal nature. With his uncle, M. de Sellon, he suffered himself to succumb to the fascination of new ideas. With Baron d'Auzers, an Absolutist by conviction, but a man of good intelligence and of agreeable company, who liked discussion even with young men, his mind was sharpened. At that school of maternal grace, when with Madame d'Auzers, who had the quick, lively, and animated nature of her nephew, and with Madame de Clermont-Tonnerre, a woman of extreme Royalist notions, but of the most perfect charity, he had imbibed a beautiful amenity and a love of tolerance, together with an easy dignity, mixed perhaps with pride, which sometimes made itself felt through all his familiar heartiness.

Let no one be deceived : with the most liberal opinions on the rights and claims of birth, Cavour was never a renegade aristocrat, denouncing the traditions of race or the spirit and customs of his family. At the highest elevation of his political fortune he was and remained the same. In the "house of the Cavours," which he did not cease to inhabit, even when he was Minister, and which was the patrimonial mansion, his eldest brother held the highest place ; and it chanced only a short time before his death, that as one day he was travelling by train a few miles from Turin, Cavour looked out on the flying landscape, and said to a fellow-traveller : "Do you see that spire half hidden among the trees ? it is the spire of the Church of Santena. There is the hereditary château of my family ; it is there that I wish to rest after my death !" Thus, before he disappeared, with the pride of a great name, he wished to give testimony to the surviving power of those first impressions which had contributed to his moral development when young.

Another perceptible influence in this supple and vigorous organisation, was the almost exclusively scientific education of the Military Academy. Indeed Cavour had but little literary instruction. "In my youth," he used to say, "I was never taught to write ; I never had a professor of rhetoric, nor even of the humanities." At times, during his active life, he has indulged in a sort of coquettish ignorance, pretending that he neither knew Latin nor Greek, and he maintained lightly that to him it "was easier to make Italy than to make a sonnet." He had supplied that which was wanting, by the determination or the curiosity of a mind which knew how to take an interest in everything, even in a new novel ; and he boldly set to work to learn English, in the history of Lord Mahon.

His intelligence was disciplined and shaped on the mathematics, which he had successfully studied at the Military Academy, under the able geometrician, Giovanni Plana : "That is what builds a head and teaches you to think. From the study of triangles and algebraic propositions, I passed to those of men and things; and now I know how useful this study has been to me, by what I am able to do with things and men." He believed himself to owe to this primary teaching the faculty " of keeping in his head a long series of theorems and corollaries which always maintained their order of battle." It is indubitable that the study of mathematics developed in him a disposition to preciseness, clearness, and exactitude ; it had given him an amazing aptitude to play with figures and calculations.

It is possible that he threw a certain amount of whim and some slight degree of affectation even into this, as he did in his pretended literary ignorance. The truth is, that the study of mathematics would not have sufficed, if this spirit of his, which all things contributed to strengthen, had not at the same time been impregnated by influences powerful in quite other ways—by experience, by his travels, by his manifold studies, and by real practical life in all its forms.

III.

The life of the real world was one of the great teachers of Cavour. Immediately upon his resignation as officer of engineers, he did not hesitate an instant ; a soldier one day, on the morrow he became a sort of steward of the much-neglected family estates.

Soldier and farmer, these, without his knowing it, were the two most instructive of the schools of politics. Agriculture had the advantage of being the only possible occupation under a government that saw revolutionary perils even in the pursuits of industry. Cavour gave himself up to agricultural life, not in distaste, nor for a pastime, but with the fire of an impatient activity; with the spirit and the resources of a nature not inclined, according to his own expression, to do things by halves, taking an increasing interest in everything about him. "I have embarked," he wrote to his friends in Geneva, "in great speculations; I have purchased a large estate among the rice-fields. I think I have done a very good stroke of business. All I am in want of is the money to pay for it; that settled, I shall make a splendid profit by it. I cannot do things by halves. Once embarked in business, I give myself up to it altogether—for that matter, my situation compels me to it. I am a younger son, which says a good deal in an aristocratically-constituted country. I must carve myself a way by the sweat of my brow." This large estate of which he speaks is Leri, created and transformed by Cavour in the middle of the Vercelli district—that Leri where he so often went to seek twenty-four hours' rest in the midst of the most absorbing affairs.

It was there, in this sufficiently monotonous district of Vercelli, in a plain covered with rice-fields and bare open meadows, that Camillo Cavour lived for years, syndic of his village, and farmer; himself directing all the details of a vast system of cultivation, seeking aid in the discoveries of science, introducing new measures and machines, thus converting a dilapidated estate into a model property. It was his work, his conquest—a prelude to many other conquests; and in proportion as success smiled on his intrepidity, he did not fear to extend his operations. He had in him activity for everything; to make a clearing of a forest, as well as to make a canal or a bank; to cultivate beetroot, as well as to establish a sugar manufactory, or a manufactory of chemical productions. One day he undertook to furnish eight hundred merino sheep for the Pasha of Egypt, and he kept his engagement, although at first he was rather put about to do so.

Assuredly this well-occupied and active life, in the midst of which he could offer his friends the free and joyous hospitality, not of a luxurious mansion, but of a well-to-do farm, was fertile for Cavour. To this he owed much of what made his peculiar originality, and his weight in politics, his familiar experience of things and men, his practical acquaintance with all special interests, and his ability and judgment in the management of the springs of a country's wealth. And withal he was the man of all others the least absorbed even when the most occupied, and while appearing to be entirely given up to his works of cultivation, he never ceased to be one among the foremost in the gay life of the world.

When he was not leading his country life he was at Turin, enlivening with his inexhaustible verve the salon of his aunt, the Duchess of Clermont-Tonnerre, or delighting and instructing himself in the shrewd, sensible, and liberal conversation of the Ambassador of

France, M. de Barante, and of his secretary, M. de Haussonville. When the air of Turin weighed on him, he went to Geneva, where he found himself near his uncle, in that cordial and intelligent society of the La Rives, the Navilles, the Lullin de Chateauvieux, amongst whom he passed evenings that he recalls, launching epigrams on the affairs of Europe, reconstructing false systems, recomposing bad ministries—in fine, arranging everything for the very best. When he ceased to feel at home at Geneva, he departed for Paris and London, the two great theatres of the world. Twice, in 1835 and in 1843, he visited France and England, as a traveller who did not lose his time.

The institutions, the parliamentary struggles, the development of national, agricultural, and industrial forces in England interested him vividly ; everything— politics and social life—attracted him in France. Welcomed for his name, his intelligence, and his cordiality in the principal salons, he fell under their charm ; it is possible that other seductions also carried him away. Well, he was in the spring-tide of his youth, fond of pleasure, priding himself little upon being a sage, and bold at the green-table, as in everything he did ; in good company not shrinking from a rubber at whist, at twenty-five louis the trick. But these wild bursts of youth did not prevent him from being an attentive observer, with a taste for serious things, above all from being impressionable to the fine and elevated charm of Parisian life ; and he wrote pleasantly from London to Madame de Circourt, with whom he was constantly in correspondence : "England is a country of enormous

resources; but what you look for in vain there is that
admirable union of science and intelligence, depth and
graciousness, of the inner and the outer, in perfection,
which is the charm of certain Parisian salons; a charm
that we regret all through life when once we have tasted
it, and that is not to be found again when we have been
removed from this intellectual oasis;" and, casting an
eye on his own country, he added: "Under certain
particulars the air of Piedmont is heavier than that of
London; the sky is pure, but the moral horizon so
obscured by the clouds developed by an intensely com-
pressing system, that the mind there has still less
elasticity than in England."

In default of elasticity, England, without doubt,
possessed merits appreciated by Cavour, though he
nevertheless preserved a distinct preference for France.
"When you shall have shown me an English or a
German Duc de Broglie, I shall begin to question my
opinion of the moral, intellectual, and political superiority of France, an opinion that every day takes
deeper root in my judgment." These excursions, in
which a life of pleasure was mingled with much studious
observation, had undoubtedly a remarkable influence on
Camillo Cavour. They initiated him, while still young,
in the heart of European affairs, the complicated interests of the world, and the various aspects of politics
in England and in France, in Belgium and in Switzerland. They gave him what I would call the exterior
and diplomatic sense of things, as agriculture, practised
in a certain extension, gave him the sense of all the
positive interior realities.

IV.

Such was, then, the life of "a young citizen of Piedmont," who, throughout the changes of an active and easy-going life, remained constantly a Liberal, flourishing in the shade of absolute government. Cavour was liberal, according to the ingenious phrase of M. de la Rive, "as he was fair, alert, and brilliant—by birth."

From his early youth he had the national and liberal instinct which governed his soul to the very latest hour, and he gives a vivid picture of the deception with which the period of 1830 afflicted him : "How many hopes deceived !" he writes ; "what illusions laid bare ! what a host of misfortunes have fallen upon our country ! I accuse no one ; it may be but the force of circumstances which has so decided it ; but the fact is, that the revolution of July, after bidding us conceive the noblest hopes, has replunged us into a state more deplorable than ever. Ah ! if France had known how to make the most of her position ; if she had drawn the sword . . . . . it might have been that . . . . . !" Entirely disconnected from the government, he did not withhold his railleries from a rule resting on Jesuitism and police, that confounded in its proscriptions the secret societies, the philosophy of Rosmini, railways, and industry—a rule with which Madame de Clermont-Tonnerre was reduced to negotiate, for a considerable period, that she might be permitted, by the medium of the Ambassador of France, to receive the *Journal des Débats.* "Science and intelligence," he said, "are deemed things infernal by those who have the goodness to govern us." Cavour loved science, and his intelligence was as free as it was clear. During these years of trial for Italy and for Piedmont, between 1830 and 1846, he often, in his private conversations, and in his correspondence with his closest friends, stirred many a deep question that he seemed but to brush in trifling ; his sharp and decisive stroke was that of a man who saw far and distinctly, nothing astonishing him.

One day, before the appearance of De Tocqueville's book, in the course of a letter to one of his friends, he described the march of new societies towards a democracy of yet unshapen outlines ; he showed the material and intellectual levelling beginning to operate between classes ; the patrician more than half destroyed ; the ancient organisations on the road to disintegration, or to transformation of some kind ; and, he added : " What is there left now to take arms against these waves of the masses ? Nothing that is solid ; nothing that has strength. Is it a good ? is it an evil ? I hardly know but it is, to my thinking, the inevitable future of humanity. Let us prepare ourselves for it, or at least prepare our descendants, whom it concerns more than us." Is it a good ? is it an evil ? He saw the inevitable circumstance, and he was of those who do not revolt against evident facts, who believe that there is nothing better than to make what you can of them by directing them. On another occasion, roused by the noise that was going on in France about the Jesuits, then masters of his little Piedmont, he wrote to a French lady : " If one would learn to know the true nature of that order, it is not where the Jesuits are struggling, and where they hold a precarious footing, that they should be studied ; they are not to be appreciated fully as they are, except where, meeting no obstacle, they apply their rules in a logical and consecutive manner. They have learnt nothing, forgotten nothing ; their minds and their methods are the same. Woe to the country, woe to the class confiding its youth to their exclusive education ! Unless it be owing to fortunate circumstances that destroy in the man the lessons imparted to the child, they will, within one century, make a race utterly debased. The opinion that I express here is shared by the most distinguished members of our clergy. . . . . The Jesuits are not dangerous in France. In a country of liberty, science, and enlightenment, they must always be compelled to shape and transform themselves ; neither in the political nor in the intellectual world can they ever obtain a real and durable empire. I wish, indeed, that, in the interests of humanity, we could come to an understanding with the Jesuits, and concede them, in the countries from which they are excluded, three, four, ten times the degree of liberty that they are willing to grant in the countries where they dominate." Observe this wish—even for the Jesuits !

V.

Yes, assuredly, Cavour was a Liberal of the early dawn, but he was always one in his own manner and in harmony with his own temperament. His was the Liberalism of a justly-poised unprejudiced brain, without fanaticism as without sourness, with nothing sickly or desponding in it; and I fancy he must have smiled somewhat when his friend Pietro di Santa-Rosa addressed him in elegiacal verses: "Camillo, for us to mourn together is henceforward the consolation of our broken spirits." He for his part never wasted much time in bewailing himself. If he had not too good an opinion of the Government, he by no means assumed the air of a victim, or of a systematic antagonist. If he was not particularly fond of those whom in his fancy French he called the *reculeurs*—backsliders—the ultras, those who from hatred or dread of revolution had retrograded to the length of one or many centuries, as little did he esteem the "fanatics"—the idealists, who, for a dream of their own, would push "Society into a fearful chaos, from which it could not be raised save by the agency of an absolute and brutal Imperialism."

He was neither of the one nor the other party; he had a natural aversion from excesses that are, more often than not, a disguise of impotence; and during one of those conspiratorial crises and reactions through which his country passed, he said: "As to me, I have long been undecided in the midst of these movements in opposite directions. Common sense counselled moderation; an overweening desire to set our *reculeurs* marching precipitated me into action. At last, after numerous and violent agitations and waverings, I finished by fixing myself, like the pendulum, between the two. So let me tell you, I am an honest middle-course man, desiring and hoping for social progress with all my might, but resolved not to purchase it at the cost of an universal overthrow. . . . . My position between the two, however, does not hinder me from wishing for the emancipation of Italy, with all possible speed, from the barbarians oppressing her; and in consequence I foresee that a tolerably violent crisis is inevitable. But I would have that crisis brought about with all the discretion compatible with existing circumstances; and besides this, I am more than persuaded that the mad attempts made by the men of action do but retard and render it more risky. . . . . "

He was already, if you will, a Liberal cloaking the man of government, or a Conservative who, in spite of his profession of the " middle-course," had nothing in him of the doctrinaire; did not take immobility for the final word of wisdom, and who meant to make of the principle of moderation a policy of initiation and action realising what the revolutionist promises, and doing it better.

There was another distinction in the Liberalism of Cavour. Others have contributed to the movements preceding Italian emancipation, and have made their way into politics through literature or by philosophy. Gioberti revived the sentiment of the supremacy of Italy. Balbo, by a series of patient and ingenious deductions, saw in the past the nourishment of new hopes. D'Azeglio wrote his romances and pamphlets with a fine, sensible, and persuasive eloquence. Camillo Cavour was neither a philosopher, an historian, nor a poet. His Liberalism was of a more practical kind, and I might almost venture to say more modern in its direction. A farmer and a man of the world, he endeavoured in his fashion to rekindle the feeling of public interests. He was always ready to seek a means to break through the network of supervision. He was one of the founders of the "Piedmontese Agrarian Society," whose statutes he had revised, from which society sprang a multitude of offshoots, where, under the pretext of agriculture, the spirit of discussion spread and sharpened. In conjunction with the Count of Salmour and others of his friends, he naturalised in Piedmont the popular institution of infant schools. Acting with the Marquis Alfieri and Count Pralormo, who represented what might be called the liberal side of the Government, he formed, at Turin, under the inoffensive name of "Whist Society," a sort of club of the Piedmontese nobility; a reunion, where men were accustomed to meet and exchange ideas. He felt the necessity of doing something; of giving a distinct shape to an activity that was beginning to disquiet the police; and when, instigated by his friends at Geneva, or excited by the wider awakening of the minds beyond the Alps, he likewise decided to take up a pen, what were the subjects he selected? They were questions of political economy, agricultural labour, and finance. He treated of the *voyages agronomiques* of M. de Chateauvieux, or of the state of Ireland; of "model farms," or of "communistic doctrines;" of "railways in Italy;" or of "the influence of the English commercial reforms."

All that was written in French, in an easy, pointed, and simple manner, without any literary style, by an observer manifestly schooled in economical problems, and taken with the great reforms, of which he hailed the victorious realisation in England, already dreaming that he might see them transported and applied in Italy.

Was he an economist? He was one after his own fashion, just as he was a farmer; as a man who constantly made use of whatsoever came in his way, without subjecting himself to a theory or to a speciality; one for whom the science of the laws of production, and the experience derived from agriculture, were useful and necessary, but secondary elements towards the art of governing. In these first pages of an amateur, writing upon questions that were special to all appearance, the politician burst forth spontaneously, so to speak, planning in a system of railways an instrument of national transformation for Italy, or in his economical liberalism the prelude of the liberalism of institutions. The man revealed himself completely by his verdicts, his ideas, and his preferences.

VI.

Unite all these features in him; they compose, if I mistake not, the characteristic physiognomy of one who is not likely to be stopped in his road. This is Camillo Cavour at the age of thirty-six, towards 1846 and 1847; it is Cavour breathing life and energy, endowed with a sort of contagious *entrain*, squandering his activity without ever exhausting it, allying discretion with audacity, flexibility with decision, the traditionary and Conservative sentiment with all modern instincts, an Italian and a Liberal, without ever being a revolutionist or a conspirator. Having a decided taste for France, and at the same time formed in the English school,

Cavour in some respects had a touch of the nature of Charles Fox. He had the ardent temperament of the great Whig leader—the power of mind, the charm of manner, and the irony without bitterness. He had yet more than Charles Fox—the instinct and the natural stamp of the man born to govern, and in his dreams of ambition he did not content himself with the part of chief of the Opposition. His leanings and his admirations were rather in the direction of those men who knew how, in case of necessity, to sacrifice their popularity for the sake of their country. "Yes, my friend," he wrote excitedly, in 1847, "Peel's reform has been the safety of England. What would have come to pass if they had allowed the too famous sliding-scale to stand? It is probable that England would have been left without resource after the recent harvest, and then what should we have seen? England owes statues to Peel; some day he will have them." If he encountered in the past, on the subject of Ireland, the figure of Pitt, he kindled, and seemed to find in himself some of the features under which he painted the son of Lord Chatham. "He had," says Cavour, "the lights of his time; he was no friend of despotism nor a champion of intolerance. This vast and able mind loved power as a means, not as an end. He was not one of those men who aim at recasting society from top to bottom, with loose conceptions and humanitarian theories of profound and frigid genius. Devoid of prejudices, he was animated only by the love of his country and of glory. If he had governed in a time of peace and tranquillity he would have been a reformer in the manner of Peel and Canning, uniting his own peculiar boldness to the largeness of view of the one, and the ableness and the sagacity of the other."

Pitt, Canning, Robert Peel—such were the men whom Cavour loved to take for models, and it was thus at the moment when the period of reforms opened for Italy, and those agitations and illusions whereof the accession of Pius IX. was the signal, that " the obscure citizen of Piedmont" found himself, better than any other, armed for public life.

On the first concessions made by Charles Albert at the end of 1847, he flung himself resolutely into this new career, not in the character of one agitator more, but as a counsellor, as a guide, by the aid of a journal, *The Risorgimiento,* which he founded with his friends, the moderate Liberals of Turin, Balbo, Massimo d'Azeglio, Carlo Boncompagni, Michelangelo Castelli. *The Risorgimiento* represented the opinions of all those who desire to maintain a good understanding between princes and people ; whose effort it was to regulate without enchaining the liberal and national movement of Italy. Cavour was not precisely a journalist ; to him journalism was only a new sphere of action, which, like all that he did, was useful to him ; it compelled him to fix his ideas ; and successively on two important occasions, the journalist, the leader of moderate Liberalism, had occasion to show that he did not shrink from resolutions of the gravest importance.

One day, early in 1848, there had been troubles in Genoa, that centre of keen passions. A deputation had gone to Turin to demand from the king, Charles Albert, the expulsion of the Jesuits and the institution of a National Guard. The public mind was in a state of excitement. The Liberal section at Turin was favourable to the Genoese deputation. Cavour instantly perceived that they were on a wrong track, and that to demand rigorous measures against the Jesuits was to run the risk of wounding the religious sentiments of the king; that a National Guard could only provoke trouble and sedition so long as a legal representation of the whole country was wanting; and he proposed to go straight to the point, without confining himself to the Genoese petition—to claim a Constitution.

While it was more daring, it was also more politic, for this was a step to flatter the pride and secret ambition of the prince whom the Constitution would elect the chief of Liberal Italy. It was in the very essence of Cavour, and, curiously enough, those who most warmly opposed him, those who refused to follow him, were men of extreme Liberalism, men of the Democratic party, Valerio and Sineo, who were suspicious of his leaning to English institutions, and ironically called him "My Lord Camillo." From that moment arose the question between constitutional policy and revolutionary policy.

Shortly after this, everything had undergone a singular change; there was no longer any question of the Constitution wrested from the vacillations of Charles Albert. The revolution of February 24 had just burst forth, everywhere kindling incendiary fires, in Italy and in Germany—at Vienna as well as at Berlin. Sicily was already in a state of insurrection. After five days' combat, Milan had expelled the Germans; while, at the same moment, Venice was setting herself free. The Austrian dominion, weakened in the heart of the empire by the Viennese revolution, had barely a hold even in its fortresses of the Adige. Amidst all these events, Turin re-echoed with impassioned appeals : Cavour was one of the first to utter the decisive word. "The supreme moment has arrived for the Sardinian monarchy," he wrote, on March 23, 1848 ; "the moment of grave deliberations ; that which decides the fortune of empires and the fate of nations. In the face of the recent events in Lombardy and at Vienna, hesitation and doubt are no longer tolerable. . . . . We, men of coolness, accustomed to follow the counsels of reason rather than the passions of the heart, after carefully weighing our words, should declare that only one course is open to the nation, to the government, and to the king—war ! immediate war ! . . . . Under existing circumstances, the highest policy is that of bold resolutions. . . . ."

Thus Cavour struck at once to the centre of the Italian movement, outstepping the boldest, and approaching— without much of illusion, perhaps, but with no vain subterfuges—that double question of constitutional liberty and of national independence which suddenly sprung up in the midst of the universal outburst.

VII.

Italy was destined to stand for mournful evidence of how a national revolution can in a few years be wrecked for want of maturity and good management—how, on the contrary, that same revolution could become successful when patiently organised and skilfully conducted. What was not known in March, 1848, the which has since been a lesson to a whole generation, was that this sudden crisis, perhaps an inevitable one, before which men like Cavour thought it their duty not to draw back, was nevertheless the most perilous of trials. Circumstances seemed, no doubt, at first to warrant audacity, and fortune seemed to smile on Italy. Radetzki's army, driven back from Milan and from Lombardy, reduced to shut itself up in Verona, in the midst of a circle of fire, and almost deserted by Vienna, was, it might well be believed, a last defence, quite inadequate to maintain the Austrian dominion beyond the Alps. On the other hand, the Piedmontese army, crossing the Ticino under the command of Charles Albert, could with a single spring reach the lines of the Mincio and the Adige. For four months it fought most valiantly, and a day came—that of the taking of Peschiera and the victory at Goito—when the cause of Italian independence seemed almost won. It was, in reality, a grand undertaking badly begun, and rendered complex by inexperience of every sort, as well as by every passion and every illusion which could lead it to a fatal termination.

The first of its dangers rested with external circumstances. The war of 1848, which broke out thus unexpectedly and with so little preparation, was intimately connected with a wide-set revolutionary situation, with an European convulsion. The result was that, up to a certain point, everything beyond the Alps depended upon what took place in Europe—upon the reactions which might, and which inevitably must, ensue. The chances of succeeding, which at the commencement of the campaign no doubt were real, diminished in proportion as events unrolled themselves.

After the days of June France was fully occupied with her own affairs. The intervention she had thought of, when she gathered together an army of the Alps, dwindled into an evasive and lingering mediation. England, an ally in this mediation, was only anxious to have done with agitations seeming to threaten the peace of Europe established in 1815. Revolutionary Germany, far from being favourable in parliament at Frankfort, openly pointed to the fortresses of the Adige as being the outworks of her natural frontiers. Austria, shaken for a moment, had time to look about her, and, by the assistance of her generals at Prague and at Vienna, to recover herself; and from the heart of the empire the poets sent forth to Radetzki, to that ancient warrior of Italy, the sympathetic war-cry,* "Austria is in your camp!" In a few months everything had changed, in so much that, before the autumn of 1848, Piedmont, flung back from the Mincio to the Ticino, reduced to undergo the humiliating armistice of August 16, stood unsupported to face a strengthened and victorious Austria, having nothing more to hope from Europe, hesitating to recommence hostilities, with

---

* Lines of Grillparzer's, very popular in Vienna at the time:

> Glückauf, mein Feldherr, führe den Streich,
>   Nicht blos um des Ruhmes schimmer:
> In deinem Lager is Oesterreich,
>   Wir andern sind einzelne Trümmer.—TR.

an army disorganised by defeat, and already powerless to restrain the passions urging it to renew the combat.

The violence of these passions, raging beneath the surface in Italy, led straight to ruin. While the army was gallantly fighting at Pastrengo, Goito, Curtatone, and Vicenza, everything was conspiring against her. The princes, on the one hand, full of misgivings and alarm, refused their alliance; the Pope, by the encyclical of April 29, disavowed the war of independence; and King Ferdinand of Naples was engaging, on May 15, in a victorious battle of internal repression, which ultimately drove Neapolitan policy to extreme reactionary measures.

On the other hand, the political doctrinaires, the abettors of sedition and conspiracy, with Mazzini at their head, were puffing the flame, adding to the difficulties of war by their divisions, and the outbreak of all the republican passions, unionist or federalist. These were really Austria's most useful auxiliaries; and the reverses of the Piedmontese army became the signal for an immense and disastrous anarchy, which extended far and wide, manifesting itself successively—at Milan, in scenes which imperilled the life of Charles Albert; at Rome, in the murder of Rossi, the flight of the Pope, and the proclamation of Mazzini's republic; at Florence, in the flight of the Grand Duke, and the advent of a noisy and confused demagogy.

Although Piedmont was protected by solid traditions, by a national dynasty, and by the "statuto,"* or royal decree, recently promulgated, it did not escape the

---

* *Statuto fondamentale*, the basis of a constitution, sworn to Charles Albert February 8, 1848, and observed by him.

universal contagion. The democratic party of the Ratazzis, the Valerios, the Buffas, the Ravinas, the Brofferias, although it did not carry a majority in the newly-opened parliament, was powerful enough to perplex the military and political action of the government, by its incoherent propositions and its declamations, aided by the clubs and an intemperate and excited press. At Turin that party was the representative or the accomplice of a turbulent democracy, the ally of all the agitators of Italy, and of all the partisans of war to the knife, of popular insurrections, and the wildest of combinations. I am but summing up the situation of 1848, in its principal external and internal features.

VIII.

In the midst of these disturbances, and in this feverish and dramatic inauguration of public life in Piedmont, Cavour fought in the front ranks, both as deputy from Turin to parliament, and in his capacity of editor of *The Risorgimiento.*

A constitutionalist and a patriot before the "statuto," and before the war, he was during the struggle the least revolutionary of men, the most reasonable, and the most liberal. Against those who feigned to bribe the union of Lombardy and of Piedmont with the simulacrum of a constituent assembly, he energetically upheld the necessity for immediate amalgamation. To those who proposed to establish a sliding-scale of taxation, he replied with the experienced discernment of a financier, a political economist, and a man of business. To those who were ever talking of recommencing hostilities with a disorganised army, reckoning on the help of France and of England, he exhibited the views of a politician sagaciously weighing the affairs of Europe. In the presence of vain and turbulent hostilities he stood by the Government. He did not fear the conflict. Without immediately obtaining the success of an orator, he soon became seasoned, making his way, and facing with an imperturbable coolness the hissing of public assemblies and the unpopularity of the streets, bearing lightly the name of *codino*, much amused with the accusation brought against him of his being an Anglomaniac. He was a frank and simple moderate, eager for the fray ; of a merciless common sense and irony towards those who believed only in " revolutionary means " without taking nature, reality, and experience into account. One day, in November, 1848, he directly attacked this shibboleth of the extreme party.

" What is it," said he, " which has always wrecked the finest and justest of revolutions ?—The mania for *revolutionary means* ; the men who have attempted to emancipate themselves from ordinary laws ; . . . . the French Constituent Assembly creating the assignats in contempt of nature and economic laws ;— *revolutionary means*, productive of discredit and of ruin ! The Convention attempting to smother in blood the resistance to its ambitious project ;—*revolutionary means*, producing the Directory, the Consulate, and the Empire ; Napoleon bending all to his caprice, imagining ' that one can with a like facility conquer at the Bridge of Lodi and wipe out a law of nature ;'—*revolutionary means*, leading to Waterloo and St. Helena ! The sec-

tarians of June striving to impose the Democratic and
social republic by fire and sword ;—*revolutionary means,*
producing the siege of Paris and reaction everywhere.
Wait but a little longer," he added, " and you will see
the last consequence of your *revolutionary means*—Louis
Napoleon on the Throne ! "

In truth he was of a just, liberal, and far-seeing
mind ; but neither Cavour, nor his friends in parliament,
nor of the press, could, placed as they were in the
centre of a circle of fire, improvise moderate views that
should yet have strength to prevail.   The movement
that was hurrying Italy away, and re-echoed through
Turin, swept off with it successively the first constitutional ministry of Count Balbo, Count Casati's ministry
of national compromise, the armistice ministry of Alfieri,
Revel, Pinelli, to fling itself into one of headlong
measures, revolutionary plots, and war at any price.

For a moment only, in the latter days of 1848,
Vincenzo Gioberti, a man raised to power through popularity, seemed called to arrest events, or to stamp them
with a new character ; at least he tried to do so, and in
so doing he soon learnt to appreciate the energetic assistance of Cavour, who had previously defended to the
utmost the ministry of Counts Revel and Pinelli against
him.

Gioberti felt the danger of a policy that was at once
coarsely revolutionary and rashly pledged to war.   He
understood that without renouncing the idea of national
independence it was possible to reach it by another road ;
and before precipitating herself upon the Austrians,
Piedmont had another part to play—that of bringing the

Grand Duke home to Florence and the Pope to Rome; and everywhere re-establish a constitutional government, —in a word, to direct the Italian movement. Piedmont would thus deprive Austria of one excuse for intervening in Peninsular affairs, at the same time conciliating and strengthening the restored princes; she would regain the sympathy of Europe, now ready to forsake her, out-wearied of so much excitement; and when her work was completed she would find herself in a better position either to negotiate with the concourse of mediating Powers, or again to take up arms.

Things were in readiness: England and France approved of the plan; General Alfonso La Marmora was approaching with a Piedmontese division from Tuscany. Unfortunately Gioberti, having come into power with the perfervid heads of the period, such as Ratazzi, Buffa, Sineo, and Tecchio, had been guilty of the error of dissolving the first Piedmontese parliament, when it had hardly been established, and to suffer a new and thoroughly Democratic chamber to be elected under the auspices of his name. Gioberti still fancied himself the master when he had ceased to be anything. At last he was left alone with his project of intervention, for-saken by a chamber to which ten elections had returned him; betrayed in his own cabinet by certain of his colleagues, and vainly supported by Cavour, who had now to defend him against his recent friends.

The defeat of Gioberti was the victory of the Demo-cratic ministers opposed to intervention in Central Italy. These, impatient to break with the armistice and all negotiations, were for immediate war. Gioberti's defeat

was the resumption of the old policy of extremes, with
an army still inefficiently reorganised, and irritated by
party insults; with a king overwhelmed with bitterness.
Placed midway between intricate complications at home
and a new war of independence, Charles Albert preferred to throw himself on the Austrian sword, heading
a country whose only cry was: "Let us make an end of
it!"   One year after first crossing the Ticino, and
the hopeful departure for the campaign in Lombardy,
Piedmont found herself again driven to the combat, to
play the highest of stakes.   The policy of "revolutionary means," to use Cavour's own words, had been permitted to see the light, to show its complete hollowness.
On March 23, 1489, it expired in the catastrophe of
Novara, where Charles Albert staked his crown with an
all but desperate heroism, and for a time the last chance
was wrecked for Piedmont and Italy.

IX.

Imagine this morrow of defeat prepared by a spirit
of rashness, and settled in a few hours.   A vanquished
nation always seems to plunge into the very bottom of
the abyss.

· The first consequence of the defeat of Novara was
the necessity for an armistice, which handed over a
portion of the country to foreign occupation.   The
Austrians, encamped on the Sesia, with power to place a
garrison in Alessandria, held Piedmont between the two
threats of an absolute invasion or a treaty of peace, of
which they would not state the conditions.   The

Piedmontese could no longer oppose any steady resistance. No doubt the army had fought gallantly at
Mortara and at Novara, under the eyes of Charles
Albert—always in the hottest fire of battle. It had
lost some of its generals and many of its officers, fallen
before the enemy. It was not the less in a condition of
extreme demoralisation, composed as it was chiefly of
recruits, and convinced that it had been forced to pay
the price of blood for the madness of political agitators.
The officers found it impossible to keep together their
men, who broke, and scattered panic all about them.

At Turin opinions wavered between discouragement
and exasperation. The clubs were noisy with passionate
rhetoric, and naturally enough there arose a cry of
treason. In the chambers, Brofferio prepared a decree
of general insurrection, and the formation in the
assembly of a committee of public safety. Motions in
Parliament rapidly succeeded one another : one ingeniously declaring the armistice to be "unconsti-
tutional," and the "statuto" in peril ; another threatening to indict the Government if it opened the gates
of Alessandria to the Austrians ; a third gravely prepared
an inquiry into the situation, and as to means for pursuing the war : all this as though the enemy were not at
hand, and ready to draw the sword of certain victory if
defied.

Matters at Turin were of small moment for the
nonce. At the first news of disaster, the populous and
fiery city of Genoa, the town of Mazziniism, caught the
contagion, passing from agitation to insurrection, and
thence to a real revolution. Either the army had

betrayed its chiefs, or it had been betrayed by them. The "statuto" had been violated. Turin was to be handed over to the Austrians, and Genoa herself was to be held as a hostage of war. It was with these reports, perfidiously spread, that agitators inflamed the public mind, and gave the signal for civil war.

The garrison, chiefly composed of reserves weakly commanded, was compelled to retire after a humiliating surrender to the rioters, who thus remained masters of the town, the arms, artillery, forts, and defences of the most important place in the kingdom. The unrestrained populace massacred a few unfortunates, among whom were a major of carabineers and the military commandant of the city; the general and his family were detained as hostages. The Genoese rabble, headed by an old *émigré,* the veteran Avezzana, constituted itself an "association of public safety"—"the provisional government of Liguria." It refused to recognise the armistice, it separated itself from Piedmont, and it humiliated the army by putting itself in opposition to the regular authorities. In truth, what took place as early as 1849 at Genoa, was an anticipatory sketch of the Commune in Paris in 1871.

This furious rabble, anxious to take advantage of the general disturbance, could not perceive that it was guilty of the crime of national treason; that in so doing it could only add to the misery of the masses, draw on Piedmont a still heavier invasion, and place the Government in a situation still more difficult. The defeat at Novara, the disorganised army, the threatened ruin of the country, agitations at Turin, civil war at Genoa, uncertainty everywhere—this was what followed the catastrophe. It was in these conditions that the young prince, destined by his birth to wear the crown of the exiled Charles Albert—Victor Emmanuel—re-entered Turin in the last days of March, 1849, to find himself so situated that everything depended on his first acts.

X.

There were two policies open to the new reign. At this decisive moment of European reaction and national confusion, Victor Emmanuel could lay aside the " statuto," and the recently inaugurated liberal *régime*, again possess himself of the blue flag of Savoy, and recover the past by shutting himself up within his frontiers, and no longer turning his attention beyond the Ticino towards Italy. Had he done this he would certainly have obtained an easier peace, and he would in his perplexity have had the support of Austria. External solicitations were not wanting—the most powerful influences sought to incline him to this resolution, which would perhaps have given him a certain momentary security,—but it is true it would have placed him in the modest condition of a subject of Austria—another Duke of Modena, or a second Grand Duke of Tuscany. Victor Emmanuel could also have manfully resigned himself to his ill-fortune, and have endured the ill results of war, without sacrificing the " statuto," or the tricoloured flag—the only two surviving representatives, the only two symbols of Piedmontese independence, and of Italian hopes, that were left.

Thus placed between divergent policies, the soldierly and princely loyalty of Victor Emmanuel did not hesitate : he accepted the part of liberal and national king; and certainly the most significant testimony that he could give of the frankness of his intentions was almost immediately to elevate to the post of prime minister him who might be termed the Knight of Italy, Massimo d'Azeglio, still lame of a wound he had received at Vicenza.

This was decisive of the fate of Italy ; this made of that dark day of Novara not only an anniversary of mourning for the bloody termination to the inconsecutive attempts of 1848, but made it also the sombre yet absolute starting-point of a new epoch. By the preservation of the tricoloured Italian flag and the maintenance of the "statuto" the future of Italy was saved. "It is a long work to recommence," said D'Azeglio, "but we will recommence it." And on the other hand, Cavour wrote about the same time to Salvagnoli : "As long as liberty exists in one corner of the Peninsula we must not despair of the future. As long as Piedmont can protect its institutions from despotism and anarchy, there will be a means of working successfully at the regeneration of the country."

It was with nothing more nor less than the "statuto" that Massimo d'Azeglio entered into office after Novara, calling to his assistance men as moderate and patriotic as himself—Count Siccardi, Paleocapa, the Venetian, the banker Nigra, and General Alfonso La Marmora, who had lately performed a national service, in suppressing, with equal judgment and promptitude,

the factious Genoese. Indeed, the task was not an easy
one ; it had to triumph over the confusion and irritation
of parties, parliamentary blunders due to inexperience,
and all possible internal and external difficulties.

Peace was the chief necessity, and D'Azeglio, in
submitting to it and negotiating for it, set an example
of resigned patriotism and courageous abnegation. It
was evident that this peace must be a hard one; it
carried Piedmont back to the treaties of 1815, inflict-
ing a war indemnity of seventy-five millions of francs
—a heavy weight on the budget of the country. After
all, it was not humiliating ; it was a necessity. It
will, however, scarcely be credited—parties played the
sad game of bargaining with that necessity, and refusing
their co-operation, at the risk of sacrificing everything.
On two occasions the Government saw itself reduced to
dissolve the House, and on the last of these two the
king himself was compelled to make a direct appeal to
the common sense of the country by the proclamation of
Moncalieri, which, under the cloak of a *coup d'état*, was
nevertheless a deed of far-sighted Liberalism. "Do not
these gentlemen perceive," said D'Azeglio, sadly, " that
the Ministry has already enough to do in upholding the
Constitution—and that *after us the Croats?*"

This was not the only task. At the time when Piedmont stood for Constitutionalism, reaction carried the day
in all parts of Europe. Piedmontese liberty seemed an
anomaly and a danger, in the midst of the absolutist
restorations which were taking place in Italy, at Rome,
at Florence, and at Milan. Austria signalised Turin as
a last incendiary focus. The Emperor of Russia declined

any intercourse with the new King of Sardinia. Even in France the Conservative party, which had lately reinstated the Pope at Rome, seemed to look upon this transalpine constitutional *régime*, which had the strange pretension of accomplishing reforms, both civil and religious, as a troublesome and importunate brawler. Piedmont encountered everywhere hostility or coldness, so that what had to be done was virtually, day by day, to wrest, as it were, from Austria, and from domestic factions as well as foreign suspicions, that " statuto " in which a well-inspired prince and wise Liberals perceived a means of reconstructing, with the aid of a constitutional monarchy, what had been cast down by revolutions and revolutionists.

XI.

Cavour was one of the most energetic supporters of this renovating policy, and of D'Azeglio's ministry. At the democratic elections which had overthrown Gioberti, in January, 1849, he had been excluded from parliament as a reactionary or *codino* ; the ·extremists had defeated him by bringing forward to oppose him an obscure nonentity of the name of Pansoya—a Barodet of the period—who only owed his celebrity of one day to that strange adventure. At the elections which followed after Novara, Cavour again found himself at the head of the poll in his native town of Turin ; re-entering the House never again to leave it ; and in this new position he rapidly attained increasing authority, warranted and confirmed by the clear-sighted decision he had not ceased to show for the space of a year; by the political spirit that never left him; and by a superiority that made itself felt in matters of public and financial economy.

He was the same frank and simple upholder of the Constitution before the crisis as after it. He held in antipathy and contempt the bragging of impotent revolutionists; and he defended and stood by the Government, more especially in the critical times immediately succeeding Novara, until the peace was definitely settled, which was only in January, 1850. But let us not deceive ourselves. Cavour, in the meantime, still remained a bold and active Liberal, accepting the "statuto" with all its conditions, guarantees, and consequences. In upholding the Ministry, he often stimulated and outstripped it; he was becoming, by degrees, the chief—the *leader*, if not, of the Conservative majority, with which he kept pace—at least, of the Liberal fraction of that majority. He was not the man to pursue a Conservative policy as a partisan of immobility and reaction; nor was he slow in showing that in him, the moderate and parliamentary man was the statesman born for power and action.

Opportunities were not wanting: they were the natural issue of that policy of day by day; and, indeed, of the constitutional system, which is perpetually bringing parties into collision.

One of the simplest consequences of this system was evidently the suppression of privileged jurisdictions and ecclesiastical immunities in the administration of justice. It was natural that the most religious and the most conservative of the men on the Right, Count Balbo and Count Revel, friends of the Ministry, should not themselves hold the principle in doubt; they only asked that negotiations should be made first with the Pope. Unfortunately, such negotiations had been carried on for two years in vain, and a longer delay would only enervate the new institutions, and allow it to be supposed that in a Liberal State there could be two laws, two jurisdictions, and two powers. It is true there were many other questions of civil reforms and ecclesiastical organisations, issuing infallibly from a constitutional *régime*. For the time being the Ministry did not go so far; it modestly contented itself with proposing the abolition of ecclesiastical privileges, of that which was called the *foro*.

Such was the bill introduced by the minister of justice, Count Siccardi—supported by all the sincere Liberals; contested dubiously by a portion of the ministerial Right; and combated with fury by the members of the reaction.

Cavour could not hesitate. He was of those who had urged the Ministry to present the bill; and when the matter was discussed in March, 1850, he seized the opportunity of claiming the civil rights of society in the face of the privileges of the Church; thus boldly to resume a true constitutional policy. He combated those who were always opposed to reforms—sometimes on the score of troubled times, at others because they were tranquil; he called attention to English statesmen, who knew how to turn the tide of revolution by the use of opportune measures; and he added: "When reforms

are effected in good time, far from weakening authority, they strengthen it, rendering the revolutionary
spirit powerless. I would say, therefore, to statesmen :
Frankly follow the examples of the Duke of Wellington,
Earl Grey, and Sir Robert Peel . . . . follow broadly
the road of reforms, without fear of their being
inopportune. Do not think that it will weaken the
cause of the constitutional throne, for it will on the
contrary strengthen it, and will strike such deep roots
into our soil that, should revolution spring up around
us, not only will it have power to dominate revolution,
but it will *gather about it all the live forces of Italy, and
conduct the nation to the destinies awaiting her. . . . .*"

This speech, one of the first in which Cavour
revealed his innermost thought, manifestly outstepped
the limits of a special question, and in determining the
success of the law in parliament, in the public mind
it left a profound impression as the revelation of a
policy, and of the man created to conduct it.

Another opportunity soon presented itself. This
time it was not one of those delicate questions which
stir every passion, but of the cruelly-embarrassed condition of Piedmontese finance—a deficit of six millions
per annum. Cavour, as we have said, stood by the
Government, brushing aside puerile charges and
chimerical schemes ; but in defending the Government,
he caused it to feel the prick of the spur. He in turn
reviewed the economical position, like a man who was
master of the facts ; touching upon them with clearness
and confident boldness ; and at the end of the list he concluded by saying nearly in these words : " Be careful ;

if in the next session the Ministry does not bring forward
a financial scheme by which to restore the balance, with
a reformed custom-house tariff, and the system of taxation which the country needs, I shall deeply regret it : we
shall, my friends and I, be compelled to abandon it. . . . . .
Although the condition of our country is serious, it
is by no means desperate ; we only need a little strength
of will and courage to make it accede to the necessary
taxation. . . . . Let us hear no more of party agitations ;
the union between the king and the nation is sufficiently
close and well established, there is nothing to fear from
extreme, revolutionary, or reactionary parties.   I do not
fear the spread of either one or the other. . . . . Proceed,
therefore ; banish alarms ; you will have the support of
parliament and of the country, even in the most dis-
tressing portion of our task—the re-establishment of the
balance of expenditure and income."

In this universal ability, firmness of mind in matters
politic, and prompt activity, we discern the man and the
minister eager to restore lost time, ripe for the work.
So clearly was this felt, that when the minister of
commerce, Santa-Rosa, died unexpectedly, in October,
1850, the name of Cavour instantly suggested itself.
Everything concurred in pointing out Cavour as his fit
successor, at a time when circumstances were full of
anguish. The unfortunate Santa-Rosa having taken part
in the introduction as well as the vote of the law of the
foro, yet nevertheless profoundly religious, was, by
order of the Archbishop of Turin, Mgr. Fransoni, harshly
refused the last sacraments of the Church. A painful
scene took place round this death-bed, of a man begging

for the prayers of the priest, while he stoutly refused to utter a recantation which he considered would dishonour his name.

At Turin public opinion was deeply moved, and not unnaturally turned towards him who had been the intimate friend of Santa-Rosa, and who more than any other had lent his aid to the success of the law of the *foro*. D'Azeglio himself desired no better than to have the support of so able and vigorous an athlete, and when he went to propose him to Victor Emmanuel, the king, without showing any more surprise than the rest, replied shrewdly : " I will accept him ; but wait a little, and he will rob you of all your portfolios." As to these conditions, Cavour had made none, neither as regarded men nor things. He knew that a minister has what power he is capable of taking, capable of exercising. Here was his old saying of the Villa Bolongaro : " We will do something." Before long, he had added the ministry of commerce to that of finance ; he held in hand the whole economic government of Piedmont, and Victor Emmanuel had said truly, that was not all !

XII.

My desire is to point out the nature of a situation in which a vanquished country has the good fortune, in the moment when most wanted, to meet with a well-inspired prince, and devoted men, who do not despair of raising it, by the aid of patriotism and constitutional liberty, from a disaster apparently irreparable.

This difficult and complicated task was not accomplished in a single day or by a single blow; it passed through many an obscure and peculiar crisis. In fact, it had two characteristic phases, of which the first is represented by the ministry of D'Azeglio, which Cavour entered in October, 1850, and which, immediately after Novara, was the true terminating point of the ruin, when things began to mend. It was really the ministry of an imperative peace, heightened and made good by the maintenance of liberal institutions.

While D'Azeglio, with his affable dignity and loyal moderation, was endeavouring to disperse external distrust, and re-establish the diplomatic position of Piedmont, Count Siccardi took the lead in ecclesiastical reforms. After having restored peace at Genoa, General Alfonso La Marmora, the minister of war, used all his efforts to reconstruct an army disorganised by defeat. Military institutions had to be modified, a new system of military instruction begun, officers' corps reconstructed, by an opening of the ranks of the regular army to most of the other Italian provinces who had fought with the Piedmontese during the war; and he inspired all with the same spirit. " I trust," said he, " that from whatever province they may come, the officers are fully penetrated with the national sentiment which makes all Italians equally devoted sons of the same great country—Italy!" La Marmora did not shrink from making himself responsible before the chambers by pushing on the fortifications of Casale, fortifications which, ten years later, in 1859, were to arrest the Austrian invasion.

In this renovating work Cavour, as minister of commerce and finance, lent important assistance, by his economic reforms, by throwing off the shackles from commerce, and by his combinations of imposts; especially by an inexhaustible fertility of resource and untiring activity, which soon gave him influence in parliament.

Piedmont started afresh. But in advancing it had to face a double difficulty; one which I should call a matter of general policy, and another of parliamentary conduct.

The question of general policy seemed decided, but it sprang up at every step and in every form, under conditions in which everything was changed. At the time when D'Azeglio's new ministry had been formed, in upholding under the hard blow of Novara the flag of the "statuto," and the Liberal cause of the nation, Cavour had been compelled to dissolve a chamber when a warlike and revolutionary opposition could only prove to be dangerous. It was not before a second dissolution of parliament, and through the intervention of the king, that he had obtained from the country a parliamentary assembly that he could work with. In this new Ministry the majority, composed of all shades of Conservatism, was immense; the Left represented a minority too small to be feared. This Conservative chamber gave Piedmont peace and good order, and saved her from perdition.

The acceptance and conclusion of peace was the signal for a totally new state of things, in which the internal affairs of the country resumed primary importance, and parties began visibly to become modified and transformed. While a fraction of the majority representing a Liberal Conservative Centre, and headed by such men as Pinelli, Boncompagni, and Castelli, did not hesitate to follow the Ministry in its attempts at reform in a wisely Liberal course, the extreme Right, with whom were Balbo, Count Revel, Colonel Menabrea and a few deputies from Savoy, offered a certain resistance. It did not wish to separate itself from the Government, nor was it other than sincerely constitutional ; but, on the whole, it was a stationary or reactionary party, which was for the " statuto," but with none of its consequences, and in supporting the Government often perplexed it.

When the Ministry presented the law of the *foro*, Count Balbo and his friends opposed it. When Cavour carried out his reforms in political economy, and was in negotiation with France, England, and Belgium for a treaty of commerce, he met with opposition from Count Revel, and from the Conservative protectionists. Although Colonel Menabrea, then a young and brilliant officer of engineers and an able speaker, was not precisely adverse, his attitude resembled that of a clerical and Conservative dissenter ; when the question of ecclesiastical privileges was broached, he had quitted the post of first secretary of foreign affairs. Meantime, in the opposite camp, a movement was taking place in a contrary direction. The extreme Left—of the Tecchios, Sineos, Brofferios—was lively, and retained its passionate and declamatory habits. But already a group was detaching itself from this Democratic party, forming, as it were, a Left Centre, with Rattazzi, Lanza, Cadorna, and Buffa. This Left Centre was gradually drawing nearer to the Government, preserving no more than an opposition of tactics, or of the occasion, and even sometimes upholding ministerial reforms with its votes.

Parliamentary conditions began to wear a strange aspect. On the one hand, the Ministry had a majority, with which it had made peace; but a portion of it seemed to resist or fall off whenever the policy of the Government followed its national and liberal course; on the other, the Cabinet had adversaries to encounter, from whom it had become estranged, chiefly in 1848 and 1849; but these had been visibly affected by the sobering influence of events. They might either become useful allies or dangerous opponents. Hence a stirring situation, dubious and uncertain. Some positive step had plainly to be taken. To remain at the disposal of the Right was to allow the policy of Government to drift towards reactions, which would one day affect the system of religious reforms, and probably, also, the liberty of the press and electoral law. Persistency in the policy that had been inaugurated was to accept in advance the necessity of making up for defections in the Right by other alliances and other support. The Ministry was not deceived, and here the question became complicated by the differences of the temperament in two men who were at the same time friends and competitors in the Government—D'Azeglio and Cavour.

XIII.

D'Azeglio and Cavour took exactly the same view of the liberal and national course to be adopted by Piedmont; but, for reasons of diplomacy, as well as from

E

personal characteristics, D'Azeglio found it hard to make up his mind to an open and avowed rupture with the Right. Devotion to the service of his country, rather than taste or ambition, had raised him to the Ministry; and he remained, when in power, the same generous and softly-mannered gentleman—clear-sighted and amiable, courageous in danger, a little languid in overcoming everyday difficulties, and easily wearied of business. Cavour had the energy and activity of a political man who had a passion for business matters, and not only foresaw coming difficulties, but instantly sought to counteract or to overcome them.

He was not insensible to the seriousness, and even the pain, of having to separate from "friends of child-hood," as he called them;[*] if the success of a liberal and national policy could only be bought at that price, he did not hesitate; he was not one to halt half way. With the instincts of a man born to govern, he often grew impatient with the perplexities caused to the Ministry by a more or less avowed resistance; he understood that, with an uncertain, shifting, and restless majority, it is impossible to govern "on a needle's point." "I have been accused," he says later, "of having separated from old friends; the accusation is unfounded. I have not left them, but they have left me. I did everything

---

[*] About that time, when in an animated discussion, he chanced to meet with opposition from old friends, he said with emotion, but resolutely: "Yes, gentlemen, I know that in entering on political life, in time of such difficulties as these, one must be prepared for the greatest deceptions. I am prepared for it. Should I be compelled to give up all the friends of my childhood; if I should have to see my most intimate acquaintances transformed into my bitterest enemies, I would not fail in my duty. I will never abandon the principles of liberty, to which I have vowed allegiance. . . . ."

to retain them, and to persuade them ; it is they who have refused to follow me. Ought I, then, to have stood alone, rejecting the co-operation of those who were disposed to follow me ? "

Those who showed themselves disposed to follow him belonged to the Left Centre, chiefly represented by Urbano Rattazzi, a man of tact and resource, a lawyer rather than a politician, but a clever orator, who might some day become a powerful auxiliary. Cavour was not forgetful of the part played by the Left Centre in the parliamentary affairs of 1848 and 1849 ; he well remembered having had to combat them, and he did so again, and as often as occasion offered, to the end. He was not, however, the man to hamper himself with irritating recollections of past divisions, and in the alliance proposed to him he saw a means of emancipating the Government and strengthening the condition of parliament, by forming among men of extreme opinions the party of all shades of Liberalism. He had no fear of these new allies ; he felt himself able to hold them in. It was all deducible to a question of *à propos* ; and Cavour, by a marvel of dexterity, chose for the more decisive affirmation of that evolution of liberal policy meditated by him exactly the moment when Piedmont was compelled to " reef sail," and pay an apparent tribute to the reactionary spirit.

Let me explain. It was when the *coup d'état* of December 2, 1851, burst upon France. The new 18th *brumaire*, appearing to Europe in the garb of a new Napoleon, was not reassuring to smaller countries like Piedmont and Belgium, where the press had full independence, and where the defeated in Paris went in search of a refuge. It was a menace to constitutional liberty wherever it existed, as well as an encouragement to the parties of absolutism and reaction. Piedmont was especially in a position to feel the double pressure of France under the *coup d'état*, and of Austria ready to take every advantage; she had to screen herself from the storm that might be drawn down on her by the vexatious imprudences of the press or refugees.

The Cabinet at Turin was sensible of the difficulties and delicacies of this situation, and as early as January 7, 1852, it hastened to justify itself to the French Government by proposing a law on the press, by which offences against foreign princes were to be transferred to the ordinary tribunals and not to be tried by jury. The Piedmontese Cabinet submitted to what could not be avoided; it made a virtue of necessity, and D'Azeglio ingeniously expressed his meaning in a transparent apologue: "Suppose we had to traverse one of those regions where wild beasts abound, and pass close to a den where a lion was sleeping, and that one of our guides told us : ' Do not speak ; make no noise, lest you should awaken him,' and if one of us were to begin to sing, I imagine we should all combine to shut his mouth. . . . . Or again : if, notwithstanding all possible precaution and prudence, the lion awakes and springs upon us, then, if we are men, we must fight!" So much for prudence ; but the bold and able deed was the taking advantage of this occasion, when a concession had been perilously made, to break with those who would fain have pushed reaction farther, establish the integrity of

Piedmontese policy, and keep inviolate the institutions of the country, by the drawing together of Liberal parties, brought about in full parliamentary combat.

This was the work of Cavour.

XIV.

There was a sort of parliamentary diversion led by Colonel Menabrea, who did not conceal his Conservative alarm, and his desire yet more to restrict the liberty of the press. Rattazzi, on the other hand, intervened, promising to support the Ministry provided it maintained a law which he considered temporarily needful, and stuck to Liberalism. Hereupon Cavour joined the debate, defending the law, and exposing the whole policy of the Government with great precision and ability, accepting offers of aid from the chief of the Left Centre, and from that moment considering Colonel Menabrea's speech in the light of a rupture.

The struggle became sharp; all the passions were alive, and joined in the *mêlée*. Peacemakers endeavoured to soften the acrimony of the combat. It was evident that no one expected this sudden change; a divorce proposed by the Right, followed by a new marriage— a *Connubio*, as Revel termed it, in recalling the events of 1848, for an argument against the new alliance. Colonel Menabrea, more surprised than anyone else at the outburst he had provoked, remarked with some sadness: "The minister of finance wants to set sail in the direction of a new parliamentary coast, and land on another shore. He has a right to act as he pleases, but I shall not

go with him. . . . ." Cavour's rejoinder was : " It is
not true that the Ministry has directed its helm towards
other shores.   It has made no movement of the sort,
but wishes to go in the direction of the prow instead of
in the direction of the stern."   With the explanations
the divisions increased, and the somewhat insignificant
matter of the law of the press became the pretext for
a decisive evolution that was well planned and resolutely
fought out in the parliamentary battle-field.

The manœuvre was certainly daring, the more so as
Cavour was binding the Ministry to more than it was at
all inclined to bind itself.   Some few of the members of
the Cabinet complained of this, whilst D'Azeglio did his
utmost to moderate the conflict and account for the words
of his impetuous colleague.   But the blow had been
dealt ; it had resounded through parliament and through
the country.   It constituted Cavour the manifest chief
of liberal opinions, the representative not of a new policy,
but of a new and more active and decisive phase of
Piedmontese policy, and the *Connubio* became more
pronounced.   The president of the chamber of deputies
died suddenly ; the minister of finance instantly supported the candidature of Rattazzi for the presidency,
and did so successfully.

A conflict so ably fought could, sooner or later, only
result in the supremacy of Cavour.   A ministerial crisis
which, in May, 1852, temporarily retarded his progress
to power, only hastened the · inevitable conclusion.
Rattazzi's election to the presidency had provoked this
new change. D'Azeglio thought his formidable colleague, the " dear inventor of the *Connubio*," as he loved

to call him, went a little too fast; perhaps he felt slightly wounded, and also dreaded the effect on the outside world of these sudden changes. Cavour saw nothing to be apprehended in his leaving the reins to D'Azeglio, while he retired for a time with the prestige of an ever-increasing authority, and, in writing to his friend Salvagnoli, in Florence, he described the recent crisis: "It was, in my opinion, not only useful but indispensable that a Liberal party should be firmly constituted. . . . . After having, at first, been convinced of such a necessity, D'Azeglio has not accepted all the consequences, and he provoked a crisis which could only result in my retirement, or his removal from power. External policy required that I should be the sacrifice. I think D'Azeglio would willingly have abdicated, but I did my utmost to dissuade him; he stayed, and we have not ceased to be friends, privately and politically. It will next be his turn to retire, and then we can constitute an openly Liberal Cabinet. In the meantime I take advantage of my new liberty for a journey to France and England. . . . ."

XV.

That this was only a truce, that this journey to England was not simply one of pleasure, can well be perceived. Cavour's intention was to see the statesmen of both countries, and disperse the prejudices of which Liberal Piedmont was perhaps the object, thus clearing a way for his own combinations. In England he found it easy to do this. Lord Malmesbury, then the head of

the Foreign Office, openly stated his hope of seeing him
come to terms with his friends—with the party he had
worked so hard to bring together.   In Paris, where he
had arranged to meet Rattazzi, he met with the warmest
reception.   He saw the Prince-president Napoleon,
whom he won by his air of easy superiority; he saw,
too, some old friends of the parliamentary world, among
others M. Thiers, who said to him: "Be patient, if
after they have given you snakes for breakfast they give
you snakes again for dinner, do not be disgusted."   In
this expedition Cavour made many new friends, and had
an opportunity of observing the situations which he
might one day have to manipulate.

In London and in Paris he kept his eyes fixed upon
Piedmont, where the Ministry seemed to be sufficiently
unsettled; and he wrote to his friends: "Instead of
combating D'Azeglio, we should lend him a frank
support; but we cannot sacrifice our good name to
him. . . . . As soon as I return we will consult together; we will see La Marmora and speak bluntly to
him.   It is time for all this to be settled.   If D'Azeglio
wishes to remain in power, let him say so, and he will
have in us sincere allies.   Should he be tired of it,
let him no longer render the problem of government
insoluble by his continual vacillations."

The fact is that D'Azeglio was bending under the
weight of government; while abroad, as at home, Cavour
was weighing upon the Ministry.   If his presence in
the Government had been a difficulty, his absence was a
still greater embarrassment.

The Ministry had not been able to live with him; it

could not subsist without him. An ally of the Cabinet, he would have absorbed and eclipsed it; as chief of the Opposition he could vanquish and render it powerless.

As soon as he returned to Turin, in September, 1852, it became evident that the question would not long be unsettled. Cavour was called to form a Ministry, of which he was to be the chief; and D'Azeglio, withdrawing from before so brilliant a rival, and without regret, wrote : " I had accepted the helm at a time when it was pointed out to me that, better than any other man, I could direct it for the country's best advantage. . . . . Now that the ship has refitted, let the winds fill her sails. I surrender my quarterdeck to another! He, whom you know, is possessed of a diabolical activity, fitted for the work both in mind and body ; and it gives him so much pleasure ! " And thus throughout a series of changes and metamorphoses, the preponderance of a Liberal Conservative is seen in sharp outline, creating, by means of alliances with the " Moderates of all parties," a parliamentary position whereon to lean, that he may put Piedmont and Italy in the track of new destinies.

CHAPTER II.

I.

WHEN, after a retirement of a few months, Cavour
victoriously returned to political life as president of the
council, he entered into power, November 4, 1852,
under circumstances which could not fail to give his
advent a more distinct character than heretofore.

At the time when D'Azeglio's ministry, which had so
patriotically handled affairs immediately after Novara,
was vanishing, a last attempt, and one not discountenanced by Victor Emmanuel, was made by Count Balbo
to reconstitute a purely Conservative Cabinet, which
might almost be called a ministry of reconciliation with
Rome. Cavour, consulted in the matter by Victor

Emmanuel, had left them to make experience of this proceeding, the inanity of which he perceived; he had then started for Leri. Balbo had exhausted all forms of negotiations and overtures, but had broken down; he had met with nothing but refusals, even from his friends, beginning with Revel, who did not feel himself equal to overcome the current of opinion. Cavour's resumption of office after this failure was all the more significant; it settled the way between the two systems, which for the space of about three years had been perpetually at conflict in Turin.

The new president of the council entered parliament under conditions that he himself had arranged, and they only needed now to be broadened and strengthened. Let Cavour's manner of going to work be noted: resolved not to allow himself to be checked by resistance from the Right—the Clerical party—he had by no means the intention of suddenly disturbing political equilibrium and separating himself from his friends—the moderate Liberals; he was careful not to "break the chain," as he called it; and, above all, he held fixedly to secure the concurrence of the principal members of D'Azeglio's cabinet, whose colleague he had been. "Without La Marmora," he used often to repeat, "I could not be minister." In his eyes La Marmora represented military reorganisation, just as Paleocapa (an engineer of the greatest eminence) represented that of progress in material works, and Boncompagni that of wise reforms in religious matters. The new ministers of foreign affairs and of the interior, General Dabormida and Count Ponza di San-Martino, clung to the same traditions. It still remained a government of the Right Centre, with a chief of firmer gait, who retained simply the financial department for himself, but was well able to undertake every ministry or government.

It was only some months after this, when time had been given to the Cabinet to consolidate, that the elevation of Rattazzi to the ministry of justice established a final alliance with the Left Centre. The change was accomplished, and it was right that it should be, by a sort of assimilation under guidance. Cavour was not at the mercy of the Left Centre; he absorbed or annexed it; and the Left Centre was wise in allowing itself to be annexed, since it was furthering the success of a fresh and fruitful idea, by the union of the whole Liberal party under the ablest of guides. Before one year had passed this idea received a striking sanction from the country, in the immense ministerial majority returned to the chamber in the elections.

From this moment Cavour might truly say that he had "raised a barrier sufficiently high for the reaction to be unable to reach above it." Henceforth he had, together with the confidence of his King, a Ministry, and a majority, that is to say, an entire parliamentary situation brought about by him, upon which to lean for the accomplishment of his designs and the progressive realisation of his policy.

II.

That policy, which commenced by creating its own instrument of action, had indeed been the original work, I might almost call it the manifestation of a man's genius. No doubt Cavour had not drawn it from his own imagination, it had been handed to him by circumstances. He was not the only one who ever thought of it; others had had a similar instinct or presentiment, but it was he who shaped it, and brought it within practical limits,. stamping it with the seal of his adventurous yet prudent mind, by changing into a reality that saying of a conquered but not despairing nation : "We will begin again !"

Cavour was one of the first to perceive the consequences of this great truth, which he summed up one day by saying: "It is impossible for the Government to have an Italian or national policy outwardly without being inwardly reforming and liberal; just as it would be impossible for us to be inwardly liberal without being national and Italian in our external relations." More clearly than any other he perceived that, if Piedmont wished, in her difficult position after her overthrow, and lying under the jealous eye of Austria, to carry out this design, she must, within her narrow compass, put forth all the energy, wisdom, and activity of a great country : "Piedmont must begin by raising herself, by re-establishing in Europe as well as in Italy, a position and a credit equal to her ambition. Hence there must be a policy unswerving in its aim, but flexible and various as to the means employed, embracing the exchequer, military reorganisation, diplomacy, and religious affairs."

Everything proceeded from a settled thought in this work, gradually revealing itself under a vigorous impulse. Economic and financial matters first engaged the attention of Cavour. Like all the vanquished,

Piedmont had to pay for defeat. The country lay under the burden of two unfortunate campaigns which, with the Austrian indemnity, had already cost it very nearly three hundred millions of francs. Thus the public debt, which before 1848 amounted to no more than five millions per annum (£200,000), was rapidly increased to more than thirty millions. The budget of its expenses, only eighty millions before the war, was above one hundred and seventy-eight millions in 1848, two hundred and sixteen in 1849, one hundred and eighty-nine in 1850, and finally it remained fixed at between one hundred and thirty and one hundred and forty millions. From almost the first moment, then, the expenses of the country had doubled; the public debt was now six times as large as before, and, in making due allowance for the time we are speaking of—twenty-five years ago —for a country of less than five millions of souls, and whose resources were still undeveloped, these figures represent a weight almost as heavy as that which has been laid upon France under still more tragic circumstances. Such was the situation.

Two systems were possible—and how frequently have they confronted one another! One scheme was, to proceed with the strictest and most scrupulous economy, keeping a modest balance, by cutting down expenses, lessening the deficit, and increasing only the most necessary taxes. But then it would be imperative to abandon all hope of playing a part in the world, to reduce the army, and abstain from the most useful public undertakings, or at least indefinitely postpone the completion of them. This was prudence of a certain kind; it was not foresight, in that it was to burden the country with an inevitable increase of charges without offering it any compensation, or doing anything that would assist the development of its vitality, or help it to support a weight that could not be lightened. Cavour had other plans; and it was he who originated the financial system of the new order of things in constitutional and liberal Piedmont, he who drew up that which, to use his own language, I will call the budget of "action and progress."

III.

Cavour's budget witnessed to a policy derived from a situation : it was the work of a man afflicted by the necessity of obtaining of the country the price to be paid for its own misfortunes, who prepared to make that forced indemnity a means of reparation. New taxes could not of course be avoided ; they were the conditions of Piedmont's credit and solvency. A combination of these new taxes with the old ones, unequally distributed in the provinces, was of the first importance. Cavour was thoroughly cognisant of the problem he had to solve, and, on his first entrance into power he had commenced the work without hesitation, without being discountenanced by the unpopularity which always awaits a minister reduced to rattle the money-box.

He, too, had to contend with propositions of radical reforms and plausible theories, even with the tax on income. He resolutely put aside unseasonable experiences as mere Utopias, to attain just to that which appeared to him possible. His whole ingenuity was exercised in wresting from the Opposition, extracting from the patriotism of the chambers, a certain number of taxes on personal property and furniture, on patents, on wills, and on registration deeds. Besides this he hoped to give to his budget a ballast of from twenty-five to thirty millions; but this was only a part of his schemes. He felt that it was quite insufficient to meet the ends of his policy. He knew that if Piedmont remained poor, taxes would always be too heavy, and that the best way of revivifying the budget and filling the exchequer was to renew the life of the country, by giving a new start to industry and commerce, by the development of its productive energies, and by all that could assist the improvement of the national fortune. This completed his financial system, or rather this was the essential and original part of it.

On the one hand, instead of retrenching expenses, at the risk of temporarily increasing the deficit by new calls on the national credit, Cavour was not afraid to devote more than two hundred millions towards the contribution of the railways of Genoa and the Lago Maggiore, Novara, Susa, and Savoy, in works of every description. He hastened the development of interior communications, everywhere favouring the spirit of association and enterprise. Again, scarcely had Cavour come into power, when he resolved to realise in little Piedmont a great idea—that of commercial freedom, which he inaugurated by a custom-house reform; and further diplomatically established by treaties of commerce with France, England, Belgium, and Switzerland. Cavour, let us add, did not proceed as a dogmatist—as a prejudiced or a whimsical freetrader; he carried out a gradual reform practically, one proportioned to the circumstances, and which was to become profitable to consumers through the diminution of tariffs; to further maritime commerce, stimulate the internal industry of the country by foreign competition, and feed it by the decrease of taxes on raw material, while it made an opening for the exportation of national productions.

To increase expenses and make new debts when it was necessary to levy new taxes; to carry out a reform of tariffs immediately after a postal reform, this together with a reduction of the salt-tax, when the budget presented a deficit, was assuredly to be bold—perhaps rash. In this difficult and complicated work Cavour exhibited an imperturbable confidence, relying on " Liberalism and the marvels it can work," to use his own expression ; with a full conviction of the vivifying influence of these particular expenditures for which he was blamed, and which he was continually compelled to stand up for, against all attacks. He demonstrated that if one or two millions of francs were devoted to the improvement of the ports, it would bring in five hundred thousand francs per annum ; that if ten millions of francs were spent in piercing the Luckmanier, it would increase the commerce of Genoa by a third, perhaps by one half. He explained that to take shares and secure an interest in the railway of Savoy, was to cause the circulation of fifty millions of francs, in a province that sorely needed capital. " In order to realise our programme," said Cavour, " and profitably cultivate the country's resources, it was necessary to give a powerful impulse to works of public utility; to work our railways with all possible circumspection, while we gave encouragement to other enterprises. . . . . In order that the position which, for so many centuries the monarchy of Savoy has maintained, should not be suffered to decline, it was necessary to reorganise and fortify our army. . . . . This scheme made it necessary for us to raise new loans, or rather to contract larger loans than they would need to have been, if we had acted on the system of modesty and economy. It consequently became necessary to increase the taxation; but that could not be done, nor could the resources of the country be developed without undertaking the reform of our economic system on a large scale. . . . . ''

This reform, undertaken to awaken the activity of the country's resources, was, in truth, not only a commercial and financial work; the diplomatic form under which it was introduced had, in the mind of Cavour, and among his designs, another character and another part to play. It was to draw Piedmont forth from the isolation in which the country had remained since its misfortunes, bringing it into closer contact with great western nations, with England and with France; in a word, it formed a bond of united interests which might grow into one of policy and of ideas. Austria was not deceived. Before he died, Prince Schwartzenberg, the Austrian prime minister, remarked, with faintly-masked ill-humour: "Piedmont intends, with its commercial policy, to purchase the support of England for Italy!" This was not absolutely true; or, at least, Cavour made no sacrifice, and sometimes he protested against having been influenced by a hidden policy in the direction of a reform which he thought serviceable to his country. In reality, he was trusting to the logic of things; he had no doubt but that, in remaining constitutional, and in adopting commercial with the other liberties, Piedmont would rapidly gain public sympathy in England, and that that would give it additional strength. "England," he said to an intimate friend, "is no longer the champion of absolutism on the Continent, and an English minister would find it difficult to take part with Austria in the oppression of Italy."

As to France, Cavour did not hide his intention of contracting a friendship with France under the veil of a commercial treaty. If that treaty was not in every point what he could have desired, and if he had been obliged to make some concessions to the French protectionist system, he made up his mind to it; he recognised a political rather than an economical advantage in so doing. "The horizon is still dark around us," he said, "and our institutions are not as yet protected from all danger. Something perhaps may chance to make us desire at least the moral support of France. Let me say frankly, in the face of impending possibilities I think it prudent, conformable with the interests of the country, to be on good terms with France. We have not neglected matters of economy, but merely left them in the background. Views of policy have caused us to accept a treaty which will strengthen a good and cordial understanding between us and France. . . . ." And Cavour adds, yet more strikingly, words that, spoken in 1851, seem almost prophetic: " Is it not possible that complications may arise, in which all surrounding nations may be concerned, in two great questions—the Eastern and the Western? Were this to happen, should we not do well to be on good terms with France? . . . ."

Thus all concurred successfully under the thoughtful and liberal direction of one who knew how to use finance, commerce, and diplomacy, in placing Piedmont on her feet again.

IV.

That which Cavour accomplished by his financial and commercial system, he not only attempted but effected, in a higher moral sphere, by his religious policy, which has been one of the clearest manifestations of Liberalism in clerical matters.

He had this problem to solve : the reconciliation of the ecclesiastical situation with the principles of the "statuto," and the maintenance of the liberal and national Piedmontese policy in its civil relations with the Church and the Court of Rome. It was ever recurring as a natural consequence to new conditions, with the decrees of the laws for the abolition of ecclesiastical privileges, that of civil marriages, the law for the reorganisation of Church property, and the suppression of certain monastic orders.

With every new project the contention became warmer; the clerical agitation, kept up by the remonstrances of Rome, was combated by the anti-clerical agitation. In parliament, the Government was accused by the Left of not proceeding with sufficient resolution and energy in religious matters ; while the Right complained that no negotiations were entered into with the

Holy See, and that the good pleasure of Rome was not consulted. Cavour's manner of handling the questions, as delicate as they were formidable, showed a mind full of decision, and at the same time absolutely free from prejudice. For a moment, no doubt, he had thought it possible to come to some arrangement with the Vatican, but he very soon perceived that it was impossible; the more so, that the religious reaction, which was spreading in Italy as well as Europe, only hardened the Court of Rome in its demands and its refusals. It was not long before he saw the Pontificate involved in dangerous fellowship with the enemy beyond the Alps by the Austrian Concordat.

He had, in reality, ceased to believe in an understanding with Rome, for the realisation of the reforms Piedmont had at heart, and as for him, he had ceased to desire it. "If we put ourselves in direct relations with Rome," he said, writing to an intimate friend, "we completely ruin the political edifice we have so laboriously erected. If we enter into an arrangement with the Pope it will be impossible for us to retain our influence in Italy. Let us not go too far, but neither let us suffer ourselves to retreat even one step. You know that I am not a priest hater, that I am disposed towards conciliation, and would willingly give the Church greater liberty than she now enjoys; you know that I should be disposed to give up the *exequaturs*, the exclusive management of the universities, &c., but, under present circumstances, I am persuaded that all attempts at concord would be to our disadvantage. . . . ." He spoke much to the same effect in another circumstance, in the heat of action : "We have to fight Austria at Venice and at Milan, and also at Bologna and at Rome!"

Thus the question of ecclesiastical reforms, the relations with the Church and with Rome, was contemplated by Cavour as being a national question, besides one of interior order—it was one of the elements of the Italian situation.   To pretend to solve that question by stratagem or compromise, would only result in endless weariness and waste of time.   With Cavour there was but one solution—liberty and complete independence of civil and religious authority ; a grand yet simple idea, which was soon to resolve itself into these few emphatic words : "A Liberal Church in a Liberal State!"   He who raised that standard in a small corner of Italy was neither a theorist nor a revolutionist yielding, at the risk of overthrowing interests, beliefs, and traditions, to a fanciful love of novelty ; neither was it the work of a puzzled tactician, trying to conceal a parliamentary campaign against Clericalism under the cloak of an epigram.   Cavour neither had the passion of a leader of a faction, the subtlety of a casuist, nor the flippancy of a thoughtless innovator.   In a liberty accepted without subterfuge, he saw a sure means of freedom for the lay portion of the country—I may call it that of the nation, since he did not separate Italy from Piedmont—without in any degree subjecting the spiritual portion, namely, the Church.

"Oh, that man," said Archbishop Darboy—the same who later fell a victim to the Commune—when at Rome, "that man was indeed of a rare sort ! he had not the slightest sentiment of hatred in his heart."

Nothing could be truer; the Liberalism of this great Piedmontese did not proceed from any sentiment of hatred or vulgar animosity. Assuredly Cavour was not what he called a "priest hater," and this it was that constituted the superiority and originality of his religious policy. He had inaugurated and started reforms wherein he saw the development of the "statuto," and he intended to carry them out; but in claiming social independence he did not refuse liberty to the Church; he left her entire mistress of her own ground; indeed he carried rather far his feeling of lay incompetency.

When some members of the Left, Brofferio and Asproni, requested that the State should supervise the education in the seminaries, he replied, emphatically: "If I had to give an opinion as a citizen, and not as a minister, I should say that the Government ought not to interfere in the teaching of theology, which it is solely the province of the bishops to watch over. Bishops should not have to do the work of members of parliament, nor deputies that of bishops. We are at liberty to believe or not to believe, and to select whom we choose for our spiritual advisers. If we are dissatisfied with the moral teaching of the seminaries, we will choose our confessors from among theologians who have attended the school of Asproni." And he added, more seriously: "How can the clergy become converted to our institutions, and how will they love them if, after having, not unreasonably, withdrawn some of the privileges which they enjoyed under the old *régime*, and just as we are about to deprive them of the few that remain, we should say to them : ' We reform, according to the principles of liberty and equality, all those points of legislation which formerly were favourable to you; but as to your independence and your liberty, we wish to preserve those traditions of the past which we call, so far as they are opposed to you, the glorious heritage of our fathers !' . . . . The best way of increasing the political influence of the clergy is to give them an exceptional position, persecute, or even subject them to petty vexations."

V.

Cavour doubtless had his own opinions upon the absolutist and theocratic tendency of the Church at that time, and the risks of such a tendency. He was under no illusion about the nature of Clericalism when combined with politics, having frequently to combat and hold his ground against it. He was careful, however, not to meet these aggressions with retaliations on the part of the Government; he continued moderate even in the reforms for which he was so vehemently reproached.

What, for instance, was that law—one of those which caused the greatest uproar—on the suppression of certain monastic orders, and on Church property ? Without affecting the rights of religious associations, it suppressed the mendicant and a few other orders, depriving them of civil status; while it sanctioned the teaching and nursing orders, especially that of the Sisters of Charity, which Cavour was foremost in defending against the attacks of the Left, declaring that nothing should induce

him to subscribe to a law suppressing charitable orders.
" I would quit the Ministry ten times," he said, "rather
than bind myself to an act that would, in my opinion,
be immensely prejudicial to our country in the eyes of
civilised Europe. . . . ."

As to the possessions of the Church, the object was
to create a special fund, endowed with the revenues of the
suppressed orders, and dedicated entirely to the clergy.

On this point Cavour did not hesitate; it was one of
the fixed ideas of his policy. He had always been
opposed to what was called the *incameration* of ecclesiastical property—in other words, to the dispossession
of the Church, transformed into a corps receiving salary
from the State; and the reason he gave for such an
opposition was a singular one from the mouth of a
minister. It was, that this measure would create the
worst form of despotism, the administrative despotism.
" I have," said he, "the misfortune—or the good luck,
which you will—to be minister in a country where a
certain degree of centralisation reigns, and where the
Government has quite enough in its hands. I declare
to you, that if you add this one of which you speak to
the powers of Government, you will give what will be
threatening to liberty. . . . ." But this was not the
chief reason; the one which determined Cavour was one
of " high policy."

His true reason was that the expropriation of the
clergy would lead to the extension and intensifying of the
spirit of caste, by the complete isolation of the clergy, in
the midst of a civil centre, and the tightening of the bonds
uniting the priest with the sacerdotal hierarchy. "It has

been," he said, "carried out on a very large scale in some European countries. In France, before the Revolution, the clergy was, if I am not mistaken, as rich as that of Spain. It was totally stripped, and was not allowed to retain a vestige of its old possessions. What ensued? I have a great respect for the French clergy, and I admit that it is more moral and also more zealous than it used to be; but no one can deny that it is also less national and less liberal than was the clergy of the old *régime*. For that was animated by a spirit of independence with regard to Rome, and a certain degree of attachment to national views; it had the instincts of liberty. Now things are different; all facts go to prove that the modern French clergy is infinitely more Ultramontane than our national clergy. It will be said: 'But there is another course that could be pursued: let us leave the followers of the faith to remunerate their own clergy.' Do you know what would be the consequence of this? A double amount of zeal, fanaticism, and Ultramontanism. Such a system exists in Ireland. There the clergy is unsalaried; its means of existence consist of charity and the voluntary contributions of the faithful. That clergy is both more fanatical and less liberal than the clergy of France."

On this point Cavour was of the same mind as De Tocqueville. Thus it was that he refused to have anything to do with ecclesiastical expropriations, or to make use of any such means for the balancing of his budget. Religious reform was to result from a legitimate and progressive secularisation of civil society, not from hostility and persecution.

Cavour was a great Liberal and at the same time a great politician. Determined to persevere to the end to keep the Liberal aims of the country free from interested motives, and to protect these formidable religious questions from revolutionary passions, he was anxious to avoid any hasty step. He was especially desirous not to cause divisions in the public mind, and he frankly stated his reasons to Sig. Depretis, who one day questioned him about it : " It is in order that the nation may be unanimous, if an opportunity should present itself of regaining our lost position by an energetic effort."

He wished neither to divide public opinion nor to allow the good name of the country to be compromised by causing useless annoyances, and when it was proposed to subject all students, including those at the seminaries, to military service, he made a firm resistance. " Your proposition will be regarded throughout the country as a revolutionary act. . . . . In the present state of things I should consider as a great evil any act that could, even externally, present the appearance of a revolutionary measure." He had no difficulty in remaining moderate, despising party excitement, precisely because he was a politician who, without paltry prejudices, followed out the realisation of a lofty scheme.

His genius was essentially tolerant and practical ; he could not see the necessity for wasting words to wound the feelings of the clergy ; he was careful rather to win them over to the reforms which he required of them, and to captivate them : and he succeeded. Witness the amazement of the head of a religious order coming from Rome at the cordial reception he met with at the hands of Cavour; who afterwards remarked with a smile : " On leaving my house that brother has gone to the Bishop's palace, where he will certainly not have had such a reception as I gave him.   He will compare the two, return to Rome, tell his story, and, if he is honest, he will say that I am not the persecuting minister and diabolical person which at Rome they imagine me to be."   This was, perhaps, not owing to a spirit of calculation ; he acted spontaneously, just as, without display or ostentation, he would distribute alms to any of the poorer clergy who asked them of him.   Sometimes in the morning, dipping into his private purse as often as into the impoverished coffers of the State, he would, with one of his fellow-workers, prepare the slender pittance that a few priests were waiting for, while he remarked, cheerfully rubbing his hands: "Ah, if the gentlemen of the Left could see us at what we are doing !"

In its very groundwork Cavour's mind was a Liberal one ; there was nothing in him of the vulgar freethinker, turning to ridicule the belief in which he has been educated ; and of this he gave a curious proof which long remained unknown.   Seven years before his death, at the time when the contest about Conventual Laws was hottest, and when a fatal epidemic was raging in Turin, Cavour had taken precautions, should he too be stricken, against the painful scenes which had occurred at the death of Count Santa-Rosa.   He wished to make sure that the ministrations of the Church would not be refused him.

One morning he had quietly ordered and prearranged everything with Fra Giacomo, the parish priest of the

Madonna dei Angeli, whom he made the confidant of his charities. At the conclusion of their interview, Rattazzi, the recently-instituted minister of the interior, chanced to come in, and Cavour, after having courteously accompanied the priest to the door, turned to his colleague and said, simply : " We have arranged everything together in case any misfortune should befall me." It is remarkable that, seven years afterwards, faithful to his promise in 1854, Fra Giacomo hastened to the death-bed of the Piedmontese minister, then prime minister of Italy. It was with this resolute spirit, a mixture of boldness, shrewd tact, simplicity, liberal confidence, and universal activity, that Cavour conducted the religious campaign which, with the Exchequer and diplomacy, expressed his policy.

VI.

To say the truth, that policy did not propel itself; it had to work its way through many a resistance, many a contradiction and passionate opposition, and Cavour had daily to contend against difficulties of every kind, both within and without.

In the early part of 1853, almost immediately after he had become president of the council, relations with Austria had undergone a first shock. Taking advantage of a hot-headed Mazzinian outburst at Milan, Austria thought fit to strike a blow at the Lombard *émigrés* at Turin ; she sequestrated the property of the Casati, the Arese, the Arconati, the Torelli, and many others. After having frankly fulfilled its duties of international police in suppressing the Milanese outbreak, Piedmont could not refrain from protesting against a measure of spoliation which affected men who not only were manifestly innocent of any offence, but who had become naturalised Piedmontese, and of whom some were members of parliament. This protest had no effect; hence arose, if not a rupture, a coldness manifested by a reciprocal recall of ambassadors.

Cavour in his heart did not regret an incident that, in less than four years after the conclusion of peace, seemed to revive the national question, and in which Austria had to bear the responsibility of a bitter provocation, condemned alike by France and England. "Austria," he said, "has managed to set public opinion and all the Governments of Europe against her. In trying to damage us, she has done us service; we will take advantage of it." Nevertheless, this half-rupture gave rise to a delicate and precarious situation; one not without anxiety, and which reactionists in Piedmont and in Europe did not fail to turn to account by representing it as due to an improvident and impatient policy of a Cabinet inspiring revolutionary agitation; but this, as yet, was nothing. In the interior, difficulties were hourly becoming more serious and more painful.

Unfortunately the new system of taxation, the financial reforms, and the commercial treaties could not be carried out without clashing with many interests, provoking much uneasinesss, and causing temporary panics. To these were added bad harvests, and diseases smiting the silkworms and the vines. The spirit of party or faction took advantage of whatever occurred. If bread rose in price, the fault was charged against Cavour and his reforms. Harangues were raised against the ministry that starved the people, and took what was theirs by right; and one evening, in the peaceful city of Turin, an excited crowd, crying "Death to him," streamed in the direction of the house of Cavour, whose windows were broken, while an attempt was made to take it by assault. This, however, was but a skirmish; it was by no means a true index of the sentiments of the people of Turin. The following day Cavour, accompanied by La Marmora, walked through the streets on his usual way to the ministry of finance, and as he went he everywhere met with signs of respectful affection.

In Savoy, reactionary newspapers endeavoured to inflame the populace and encourage discontent by a perfidious comparison between the old and the new rates of taxes. Cavour was publicly accused of crushing the artisan and the labourer with imposts that he might prosecute his Utopias about Italy. The municipal council of Chambéry, altogether under reactionary influence, almost gave the signal for a refusal to pay the levy. The National Guard declined to be present at the rejoicings in honour of the "statuto." A Savoyard wrote to Cavour: "If you are obstinate we are doubly so; it is not in Savoy that heads are weathercocks."

Cavour's religious policy was made a pretext for still greater excitement. External agitation kept pace with the parliamentary combat. The Government which was leading Piedmont "to schism, anarchy, and destruction," was threatened. The execution of the law for the suppression of certain convents provoked painful scenes of resistance. Epidemics and famines were declared to be a visitation from heaven for the institution of sacrilegious laws. How much more so was it when misfortune fell on the royal family itself; when death removed the queen's mother, the queen, and the Duke of Genoa in the space of a few days? These unforeseen occasions for mourning were spoken of at the court, among those immediately about the person of the king, as warnings from heaven.

In this tangle, although Cavour did not waver an instant, he was sometimes anxious: "Policy is becoming more and more perplexing," he wrote to his friends at Geneva; "we have to contend against famine, new taxes, priests, and reactionists. . . . . Nevertheless, I do not relinquish hope." Another day he wrote thus from Leri, where he had gone to enjoy a few moments' needful rest: "After a desperate struggle, in parliament, in the salons, at the court, as well as in the streets, to which are added a number of lamentable circumstances, I found I had reached the end of my intellectual resources, and I have come here to restore them by a few days' rest. Thanks to my natural elasticity of fibre, I shall shortly be able to resume the weight of affairs; before the week is out I hope to be back at my post, where difficulties await me, giving rise to a political situation likely to become more and more strained. . . ."

It was a laborious and an unceasing struggle, combined, as it was, with intricacies and vicissitudes, to which a prime minister of less "elasticity of fibre" than he must have succumbed.

This stoutly-contested policy, nevertheless, began to make itself felt and seen in its primary results, and in a few years it began to bear fruit. On all sides the movement was discernible. With his persevering and methodical energy, and by the help of a minister of finance who did not begrudge the money necessary, La Marmora had already had time to reorganise the military institutions, and construct an army, which, although it could not be numerous, was nevertheless able to bear with dignity the Italian standard. Nor was the new economic management sterile. Stimulated by liberty, national activity manifested itself in every form of industry and commercial enterprise. The works of public usefulness, when completed, were a source of wealth. At the beginning of 1854 the Genoese railway was opened; cutting its way through the Apennines to that Gulf of the Mediterranean, where Cavour was proud to have arrived on the first locomotive.

By small degrees Piedmont began to present the appearance of a little country full of life, quick to spring to her feet, knowing how rightly to make use of the freedom of a constitutional rule; and she soon acquired an honourable name in Europe; and in France, as in England, the country won attention and sympathy.

Cavour himself was visibly rising in public consideration. The ability he displayed in the management of struggles, out of which he always came the stronger, inspired a growing interest and confidence in those around him. In the midst of all these affairs, his thoughts remained fixed on the momentous enterprise before him;

he did not overlook the serious character of it, and, in a
private letter to Madame de Circourt, in 1854, he wrote
as follows :

"Circumstances have led Piedmont to take a
clear and positive position in Italy. I know that it
is not without danger, and I feel all the responsibility
that it imposes on me ; but honour and duty have laid
the burden on us. Since Providence has so willed it that
Piedmont should alone be free and independent in Italy,
it is the duty of Piedmont to use that liberty and independence in pleading the cause of our unfortunate peninsula
before Europe. We will not shrink from that perilous
task ; the king and the country are determined to accomplish it to the uttermost. Maybe your friends, the
doctrinaires and the Liberals, who deplore the loss of
liberty in France after they have helped to stifle it in
Italy, will consider our policy absurd and romantic. I
am resigned to their censures, feeling certain that
generous hearts like yours will sympathise with our
efforts to recall to life a nation for centuries buried in a
frightful tomb. If I should fail, you will not refuse to
give me a corner among the eminent vanquished who
fly to group themselves about you. . . . . Take this
confession as the avowal that my whole life is conse-
crated to one object—that of the emancipation of my
country. . . . ."

This, then, was his avowed aim and object ; but in
order to reach it Cavour knew there must be many a
halting-place ; there might still be more than one road
to it, and the result of the policy he had been following
for more than four years, and by which he was raising

himself in raising his country, was precisely that one which was to enable Piedmont to reach its aim by any road, taking advantage of any favourable opportunity that might offer. When such an opportunity should present itself, Cavour was not the man to let it pass.

VII.

What Cavour had foreseen as early as 1851, when he spoke of the diplomatic advantage of a treaty of commerce, was at hand. The Russian war with France and England was the event which might involve the interests of all countries, and divide " into two camps the East and the West." From the first Cavour watched the great conflict with an attentive eye ; he apprehended its inevitable extension, and was, as it were, fascinated by it. In the spring of 1854, when the armies of France and England were making for the Black Sea, one evening in the company of Count Lisio, at the house of his niece, Countess Alfieri, in whose society he loved to seek repose, Cavour appeared absorbed. " Why should you not send ten thousand men ? " said his niece to him, suddenly, as though guessing at what was in his mind. " Ah ! " he replied, eagerly, " if everyone thought that, it would already be done." Every now and then the Countess Alfieri, a woman of intelligent mind, and well fitted to understand her uncle, would ask : " Well, are we ready to start ? " and he would only reply, with a smile : " Who knows ? "

The truth was that Cavour was entirely in favour of such a scheme, and if it had rested only with him he would have been one of the first to join the Western alliance, thrown open by the Anglo-French treaty of alliance of April 10, 1854. Piedmont could well do as she would ; she had not been in direct relations with Russia since 1848. Perhaps, from antipathy to the Liberal Government of Turin, and also no doubt with a view to pleasing Austria, the Emperor Nicholas had not even vouchsafed a reply to the first official notifications of King Victor Emmanuel. Piedmont's liberty of action and sympathies with the Western cause were therefore under no restraint ; but Cavour was not acting alone. Besides the king, whom he first brought round to his views, there were his colleagues, nearly all stubborn men, to win over—the minister of foreign affairs, Dabormida, Rattazzi like the rest—then parliament, then public opinion.

It must be admitted that when at first the report of this project spread abroad in Turin, it produced an impression that it was the madness of an adventurous spirit. Why throw the country into this far-off enterprise ? What place would little Piedmont take beside the two greatest Powers of Europe ? What the part of the modest Sardinian contingent among the armies of France and of England ? Was it a time to impose new sacrifices on the country for a ruinous piece of folly, when it was so difficult to meet the deficit of the budget ?

Without being insensible to oppositions of which he could not be independent, Cavour did not relinquish his aim. He saw an opportunity of blotting out Novara and bringing forward the new Sardinian army, while securing the support of England and France, and acquiring for Piedmont both moral and diplomatic credit. He centred all his energies in popularising his scheme and in gaining allies; and, at one time, persuaded that another might be more successful in the matter than himself, he proposed to Massimo d'Azeglio that he should take his place as president of the council, while he served under his orders, or even, if necessary, quitted the ministry. "Do what you think best," he wrote; "I will support you through and through, provided you make the alliance." D'Azeglio promptly declined, promising to give his fullest aid to a policy of which he appreciated the greatness, and feeling that none could conduct it more sagaciously than he who had conceived it.

In the midst of his perplexities Cavour's eye was on Austria, when suddenly the news went forth at Turin that the Viennese Cabinet had signed the treaty of December 2, 1854, with France and England, by which it both did and did not bind itself. From that moment the question became urgent. If, before going any further, the scheme of Austria was to cause her assistance to be purchased at Paris and in London by pledging her Italian possessions, it would be the interest of Piedmont to counteract it by an immediate alliance with the West; if, on the other hand, Austria intended to drag on in an equivocal neutrality—and this the penetrating eye of Cavour foresaw—the Cabinet of Turin would necessarily gain an advantage by outstepping it with a frank and bold resolution. Lastly, if Austria through some unexpected circumstance threw herself towards Russia, then all would be for the best, and the Italian question would spring up of itself. In any case

no hesitation was possible, and at the last moment
Cavour was encouraged by one who ever remained
his devoted friend, Sir James Hudson, the English representative at Turin, who had just received from his
Government the order to propose, in conjunction
with the minister of France, a treaty of alliance with
Piedmont.

As long as the conditions of the alliance were not
fixed there would of course still be difficulties to contend
with. Would the Sardinian Government be satisfied by
sending a contingent for an auxiliary corps in the pay of
England ? The Cabinet of London seemed to have
understood it thus ; but neither Cavour, who held to the
independence of his policy, nor La Marmora, who felt a
just pride in the small expeditionary corps of which he
was to be chief, would ever consent to lend themselves
to that arrangement. They would admit of no other
part for Piedmont than that of one ally negotiating with
another, defraying its own expenses, and preserving the
dignity and disinterestedness of its co-operation, that it
might retain equal rights. All that was asked of the
English Cabinet was the facilitation of a loan.

On the other hand, the ministry of Turin would
evidently have preferred some guarantee for Italy, or, at
the least, some sort of ostensible pledge of sympathy.
It would have wished England and France to bind
themselves to claim at Vienna the raising of the decree
sequestrating the Lombard estates ; but to this condition,
which the Sardinian Government held to in a spirit of refined generosity, neither France nor England could agree,
and the question might perhaps have proved serious,

had it not been happily put an end to by the principal Lombard *émigrés*, who, in the interests of the negotiation, begged that Cavour would not trouble himself about them.

At the eleventh hour, on the refusal of General Dabormida to yield the point of the guarantee, Cavour was compelled himself to take the management of foreign affairs, in order to sign without conditions : and thus, out of much perplexity and much deliberation, was concluded the treaty of January 10, 1855, uniting Piedmont to France and England, and which Count von Usedom called "a pistol fired in the ear of Austria."

VIII.

There was yet another battle to fight in parliament, and Cavour had clearly to face every sort of opposition. In the camp of the Right the Piedmontese intervention was looked upon as a totally unnecessary adventure, which might prove ruinous, and which would condemn the country to waste of money, while it caused the army to play an ill-defined subordinate part. And more : that which Cavour had so laboriously effected was termed an act of weakness, the enforced penalty of the revolutionary policy of the Cabinet, the consequence of the change to Liberalism of the president of the council, and his alliance with the Left Centre, or party of action. It was said that France and England, in directing their arms to the East, had been unwilling to forego the chance of complications in Italy, and had therefore insisted on binding Piedmont. That treaty was on their part a precautionary measure; an imposed guarantee.

In the camp of the Left things were still more extra-ordinary. The entry of Piedmont into that "European concert," in which Austria was to be one of the principal "performers," was sneered at. A treaty with the Western Powers was a desertion of the national cause. "The alliance," said Brofferio, "is economically charge-able with rashness; militarily, it is a piece of folly; and politically, it is a wicked act." It would surely lead to a desertion of Liberal principles! The extreme Liberals went so far as to provoke among a few misled subaltern officers a protest, in which it was stated that "no Government had a right to dispose of Italian soldiers to fight in an anti-national war;" and it went on to say: "Let us rise, and swear that we will only consent to fight for the unity of Italy, and for those people who aspire to defend their nationality! . . . ." The more moderate, and those who had a certain pretension to shrewdness, complained that for a time at least neutrality was not maintained, an armed neutrality, which could seize its favourable opportunity in the midst of the complications with which Europe was threatened.

Neither one side nor the other seemed to see that there was yet another means of serving Italy. Cavour let them have their say, and then he laid before them his policy in a speech which was animated with the breath of a new life. He showed them that neutrality could not be other than a dangerous falling into the back-ground; that to stop the progress of Russia towards the Mediterranean was more in the interest of Piedmont than in that of any other nation ; and, making straight at the knotty point of the matter, he asked whether the alliance would be favourable or injurious to Italy ?

Here was the whole question : "We have joined the alliance," said he, "without relinquishing our exterior sympathies any more than our interior principles. We have not hidden our anxiety for the future of Italy, or our desire to see its condition ameliorated. But how, I shall be asked, can the treaty serve the cause of Italy ? It will serve it in the only way possible—in the actual situation of Europe. The experience of these last years, as well as that of centuries, shows how little Italy has benefited by conspiracies, plots, revolutions, and futile excitements. Far from bettering her condition, they have been among the greatest evils which have befallen this beautiful portion of Europe, and that, not only on account of the innumerable misfortunes to individuals resulting from them, but because these perpetual schemings, these insurrections and uprisings have resulted in a diminution of the esteem and sympathy which other nations might have entertained for Italy. . . . . And now the first of conditions for the good of the peninsula is the restitution of her good name. . . . . To effect this, two things are necessary : first, we must prove to Europe that Italy has sufficient civil sagacity to govern herself liberally, and that she is in a position to give herself the most perfect form of government ; secondly, we must show that our military valour is still what it was in the time of our ancestors. In the last seven years you have done much for Italy. You have proved to Europe that the Italians can govern themselves sagaciously. . . . .

But you must do more. Our country must give evidence that her children can fight courageously on the field. Believe this, that the glory our soldiers will know how to achieve on the Eastern coasts will do more for the future of Italy than all the noisy talking in the world. . . . ."

In speaking thus, fascinating the Chambers with the patriotism of his ideas, and in carrying, not without some trouble, a disputed vote, Cavour was not unaware that he was playing a formidable game. He had said to a friend, to whom he wrote immediately after signing the treaty: "I have undertaken a terrible responsibility; but, come what may, my conscience tells me that I have fulfilled a sacred duty!"

After that day of April, 1855, when La Marmora and his 15,000 Piedmontese soldiers were making their way towards the Crimea, Cavour was many a time affected with the consciousness of responsibility.

The little army was showing itself worthy of a place side by side with the allies before Sevastopol, and it had the instinct that it was there for the fulfilment of a great idea. On one occasion, when a poor soldier was struggling with deep mud in the trenches, a young officer cheerfully rallied him with the words: "Never mind, it is with this mud that Italy is to be made." Nevertheless, Cavour was deeply anxious, for, before fighting the Russians, the little Piedmontese army had, on its arrival, to contend with disease—with cholera. The epidemic struck its heaviest blows in the Piedmontese camp. At one time, in summer, a constant succession of deaths was recorded in Turin.

Major Cassinis, Victor de Saint-Marsan, and a Casati—all these fell victims to an obscure death in the flower of their youth. General Alexander La Marmora, brother to the commander-in-chief, was the next to be taken away.

The truth was sad enough, but public rumours exaggerated it; those foretellers of evil who had tried to hinder the expedition already triumphed over what they now, more than ever, called a mad enterprise. Cavour anxiously watched the course of events, writing to La Marmora: "We often meet together, and we always speak of you. Our thoughts and our best wishes are with you in that glorious but hazardous campaign to which your devotion to your country has led you." He never doubted the result, but he began to find time hang heavily; his mind was full of anxious apprehensions, of which he spoke when sitting one Sunday under the trees at Santena, whither he had gone with Sir James Hudson, Rattazzi, Minghetti, and Massari. "I knew it," he said; "when I advised the king and the country to venture upon this great enterprise, I was sure that we should meet with many heavy obstacles, and be sorely tried; but this battle with disease fills me with alarm; it is an evil complication. Let us not be discouraged, however; now that we have thrown ourselves headlong into the fight, it is useless to look back. I know that, when dying, Rosmini expressed a presentiment that the Western Powers would conquer. I hope so; and I, too, believe it. Never mind, we are but under a cloud." Those around him, and who heard him, could perceive a dramatic and patriotic conflict taking place between the anxiety of a serious man, and the unbounded confidence which never quitted him.

On that day Cavour might be said to have reached the eventful moment in a lifetime where everything depends on the success or failure of one event; where a minister who has played with fortune has no other alternative than to be either shunned and disgraced as an adventurer, or be a great man. Had he failed, there would, it is true, have been nothing in the spirit of vulgar adventure in what he attempted; but he was of the order of those who succeed, because they know how to deserve success; because they know how to combine judgment with boldness in their schemes; and when he himself still seemed uncertain of succeeding, he was on the eve of seeing his policy come victoriously out of the ordeal, to be crowned with all that can reward success.

IX.

The first satisfactory sign was the simple and laconic message which Cavour received the day following the battle of August 16, 1855 : "This morning the Russians, with 50,000 men, attacked the lines of the Tchernaya. Our pass-word was, 'King and country.' This evening you will know by telegram whether the Piedmontese were worthy to fight beside the French and the English. We have two hundred dead. The French despatches will tell you the rest." Piedmont was thus relieved of its heavy load of fears; it gladly welcomed this good report with a zealous, patriotic pride. As to

Cavour, he felt as much pleasure in the success of La Marmora as in his own. The brilliant conduct of the troops, and of their leader, not only justified the treaty, but it also justified the president of the council in the eyes of all those who had accused him of neglecting to settle the position of the Piedmontese general in the midst of the allied forces. Cavour had left nothing undone; in a delicate situation he had exhibited confidence, under which great good sense was hidden. He had said to himself that if, as was reasonably hoped, the army proved true to itself, and worthy of its country, its leader would naturally be raised to the position he had been able enough to win, and which no one would think of refusing him: in the contrary case, all diplomatic stipulations would be useless. He had placed confidence in the army and in La Marmora, and he had the delight of seeing it justified. The army was making a good appearance in the great conflict. With his military qualifications, and his spirit of command, La Marmora had had no difficulty in taking rank beside the generals of the allies in the Crimea, just as a little later he took his place in a council of war assembled in Paris. The military result, which formed a part of the scheme of Piedmontese intervention, was therefore attained by the courage of the combatants on the Tchernaya, and by the attitude of their leader, in whom Lord Clarendon recognised the bearing " of a soldier, a gentleman, and a statesman."

The next encouragement for Cavour's policy was Victor Emmanuel's visit to Paris and to London in the latter part of 1855, which proved how Piedmont had progressed in a short time.   Instead of being an obscure and insignificant State, lying hidden and forgotten at the feet of the Alps, Piedmont was gaining a firm footing on the European platform ; she was bringing herself into notice, and being talked about.   Victor Emmanuel was everywhere welcomed as the sovereign of a small kingdom which had known how to take a great and important step.   In Paris he soon became popular ; in London he was made much of, not only because he was a Crimean ally, but also because he was a constitutional king—the legal prince who had made Piedmont into " a small England in Italy."

Victor Emmanuel was accompanied in his travels by D'Azeglio, to whom Cavour had assigned a special mission.   " His presence is necessary," he said cheerfully, " to prove to Europe that we are not infected with revolutionary leprosy."   To this D'Azeglio lent himself with the delicacy and good-nature of the most genuine patriotism.   Cavour himself was naturally of the party, and had his share in the rejoicings and ovations of the occasion.   Once more he found himself in Paris—he had not visited it since 1852—which he now entered as a negotiator for the French alliance, an all-powerful and able minister, and a political personage of refined and fascinating manners.   From the Tuileries, where he held counsel with the chief men of the day, he would go to the house of Madame de Circourt, where he often met the representatives of the beaten parties.

" From six o'clock in the morning until two hours after midnight," he wrote, " I am always about ; I have never led so unquiet a life or one so useless : patience, however. . . . . The king is in good health and in the best of tempers. To-day there is a grand review, to-morrow a ball at the Hôtel de Ville, and Thursday we leave. I send Cibrario the programme of our stay in England; it is not an amusing one. When I shall reckon up my various rights to a retiring pension, I hope that the present trip will be counted as a campaign. . . . . I have seen Thiers; he approves of the war, but he would now desire peace. He despairs of his party, and almost despairs of parliamentary rule. Cousin has become a fusionist. . . . . I chanced to meet with Montalembert, and, notwithstanding the small amount of sympathy existing between us, we shook hands. I have also seen the Nuncio, and told him that we should wish for an agreement on the same basis as the French system; he pretended not to understand me. . . . ." Cavour saw much society; he saw every branch of Parisian society, and he even sometimes regretted not being able to escape the turmoil of official visits and receptions, to go to the theatre and be cheered by the sight of the "nymphs of the ballet."

In all these diversions, however, he never lost sight of the one essential point, the fixed subject of all his thoughts, and it was about that time, in the interviews he had with Napoleon III. at the Tuileries, that for the first time he heard those words which were to be the prelude to many an important event : " What can be done for Italy ? " It was perhaps only lightly uttered, perhaps merely a vague manifestation of sympathy and courtesy; but he who heard it, in December, 1855, was not a man to let it fall unheeded, and, if the stay of

Victor Emmanuel in Paris and London could have no immediate results, it was still the sign of a new era for Piedmont. It was like a sort of prologue or preparation for the more serious moral victory that Cavour was on the eve of securing at the Congress of Paris, by means of the general negotiations which were for a time to restore peace to Europe.

X.

Let me summarily recall the facts. Up to that time the war had been circumscribed in the East. The fall of Sevastopol, on September 8, 1855, had in reality brought the Crimean campaign to an end; and since that bloody and glorious feat of arms, the presence of winter had produced a tacit suspension of hostilities. It was now a matter of speculation whether the war would rekindle in a still more violent form, what point it would select, and what new direction it would take; and it was there that all interests met in a conflict half veiled between pacific and warlike influences. Russia appeared disposed henceforward to pay for her defeat by concessions in the East. England was the least anxious to lay down her arms, but she could do nothing without France, and France began to incline for peace. Austria, not having engaged her army, felt herself compelled to take some decisive measure, and was doing her utmost to bring about a settlement: and from all this an armistice came, with the preliminaries of peace. Such was the situation.

Cavour would, at heart, have desired a continuation

of the war. In a prolongation of it he perceived a further chance for Italy. Intervention and diplomacy were to him only a delusion. But, after all, if instead of war there was to be an armistice, he felt he must make the most of it, and hold himself in readiness for the negotiations which were about to commence at the European congress assembled in Paris.

The selection of a suitable agent had been a cause of considerable perplexity at Turin; D'Azeglio was pointed to as the probable plenipotentiary. To say the truth, everybody was a little frightened by the difficulties; the more so as no one saw very clearly in this new diplomatic phase. It soon became evident that Cavour alone could bring to happy issue a matter which he had been chiefly instrumental in promoting and directing. After hesitating a moment, he consented to start for Paris as chief Sardinian plenipotentiary, and from the moment of his arrival there he had to settle questions of the greatest importance. What part was Piedmont to play? What was to be her position in the congress? Nothing had as yet been decided. What Cavour had done for the Piedmontese general in the Crimea, he did for diplomacy, and he said: "When the king's government signed a treaty of alliance with England and France, it did not think fit positively or particularly to state the position to be assigned to Sardinia in the congress. The Government was convinced that, with nations as with individuals, influence and public esteem depend on conduct and reputation more than on diplomatic stipulations.

In Paris he relied on his natural resources, as he had

relied on La Marmora in the Crimea; and he was not deceived. Austria vainly tried to persuade France and England that Piedmont could take part in the war and not have a right to be represented at the congress; that she was only a state of the second order—an intruder in European affairs; Austria did not succeed. Neither France, England, nor Russia would consent to so humiliating an exclusion. This was the result of the "acquired status" of Piedmont, and also an opening victory for Cavour, who entered the congress on the same level as the representatives of the greatest Powers; and that day the Austrian plenipotentiary, Count Buol, might well fear that he would have, as he called it, a web to unravel. The position was still full of difficulty for one who, entering a congress with a contested right to his place there, had some day or other to introduce a personage even more objectionable—viz. Italy. It was in this that Cavour gave special evidence that he could mount with the occasion. Placed for the first time in the highest political position in Europe, and mixed up with matters of the greatest importance—as arbitrator of war and of peace—he proved himself equal, without effort, to everything required of him.

Perfectly master of himself, courteous with everyone, patient and shrewd, he chose to keep in the background at the few first meetings of the Congress; he spoke little, and when obliged to give an opinion on the matters under discussion—the free navigation of the Danube, or the neutralisation of the Black Sea—he gave it concisely and clearly, always taking the most liberal view. He very soon won golden opinions from his colleagues, astonishing them with the variety, justice, and depth of a mind that nothing seemed ever to take unawares. In the midst of this assembly, where so many interests met, and where policies were antagonistic or jealously eyeing one another, Cavour found no difficulty in taking a clear course, and in seizing affinities and antipathies in different natures ; nor was he slow in taking advantage of them, always being particularly careful not to separate himself from France and England.

As it appeared that peace was seriously contemplated, he saw no reason to wound the pride and feelings of Russia, plus the conditions already imposed upon her, and the more Austria was tenacious, the more lenient he became. By a singular contrast, Austria, which had done nothing and not lost a man, held rigidly and inflexibly against Russia, while Piedmont, which had bravely sent her soldiers to the fight, maintained a perfect moderation in the common victory of the Allies.

This difference in the attitude of the representatives of Austria and Sardinia did not fail to strike the Russian plenipotentiaries, and Count Orloff was grateful to Cavour. The friendliest understanding existed between them. One day, when the question of the neutralisation of the Black Sea was mooted, Count Orloff turned to Cavour and said, loud enough to be heard: " Count Buol speaks as though Austria had taken Sevastopol !" On another occasion, when the Austrian plenipotentiary was insisting on the subject of a small cession of territory— which by a diplomatic euphemism would be termed a " rectification of frontiers "—in Bessarabia, Count Orloff said to Cavour in a significant tone : " Austria's plenipotentiary does not know how much blood or how many tears this rectification of frontiers will cost his country." Assuredly the Piedmontese took no measures to soften the resentment of Russia towards Austria.

Before a month was out Cavour had solved the problem how to establish his position and acquire real authority, by the frankness and graciousness of his manners, as well as the superiority of his mind; and while the Congress was considering the question of the East and the Black Sea, the energetic plenipotentiary of Victor Emmanuel did not lose his time. Besides the official negotiations which were to be crowned by the treaty of peace of March 30, 1856, he had his own work to carry out. He had interviews with the Emperor at the Tuileries, with Lord Clarendon, Lord Cowley, and the representatives of Russia ; from some he secured support, from others co-operation, or at least a benevolent neutrality. His effort was to get the congress to consider the Italian question—that was the only question he had at heart, and he burned to be the champion of it before Europe. There indeed was the difficulty.

The Italian question was not discussed ; it did not exist officially ; it could not therefore present itself under a diplomatic and regular form. The " principle of nationalities " had not its accredited plenipotentiary.

The yoke of the foreigner could not be spoken of ; Austria would have had a right at once to protest against the discussion of such a matter in a congress. assembled to consider the Eastern question. Doubtless, this great Italian question, so difficult to lay hold of, had one vulnerable point ; it was a permanent violation of the treaties which diplomacy was accustomed to regard as the basis of the peace of Europe. A French army occupied Rome, and the indefinite prolongation of that occupation was a living testimony to the incapacity of the Papal Government to support itself. The Austrians had occupied the Legations ever since 1849, and appeared to be in no way disposed to quit Bologna. The Austrian dominion, a legal government in Lombardy, extended by an abuse of treaties to the duchies of Modena and of Parma as well as to Tuscany. The king of Naples could only sustain himself by acts of extreme arbitrary power. Hence a state of things chaotic and violent, which was dangerously favourable to revolutionary intrigues, and even menacing to Piedmont. In this direction it might be possible to strike on the Italian question, and bring it under the observation of diplomacy. Cavour left no stone unturned, and from the moment that he set foot in Paris he prosecuted the matter with indefatigable activity.

To the question which Napoleon III. had asked him— " What can be done for Italy ?" the Piedmontese minister replied by handing in a statement remarkable for vigour and lucidity. On the eve of the signing of peace, on March 27, he sent to his allies, France and England, a note, representing the situation of Italy under a new aspect ; he proposed for the Roman States—at least for the Legations—plans that were perhaps impracticable, but which might be at least a point from which to start and make a beginning. The more the congress advanced on the road to peace, the more Cavour became pressing, as though he felt that the opportunity purchased at such cost was about to escape him. In the end he won his mark. He succeeded in rousing Napoleon III. and fascinating Lord Clarendon, and in securing at least a certain favourable neutrality of the Russians.

Meantime the Emperor commissioned the French plenipotentiary, Count Walewski, to kindle the powder Cavour had amassed, and thus it was that eight days after the peace the Italian question was suddenly exploded in the congress at Paris, in that sitting of April 8, 1856, when Austria was for the first time compelled to hear the announcement that after Russia she might have to pay the expenses of the next war to come.

XI.

The sitting that day was very curious and memorable, from the consequences that ensued. The French plenipotentiary called every diplomatic euphemism to his assistance; he took advantage of the congress to provoke "an interchange of ideas on different subjects which were waiting to be settled, and which it would be well to take into consideration in order to prevent fresh complications." He mixed all the questions together, the occupation of Rome by the French troops, the occupation of the Legations by the Austrians, the situation of the kingdom of Naples, the anarchy of Greece, and the excesses of which the Belgian journals were guilty.

What the real question was it was easy to perceive, and Austria was the last to misunderstand it Count

Buol immediately protested the incompetency of the congress, and declined all discussion on the affairs of Italy. He would have no explanation, no manifestation whatever; and by his very attitude he forestalled any possibility of a practical solution. He very well perceived whence the blow came : up to a certain point he could evade it officially, but he could no longer prevent the outburst. Count Walewski said some hard words about the interior government of the king of Naples, and he admitted that the situation of Rome and the Roman States, reduced as they were to live under foreign protection, was "abnormal." Lord Clarendon, still more severe upon the king of Naples, plainly declared that the Pontifical government was the worst of all governments, and that the condition of the Romagna, hovering between a state of siege and one of brigandage, was frightful ; adding that the only remedy for such a state of things was secularisation, liberal reforms, and an administration conformable to the spirit of the age. Cavour, whose game was being thus so ably played, came forward in his turn to corroborate all that had been said, and to show that yet more wanted doing. He demonstrated that the " abnormal " was not only the situation of the Pontifical States and of Naples, it was that of the whole peninsula ; and that Austria, stretching her power from the Ticino to Venice, encamped at Ferrara and Bologna ; mistress of Placenza and possessing a garrison at Parma, destroyed the political equilibrium of Italy, constituting a permanent danger for Sardinia. "The Sardinian plenipotentiaries," he said, as he faced Count Buol, " therefore think it their duty to call the attention of Europe to a state of things so abnormal ; that which results from the indefinite occupation of a great portion of Italy by Austrian troops . . . . ."

What he uttered at the congress on April 8, he energetically confirmed a few days later in a communication to France and England on April 16, in which he stated that the condition of Piedmont was becoming insupportable, and that if nothing were done she would be driven to the terrible alternative of bending, like the other Italian States, under the yoke of Austria, or taking up arms. " Internally troubled," he went on to say, " by the action of revolutionary passions instigated around her by a system of violent compression and by foreign occupation, menaced with a still greater extension of Austrian power, the king of Sardinia may from one moment to another be compelled by an inevitable necessity to adopt extreme measures, of which it is impossible to foresee the consequences. . . ." It was, in a word, the exposure of a whole situation, and of a policy laid before all Europe by the most strenuous of men; and if for the moment nothing came of it but an empty protocol, the energy with which the question had been started revealed the growing gravity of Italian affairs.

But had not Cavour hoped for something more than a protocol? Was he not deceiving himself? No doubt he too, in spite of the high balance of his mind, was sometimes carried away in action. After having succeeded as far as success was possible for the moment, he thought he had not done enough, and then, side by side with official diplomacy, there was another chapter, showing him the victim of fits of impatience and frenzy.

Quick though he was to control himself, Cavour was subject to these hot moods; he felt it himself, and in a hurried account which he sent to Turin of all that he was doing and attempting, and of his mental agitation, he says : " I trust that after reading this you will not imagine that I have brain fever, or that I have fallen into a state of delirium ; on the contrary, the condition of my intellectual health is excellent. I have never felt more calm ; I have even obtained a great reputation for moderation. Clarendon has often told me that Prince Napoleon accuses me of being wanting in energy, and even Walewski praises my behaviour ; I am really persuaded, however, that boldness might not be unattended with success."

XII.

The fact is that for part of April, 1856, Cavour was mentally revolving every kind of plan. He did not even shrink from an immediate war with Austria ; even flattering himself into the belief that he could drag France and England into it too. His secret diplomacy was raised to a singular pitch, chiefly in two letters, certainly expressing the most curious of his mental preoccupations, and even of his particular situation, immediately after the congress.

" Yesterday morning," he says in one of his letters, " I had the following conversation with Lord Clarendon : ' My lord, that which took place at the congress proves two things—1st. That Austria is determined to persist in its system of oppression and violence towards Italy ; 2ndly. That diplomatic efforts are quite inefficient to modify that system. The results to Piedmont are extremely injurious. What with party irritation on the one hand, and the arrogance of Austria on the other, there are but two courses open to us; either to become reconciled with Austria and the Pope, or to make preparations for the declaration of war with Austria at no distant period. If the first alternative is the better, I ought, on my return to Turin, to advise the king to call to power the friends of Austria and the Pope. If the second is preferable, we shall not fear, my friends and I, to prepare ourselves for a terrible war—for war to the death !' Here I stopped, and Lord Clarendon, without expressing either surprise or disapprobation, then said : 'I think you are right, your position is growing critical ; I can imagine that an outburst may become inevitable ; only the time to speak of it openly has not yet come.' I replied : 'I have given you evidence of my moderation and prudence ; I think that in policy one should be excessively reserved as to speech, and exceedingly decided as to deeds. There are positions in which less danger will be found in an excess of audacity than in one of prudence. With La Marmora for our commander-in-chief, I am persuaded that we are fit to begin a war, and if it should last long you will be forced to come to our assistance.' Lord Clarendon eagerly replied : 'Oh, certainly, if you should be in trouble you can rely upon us; you will see how energetically we shall hurry to your aid.' . . ." Cavour did not doubt that these words, coming from so reserved a man as Lord Clarendon, showed that England was ready to let herself be drawn into a war having for its aim the freedom of Italy. But here began his illusion, and perhaps he exaggerated to himself the real meaning of Lord Clarendon's words, and the extent of his sympathy in this matter.

In another of Cavour's letters about the same time he gives an account of a visit he paid the Emperor, describing that busy mode of life so full of succeeding impressions, and in which he throws some light on the relations existing between the Piedmontese and the Austrian plenipotentiaries. "I have seen the Emperor," he says, "and I said much the same thing to him as I had said to Clarendon, only putting it a little more mildly. He listened courteously, and added that he hoped to bring Austria to a better view of things. He told me that on the occasion of last Saturday's dinner he had said to Count Buol that he deeply regretted to find himself in positive contradiction to the Emperor of Austria on the Italian question; upon which Count Buol immediately went to Walewski to tell him that Austria's greatest wish was to comply with the Emperor's wishes in every respect, that France was her only ally, and that it was therefore imperative that she should follow the same policy. The Emperor appeared pleased with this mark of friendship, and he reiterated that he would take advantage of it to obtain concessions from Austria. I showed myself incredulous, I insisted on the necessity for adopting a decided attitude, and I told him that to begin with I had prepared a protest which I would hand to Walewski the following day. The Emperor hesitated long, and finally said: 'Go to London, come to a clear understanding with Palmerston, then come and see me.'　The Emperor must have spoken to Buol, for he came to me with a thousand protestations about Austria's good feeling towards us, her desire to live peaceably with us, and to respect our institutions, &c. &c., and more humbug of the sort. I replied that he had not given much evidence of such a wish when at Paris, and that I was leaving with a conviction that the understanding between us was worse instead of better.　The conversation was a long and animated one, but always in a tone of urbanity and courtesy. . . . At parting he shook my hand, saying : 'Allow me to hope that *even politically* we shall not always be adversaries.'　I conclude from these words that Buol is somewhat uneasy at the exhibitions of opinion in our favour, and possibly also at what the Emperor may have said to him. . . . Orloff made a thousand protestations of friendship—he agreed with me that the condition of Italy was insupportable. . . . Even the Prussian speaks ill of Austria.　After all, if we have not gained anything practically in the eyes of the world, our victory is complete. . . ."

It was evident that this idea of a coming war with which Cavour flattered his mind could not long. be indulged.　It met with no encouragement in Paris, and Cavour soon perceived that nothing was to be gained from that journey to London which the Emperor advised him to take.　A gracious reception from the Queen and the Prince Consort, who exhibited a somewhat platonic interest in the affairs of Italy, an invitation to be present at a naval review, protestations of sympathy from Tories as well as Whigs for the Piedmontese

Constitutional Government—all this he met with in London; but beyond this he found the English very little excitable in favour of the national question. In fact, he was able to see but very little of Lord Palmerston, and such an interview as he had had in Paris with Lord Clarendon was not renewed in London. Cavour's steady mind soon reverted to the practical truth and a just appreciation of circumstances. But though the war which he had been prematurely dreaming of kindling, immediately after a recent peace, was only an illusion of a moment; and though he could not have all that he wished, what he had actually obtained in reality was nevertheless very real and singularly encouraging.

What more was wanted? Piedmont had united her arms with the arms of the greatest nations in the world, and wiped away the painful recollection of her defeat; she had offered in the fire of great battles the spectacle of what one of the French generals, Bosquet, called "a jewel of an army." She had taken her seat round the green-table of a congress, beside France, England, Russia, Austria, and Prussia. She had made herself one of the European Powers, and shown that the importance of a country is measured rather by its ability and valour than by extent of territory. She had acquired the right to touch upon forbidden questions, to speak for Italy, and constitute herself Italy's plenipotentiary.

This was the result of a policy as consecutive as it was resolute; and when Cavour returned to Turin after the congress, and there met with the same opposition which had assailed him before the Crimean campaign, harassing him anew with questions as to what he had gained, he was able quietly to reply: " We have not reached any very definite object, it is true ; but we have secured two things : In the first place, the anomalous and unhappy situation of Italy has been laid before Europe, not by demagogues or hot-headed revolutionists, nor again by excited journalists, but by the representatives of the highest powers of Europe ; by statesmen who govern the greatest nations, and who are accustomed to take council of reason rather than emotion. In the second place, these very Powers have declared that it was not only in the interest of Italy, but in that of Europe, that the ills of Italy should be remedied. I cannot believe that a judgment passed and a counsel given by such powers as those of France and England can be barren of good results. The principles which have guided us in these last years have enabled us to make a great advance. For the first time in the whole course of our history the Italian question has been broached and discussed in a European congress ; not as formerly at Laybach and Verona, with a view to aggravate the evils Italy had to bear, and put new chains about her neck ; but, on the contrary, with the openly-avowed object of finding some remedy for her oppressed condition, and to exhibit the sympathies of great nations towards her. The congress is ended, and now the cause of Italy is brought before the tribunal of public opinion. The action may be long, and the shiftings many. . . . . . We await the issue of it with an entire confidence. . . . . ." Thus spoke Cavour before the Chamber on his return to Turin. He was popularly recognised as the representative of a revived and strengthened Piedmont, and Italians hailed him as the hope of Italy.

CHAPTER III.

PARLIAMENTARY REIGN OF CAVOUR—PREPARATIONS FOR WAR.

A Pause after 1856—New Situation of Piedmont—Moral Headship of Cavour—Portrait of the Man—His Character—His Speeches—A Parliamentary Reign—Watchword of the New Phase—*Alere flammam!*—Activity in Turin—The Fortifications of Alessandria—Maritime Arsenal of Spezzia—Boring of the Mont Cenis—Piedmontese Policy in Italy—Cavour and Daniel Manin—Piedmont before Europe—Relations with Russia, with England, and with France—Crisis in Piedmontese Policy—Elections of 1857—The Crime of Orsini in Paris—Effects in Turin—Official and Secret Diplomacy—Speech of Cavour on the Alliances—Private Communications of the Emperor—Negotiations—Interview at Plombières—Secret Treaty—Scene on the 1st of January, 1859, at the Tuileries—Speech of King Victor Emmanuel before Parliament—Prologue of the War.

I.

It was a particular element of strength in Cavour, that he kept a definite object in view, obscured, it may be at times, by passing events, but ever present to his mind. His courage, though great, was surpassed by his presence of mind and political tact, by the art, which he possessed in an eminent degree, of suiting his actions to circumstances. Manzoni used to say of him that he was every inch a statesman, with " all a statesman's prudence and even imprudence." He could be prudent or imprudent as circumstances required. After the Paris congress, he found himself in a position equally brilliant and difficult. He had sown seed assiduously, and with a careful hand, and he looked for a harvest. But if, in the midst of all his excitement in Paris, he had indulged a hope of the possibility of a war of liberation being speedily entered upon, he had soon been obliged to recognise that, for one campaign, it was enough to have introduced the subject of Italy in the midst of the congress; that further steps in the same direction would only for the present set France, England, and the whole of Europe—slowly recovering from a recent conflict—against his scheme. He had quickly understood that the new situation, inaugurated by the peace of March 30, 1856, was still immature; that it was needful to give to all political views, all alliances and conflicting interests, time enough to assume a definite shape, by familiarising public opinion with the Italian question, which had been so suddenly brought forward. He had seen, in a word, that no decisive step could be taken for some years to come—perhaps two, or even three; and that until then the struggle must be continually renewed, in order, not only to keep possession of the ground already gained, but also to prepare for an onward march. One thing remained certain: the Paris congress had left the Italian question an open one; beyond the Alps, Piedmont and Austria now stood opposed face to face. On his return to Turin, Cavour remarked: "The Sardinian and Austrian plenipotentiaries, after sitting side by side for two months, parted without personal animosity, but thoroughly imbued with the conviction that the two countries were farther than ever from political union, and that the principles professed by the two States are irreconcilable." This avowed antagonism, thus laid before the whole of Europe, and accepted by Piedmont, was felt by Austria with all the rancour of a Power that has been set at naught; irritated by an antagonism which she rightly qualified as unequal, so long as only insignificant Piedmont was concerned in it, she increased the evil by her complaints and accusations. A few months later the quarrel would receive the perilous emphasis of a diplomatic rupture.

Even before the war in the East, in 1853, Austria had recalled Count Appony; after the war, early in 1857, she recalled Count Paar, recently sent as envoy to Turin. This was not yet a declaration of hostilities, but it was an acknowledgment of incompatibility between the imperial supremacy established at Milan, and the only free State in the Peninsula. To say the truth, this rupture could excite neither surprise nor emotion in Cavour, who had foreseen it, and was relieved by it, but desired to lay all the responsibility of it on Austria. He did not ignore " the difficulties and dangers " of ever-increasing tension in the relations between the two Powers; he saw in it one of the inevitable consequences of the situation accepted by Piedmont, one condition of the new campaign he had opened by the bold initiative he had taken at the Paris congress. To sap the Austrian domination morally, without affording her the pretext for a rash attack—to maintain the Liberal ascendency of Piedmont, though at the cost of much effort—to rally Italian patriotic sentiment around the banner of Victor Emmanuel without committing himself with the different Governments—to obtain allies by any means, while leading Europe gradually to consider the liberation of Italy as important in the interests of conservatism—to prepare for war under cover of peace—and to pursue all these objects in the midst of conflicting parties, and of incidents equally new and unforeseen : such was Cavour's work during the two or three years following 1856. A task so bold and intricate could only be carried on to the end by a man who had succeeded in obtaining a real preponderance, a sort of parliamentary kingship or dictatorship, an instrument powerful and supple to his hand. Few of the phenomena of contemporary parliamentary history are more striking and original than the power thus obtained by one man through parliamentary action.

II.

" We have a Government ; " so said the Turinese at this period ; " we have Chambers of representatives ; and we have a Constitution : the name for all that is— Cavour." The playful turn of the remark did not trifle with the truth of the matter. The fact is that at one time it was Cavour's fortune to eclipse, or rather to personify the Piedmontese constitutional *régime*, which owed him all its lustre and efficiency. Assuredly he was not alone in a country which numbered among its senators D'Azeglio, Count Sclopis, Count Gallina, Marquis Alfieri ; and among its deputies Balbo, Revel, Menabrea, Boncampagni, Rattazzi, Lanza, Mamiani Farini. More rapidly than the rest he had obtained the exceptional position of a man reigning in and by the Chambers, ruling parties and leading public opinion, which followed humbly in his train.

As the complication of events increased, and combinations of internal policy were added to diplomatic action, Cavour's influence increased also to an extraordinary degree. The Chambers shrank from refusing him anything he asked for; and if some eccentric members of the Radical or the Absolutist party, if Brofferio or Count Solaro della Margherita worried him with their conflicting attacks, they gave him but fresh occasion to strengthen his ascendency. Deputies who had come prepared to question anything and everything were frequently reduced to silence by a gesture or a keen glance from him—like the worthy tradesman of the Via di Po, who, one day while exhibiting his wares to the Countess Stackelberg, suddenly vanished into the colonnade, but as quickly reappeared, saying: " Pray excuse me, but I caught sight of Count Cavour, and I wanted to see how matters are progressing. He looked cheerful and smiling, so things must be going on all right; I feel comfortable now." It was thus in parliament; the habit was contracted of judging things by the countenance of the President of the Council.

Call it a dictatorship: but it was a most exceptional one, daily granted and hourly assented to; continually exercised under the control of the Chambers. Under the eye of a free nation Cavour, with a confidence which he knew how to impart to those around him, accepted all the conditions of a parliamentary life which he loved, and the strength and dignity of which he appreciated. Neither the conflict nor its consequences repelled him. On one occasion, on its being pointed out to him that a measure to which he attached the highest importance would already have been carried had he but been a minister of an absolute Government, he replied with great animation : " You forget that under an absolute Government I neither would nor could have been minister at all. I am what I am because I am fortunate enough to be a constitutional minister. A parliamentary government has its drawbacks like any other ; and yet, with all its drawbacks, it is worth more than all the others. I may lose patience with the opposition I meet with, and resist it energetically; but then, on reflection, I am thankful for such opposition, since it compels me to make my views clearer, and to renew my efforts to convince the majority. An absolute minister commands ; a constitutional minister, in order to be obeyed, must persuade: and I mean to persuade the majority that I am in the right. Believe me, the most inferior chamber of representatives is preferable to the most brilliant imperial anteroom." Thus he who appeared to be a dictator was in truth only the head parliamentary official, putting honestly into practice, with equal fidelity and liberal confidence, the *régime* which he appeared to overshadow.

No doubt Cavour owed the authority he had thus obtained to his success, to his being leader in an onward movement, and to the pre-eminence he had been able to give his little country in the settling of European difficulties. He owed it also to his genius for business, to the breadth and versatility of his mind, to a marvellous fertility of expedients, to the ready influence exerted by a sympathetic nature, at once amiable, easy, and forceful. Be sure it was no ordinary party-chief who could be at once Minister of Commerce, Minister of Finance, Minister of Foreign Affairs, Minister of the Interior, and even at a given moment, Minister of War; bearing all these burdens without bending under them, with never-failing aptitude and unwearying activity. Whether in parliament or directing business, Cavour reaped the advantages of his early practical training. He combined the superiority of a politician pursuing the realisation of an idea, with that of a man who had mastered all the details of administration and of political economy. Completely identified with his country, he was as well acquainted with every province and town of Piedmont as with his own estate at Leri.

Agriculture, commerce, industry, maritime interests, state finances, and even the finances of the communes—none of these came amiss to him. He often amazed and disconcerted his enemies, proving to them with playful gusto that he knew the affairs of their particular locality better than they did. He had the art of interpreting dry financial statements, so grouping facts and figures as to lend them a living interest. In the endless discussions upon the new taxes, he would give a graphic and animated description of what the people had to pay for these terrible taxes, and, on the other hand, how much they had been the gainers by the diminution of tariffs, by increased facilities of traffic, and by railroads; and he would depict with a master-hand the increase of national prosperity under the happy influence of this system of economical Liberalism so much cried down by its opponents. To a member who was complaining on behalf of his provincial district, the fertile regions of Monferrat, so rich in wine and cereals, Cavour replied, without hesitation: " The honourable member who has just spoken on behalf of the Monferrat agriculturists must be himself a skilful cultivator, and doubtless he makes thirty-one hectolitres of wine per hectare. The means of communication between Nice (in Monferrat) and Alessandria give him a profit of at least 1f. 50c. per hectolitre, which represents 45f. per hectare. I beg him to inform us whether he pays 45f. per hectare in taxes." Much laughter greeted this home-thrust by way of demonstration. Cavour possessed the advantage of a thorough acquaintance, of the most precise and intimate kind, with all that concerned his country. This was no doubt one of the causes of his ascendency; but it was far from being the only one, nor even the truest, or, if the word is allowable, the most human.

III.

The real cause of Cavour's superiority and authority in parliament, as well as at the head of affairs, was the quality of the man—the attractive originality of his marvellously well-balanced nature. Cavour had nothing in common with the mediocre statesman, ambitious of power, and yet encumbered with it; full of his own importance, exhausting subtleties and complications, and, with much labour, achieving infinitesimal results. In him there was no arrogance, no strain, no uncertainty. He was the most natural and straightforward of politicians, carrying out his innumerable engagements with the greatest case; doing the most engrossing work without effort or fatigue; holding cheaply all etiquette and regu-

lations; cordial and pleasant in all his relations with
men.   He shrank instinctively from whatever savoured
of affectation or display; and when, after having been
hard at work ever since daybreak in sending off despatches or receiving visits, he went on his way along the
colonnade of the Via di Po to the Office of Foreign
Affairs, or that of Finance, he seemed only a worthy
citizen of Turin, bowing to an acquaintance here, or
talking to one there, affable with everyone.   In the
midst of the most important affairs he had the gift of a
cheerful animation, the wholesome brightness of an
elastic temperament and a well-regulated mind; a
cheerfulness which manifested itself in a hearty laugh, or
in a way of rubbing his hands in a certain manner which
has become traditional.

Thus endowed with a happy spirit, a ready intelligence, and a great enjoyment of life, he never knew
what *ennui* was, any more than rancour or bitterness.
He used to say that rancour was absurd, and that nothing
need ever be wearisome.   Thus he would pass with
perfect equanimity from the study of some profound
political problem to the reading of a novel or a newspaper article; from conferring with an ambassador to
conversing with some humble peasant or modest appli-
cant for office; from the most complicated state affairs
to mere parish matters.   This was the man who, in the
gravest crisis in his career, between the ministry of yesterday and the ministry of the morrow, could write from
Leri to one of his friends : " Do not be vexed with me if
I don't write to you.   It is because I don't wish to entertain you with the discussions of the vestry-meetings

of Trino, of which I am a very active member.   Don't lose this letter; it contains the direction of the apothecary who sells chestnut-oil to cure gout.   At Leri one has leisure for everything, even for reading Madame de S.'s prosing.   Here I am, shelved for an indefinite time. . As far as I am concerned, I am quite content, for this life suits me perfectly.   I am quite happy by myself, or with the worthy agriculturists amongst whom I live."

He could indeed find time for everything, because he took an interest in everything, and he could find good in everything.   He despised neither men nor things, and he used to say wittily that many card-players only lose because they have no regard for the small cards; as for him, he knew the value of the small cards—of insignificant people, even of counsels and remarks which he would call forth and listen to and make his own.   But under this apparent facility and good humour, Cavour possessed the highest qualities of a statesman; clearness and precision of ideas, and a strength of will which at times could make all give way before it.   Neither peril nor difficulty proved an obstacle to his will.   Only, this iron will was clad in graciousness, the sharp outline of his ideas was veiled in the garb of amiability; his practical good sense, so unerring and fully developed, was combined with great and broad conceptions; and thus this gifted nature—hearty, liberal, impetuous, and fascinating—became irresistible : friends, adversaries, dissentients, all were attracted and carried along by it.

The innumerable speeches by which Cavour defended his policy, and which subsist as a monument of the parliamentary *régime*, represent faithfully his character and tone of mind. Cavour was not a born orator, and at the beginning of his career he obtained a hearing with some difficulty. His voice was rather harsh; there was a certain sharpness in his tones, not abated by the wear and tear of conflict; and he never lost a slight .cough, which at times interfered with his well-rounded periods, and which, indeed, he knew how to turn to account when necessary. Besides this, he had to acquire the habit of speaking Italian, and he rather piqued himself upon his literary inability; he used sometimes to pretend to consult his friends as to the correctness of some sentence; but he rapidly became the first debater in the Piedmontese parliament, riveting attention by the reliableness of his views and the substantial soundness of his elucidations; fascinating his hearers by the subtlety of his reasoning, and making himself formidable by the brilliant sarcasm of his repartees.

Usually he would allow the discussion to develop itself, and speakers to follow each other in succession, while he betrayed emotion or impatience, or appeared to listen with smiling animated *bonhomie*; for in him all was life and action. When the discussion seemed to be at an end, when everyone else had spoken, he would enter the arena with one of his telling speeches. He never wrote them down beforehand; a few hours' meditation was sufficient preparation; he relied for the rest on the inspiration of the moment, like a man master of his thoughts. Cavour had the art of grasping a question, at once elevating and simplifying it, answering each interruption without breaking the order of his ideas, combining the superiority and novelty of his views with the accuracy and abundance of his facts ; and this too in the most natural language, without declamation or literary artifice, with a logical clearness of demonstration which vanquished his enemies, captivated and encouraged his friends, and satisfied and reassured public opinion. Was he a witty or an eloquent man ?—He was essentially the richly-gifted politician, making use of wit and eloquence ; an orator with a practical aim ; with a comprehensive grasp of every subject, quick to disengage whatever was practicable, and to seize the gist of the matter ; enlarging his own influence while enlarging his sphere of action. He was always on a level with the situations which his own inventive genius had created, and equal to all the difficulties which he did not shrink from provoking.

For Cavour the parliamentary *régime* was by no means a mere medium for his eloquence or an arena of party stratagem ; it was a powerful lever for practical government, a means of awaking public opinion, and associating it with the progressive realisation of an ever-active idea. Cavour would sometimes say : "I am willing to lead and even to spur on the country, but the country must back me up ; between it and me there must be no rupture. Should any such rupture arise, not only could I no longer indulge the hope that my political plans would ever prevail, but I could no longer be minister." To precede and direct public opinion, without ceasing to be in living contact with it, to know on occasion how to wait, this was his grand secret ; the secret of a great Liberal who only obtained the voluntary

confidence of his country by proving himself a far-sighted
and able promoter of a national work; and not a mere
partisan or faction leader. Such was his view of the
parliamentary *régime* of which he made such happy use
in order to take the first forward step. And he had
more than ever to make use of it after the Paris congress,
in a policy comprehending at once internal and external
action : Piedmont, Italy, and Europe. On these three
points he had to concentrate his efforts.

IV.

The position attained by the Cabinet of Turin, through
its co-operation in the Crimean war and the general
negotiation for peace, was certainly flattering to the
pride of a small country. The point was to maintain,
strengthen, and extend it for further progress.

Cavour knew well that there could be no drawing
back ; that after having raised Piedmont to a certain
level, he could not allow it to decline again ; and that
after having excited the hopes, interests, even the
impatient expectations of his country, he could no
longer extinguish the flame he stood in such need of.
Immediately, therefore, upon his return to Turin, after
the Paris congress, he busied himself with giving a fresh
impetus, that he might enable Piedmont to keep up her
ambitious *rôle* of a small power bent upon becoming a
great one. "*Alere flammam*" was his motto. It was
necessary to go forward, to do something ; to prove the
omnipresence and activity of the Piedmontese leadership, which had to manifest itself in every possible way.
In less than two years, amid a multiplication of enter-

prises and projects, Cavour had fortified Alessandria, created a great marine arsenal at Spezzia, and urged on the boring of the Mont Cenis tunnel—all this at the risk of appearing to exceed the stretch and force of a small nation by a policy of moral action or of military preparation which told heavily upon its exchequer, and necessarily called for fresh loans.

The fortifications of Alessandria, and especially the national subscription for one hundred cannon, set on foot by Italian patriotism, to mount on the Piedmontese citadel, might well, and with more reason than the alliance with the Eastern Powers, pass for a " pistol-shot," or indeed a cannon-ball, fired in the ear of Austria. Cavour denied nothing, asserted nothing ; he did not deny the moral bearing of the demonstration, though still avoiding anything that would have seemed like a direct provocation. He got out of the difficulty by representing the fortifying of Alessandria as the carrying out of an old scheme, and brought forward, in his light-hearted way, his former terrible colleague of the War Office, La Marmora. " When I was Minister of Finance," he said, " he was always tormenting me ; and I remember well, that on his departure for the Crimea, his last words to me were : ' Do not forget that if you fail to look to the fortifications of Alessandria, some fine day I shall protest formally and publicly against you.' " In like manner, on the subject of Spezzia, he would repeat : " When peace was made, my colleague La Marmora, who is at heart as tenacious as myself, said to me as he turned into the War Office : ' Alessandria and La Spezzia ; ' to which I replied, ' La Spezzia and

Alessandria.'" The fortifying of Alessandria, by completing the fortifications of Casale and of Valenza on the Po, made good the defence of Piedmont against the first shock of an attack; and, in truth, it was this *ensemble* of public works suggested by far-sighted wisdom, which, in the decisive epoch of 1859, were destined to save Turin, by arresting the Austrian invasion, and leaving the French army time to arrive.

The creation of a great arsenal at La Spezzia, at the utmost limit of the kingdom, a work which Cavour did not shrink from attempting, even after Napoleon, would evidently lead to vaster combinations, which comprehended at least the whole of Northern and Central Italy. Under diverse forms, these two projects of La Spezzia and Alessandria, strongly opposed, and carried almost arbitrarily, were in truth military works, a sort of making ready for the conflicts of the future, perhaps of a speedy war. The boring of the Mont Cenis tunnel represented another side of this indefatigable policy : the thought of aggrandisement by moral action, by a fertile initiatory movement, by the extension and ever-increasing facility of intercourse between the nations. It was indeed a great enterprise for an insignificant country, this attack upon Mont Cenis; this gigantic speculation, in which political and financial questions were mixed up with the original and purely scientific aspect—that of the possibility of its execution, and the means by which to carry it out. Cavour was undismayed by so venturesome an undertaking. His keen glance no doubt apprehended its practical benefits, the happy consequences which must ensue for the sub-Alpine population, for the national industries, and for the part his small country would have to play in the world's onward progress. He reckoned with the precision of an economist, like a long-headed financier, all the material advantages of the Mont Cenis tunnel ; but at the same time he was, perhaps, especially alive to the honour Piedmont would achieve by this proof of indomitable resolution. He threw himself into the enterprise with all his accustomed ardour ; and one day, on the Piazza d'Armi of Turin, pointing in the direction of the amphitheatre of Alps which shut in the horizon, he observed to his friends : " If Louis XIV. said the Pyrenees would be no more, I hope some day to say with more truth that the Alps are no more. People speak of the great obstacles in the way, and I admit them ; they say also that we are still too small a State to attempt an enterprise of such magnitude. I reply that, as for the obstacles, we shall surmount them, and in order to become great we must do this. The Alps must actually come down." And, thus saying, his looks revealed the ardour and power of will animating him.

Cavour had from the first taken the greatest interest in this undertaking. He followed with deep attention all the experiments of Sommeiller, the able Savoyard engineer, who, after distinguishing himself in the works among the Apennines, in the line to Genoa, applied all the power of his genius to the solution of the problem of employing compressed air in the boring of Mont Cenis. Cavour not only seconded Sommeiller in his ministerial capacity, he also upheld him by his own faith in the scheme ; and just as in La Marmora he had always found an equally faithful and active fellow-worker, so in the matter of the Mont Cenis, his associates and supporters were his colleagues in public works—Paleocapa, and Menabrea, who laid aside his political views in order to aid in so great an enterprise. Cavour busied himself with all that could insure success, defending with equal energy the engineers, the means of execution, the necessary loans, or the treaties signed with the Savoy Railway Company ; smoothing down all difficulties, and winning over all hesitative opinions. " I trust," he energetically declared in parliament, "I trust none of you will belie what you have already done at the close of this laborious session of the Legislature ; I feel sure you will follow out a frank and resolute policy. If you should adopt another proposition, you would inaugurate a totally different system ; and I should indeed deplore this, not only because a great work would be compromised, but because it would be a fatal omen for the future political system of parliament ; we had the choice between two ways, and we preferred the bolder and hardier of the two ; we cannot now stop half way. It is for us a condition of existence, an unavoidable alternative—On, or perish ! I firmly believe that you will complete your work by the greatest of modern enterprises—by voting for the tunnelling of Mont Cenis." It is thus that success is won, and when short-sighted opponents troubled Cavour, asking him to what lengths he intended to go, and pointing out the danger of placing the strongest military establishment at the extreme end of the kingdom, multiplying fortifications and armaments, engaging Piedmont in enterprises quite beyond its strength, and when they accused him of creating an artificial and

hazardous situation which could not last, he did not
always reply, although he was not one to disavow his
thoughts.   He well knew all that could be said on the
subject.   For the present he had attained the more
obvious aim of his policy, since at the cost of efforts and
sacrifices, the greatness of which he did not deny, and
the justification of which he left to the future, he was
able to present Piedmont as the active, acknowledged,
and ever-advancing representative of the liberal and
national idea.

V.

The problem for Cavour was not only at Turin : from
henceforth it extended beyond the Alps.   This problem
consisted in penetrating Italy with the new spirit which
animated the Piedmontese policy ; rallying, organising,
and disciplining Italian patriotism under the tricoloured
flag waving in the hand of a popular king.   Cavour
knew what had been the cost of dreams, chimerical ideas,
factions, secret societies, and revolutionary movements
to Italy.   His one thought was to break with such
disastrous associations, disengage the cause of Italy from
all that had compromised it, set it free from revolutionary parties by maintaining its character of a just
and honest work of restitution, and carry on the work
he had begun at the Paris congress.

He relied upon the propaganda of his liberal and
national policy, not upon revolutionary dreams, the
fatal sterility of which he knew and repudiated.   He
would say, speaking of the Mazzinians : " I admire their
devotion to an idea ; I abhor their fanaticism."   An

attempt upon the life of the king of Naples by the ·soldier Agesilas Milano excited nothing but disgust in him, nor would he have dreamed of making a merit of his indignant repudiation of it.

To those who reproached him with not favouring all attempts at insurrection in the other Italian States, or who .in his presence applauded deeds of murder or incendiarism, he replied in parliament : " Our speeches and our policy are not intended to prompt and foster rash enterprises, vain and foolish attempts at revolution in Italy. It is quite otherwise that we understand the regeneration of the country. We have ever followed a straightforward and loyal policy, and as long as we shall be at peace with the other sovereigns of Italy, we shall never employ revolutionary means nor promote disturbances. As for Naples, mention has been made of recent and painful facts : the explosion of a powder magazine, and of vessels of war; a horrible outrage. Some have spoken in such a way as to throw the credit of these deeds upon the Italian party. I repudiate them ; I repudiate them utterly, and for Italy's own sake. No; these are not deeds that can be attributed to the national Italian party, they are the isolated acts of some misguided wretch, which must be stigmatised by all good men, especially by those who value Italian honour and welfare."

Words like these, uttered by him who had introduced Italy into the congress of European Powers, awakened deep and salutary sympathy beyond the Alps. They renovated public opinion ; they had the advantage of depriving the factions of their plea that they conspired for the national cause, and the other Powers of any pretext to charge the national cause with the blame of conspiracies commonly resulting from the violence of measures of repression. The factious spirit was not to be lightly overcome. Its adherents felt that this minister of a constitutional monarchy was their worst enemy; and at the very time Cavour was thus disowning revolutionary means, Mazzini, on the Piedmontese territory itself, at Genoa, was making a last effort to regain his influence. Mazzini's wild attempt at Genoa failed miserably, thanks to the good sense of the public, more surprised than alarmed at this outbreak. It was only one more proof that the power lost by the factious party was steadily being gained by the party of national Liberalism.

In proportion as it became more marked in word and deed, Piedmontese policy had the happy result of reviving everywhere a belief that the work of liberation was to be brought about by open and regular means. And in this work Cavour quickly found allies or fellow-workers, who flocked to him from all parts of Italy, sometimes without his seeking them or knowing them. The national society formed at this period, organised by Giuseppe La Farina, a Sicilian emigrant, was one manifestation of this new phase in Italian affairs. Cavour found in this society an independent auxiliary, rather a dangerous one at times, perhaps; but it had the advantage of bringing back into the great patriotic current many honest minds until then entangled in Mazzinian "affiliations." Cavour had especially won over the most generous and powerful of allies, Manin,

living in retirement in Paris ever since the fall of
Venice.

Although placed under such different conditions, the
one in all the *éclat* of an official post, the other an exile,
these two men were made to understand each other;
they had numerous points in common : impassioned
patriotism, clear-sightedness, and a keen and practical
insight into events. At the time of the congress Manin
had an interview with Cavour ; he had speedily apprehended the meaning of the Piedmontese minister's
policy, and in spite of his Venetian predilection for
Republicanism, with the resolution of a man " in search
of that which is practically possible, loving Italy more
than the Republic," he did not hesitate to declare himself
in favour of a policy whose success he had hailed in the
Paris negotiations. Broken by family affliction—the
death of a daughter, who was in his eyes the pathetic
image of his beloved Venice—suffering already from the
malady which carried him to the grave, he was spending
his remaining strength in developing his ideas, his programme for the future. It was he who had promoted the
subscription in Paris for the hundred cannon of Alessandria, concerning which a particular significance was
found in the toleration extended to it by the French
Government. He wrote innumerable letters and mani-
festoes upholding the alliance with France ; warning his
fellow-countrymen against old divisions and sterile party
conflicts; repudiating especially, as did Cavour, assassination and the stiletto of the conspirator; urging Mazzini
to give up his plots, and to retire from an arena where
his presence was only an obstacle. "I accept the

monarchy of Savoy," he said, " provided it will help loyally and efficiently in the making of Italy. The Piedmontese monarchy, in order to be faithful to its mission, must ever keep in view the final goal—the independence and unification of Italy. It must make use of all the means which will enable it to advance one step in the way leading to that goal. It must remain the kernel, the centre of attraction of Italian nationality."

Manin could not know that before the close of four years from that date what seemed a dream would have become a reality—which he was not destined to see. His dying eyes and longing heart anticipated and embraced the future in its ultimate issues.

Cavour, for the time being, could not keep pace with him, or at least he could not acknowledge that he did so. He felt the danger of moving too fast; he was accustomed to repeat in his own intimate circle : " We can do but one thing at a time. Let us begin by turning the Austrians out of Italy ! " Being the minister of a regularly-constituted State, he believed himself bound to allow for certain necessities of government, to avoid false steps and useless or premature complications.

When France and England, in 1856, engaged in a diplomatic intervention, to moderate the rigorous despotism of the king of Naples, Cavour kept out of it ; not because he was not tempted to make the best of such an occasion, but because he could not see how far the two Powers meant to go, and because he dreaded an inefficient demonstration, by which Piedmontese credit would suffer without compensation. When, in the summer of 1857, Pope Pius IX. went to Bologna, Cavour did not consider himself free from the obligation required by custom; he sent Boncompagni, then representing Victor Emmanuel at Florence, to greet his Holiness. He considered such homage due to the head of the Church and the Piedmontese Catholics, whom he would not slight unnecessarily. Cavour was a minister who kept on good terms with governments and tradition, but that did not hinder him from following his own path.

His words as well as his deeds continually strengthened the ascendency of his policy on the other side of the Alps, and from this tendency of Cavour, from the impulse given by Manin, from the manifold action of the National Society, there sprang the new and rapidly-growing Italian Party, prompt to submit to the discipline and march under the orders of him of whom the brilliant and accomplished Florentine, Salvagnoli, used to say: " After a conversation with that man I breathe more freely; my mind dilates."

VI.

For the parliamentary leader to have won over Piedmont and Italy by the attraction of a national policy was much, but more was needed. Cavour had to obtain allies by taking advantage of the somewhat critical situation in which Europe found itself immediately after the Paris congress. The peace of March 30, 1856, had left a certain number of points unsettled— the limitation of the new Russian frontier in Bessarabia; the possession of the Isle of Serpents at the mouth of the Danube; the regulation of the navigation of that river; the organisation of the principalities of Moldo-

Wallachia—and the solution of those complementary questions was almost as delicate and thorny as the peace itself. It was rendered all the more so by the interests and resentments that it brought into play, and by the disturbing of alliances which might come of them. One thing was certain—there were mutual misunderstandings. European diplomacy was divided into two camps. In the one, Austria, rather suspicious in its attitude towards Russia, and holding to the conditions of the peace with the utmost rigour, had the support of England and Turkey ; in the other, France showed a visible inclination for Russia, putting the most favourable interpretation on the conditions, and, seemingly anxious to flatter the nation she had lately fought. Peace had hardly been signed a few months, and already the allies of Cavour seemed no longer in harmony.

At first Cavour only interfered with much reserve in these private dissensions, wherein he feared to find division, if not hostility, between two powers, England and France, which he would fain have conciliated equally. If his intervention soon grew more active, it was because he was called to action by what he considered a political necessity, and by the confidence of the Cabinets, who grew more and more in the habit of referring to this clear and creative mind. He acted the part of a kind of mediator or peacemaker in the conferences held at Paris or at Constantinople. Thus, in the matter of boundary, known under the name of the " *question de Bolgrad,*" it was he who suggested an arrangement desired by France, destined to accommodate Russian susceptibility, and be definitively accepted by England.

When the organisation of the Principalities was being settled, he sided with Russia and France for the union of Moldavia and Wallachia; he considered this a due recognition paid to nationality, and he showed himself the more resolute when Austria proved hostile. Count Buol had said: "We have quite enough with one Sardinia at the foot of the Alps, without having another at the foot of the Carpathians."

These questions were of importance in his eyes only in proportion as they tended to strengthen Piedmont, concerned Italy, and helped the latter to attain the object in view; which was, to gain fresh allies or sympathies against the enemy he had to combat. It was the ruling thought in his diplomacy in the midst of all the European incidents which he endeavoured to turn to account, in order to create, as he said, an atmosphere favourable to Italy.

In fact, by his readiness and wise moderation, he had first won over Russia, which displayed towards Piedmont a marked cordiality, if only to show hatred of Austria. As soon as the intercourse between the two countries had been renewed, Prince Gortchakoff said to the representative of the court of Turin: "I do not wish to enter into recriminations. We have been ill-advised since 1849 in our refusal to allow you a Russian legation at Turin, and in refusing to grant you a legation at St. Petersburg. We have been too much influenced by Austria; I never approved of it. Now the path is open before us; we may, if we choose, be friends. Let me say that Russia and Piedmont are natural allies. We are very well pleased with your attitude towards us."

The Emperor Alexander II., during the festivities of his coronation at Moscow, had spoken in most flattering terms to General Broglia, ambassador of Victor Emmanuel, purposely raising his voice in order to be overheard by the Austrian ambassador. Shortly afterwards, the Czarina, mother of Alexander, had gone to spend the winter of 1857 at Nice, where she had been treated with marked consideration and deference. The Grand Duchess Helena paid a visit to Piedmont. The Grand Dukes Constantine and Michael, who were going on a visit to their mother, had been to Turin, where princely honours were shown them. They had gone with Victor Emmanuel to a State representation at the theatre, and these demonstrations were all the more significant in that they coincided with the diplomatic rupture which had just taken place between Austria and Piedmont.

Meanwhile, the Russian diplomatists repeated to the Sardinian representatives : " Piedmont must have a more extended territory, even in the interest of Russia. But this must be brought about independently of revolution ; the initiative must come from above. Pending this, let the Sardinian Government continue to prove to Europe that it is capable of maintaining order ; let it abstain from disturbing the other Italian States. If Piedmont can calmly await the great day, that day will come, and Russia will assist her in driving Austria out of Italy." These promises and demonstrations might indeed be rather flattering than efficacious. In any case, they marked the culminating point of the relations between Russia and Piedmont about the year 1857, and were of sufficient importance to encourage Cavour, at the

risk of offending Lord Palmerston, to yield to the Czar
a permanent right of anchorage in the Mediterranean,
in the harbour of Villafranca, and Russia's hatred of
Austria was at least the earnest of a sympathetic
neutrality when a conflict should take place.

VII.

There remained now only England and France, the
two great allies whom Cavour kept continually in view,
from whom he expected more direct and active support,
without knowing to what extent it would go. Evidently
his ideal would have been to maintain the alliance
between these Powers in all its integrity, while he
cherished the hope of one day making use of it for the
cause of Italy. It was a dream, as he had lately been
made aware in the negotiations set on foot after the
Paris congress. As soon as difficulties arose, England
had turned towards Austria, and England had assuredly
not allied herself with Austria in affairs of the East in
order to abandon her in the affairs of Italy.

The policy of England, that of Liberals and Conservatives alike, could be lavish in encouragement, and
in proofs of the warmest sympathy towards the constitutional government flourishing at Turin ; it was willing to
call for internal reforms in the other Italian States, to
lecture the Pope and even the king of Naples ; nay, if
need were, it would not refuse its help to Piedmont if
it were attacked : but it would go no farther. The
words of Lord Clarendon, which had for a time misled
Cavour, did not go beyond this limit.

England, bound traditionally to the treaties of 1857, desired neither war nor a readjustment of territory for Italy. She took especial umbrage at any complication offering France occasion to interfere beyond the Alps. Accordingly Cavour met with demonstrations of friendship and of much consideration at England's hands, but scarcely of encouragement, rather mistrustful and irritating advice. In spite of all his efforts he gained no ground; he had perhaps excited suspicion by yielding to Russia the right of anchorage in the Mediterranean harbour of Villafranca. Lord Palmerston had said sarcastically: "Really, I did not expect Count Cavour to become Russian." To which Count Cavour, when told of it, replied: "Tell Lord Palmerston that I am Liberal enough not to be Russian, and too much so to be Austrian."

When the diplomatic rupture between Austria and Piedmont was at its height, at the beginning of 1857, the Sardinian ambassador to London, the Marquis Emmanuel d'Azeglio, had a decisive explanation with Lord Palmerston: "Your error," said Lord Palmerston, " lies in believing that in order to promote the good of Italy the best way is to be on bad terms with Austria. With the means of action Austria has at command, she will turn the other Italian States against you, and will be an irreconcilable enemy to all your plans of reform. Would it not be better to disarm her opposition by taking from her every plausible pretext of combating Piedmontese policy?" "But, my lord," replied the Marquis d'Azeglio, "we shall never see Austria concurring with us to ameliorate the situation of Italy.

She has all the Governments on her side—we have the people. She says to the former : 'Will you have my protection ? I grant it you. Do not forget that I represent absolutism, the reign of the sword, and Catholic intolerance.' But as for us, we say to the people : 'Follow us; we have Italian blood in our veins; we uphold the flag of independence, religious toleration, free institutions, and moral and material progress.' It remains to be proved which of these two policies England will be inclined to support.". . . . Lord Palmerston did not answer, or at least he only answered by evading the question, leaving to Piedmont the responsibility of its own policy and of "the consequences, good and bad," that might result therefrom. In default of England, Cavour might hope for more success with France. He daily felt more and more that the great and decisive succour for Italy must come from that quarter. It was no new thought for Napoleon III. The independence of Italy had been one of the cherished day-dreams of the young insurgent of the Romagna in 1831—of that man whom Pius IX. used to speak of long afterwards, when he was at the summit of his greatness, as "the conspirator of Forli." The Paris congress had but laid bare the intentions or desires of which Cavour hastened to take advantage, and which he attempted to make permanent in spite of the difficulty of the task. It is quite evident that at one time there was between Cavour and Napoleon III. a sort of mysterious intelligence, unacknowledged, and only revealing itself by degrees. As is now well known, it was at the instigation of the French sovereign, in consequence of a private conversation between the Emperor and Count Villamarina at Compiègne, that the Cabinet of Italy took the initiative in the combination which settled the last conditions of the peace in a manner that proved favourable to Russia and acceptable to England.

The Emperor had made use of Cavour in order to save, as he said, the Anglo-French alliance without alienating Russia; and what had been done by Piedmont Napoleon III. considered a personal service. A few days later Count Walewski observed to Villamarina: " The Emperor has ordered me to testify his gratitude and satisfaction to Count Cavour as well as to yourself, and to tell you from him—pray take note of his words —that all this will not be in vain; that he will never forget it."

The representative of Victor Emmanuel in Paris was desired to make the most of these friendly dispositions, and about this time he wrote to Turin: " Napoleon wants time to insure the success of his favourable intentions towards Italy. Allow me, therefore, to express my earnest hope that the Italians will not by any ill-timed movement compromise the future which Sardinia has prepared for them by her sacrifices on the battle-field, and by her success at the Paris congress. For the present we must have patience, and await the course of events. We must show great faith in the Emperor's personal policy, and not put any hindrance in his way. Napoleon and the times are in favour of our cause and Italy's; I maintain this assertion, even at the cost of being considered a mere enthusiast." These Italians were clear-sighted people.

But what increased the difficulties of the situation was that the France of 1857, whose alliance and co-operation Cavour sought and hoped to obtain, was for the time being singularly involved and embarrassed. France presented the phenomenon of a sovereign favourable to Italy, with a personal policy which was shrouded in mystery; and of ministers who seemed to follow another policy, unheeded by the sovereign. And then, outside the official regions, in Parisian society, in the old parliamentary world, there reigned a tone of opinion somewhat affected by the manifestations of the congress on the Roman question, hostile to the empire and rather adverse to the cause of Italy. Cavour knew all this. If, justly enough, his first care was the management of the taciturn sovereign on whom everything depended, he had also each day to encounter the discordant elements, the conflicting influences, and the private difficulties which characterised the internal *régime* of France, and might at any given moment turn aside or thwart the designs of the Emperor. Moreover, he was not ignorant of the fact that this imperial alliance, if it acquired weight, might endanger or threaten the constitutional liberties of Turin.

VIII.

Cavour's situation had now become a very extraordinary one, both as minister and man. If he turned to England, he found there a government, statesmen, Conservatives and Liberals alike, openly declaring themselves in favour of all liberal progress in Italy, but utterly discountenancing any policy of national liberation. If he turned to France, he found an all-powerful sovereign, enigmatical, secretly disposed to favour the triumph of Italian independence, but suspected of wishing to give his help in this national work at the cost of sacrifices of internal liberty, which Italy neither could nor would make.

In the midst of these difficulties and apparently insurmountable obstacles, Cavour neither allowed himself to be troubled nor checked. He pursued his course, preparing the Napoleonic alliance, with the fixed resolve to surrender no vital liberty; possessing himself more and more of the confidence of the Emperor, with whom he had already private communications, besides the usual diplomatic means; transacting business with the imperial ministers, who sometimes were not made fully aware of what was taking place, and endeavouring to conciliate or reassure the French Liberals. He had full need of all his dexterity, in a work often interrupted or resumed. On this complex matter he brought to bear such sagacity, such well-directed firmness, such fertility of expedients, such an art in handling affairs and men as made old Prince Metternich, then still living, remark: " Diplomacy is dying out; there is only one diplomatist left in Europe, and unfortunately he is against us; I mean Count Cavour."

Skilful diplomatist Cavour certainly was; sufficiently so to rank among the first of all diplomatists; and yet when everything was said and done, beyond that mere confidential part in which discretion is one more means of insuring success, the strong point of his diplomacy was frankness and open dealing. He spoke out his opinions and aim with an openness which awakened surprise, and was sometimes mistaken for cunning; and when once the Prussian envoy at Turin, Count Brassier de St. Simon, astonished at Cavour's freedom of speech, was searching for some hidden meaning in his words, Cavour replied quickly: "Do not deceive yourself. I say only what I think. As for the habit attributed to diplomatists of disguising their thoughts, it is one of which I never avail myself." He used often to say laughingly to his friends: "Now I have found out the art of deceiving diplomatists; I speak the truth, and I am certain they will not believe me."

Thus, besides his diplomacy as courtier and chancellor, he had another at command, a diplomacy without reticence or *arrière-pensée*, which after all was but the commentary and complement of the negotiations he pursued in secret. More than one of his notes was written less for the Cabinets than for the public of Europe—for general opinion; for if he studied to convince or to manage the divers governments, he wished also, as he said, to prepare matters in such a manner that Piedmont, the day she entered the lists, should find European public opinion favouring her.

The danger of this policy, doubtless straightforward alike in its principle and its aim, but to all appearance intricate, consisted in its being liable to misconception, and dependent upon a multitude of circumstances. It was only a great promise before it became a reality, and meanwhile it began to weigh heavily upon the small State of Piedmont, which had so great a stake in what might after all prove to be but an adventure. The results might yet be far distant, and were quite indefinite; the sacrifices required were positive, immediate; and the extreme parties, equally hostile to the new policy prevailing at Turin, were necessarily always ready to make the worst of mishaps, incidents, or any more or less specious causes of complaint. Irreconcilable revolutionists, like Mazzini, never ceased to agitate, trying to rally all the demagogic passions at once excited and suppressed by Cavour's national Liberalism. The reactionary parties in their turn made the most of the threats of revolution, the taxes, the loans, the rash enterprises, the suffering of the populace—which they attributed to a permanent system of high pressure. At the least sign of vacillation in those in authority, the public mind was in danger of being unsettled.

This was precisely what appeared to take place towards the end of 1857, after Mazzini's wild outbreak at Genoa; the election of a new parliament seemed to indicate that a reaction had set in. The Liberal majority was still numerically of good proportions, but morally it had suffered loss in the contest. The Minister of the Interior, Rattazzi, and Lanza, Minister of Public Instruction, were only elected by a second ballot. One of the chiefs of the extreme Right, Count Solaro della Margherita, had votes enough to elect him four times over. A certain number of canons, men notorious for their reactionary opinions, now entered parliament. Savoy had made herself conspicuous by returning deputies who almost all of them belonged to the Clerical party. What was the signification of this result of the elections ?—It was no doubt due to very special circumstances. Aristocratic and religious influences had been at work for the first time, even over-acting their part, in the elections. The Liberals had become divided, relying rather too much on their ascendency. The Minister of the Interior had been at any rate unfortunate, if not imprudent, in the affair of the sedition at Genoa, as also in directing the operations of the elections. The explanation given softened without cancelling a result that at first gave Cavour deep pain. " We have got into a bad way," he said that evening to a friend. " The policy of an eight years' reign is in danger of being forsaken, and then what will become of our poor Italy ? What can the king do, who is pledged to the triumph of this policy ? He will abdicate, and then what will follow ?— *Coups d'état ?* I shall never advise *coups d'état* even in the interest of the Liberal policy. Dissolve the Chamber. That might be done ; that is constitutional. And then, if the same Chamber should be returned, or a worse one ? This eight years' policy, it goes to my heart to think we need ever forsake it ; but no, no, it cannot be. Good sense always helps Gianduja (the Piedmontese John Bull) at critical junctures. No, no, we will not forsake this policy ; we will have recourse. to no extraordinary means to preserve it ; we shall gain the day by constitutional and legal means, wherein our strength lies. Do not doubt it ; remember the red crisis of 1849 : it was alarming and very serious, but we surmounted it. Well, we shall also surmount the black crisis of 1857." It was in any case a warning which

Cavour would certainly not disregard, especially at a time when he needed more than ever the reconstruction of a majority that would remain faithful to him. The first emotion over, he looked things in the face; he quickly realised that this apparent hesitation in public opinion was not the disavowal of "an eight years' reign;" that his personal influence was untouched; and that faults really had been committed; and, in order to save his policy, he allowed the fall of Rattazzi, who, though somewhat bruised, was not yet transformed into an enemy by it. Cavour himself took the Ministry of the Interior, as he had already taken in succession the Ministry of Finance and the Ministry of Foreign Affairs. "This change," he wrote to Paris, "has been forced upon me by the necessity of raising the *morale* of the administrative body, which has been depressed by a series of vexatious circumstances. We thought it would not be expedient to introduce into the Cabinet a new element that would have led to the belief that the minister inclined to the Right or to the Left, whereas he perseveres in the line of conduct he has pursued until now without the least deviation."

Very soon matters returned to their former condition; Cavour found his authority ever on the increase, rising more and more above the level of parties, drawing to his assistance the "moderate men" of all shades of opinion, Right as well as Left. He was now more than ever master of the field; and against the Clerical absolutists, who persisted in their opposition to him, he called to his assistance the most unlooked-for accomplice, Joseph de Maistre himself, whose diplomatic letters, abounding with such sentences as the following, he caused to be republished : "The diameter of Piedmont is out of proportion with the grandeur and nobility of the House of Savoy. · As long as I breathe I shall repeat that Austria is the natural and eternal enemy of His Majesty. If Austria rules from Venice to Pavia, there will be an end to the House of Savoy : *Vixit !* Mark well the Italian spirit ; it was born of the revolution, and will soon play a tragic part. Our system, timid, neutral, hesitating, groping, is fatal in the present state of things. Let the king put himself at the head of the Italians, and let him employ revolutionists, indiscriminately, in all civil and military posts. This is essential, vital, paramount. This is my ultimate view of the matter ; if we remain or become an obstacle, *requiem æternam,"* &c.

What more was the Piedmontese premier saying and doing in 1857, half a century after Joseph de Maistre had uttered these words, which now came back sounding like an importunate tocsin in the ears of the reactionary members of the Right ?

IX.

Doubtless Cavour was not mistaken ; this "eight years' policy," guided with such consummate skill through so many complications, was not in danger of foundering because of an electoral mischance. It emerged from the crisis as it did from many others ; and by one of those happy strokes of fortune which befall none but able men, that which seemed likely to destroy it, much more than the passing disturbance of the election, on the contrary, tended to hasten its success, by making good fortune issue from the most sinister of events.   Something very similar to what took place at the beginning of 1852, the day after the 2nd of December, but far more serious and threatening now, gave Cavour the opportunity of displaying the same dexterity, attended by the same good fortune, and enabled him to steal a march triumphantly on the enemy.

This alarming and unforeseen event was the attempt made at Paris on the evening of January 14, 1858, to assassinate the Emperor and Empress as they entered the Opera House.   At the first intelligence of it transmitted to him by telegraph, Cavour exclaimed: "Provided only the assassins be not Italians !"   Unfortunately they were Italians.   The rash originator of this criminal attempt, Felice Orsini, was an emigrant of the Roman revolution, known to have made a romantic escape from his Austrian prison, affiliated with the secret societies, and a man from whom the Piedmontese premier remembered to have lately received a letter to which he had returned no answer.   What was now to happen ?

All might undergo a change ; the fanaticism of a handful of conspirators might defer for a long time the fulfilment of Italian hopes.   A reaction probably, nay, almost inevitably, would destroy all that had been done. Cavour was soon aware that influences, all of them hostile to Italy, surrounded Napoleon III.   The Papal nuncio had not hesitated to tell the Emperor that " these were the fruits of the revolutionary passions fostered by Count Cavour."   The ambassador of the Emperor Francis Joseph had immediately asked whether the time had not yet come in which to "establish between France and Austria a mutual understanding, in order to constrain Piedmont to leave off protecting the machinations of the refugees and the licence of the press."   On the other hand, the President of the Council received from London and Geneva, as well as from Paris, the assurance that the revolutionists had not lost hope ; that they were preparing new plots against the Emperor, and even against Victor Emmanuel.   Cavour, without letting himself be intimidated, was quite aware that a storm was raging. "The present time," he wrote, "is full of perils and difficulties, daily on the increase.   The fury of factions is unbridled ; their perverseness adds to the forces of the reactionists, who become daily more formidable.   If the Liberals get divided among themselves they will be lost, and the cause of Italian freedom and independence will fall with them.   We will resolutely stand in the breach, but we shall assuredly fall unless our friends rally round us to help us against the attacks besetting us on all sides."

The situation was indeed a perilous one, and foremost among the causes of alarm was the panic which appeared to prevail at Paris.   The French Government needed no fresh stimulus.   In the face of a murderous plot carried out by Italian hands, prepared in England, pointed out as the premeditated deed of revolutionary cosmopolitanism, pledged to conspiracies and assassinations, it was for the time convulsed, as it were, with the spirit of reaction.   While a general was being appointed Minister of the Interior, Count Walewski, the head of French diplomacy, was writing in all directions : to

London, to Brussels, to Rome, to Turin, calling for acts of repression, guarantees, assurances against the right of refuge, against emigration, and against the freedom of the press. The French Government so far forgot itself as to even insert in the *Moniteur* certain military orations, animated by a spirit of bravado, alike useless and offensive to England.

In London, the French demonstrations resulted only in awakening English susceptibility and hastening the downfall of Lord Palmerston's cabinet, which was replaced by a Tory administration. In Turin the French minister, Prince de Latour d'Auvergne, was commissioned by Count Walewski to demand from the Piedmontese Government a number of measures due to the occasion : the suppression of Mazzini's organ, the *Italia del Popolo* ; the banishment of dangerous refugees ; a new law to regulate the press ; the prohibition of refugees to write articles in the newspapers, &c. To say the truth, though disguised under the appearance of courtesy and friendliness, this amounted to a command. Cavour, who was prepared for every emergency, was willing to satisfy the French Government as much as lay in his power by an increased surveillance and a moderate reform in the laws regulating the press, but he unhesitatingly refused to lend himself to any arbitrary proceedings, such as the suppression of newspapers, which would amount to *coups d'état*. Especially did he resist any measure which bore too visibly the stamp of an attempt at foreign interference. To avoid making matters worse, he prudently abstained from all diplomatic controversy ; he contented himself with giving verbal answers, offering promises and protestations, with which Walewski refused to be satisfied, and which only provoked more urgent representations.

The Emperor himself, soon after Orsini's attempt, had a singular and significant conversation with General della Rocca, whom Victor Emmanuel sent to congratulate him on the failure of the outrage, and also, perhaps, to appease him. "Do not believe," said Napoleon III. to the General, and to Count Villamarina, "do not believe that I wish to put any pressure upon your Government. In the many vicissitudes of my life, I have had occasion to learn to esteem highly the dignified attitudes preserved by small States with regard to the demands of their more powerful neighbours. But these things that I ask are easily carried out, and might be acceded to by any allied government, even by one which cared but to see justice done. Let us suppose that England refused to grant my legitimate demands, the intercourse between the Cabinets of Paris and London would soon cease, and the next step would be a declaration of hostilities. If that should ensue, let us consider honestly what would be the condition of Sardinia. There are two alternatives: she would be for or against me, but you must not deceive yourselves. The realisation of your hopes and your future are in the French alliance, which alone can support you efficiently. Well, in order to be with me in that day, it is indispensable that you should accede to my present demands. If you refuse, you set yourself against me, you will be with England, and what advantage can you derive from that? What good will you get from a few English war ships at La Spezzia or at Genoa, if England cares to keep the treaties of 1815 in all their integrity? In that case, much against my will, I should be constrained to lean upon Austria, and once embarked in that policy, I should be forced to give up my most cherished day-dream, my dearest wish—I mean the Independence of Italy." These words, equally persuasive and menacing, left Piedmont in a cruel dilemma.

X.

In short, during several days a crisis reigned of the most gloomy, violent, feverish description, between Turin and Paris. More than once the official attitude of the French Ministry made Cavour think all was lost, and the king conceived that he must again have recourse to a great stroke.

Of his own accord, as from sovereign to sovereign, Victor Emmanuel wrote a confidential letter to Napoleon III., in which he expressed himself openly, protesting his attachment and his desire to please the Emperor, but at the same time declaring, with dignified emotion, that there were concessions he could not make ; that if he were driven to it, he, like his ancestors of Savoy, would go and fight on the Alps to defend his crown. In commenting upon these words, the President of the Council likewise wrote to his representative at Paris : "Stand firm, and hold your ground with dignity and moderation ; do not draw back a single step. His Majesty has written to the Emperor in terms of the most cordial friendship, but as a king who will stand upon his rights. In order to save the independence and honour of the country he will shrink from nothing, and we are ready to follow him. The Emperor has evidently been persuaded that we have become more friendly with England since Orsini's attempt. Nothing can be farther from the truth. I have written nothing about our difficulties with France to our envoy in London, and I have not even whispered a word about them to Sir James Hudson." This was when the crisis was at its height.

Soon, however, the pressure began sensibly to diminish. The mere confidential diplomacy was telling upon the official diplomacy, and was effectually averting all danger of a possible rupture. The Emperor's anger was also gradually dying out; even he admitted that if there were any conspirators it was not Piedmont, but the hazardous situation of Italy that was to blame. At the Tuileries it had come to be repeated that : " So long as there should be Austrians in Italy there would be attempts at assassination in Paris ; that Count Cavour was in the right, and ought to be seconded." Napoleon III. had finally written to Victor Emmanuel that it was only between great friends that it was possible to speak out ; he bade him do what he could, and not trouble himself further. And now comes the most singular part of this crisis in the relations between Paris and Turin. While the Emperor was growing more and more calm, and was ceasing to interfere at all in a matter which he had learnt to see in a new light, the French ministry persevered increasingly in the demands with which it stormed the Turin Cabinet ; it doubled the number of its almost threatening communications, until at length matters reached the climax. Prince de Latour d'Auvergne had been requested to read a fresh and still more peremptory despatch to Count Cavour. The latter listened calmly and patiently, until, the reading over, he replied with the utmost tranquillity and a tone of friendly sarcasm : " But the affair is over ; the King received yesterday a letter from the Emperor which terminated all." It was literally true ; and Prince de Latour d'Auvergne, a benevolent and enlightened man, who faithfully carried out his instructions, but was growing sceptical on many points, had only to fold up his despatch and return home, pondering on the difficulty of serving princes who have two kinds of diplomacy.

Cavour's invariable policy was to preserve the alliance with France without sacrificing the honour and freedom of his country. Let the inviolability of the " statuto " and the national liberty be secured, and he never hesitated to seek any means of giving the Emperor satisfaction or guarantee. It was in his interest to do so, were it only by way of open protest against sinister plots.

He found his justification in the sufficiently scandalous acquittal of a Turin newspaper, which at that very time indulged in a justification of the outrage of January 14. The President of the Council hoped to have found the means of keeping Piedmont within the bounds of rightful authority, by proposing a law which increased the penalties to be inflicted on persons conspiring against the life of foreign monarchs, or defending political assassination, and choosing a new jury for cases of transgression of the law on the part of the press. This new law was not in any way exceptional ; it interfered neither with the " statuto " nor with the essential conditions of

the freedom of the press, nor yet with the principle of
trial by jury : its value lay in its moral influence ; it
protected the responsibilities of Piedmont.

It was difficult, notwithstanding, to obtain so simple
a measure from a parliament which was not and could
not be made aware of all the circumstances of the case.
Cavour lost no time, and while he pursued his diplomatic
work he brought all his activity and authority to
bear upon the task of reconciling his opponents, and
awakening all to a sense of the gravity of the situation.
He gave numerous audiences, in which he displayed an
inexhaustible. vein of good sense and patriotism. As a
matter of course, he met with strong opposition, which
he was quite accustomed to overcome. The one accused
him of carrying out his bold and dangerous policy at
the cost of the humiliation of Piedmont by foreign
Powers ; others brought forward against him the old and
hackneyed accusation of not seeking his support in the
people and in the revolution, instead of buying over the
dangerous co-operation of despotic Governments.

Virtually, however, an immense majority in the
Chambers was predisposed to side with him, feeling
more than ever how indispensable and secure was his
guidance. The one question with Cavour was, how to
give this majority an occasion of declaring itself. He
hoped to do this in the public discussion shortly to be
opened, and which insured his victory. Once more, in
a few master-strokes, he set before them that " eight
years' policy," which had begun so humbly, but had
spread and increased and culminated in that " system of
alliances," which the new law was intended to strengthen.

Cavour did not attempt to conceal the truth, that this law, proposed and defended by him, had two essential objects. The first was to achieve the definitive conquest of the French alliance; not by any act of subordination or abdication of dignity, but by a reliable and spontaneous proof of good-will : and to those persons who despised all alliances, or proposed to wait until a change of government should have taken place in France, he responded by an explanation equally luminous and astute ; a very model of rational policy and profound diplomacy.

The second object was to set Italy free from all dangerous secret societies ; and to those who persisted in confounding the cause of Italian emancipation with insurrectionary movements, in short, with universal revolution, he replied with emotion: " How senseless ! to believe that the revolution which would again imperil the great principles of social order could be favourable to the cause of liberty. How senseless ! not to perceive that the effect would be the destruction of every vestige of liberty on the Continent. How senseless ! those who betray that their aspirations are revolutionary rather than patriotic ; that they love the revolution better than they do Italy." And, going on directly to the situation of the moment, he pointed out the harm which factions had ever done to Italy ; the harm they had again done her by carrying out their principle of assassination. " It is a mournful and deplorable fact," he exclaimed, " deplorable beyond all expression, that an Italian faction should be known to profess and practise such horrible maxims. In the face of such facts we have felt that it was absolutely necessary for the good of Italy that in the one Italian State which has a Liberal Government a voice should be lifted up, not only by the Government, but by the nation represented by its Chambers, in solemn and indignant protest against these criminal doctrines of political assassination."

XI.

While Cavour spoke thus, carrying his parliament with him by the sheer force of reason and patriotism, he had gained his cause already in other quarters where he most felt the importance of gaining it.

The Emperor was grateful to him for what he was doing. The question had lost its threatening aspect; but what was not yet known, nay, could scarcely be gathered from certain obscure indications, was that the crime of January 14 was about to form the strange and mysterious commencement of a new phase of Italian affairs. The question has often been asked, what part the attempted assassination in the Rue Le Peletier really had in the preliminaries of the war of 1859. The sudden impression of terror it awakened certainly did not give birth to an idea which existed already; the attempt on the Emperor's life was but the pretext or the occasion of an incident equally strange and significant. While diplomatists and parliaments were still discussing various small amendments or unimportant articles of legislative measures — this was what was taking place.

Felice Orsini, the man who had not shrunk from

scattering death around him in order to take the life of the only sovereign likely to help his country, was doubtless a great criminal—a murderer from sheer fanaticism—but there was nothing of the mere vulgar assassin about him; he stood high above his obscure accomplices, and by one of those strange revulsions of feeling which a violent crisis will sometimes bring about in the mind of a fanatic, the presence of death restored to him a stoical clearness of vision. He had written from prison a letter to the Emperor Napoleon which was produced in his defence, and even published in the *Moniteur*, in which he implored Napoleon to deliver Italy. "Let your Majesty call to mind," he wrote, "that the Italians, among whom was my father, shed their blood freely and joyfully for Napoleon the Great, that they continued faithful to him until his downfall. Let it not be forgotten that the peace of Europe and that of your Majesty will remain a mere chimæra as long as Italy is not free. If your Majesty will but deliver my country, the benedictions of twenty-five millions of men will resound from generation to generation."

This was not all: at the last moment, without attempting to escape from the supreme expiation due to so many victims, without flinching in any way in the very face of death, Orsini had written a second letter, a sort of last testament, in which he said: "In an hour or two I shall have ceased to be; but before I breathe my last I wish to make it clear, nay, I would affirm it with all the frankness and courage which until now have never failed me, that assassination, however it may disguise itself, is no principle of mine, although in a fatal

moment of mental aberration I allowed myself to be
drawn into organising the attempt of January 14.
Instead of having recourse to a system of assassination,
may my fellow-countrymen reject it far from them ;
may they learn that redemption can only be obtained by
abnegation, and by a constant union of efforts and
sacrifices, without which Italy can never be made free.
As for the victims of January 14, I offer my life as an
expiatory sacrifice, and I implore the Italians, when once
they have become independent, to give some worthy
compensation to those who have in any way suffered."
These words of retraction had visibly affected the
Emperor, who charged one of his most trustworthy
secret agents to place Orsini's papers in the hands of
Count Villamarina, with orders to send them to Turin.

Why should the Emperor have been so anxious to
send these documents to Turin ? What could his aim
be ? Was it one of the eccentric proceedings of a complex mind, trying all paths, however devious, in order to
reach a goal as yet but dimly perceived ? Be it as it
may, one morning, towards the end of March, Cavour
suddenly received this unexpected communication. In
vain he sought for an explanation of it. He had dis-
approved of the insertion of Orsini's first letter in the
Moniteur, but on receipt of the packet, all hesitation on
his part ceased. Next day the official gazette of Turin
published all the papers, including the testament, which
was new to the public, accompanied by a note, asserting
the retractation and repentance of the criminal, and his
counsels to trust in " an august Will propitious to Italy."
This unexpected publication, which sceptics at first took

for a mystification—it appeared on April 1 !—produced everywhere a rapid and profound impression, and as it only preceded by a few days the discussion on the law of the Press, and on " conspiracies against foreign sovereigns," it greatly tended to insure success, the spirit of it animating the debate which followed.

The President of the Council naturally abstained from touching upon the point, and involving himself in explanations which, for that matter, he could not have given.   He knew nothing for certain ; he had only seen in the communication he had received a kind of indistinct encouragement, or a sign of intelligence from the Emperor, and this was much.   It was evident that from this time he felt greatly reassured ; he was in a state of suspense when, soon after, towards May, he received from another quarter, from a friend living in Paris and familiar with the Palais Royal, a fresh letter, containing a well-defined plan of alliance between France and Piedmont, the conditions of arrangement, the reciprocal advantages, and even a project of marriage between Prince Napoleon and a daughter of Victor Emmanuel. The writer was a friend to Italy and the Piedmontese Ministers, and spoke like a far-seeing man of the possibility of a decisive negotiation.

This looked pregnant with serious matter.   The President of the Council submitted everything to the King.   The first question was how far the letter was to be depended on, and Cavour decided to send to Paris a young man, Cavaliere Constantine Nigra, for some years past his confidential secretary, whom he knew to be capable of carrying out the most delicate of missions.   It was placed soon beyond a doubt, and this on the authority of a confidential agent of the Tuileries—the same who had despatched the Orsini documents—that the letter received at Turin, without having had any direct sanction, faithfully interpreted the Imperial mind. Napoleon III. was quite disposed to act, but nothing could be done without an interview, which was to be arranged in such a manner as to disarm all suspicion. Dr. Conneau, on pretext of a pleasure trip to Italy, was about to pass through Turin, where he accordingly appeared in June : he had an interview with the King and the President of the Council, and a quiet excursion was planned for Count Cavour to Plombières, whither the Emperor was proceeding soon to take the waters.

XII.

While this interview, the veiled preliminary step to such remarkable and important events, was being arranged, Cavour was terminating a long session which placed no more hindrances in his way, but left him wearied with the hard winter's work of 1858. He had passed through trials of all kinds, diplomatic struggles, parliamentary conflicts, and with his accustomed energy and flexibility had remained master of the situation. Perhaps he was getting a glimpse of the end of what would restore to him his lost vigour, and reward him for all his labours ; but not a word of it escaped his lips, he spoke only of his weariness and want of rest ; he hoped to be able to forget all for a few days, as might well be believed, and it was on July 7, the eve of his journey to Plombières, that he wrote to his friend, Madame de

M

Circourt, in the pleasing, careless tone of a wearied politician, or a diplomatist out for a holiday :

"Were I free to turn whither my sentiments and desires would lead me, I should certainly take advantage of my vacation to come and crave your hospitality at Bougival ; but, chained as I am to my political chariot, I may not turn aside from certain paths. If I were to go to France at this moment, where diplomatists are vainly trying to solve a problem that they themselves have rendered insoluble, my journey thither would give rise to all sorts of comments. When once the session is over I shall go and inhale the fresh mountain air of Switzerland ; far from men whose minds are crammed with petitions. I intend staying a few days at Pressinge ; I shall not be suspected of conspiring with my good friends the De la Rives, against the peace of society. We shall often speak of you ; we shall travel in spirit to the charming hermitage you have turned into an earthly paradise for your friends' enjoyment."

The fact was that matters had been kept quite private ; no one knew anything either at Paris or Turin, while Cavour, who was " going to inhale mountain air in Switzerland," and who really had passed through Pressinge, was quietly making his way to Plombières, where he arrived on July 20. As he had no passport, prime minister though he was, he might have been arrested on landing by an officious gendarme, had not an imperial agent happily been present to extricate him from his difficulty.

Immediately upon his arrival, after breakfast, the Emperor, on pretext of showing him some works in progress, took him out into the country in a small chaise, driven by himself, and it was during this *tête-à-tête* of three or four hours' duration, that the general conditions of an alliance were agreed upon ; it only needed a few conversations to define them more precisely. Events, while somewhat modifying, afterwards revealed what these conditions were. At that time they were as follows : A war with Austria ; the formation of an Italian kingdom of eleven millions of souls, or thereabouts ; the cession of Savoy and Nice to France. The marriage of Prince Napoleon with Princess Clotilde was foreseen and wished for at Paris, and agreed on at Turin, but it was to remain an incident, not a condition. Cavour did not stay longer than twenty-four hours at Plombières. The Emperor treated him in so cordial a manner as to surprise his courtiers ; he "laid himself out to please," it was said. He felt more than regard for the Piedmontese minister ; he had as much confidence in him as he was capable of placing in anyone. During Cavour's stay at Plombières Napoleon III., who had just received a despatch, turned to his guest, and said with a smile : " Here is Walewski announcing your arrival to me "—thus in one word illustrating the situation.

The presence of Cavour at Plombières could not fail soon to transpire ; and in order to lessen the effect it might produce he hastened to leave, as though he were continuing his travels. He went as far as Baden, where he encountered the Prince Regent of Prussia, the future Emperor William, who, after having seen him, declared : " But he really is not such a revolutionist as people make him out to be." Thence, returning through

Switzerland, he halted at a wayside inn, where he wrote out at length the memoranda of his conversations at Plombières, and of the arrangements decided upon there.

In the midst of all this, meanwhile, would the reader learn how Cavour employed his leisure moments? On his passage, at Pressinge, he had taken up a thick book, Buckle's "History of Civilisation," and he read it, take my word for it, thoroughly. Six weeks later he apologised for not having returned it. "I wished," he said, "to read it from end to end, no easy matter when one has two ministerial portfolios on one's hands. In spite of its deficiency of method, its lengthiness, and its want of clearness, this book deserves to be read; for, to my thinking, it denotes an evolution in the English mind that will necessarily entail remarkable consequences. If I were not a minister I should try to write an article on the book." This man was one certainly who found time for everything.

Cavour, being a minister, might well dispense with writing an article on Buckle's book. For the time being he had other matters on hand; he was engrossed by the combinations he had assisted in forming, and the hopes he had a right to entertain. He had returned from Plombières, having laid aside all his weariness, silent about matters needing to be kept secret; but full of vitality, and inspiring life and confidence in all around him. He employed the autumn of 1858 in completing his work; he sent to Paris the memorandum he had prepared, containing a *résumé* of the ideas exchanged at Plombières with the Emperor, who found only a few insignificant details to modify in his manuscript. Throughout these months, Cavaliere Nigra, Cavour's young messenger, travelled backwards and forwards between Turin and Paris, like an incarnation of diplomacy, transmitting the words of each to each with equal fidelity and intelligence. The result was a secret treaty of alliance, offensive and defensive, between France and Piedmont; until then there had been merely verbal conventions.

Cavour and the Emperor were in perfect accord together, as was shown by an incident which now appears somewhat strange. The Prince Regent of Prussia had lately placed Prince Hohenzollern at the head of affairs at Berlin. Cavour conceived the idea, on an understanding with Napoleon III., of sending the Marquis Pepoli to Germany; the marquis being a connection not only of the new Prussian premier, but also of the Napoleons.

Pepoli, who took his instructions from Paris as well as from Turin, was ordered to flatter Prussia, awaken her ambition, detach her from Austria, and draw her into the new-made alliance. Prince Hohenzollern declined these overtures, giving in return vague expressions of sympathy, accompanied by protestations of respect for the treaties. A common enterprise of this sort was surely a strong proof of the growing intelligence between the allies of Plombières.

One point remained undecided in these arrangements, otherwise so nearly completed. The Emperor, who wished or believed himself to be master of the situation, had reserved to himself the right of choosing the time

and the manner of starting the question, and Cavour at
times was anxious and troubled by a state of uncertainty
which after all might end in an adjournment *sine die*;
it is evident, however, that when such warlike combinations are made, they tend fatally towards their object.
Secret alliances get noised abroad, men's minds are disturbed, relations are embittered, and this came to pass
towards the end of 1858.

Italy, thus skilfully worked upon, was thrilled with
excitement, and earnestly desired the conflict. France,
somewhat astonished and ill-informed, was reduced to
consulting the oracles of the imperial policy. Europe
felt an uneasiness, the cause of which was not as yet
perceived by her, when suddenly the nature of the
situation was made known by two events happening
almost simultaneously; or, if you will so call them,
speeches.

On January 1, 1859, Napoleon III., giving audience
to the Diplomatic Corps, testified in a brusque manner
to the Austrian ambassador his regret at the hostile
spirit prevailing between Paris and Vienna. A few days
later, at the opening of the Chambers, Victor Emmanuel
remarked : " Our horizon is not at all clear. Our country,
small indeed territorially, has yet become influential in
Europe, through the greatness of the ideas it represents
and the sympathies it inspires. This situation is by
no means without its dangers ; for while we would respect
treaties, we cannot remain insensible to the cry of
anguish which reaches us from so many parts of Italy."
Victor Emmanuel could not, it was understood, speak
thus without an understanding with his French ally.

On the evening of the day on which this speech, so full of warmth and colour, was uttered, the Russian minister, Count Stackelberg, while complimenting the President of the Council, observed: "It was like a crimson aurora." Count Cavour replied that the colour was not the artist's work. "It is the landscape," he said, "which glows with sparks and flames;" on which Sir James Hudson remarked: "It is a flash of lightning striking the treaties of 1815." It might indeed be all these; but above all it was the first result of the secret understanding and treaty at Plombières, or rather the fruit of a policy which, before reaching its goal, had still many a trial to undergo and many a battle to fight.

CHAPTER IV.

I.

Now that the national drama of Italy hastens to its crisis, let us recall two dates to the mind's eye, and compare them. On March 23, 1849, Piedmont fell vanquished on the battle-field, with nothing left in her grasp save a broken sword and a torn flag. She had no allies and but few friends remaining; friends, too, more disposed to blame her rashness or compassionate her want of military success than to assist her. Austria triumphed by her armies; the reactionary party triumphed through the invariable logical result of disorderly revolutions. For a long time all seemed lost on the other side of the Alps. In the first days of 1859 all was won back again. All had changed. The cause of Italy had regained the attention of Europe; it engrossed Governments and public opinion alike.

Such was the work of the policy started at Turin and stoutly pursued during ten years : the policy which guided Piedmont from Novara to the Crimean war; from the Paris congress to the negotiations of Plombières. This ten years' policy succeeded in isolating Austria within her contested dominions; it rallied all Italian feeling around a national monarchy; it separated the question of independence from that of revolution, and it awakened the Foreign Ministers. Its success was due to an amazing combination of circumstances, cleverly prepared or still more cleverly laid hold of; and at the given hour, it found supporters in two men who, different as they were in position, character, and mind, were yet able, by supplementing each the other, to render the most difficult of enterprises a thing of possible achievement. Napoleon and Cavour meet and come upon the scene !

There was assuredly but little resemblance between these two men ; they stand before us rather in vivid and mysterious contrast with each other. They came into collision more than once, but nevertheless they mutually attracted each other, each feeling that the other was necessary to him.

For Cavour, Napoleon III. was the powerful, perhaps dangerous, but indisputable ally, the head of one of the foremost of Continental nations and of an army still reputed irresistible. For Napoleon III. Cavour was the Foreign Minister and instrument of his enigmatical views with regard to Italy, the man best calculated to sweep him on, to oppose him if necessary, and ease him of the burden of his irresoluteness by putting pressure upon him, in offering him in a variety of ways the occasion of deciding and acting upon his decision.

It was said that during the interview at Plombières, the Emperor, then credulous of his own omnipotence, observed to Cavour: " Do you know that there are but three men in Europe, we two and a third whom I will not name?" Who was this third person? No one knows. Out of this meeting of the other two "men," in the little town of the Vosges, originated, in the beginning of 1859, the coincidence of the scene of January 1 at the Tuileries and the thrilling speech of Victor Emmanuel in the Turin parliament on January 10.

Cavour, without any previous warning, had necessarily at once divined the meaning of the words carelessly spoken by Napoleon III. to M. de Hubner, and on hearing them he remarked with a smile: " The Emperor means to go ahead, it appears." As for Victor Emmanuel's speech a week later, the Emperor had known and approved of it beforehand. It was a part of his tactics that his ally should say what he would not or could not as yet say himself.

Some few days subsequently another incident startled the world as with a fresh revelation. It became known almost simultaneously that Prince Napoleon, accompanied by General Niel, had left Paris for Turin, and that the marriage of a Bonaparté with Princess

Clotilde of Savoy was accomplished. All was settled before January 30, at Turin, where an excited public regarded this union of the dynasties as the promise of events at hand. From this period, dating January 18, the previously personal and implied understanding between the Emperor and the King took a more distinct diplomatic form, and grew into a regular alliance, founded on the apprehension of an attack on the part of Austria.

For a final *coup de théâtre* : on the morrow of the marriage of Prince Napoleon and the Princess Clotilde, there appeared suddenly in Paris a startling pamphlet, "Napoleon III. and Italy," known to be inspired by the Emperor, and in which was traced a whole programme of Italian reorganisation by national federation, independent of the foreigner.

Thus within a narrow period consecutive events were crowded. The words spoken by Napoleon III. to Baron Hubner found their supplement, a sort of swelling echo, in the speech of Victor Emmanuel, and these two public acts were crowned by the family alliance, and by the imperial manifesto, which raised the problem of the destinies of Italy before Europe, as though the treaties of 1815 were not in existence. A few weeks, it might be said a few days, sufficed to bring the crisis to a head. Meanwhile nothing was decided, and the question still was whether the knot would have to be finally cut by the sword, or whether, by a last effort, the Governments would succeed in conjuring the storm which, gathering its ominous black masses to all appearance over Austria alone, threatened the whole Continent. During this

winter of 1859 the struggle continued between the warlike and the pacific currents; a confused and agitated
prologue to the great drama.

II.

It was indeed a most strange situation, where everything seemed to lead fatally to a conflict, and the definite
point of the discussion remained obscure; where diplomacy knew not how to touch this Italian problem, which
had undoubtedly its origin with bad government in
the Legations and in the Duchies, but was also above all
attributable to the domination of the foreigner; that is to
say, to a condition of things presenting difficulties only to
be settled by an appeal to force.   We see, for an example
of this curious phase in modern history, Cavour himself,
the only one of all the actors who was in the secret of
what he wished, passing nearly four months between a
national movement, alternately stimulated or bridled by
him, and the perplexities assailing him from Europe,
projects of negotiations on all sides rising to bar the road
to him.

Had Austria possessed more initiative and more.
pliability, she might easily have simplified the question,
greatly to the confusion of her enemies.   She seemed
once to be awake to the idea, and the episode glances
with a covert melancholy before plunging into the torrent
of events.

Some short time previously, in the year 1858, the
Cabinet at Vienna had despatched the Archduke Maximilian as Viceroy to Lombardy, on a mission of peace

and conciliation. The ill-fated prince, doomed to the Mexican tragedy, arrived at Venice and Milan full of liberal designs. He had youth in his favour, a very cordial and gentlemanly manner, Austria to back him, the good counsel of the prudent Leopold of Belgium—whose daughter he had just married—and through King Leopold the best wishes of England in his favour. Maximilian had taken up his task in earnest. In the course of an excursion on the Lago Maggiore, and in a conversation with the Prussian minister at Turin, Count Brassier de Saint-Simon, he spoke of Cavour in the warmest terms. "I greatly admire Count Cavour," he said; "but as the business in contemplation is a policy of progress, I shall not let him outstrip me." Cavour, who gave ear to everything, disdaining nothing, was not insensible to this attempt, which might have disconcerted all his plans; and subsequently he confessed that the mission of the Archduke Maximilian had caused him the liveliest anxiety.

Suppose for a moment that Austria, strong in her incontestable territorial rights, and a military power permitting her to make concessions that could not be deemed dishonourable, had persisted in this Liberal idea, diverting and weaning the national Italian sentiment, softening her rule, and taking Europe to witness to her generosity : do but imagine this drama turned to a reality under the quieting administration of an Archduke; how different might events have been from the war of 1859 to the war of 1866, and all that since ensued—not forgetting Mexico.

Though she should not have succeeded in it, the

policy was at least worth making a trial of; but owing to one of those fits or false calculations, of which she has given more than one example, and which have always cost her heavy, at the first signs of a public crisis, Austria fell back affrighted on her traditions of immobility and repression. She did not confine herself to cancelling the mission of the Archduke Maximilian, but exaggerated her military rule in all her Italian possessions. She had already commenced her preparations for war before January 1, 1859; she hurried them forward feverishly on the morrow of this date, despatching army corps upon army corps into Italy, organising her forces as on the eve of a campaign, and going so far as to take a position on the Ticino, in face of Piedmont. Some of her officers, carried away by their bellicose fury, were guilty of acts of grave imprudence. At their banquet-tables in Milan, they talked of nothing less than a speedy departure for Turin, which was to be the first stage of a march on Paris.

Austria did not see that by her precipitancy and her excitement she compromised everything, disarmed in advance those who were striving for peace, and placed herself in a position that from one day to another exposed her to a fit of rashness, by the excess of her military display and of her expenditure. She was unable to perceive that she played the game of her enemies, and might possibly be tumbling into a pitfall; and in any case she began by offering Piedmont a pretext that, finding herself supported, the country did not fail to profit by. Piedmont replied to armaments by armaments, to demonstration by demonstration, putting the fortresses of Alessandria and Casale in a state of defence, and getting together her regiments scattered on both sides of the Alps. The parliament voted a loan of two millions sterling, ostensibly necessitated by the "provocation of Austria," so that the two Powers were already all but front to front; or at least the question of peace or war became terribly vexed and envenomed when diplomacy went to its task of holding back issues on the verge of explosion.

III.

What was it that diplomacy sought to do, or rather, what could it do in the state to which affairs had come? All these incidents whirling about had not failed to produce an impression revealing a positive danger of war. The wish was for peace, and diplomacy strove to preserve it.

England, represented by the Tory ministry of Lord Derby and Lord Malmesbury, held to peace more than the other Powers. Unhappily, Europe was deeply divided, and England herself, upon whom the initiative of discussion and negotiations devolved, was full of perplexity. She felt herself divided between her traditional Continental policy, which held her to the treaties of 1815 and Austria, her sympathy with the cause of freedom, which made her lean to Piedmont and Italy, her interests as a commercial Power, and her anxiety regarding the designs of France, whose growing intimacy with Turin filled her with misgivings. She would have conciliated everything—peace and that which menaced peace—Austria, France, and Piedmont; and she could not discern that her urgent applications to one and the other imperilled her chances of success with them all.

When England appealed to Vienna, Count Buol Schauenstein, minister of the Emperor Francis Joseph, replied impatiently: " You are mistaken, it is not here that you should come with your entreaties and your counsels; go to Paris and Turin, and speak your mind out plainly there. Let the Emperor Napoleon learn that, if his army crosses the Alps, England will not look on quietly; let the King of Piedmont know that England sanctions no plundering of the Austrian possessions in Italy. If the Queen's ministers hold a resolute language we shall have no war. Italy is not in want of reconstruction; let them cease to stir her up, and we shall hear no more of it."

Turning to Turin, the English Cabinet was told that, if it desired peace, it had better apply to Vienna; that the source of the evil lay in the foreign lordship in Italy, which was a dangerous friend to bad governments, a menace to Piedmontese constitutional liberty, and the perpetual fosterer of revolutionary passions; it was explained that, taking Austria to be on the legal ground of 1815 in Milan, she was not so in her occupation of Bologna and Ancona for a period of ten years, binding the Central Duchies to terms amounting to vassalage, and turning Piacenza into an imperial fortress on the frontier of Piedmont.

When England put her questions to France, the Emperor gave her every encouragement in her peaceful mission, disavowing the barest idea of aggressiveness, and assuming the air of a prudent friend by whom

Piedmont was kept back, while in the main letting certain ideas be seen, with regard to Italian affairs, that had small chance of being accepted by Austria.

England might have found a lever in the neutral Powers; but the assistance with which Prussia favoured her was sufficiently platonic; and as to Russia, Prince Gortchakoff, from the very commencement, held these words to Sir James Crampton, the English minister at St. Petersburg: " Decidedly Russia wishes for peace, she has need of it; but allow me to tell you with my habitual frankness that we are unable to look with the same eye upon France and Austria. We are upon terms of close cordiality with the former; as to the latter, it is the contrary. The Court of Vienna has behaved disgracefully in return for our services to her. In other times Russia offered her counsels to her allies, she refrains now from counselling whomsoever it may be. If we are asked for an opinion, our reply is favourable to peace: so far we go and no farther. Be good enough to understand that, if the peace of Europe is disturbed, I do not tell you on which side you will find the Russian arms. Upon this head we have determined to remain quit of any engagement."

Beset by such contradiction and confusion, England had reason to be embarrassed, but she did not lose heart. She had commenced by trying since the month of January to bring Napoleon III. to specify his views. She soon took another step: before the end of February, the Queen's ambassador at Paris, Lord Cowley, was despatched to Vienna with a sketch of negotiations, and instructions to do his utmost to bring Austria to agree to them. In this first programme it was a question of the abandonment of the military occupation of Bologna and Rome, the abrogation of the Austrian treaties with the Duchies, the establishment of a system of liberal reform in the Italian States, and, above all, the putting of the relations between Austria and Sardinia on a proper footing.

Lord Cowley's mission was not much of a success; nor, in fact, had it altogether failed—or at least the English Cabinet fancied it had not, and possibly flattered itself already that it would be able to command events by means of mediation, when suddenly, on or about March 20, Europe was startled by the proposition of a congress, coming from St. Petersburg, in reality responding to the secret wishes of the Tuileries. It was the first apparition of that idea, or it might be said chimæra, of a congress, so frequently and so vainly pursued since by Napoleon III.

A congress to consider the Italian problem! Under what conditions and where should it sit? Of whom should it consist? Was it to treat of Italian affairs without the Italians? Was the congress to open to the sound of armaments that were still being pushed on hard and fast on the Ticino? Plainly the question, far from being simplified, became more complicated by the bringing of these European inconsistencies into broad daylight, and entering on a path devoid of outlet. An acute diplomatist remarked: Behold a congress that will never sit!

IV.

It was in the midst of difficulties like these that Cavour was plunged between January 1 and April, 1859. For him the main trial of his dexterity was not simply to lead to war out of such a state of confusion; it was to gain his end without too much separating himself from Europe; above all, without for a moment losing his junction with France, whose vanguard he was across the Alps. The prime task for Cavour was to reconcile the interior movement upon which he leaned—of which, more than ever, he was now the prudent and impassioned guide—with the exterior difficulties that could not be avoided. In this double labour he spent four months of an inexhaustible and lively activity, always with an eye on the Ticino and on Austria; passing from a diplomatic conference to an inspection of the fortresses of Casale and Alessandria, watchful over every service, and re-ceiving all the world, inspiring everyone about him with his own spirit and fire.

The first incidents of the new year, the moment when, to use the expression of the period, "the bomb had burst," had shaken Piedmont and the whole of Italy with deep commotion. It was understood that the hour had come, and there was from that time but one thought for all. D'Azeglio, the knightly man, ever prompt to generous resolves, had hastened to write to Cavour: "It is no longer the hour for the discussion of politics, there is nothing to be done but to succeed; make what use you will of me."

The words of D'Azeglio expressed the universal sen-timent. From all parts a stream of frank confidingness, so to speak, flowed towards Cavour. Those whose thoughts were set above all upon independence turned their faces to Turin ; and from Lombardy as from Tuscany, from the Romagna and from Modena, shoaled hosts of young men eager to be enrolled under the banner of Victor Emmanuel. There was nothing of the turbulence of 1848 in these manifestations ; on the contrary, they were signalised by a formal and serious spirit, even in the excitement of the national emotion. It was like a conspiracy of a novel order, whose word of command was to shun the errors of the past, and to rally without bargaining round him who had carried Italy so far on the road.

Cavour took joy in a movement that was a work of his own creation ; it responded to his heartiest wishes, and he designed to make the best use of it by organising it. If, on the one hand, the supple and forethoughtful patriot had done his utmost to procure a powerful ally, he was not, on the other, ready to consent that everything should be owing to this ally. He wrote to La Marmora : " In order that the war may come to a fortunate issue, we must prepare for greater efforts. Woe to us if we triumph solely by the aid of the French !" For the sake of national dignity, as well as for the independence of his policy, he stood for not receiving freedom as a gift. To this end he was diligent in the moral and material preparation of his country, and strove to the utmost to associate Italy with Piedmont. At the risk of embroiling himself with diplomacy, he busied himself in creating, under the title of " Chasseurs of the Alps," the battalions destined to form *cadres* for the Lombard and Tuscan youth pouring into Turin, to place them beside the Piedmontese army; and, intrepid as he was, he did not shrink from the idea of entrusting these battalions to Garibaldi.

One morning in the winter of 1858–59, before break of day, an unknown visitor had presented himself at the house of the President of the Council, who had been immediately informed of the visit by his valet somewhat in alarm. "Who is the man?" said Cavour. "He has a broad hat, a big stick in his hand, and he will not deliver his name; he says that your excellency expects him." It was Garibaldi, who had come to arrange with Cavour for putting himself under the orders of Victor Emmanuel. But as his name was still sufficient to scare many, Garibaldi quitted Turin for Caprera, leaving behind him Colonel Medici to organise the Chasseurs of the Alps; and in Medici Cavour soon found a zealous and devoted auxiliar. No doubt it was a risk to run, and it was not impossible that such a coadjutor might prove an embarrassment in the future. Cavour alone could manage these elements and throw the die; he saw herein the means of reuniting all the forces of the country, to annul or rally the Republicans, leaving aside only the inveterate disciples of Mazzini; and as to these, he did not hesitate to declare that, if they stirred a step, he would shatter them with grape as pitilessly as he would the Austrians.

v.

The gravest difficulty for Cavour lay outside the kingdom, with England, and even to a certain degree with France.   England, finding him always in the way of her negotiations for peace, treated him roughly.   Lord Derby and Lord Malmesbury did not cease to worry him with their recriminations and admonitions, which his friend, the brilliant Sir James Hudson, delivered with more fidelity than of personal share in them.

The English Cabinet beheld in him, and not without some truth, the great agitator and constant provoker of Austria, the most dangerous adversary of all endeavours after peace.   Cavour, for his part, listened patiently, sometimes anxiously, decided both to resist the wishes of England and not to wound her.   Upon occasion, if he was pushed too far, he burst out, replying boldly to an English diplomatist, who told him that public opinion in London accused him of imperilling the peace of Europe by his Italian policy : "Admirable ! and I, on the contrary, think that the most serious responsibility for the troubled position of Italy rests with England, her parliamentary orators, her diplomatists, and her writers, who have been labouring for years to excite political passions in our peninsula.   Is it not England that has encouraged Sardinia in her propaganda of moral influences opposed to the lawless preponderance of Austria in Italy ?"

Susceptible as he was to the rebukes of the English Cabinet, Cavour still exerted his utmost wariness in dealing with England, trying all he could to win her by allusions to her previous good favour, her liberal traditions, and her sympathies for Piedmontese Constitutional Government.   He seized opportunities for addressing his speeches in parliament to the English people; he reminded them that every just cause—emancipation in Ireland, and negro emancipation—had finished by triumphing ; and he exclaimed : " Can it be that the cause of Italy is less holy than that of the Irish, or that of the blacks ? And she also, Italy, will vindicate herself before English public opinion. I can never believe that a man so distinguished as Lord Derby, presiding over the counsels of England, will, after having affixed to the great act of negro emancipation the name transmitted to him by history, conclude his noble career by complicity with those that would condemn the Italians to eternal servitude."

The astute minister was at that time graciously giving receptions at Turin to many eminent Englishmen, among others, a member of the Whig party, General Fox, and Mr. Gladstone ; the latter had recently left the Ionian islands, where he had completed an official mission, and returned through Venetia and Lombardy, which he found in full military occupation. Cavour neglected nothing in indicating to his guests that England was mistaken when she identified peace with Austrian domination. " You have been privileged to see," he said to Mr. Gladstone, " that Austria threatens us ; here we are tranquil, our country is calm, we shall do our duty."

He knew what he was about ; if he could not have England for friend he would not have her for an enemy, and he sent her as ambassador-extraordinary the man best calculated to reawaken her sympathies and liberal instincts, Massimo d'Azeglio, saying of him hopefully : " There is the father of the Italian question ; he is a

Moderate; they will not be suspicious of him. His presence in London should be of first-rate service among all who are not of pure Austrian blood."

And D'Azeglio departed for London, fresh from his journey to Rome, whither he had been despatched to decorate the Prince of Wales with the collar of the Order of the Annunciation on his visit to the eternal city.

The relations of Cavour with France were of a different character, without being less complicated and laborious. The dauntless Piedmontese had found, it is true, a friend of the Italian cause in Napoleon III., an ally more than half pledged to him, and after the month of January the marriage of Prince Napoleon with the Princess Clotilde gave him a firm auxiliar in one who had become a member of the royal family. His relations with the Tuileries continued close and secret through the Count of Villamarina, above all through the Cavaliere Nigra, his young and trusty lieutenant, whose private mission circumstances were rendering important.

The influence of Turin on Paris was as real and as active as that of Paris on Turin. The alliance, contracted and close-linked six months ago, was untroubled; but Cavour was not unaware of the uncertain and shifty character of Napoleon III., nor of what difficulties beset the master of France. In fact, the policy indicated from the date of January 1 had raised a storm of opposition in a portion of French society—in the religious world, among the veterans of the parliamentary world, and even in a certain set of the friends of the Empire.

Some of the more thoughtful minds apprehended, in this war which was approaching, a destruction of equilibrium that could not but be harmful to the traditional interests of the country. Others foresaw danger for the temporal power of the Pope in an Italian war. Worldly Paris, the ardent and hot-brained city, little heeded by the Empire, though it exercised its influence on opinion, was for peace. Cavour knew it well, and did what he could to win the support of liberal minds; but the views of a good part of Parisian society were notorious, and he knew also that in the Imperial councils the Minister of Foreign Affairs, Count Walewski, shared those views so little favourable to the striking of a blow for Italy. Napoleon III. was manifestly attached to the cause for which he had made the alliance of Plombières and Turin, while Count Walewski talked and behaved like a minister pursuing a directly opposite line of policy—the policy of objection to war with Austria, severity towards Piedmont and Italy, suspicion approaching almost to personal hostility to Cavour : and the singular thing was, that in a despotic government there was a sort of conflict going on, under shelter of which the Emperor, acting either from indolence or calculation, allowed his minister's pacific efforts and declarations to proceed publicly, without interposing the decisive word.

Napoleon III. likewise was anxious to calm the mind of England. He wished to appear forced into war, taking up arms only in the interests of peace, conservative principles, and the European equilibrium, transparently compromised or threatened by Austria in Italy. He suffered Count Walewski to perform with perfect sincerity on the *thema* he had selected, insomuch that Cavour, already embarrassed by England, found himself in addition face to face with this crack-skull of a double-headed French policy. The Emperor who sustained him was not given to speak every day, and, on the other hand, he had to deal with the salons, the financial powers, religious influences, and official diplomacy, which, in the prolonged intervals of the imperial silence, made themselves heard.

VI.

Often during these laborious and agitated weeks of the beginning of 1859, obliged as he was to show front to all difficulties and perils, Cavour underwent woful anxieties, owing to the ceaseless contradictions tormenting him. He did not let them thwart him. He pursued his course through all these entanglements, multiplying as they continued.

The situation began to be really critical towards March 20, when the proposition of a congress startled the world. There was a sharp scene in Paris between the French Minister of Foreign Affairs and the Sardinian envoy, Count Villamarina. Count Walewski, in a fit of ill-temper, possibly designed to intimidate the Cabinet of Turin, allowed himself to be carried away so far as to say that : " The Emperor would not make war to favour the ambition of Sardinia ; and that all would be settled pacifically at a congress, in which Piedmont would have no right whatsoever to participate." At the same time Prince de la Tour d'Auvergne, under the directions of Count Walewski, held disquieting language though it was without acerbity. Cavour stood ready to face the storm. He wrote to Prince Napoleon, and transmitted a letter from the King, that Cavaliere Nigra was deputed to hand to the Emperor; and he added his instructions to Nigra to speak "energetically to his Majesty; telling him that Count Walewski writes to the minister of France at this Court in a manner to dispirit us and push us to acts of despair." The Emperor replied: "Let Count Cavour come hither to Paris, without further delay." The summons brought Cavour to Paris on March 25.

No sooner had he arrived than he saw himself in the presence of machinery labouring not only for the maintenance of peace, though it should be at the sacrifice of Piedmont, but to have him thrust aside, as the chief obstacle in the way of peace. More than ever he was the great suspected!

Count Walewski's reception of him was courteous and cold. Lord Cowley also was sufficiently serious. At the Tuileries his welcome was cheerful and trusting, as it had been at Plombières. He enjoyed repeated interviews with the Emperor, and the few days he spent in Paris were not lost time for him; he employed them in reconnoitring the situation, and studying the game of Parisian politics, never losing his independence of mind and natural airiness. "I should certainly come to see you," he wrote to Madame de Circourt, "but I dread finding in your salon the frantic partisans of peace, who would be mortally shocked by my presence. In spite then of my warlike disposition, as I do not wish to make war on your friends, I shall not present myself to you save on your promising to receive me privately, or in the presence of those who will not tear out my eyes for the love of peace."

One morning of this end of March, a financial sovereign, Baron James de Rothschild, called on Cavour, whom he had known for some period, and a curious dialogue ensued between them. The all-powerful banker, strongly opposed to war, and desirous to know how far things had gone, became pressing. " Well," replied Cavour, " there are many chances in favour of peace, and there are many in favour of war." " Always joking, M. la Comte !" " Look here, Baron, I will make you a proposal ; let us buy together in the funds ; we'll buy for a rise ; I'll resign my post and there'll be a rise of three francs." " You are too modest, M. la Comte, you are worth fully six francs ! "

The fact is that at the moment when Baron Rothschild received this waggish confidence, there was really in Europe a man disposing of peace or war, and this was the prime minister of Piedmont ; and the truth further is that when he spoke thus, Cavour was not much wiser in the matter than his interlocutor. He carried back a lively sense of the gravity of the situation to Turin, where he had returned on April 1. He saw the business badly begun. Without suspecting the Emperor, he apprehended difficulties and delays, which might indeed be sharply abridged by Austria, if only Austria would do him the good service to commit herself to some rash step.

The matter could not long remain undecided. From the first days of April it narrowed more and more, and concentrated definitely in two points, which were but one—the congress and the preliminary disarmament. It was there that the understanding was next to impossible. Austria on her part would not have Sardinia admitted to the congress, and besides, she demanded irritably and haughtily the disarmament of Piedmont in advance of any European deliberation. Cavour, on his side, looked with an evil eye on this sudden apparition of a congress, and in any case he could not consent that Piedmont, after for three years joining in all the deliberations of Europe, should be left at the door of later conferences on Italian affairs.

He had declared from the first moment that " the congress must have a disastrous effect on Italy if Sardinia were excluded," and that he should be drawn or forced to send in his resignation. As to disarmament, he would not hear of it ; he wrote resolutely to Prince Napoleon : " We will not disarm. Better fall vanquished, sword in hand, than perish miserably in a state of anarchy, or see ourselves degraded to maintain public tranquillity with violence, like the king of Naples. To-day we have a moral force worth an army ; if we abandon it, nothing will give it us back."

How was conciliation practicable between such opposing pretensions ? Diplomacy was bewildered; for if Piedmont was refused a seat at the congress, it was difficult to insist on her disarming ; and if she was asked to disarm, it appeared simply justice to invite her to the congress. Out of this came a combination put forward by England, modified and shaped by France ; it was to be a general disarmament, in which Piedmont was to participate on her admission to the congress with the other Italian States. The Cabinets made the last throw for peace in this scheme. It was not at all to the taste of Cavour, who watched the latest labours of diplomatic expedients most anxiously. So long as he had to do only with England on the question of disarmament, he could shuffle from the pressure of English diplomacy, and dexterously elude replying. When the official proposition to disarm came to him from France, he was seized by a strong emotion, as in the very crisis of his life.

VII.

On the evening of April 18, towards midnight, a secretary of the French Legation had brought him a brief and peremptory telegram, in which the French Cabinet demanded his immediate adhesion, and on reading it he exclaimed in a paroxysm, "that there was nothing more for him to do but to blow out his brains." He fancied all was lost; that the Emperor had forsaken him in the heat of the crisis; and he felt his soul overwhelmed with patriotic anguish at the idea of this work, at which he had laboured for six years, and which had seemed so near succeeding, being jeopardised. But the first dolorous instant passed, his natural elasticity, that never gave him time to blow out his brains on any of the occasions when the thought of it came to him, revived, and he began to reflect.

Every possible scheme and resolution worked in his brain. "It is true," he said animatedly to his friends, "true that we are unhurt on the score of our personal pride. England first stipulated for a preliminary disarmament, and we replied in the negative ; she then asked us to subscribe to the principle of disarmament, and this likewise we declined. To-day, if we adhere to a proposition to disarm on the condition of being admitted to the congress, we submit to a demand addressed to us by Europe. Our honour is safe. We resisted as long as we could. Nevertheless our situation is grave : not desperate, but grave."

Cavour had more than one good reason for calming himself and believing that things were not desperate. Despatches and telegrams received by him on the morrow from London, above all from Paris, helped to reassure him. There was also another point of which he had not at first seized the importance : the adhesion demanded of him, which he had sadly transmitted by the telegraphic wire—what value was there in it if not completed by the adhesion of Vienna? He had most prudently made his sacrifice to be in accord with Europe, not to separate himself from France. Would Austria likewise submit? Far from being decided, the question became more than ever doubtful. During the first days nothing was known, and Cavour himself began to say : "Austria does not speak; if she should refuse, Napoleon must have divined her! In truth the Cabinet of Vienna did not speak, and it remained mute because it had already come to its resolve.

Was it that Austria yielded to a movement of wounded and angry pride? Did she see in the proposition made to her a merely captious expedient, invented to gain time ? Did she suppose herself ready to be ahead of her adversaries in the battle-field, and undo their plots by the swiftness and vigour of her blows? However it may be, during these latest negotiations, when diplomacy imagined that a solution had been found, Austria prepared to force events. She likewise had made a last effort at Berlin to endeavour to interest Russia and Germany in her cause, by widening the war, and proposing to open the conflict on the Rhine as well as on the Po. Though unsuccessful, she let herself be carried away by a warlike mood. She wished to have done with it; and without waiting further she determined to address an ultimatum direct to Turin, summoning Piedmont to disarm, and allowing her a delay of three days to reflect on it. Cavour could have wished for nothing better in his dilemma, and his sole fear was to see Austria stop short.

He still knew nothing certain on the 19th April. He could not know that the ultimatum that very day was ready to be launched at him from Vienna. On the 20th he began to gather the first signs of the coming *coup de théâtre*. He was in the Chamber of Deputies at the Carignano palace on the 23rd, when a word written in haste by one of his intimates informed him of the arrival of Baron Kellersperg, bearer of a communication from Count Buol; and shortly afterwards at the Ministry of Foreign Affairs, at half-past five of that afternoon, he received from the hands of the Austrian envoy this communication, which was nothing other than the command to disarm. Three days later, at the same hour—being the term of the delay granted—he delivered the reply of the Piedmontese Government to Baron Kellersperg, whose hand he courteously pressed in assuring him of the happiness he would have to see him again "under more favourable auspices." Immediately he gave his final orders to Colonel Govone, deputed to accompany the Austrian officer to the frontier; then, turning to some of his friends who were waiting for the end of the scene, he cried with friendly familiarity, the natural key that never forsook him: "It's done; *Alea jacta est!* we have made some history, and now to dinner!"

Austria might justly declare that she had been pushed to extremity. She had some reason to say and believe that she was only defending herself in appealing to arms to decide a question threatening and harrying her on all sides. Still it was in a measure her fault that it so befell that the provocation coming from her should alienate Europe, chill England, and disengage Piedmont in assuring the latter, as the word flew instantly from Paris, "the fullest aid from France." Of this long and laborious diplomatic imbroglio of three months, there remained nothing but a defiance to war, flung down hastily, caught up with feverish zeal, and opening the road of events to Italy and the brave statesman, who had worked for it ten years, and had gone to the Crimea and to Plombières to prepare this crucial hour.

VIII.

When, dating from the morning of April 30, the first French columns descended from the Alps, and debouched in the Piazza Castello of Turin, in the midst of an excited population, Cavour stood on the balcony of the Ministry of Foreign Affairs with other persons of distinction, French and Italian, and Sir James Hudson as well. He had verily good reason to see the march of his own policy in this thrilling spectacle. A few days later Napoleon III. disembarked at Genoa, and did but express a manifest truth in saying to him : " You ought to be satisfied, your aims are being realised."

Under this aspect, war was doubtless a blessing, for it delivered him from uncertainties, by making his long ten years' dream a living and striking reality. War was not, as may be imagined, a time of repose for him, more especially in the earlier period, when Turin expected at any day to sight the enemy, and the Austrians might, with a little dash, have undone the combinations of their adversaries, before the junction of the armies of Piedmont and France.

Much was at one moment to be feared, in fact, if the Austrians, having crossed the frontier, had known how to profit by their weightier numbers in resolutely marching on Turin : if, after committing an error of diplomatic precipitancy, they had not been guilty of another and stranger, by faltering in their military steps. What prevented the war from leading off with a disaster for the Allies ? It may be entirely the fortunate inspiration of Marshal Canrobert, who, on his arrival on April 29, took upon himself to throw out his first French lines to Casale, in a manner to deceive and intimidate the Austrians. Cavour stood ready for the worst, shrinking neither from the determination to defend Turin to extremity, nor, in case of need, from the cruel alternative of inundating the Lomellina to arrest the foe. There was enough all about him to kindle and occupy his wakefulness in this war he had challenged, and whose risks and troubles he encountered with an intrepid heart.

Remaining alone at Turin, while the King and General La Marmora went to the camp, he was President of the Council of the Ministry of Foreign Affairs, Minister of the Interior, Minister of War, Minister of Marine—everything, and equal to all his duties. He lived in the centre of the fire of these devouring labours. His bureaux were his field of battle, which he worked in night and day, and, after his fashion, may be said to have fought in ; having at once to arrange for military transports and provisioning, to reply to petitions for instructions pouring in on him from all sides, to maintain his diplomatic correspondence, and look to his relations with the French army.

Nothing dashed him, nothing perplexed. Witness that day of the month of May when, within four-and-twenty hours, he found means to solve the problem of feeding the French army, reduced to extremities. According to special arrangements, the Piedmontese Government had undertaken to provide for the wants of the French troops up to a certain date. The day had come, and the French military administration found itself painfully embarrassed in considering of the morrow. The Emperor, in camp at Alessandria, surprised by such annoying intelligence, could think of nothing better than to despatch Cavaliere Nigra, whom he kept near his person, to Turin. Cavour, after some show of vexation at the bad management, did not the less hasten his measures to amend it. He at once put in motion the whole body of mayors of the communes within reach of the lines of rail; he gave them orders to requisition all the meal they could lay hands on, heat the bakeries, and make as much bread on the spot as they could; then, without loss of a minute, to the nearest stations—and behold, next morning there was provision beyond what was needed at Alessandria! This is but one of many instances of his indefatigable promptitude in regard to administrative and military business.

IX.

The gravest point ahead was in the political bearings of this war, which opened with numerous victories, and from Montebello, Palestro, Magenta, Melegnano, carried the allies to the Mincio.

There can be no doubt that the agreements between Cavour and Napoleon III. remained at first intact with the original programme of the war. The Emperor, before leaving Paris, had himself declared in a proclamation: "Austria has brought things to such a pass that *she must lord it up to the Alps, or else Italy must be free up to the Adriatic*: for in that country every nook of earth holding independence is a danger to the power of Austria. . . . . . The aim of this war is to restore Italy to herself, not that she should change masters, and we shall have on our frontiers a friendly people, owing their liberty to us." The Emperor added also, it is true: "We do not enter Italy to foment

disorder, nor to shatter the authority of the Holy
Father, whom we have replaced on his throne, but to
relieve it of a foreign burden weighing upon the whole
peninsula."

Shortly afterwards, at Milan, following the victory
of Magenta, which gave Lombardy to the allies, Napoleon III. addressed far more serious words to the
Italians, telling them : "Providence sometimes favours
a people by giving them the opportunity to spring
to life at a blow, but it is on the condition that they
shall know how to profit by it. Profit, then, by the
good fortune offered to you! Unite in a common aim
—the deliverance of your country. Give yourselves
military organisation. Fly to the banner of Victor
Emmanuel, who has so nobly shown you the path of
honour ; . . . . . and animated by the sacred fire of
patriotism, be but soldiers to-day : to-morrow you will
be citizens of a great country."

So spoke the Emperor, and naturally what was to be
anticipated ensued. Already in the last days of April,
at the opening of the war, Florence had made her
revolution, letting her Grand Duke depart in peace
and find an asylum in the camp of the Austrians. The
Governments of Modena and Parma had melted away.
Towards the middle of June, the Austrians, anxious
to have all their forces on the Adige, hastened to quit
the Papal territory, Ancona and Bologna, which they
had occupied for ten years, and immediately, with a
spontaneous outburst, the Romagna joined the movement.

All these things were accomplished without a

struggle, insomuch that in the track of the armies there was a half-emancipated Italy turning to Piedmont. Here was the most delicate part of the programme of the war, and Cavour watched it keenly. Day by day he marked the successive steps of this work of liberation; it had all his sympathies, and he strove to keep it in good order, for it was one of the sources of his strength. He had sent Count Pallieri to Parma, the ardent and devoted Farini to Modena, and to Florence the sagacious Boncompagni. He reserved for Bologna, a difficult position, the person the best fitted to exact obedience by the authority of his name, his noted loyalty, and his lofty mind—Massimo d'Azeglio.

What was to be done with these provinces, for the moment delivered up to themselves, was the business of the war. The men he forwarded represented among them the lordship they had besought of Victor Emmanuel. He gave similar instructions to each of them: "Repression in the cause of order, activity on behalf of the war; what remains leave to the future." His principal care was to allow no opening for agitation and declamation, and it was with this mind that he wrote to Signor Vigliani, a Piedmontese magistrate, of a liberal and conciliatory disposition, whom he had made governor of Milan: "We are not in 1848; we permit of no discussion. Take no notice of the excitement of those who surround you. The smallest act of weakness wrecks the Government."

His lieutenants were everywhere, even in the camp of Garibaldi, whither he had sent a young Lombard,

Emilio Visconti-Venosta—who has since been Minister of Foreign Affairs—who there served as Royal Commissioner with the Chasseurs of the Alps, with whom he made the campaign. In a word, the armies marched, Italy was in movement, and Cavour inspired and directed all, while holding himself as much as possible within the bounds of the imperial programme. The culminating point was about to be touched—Solferino!

X.

But already, before this more bloody than decisive battle of June 24, there had been some clouds in the camp of the allies.

With the progress of events the situation grew more complicated. In approaching the Mincio and the Adige, the armies of France and Piedmont had heavy operations in view instead of battles; they had to conduct sieges and carry formidable positions: they were soon to be in the presence of the Quadrilateral. European diplomacy, at the same time, after leaving the war to its first shots, appeared disposed to resume work; Prussia, without showing any hostility, seemed inclined to play a more active part. On the other hand, the successive movements in Italy, troubling the provinces of the Pope, awakened suspicions and animosities against what was called "Piedmontese ambition;" and all these circumstances tended to feed certain busy efforts, having their centre in Paris, which were soon to reach the headquarters of Napoleon III. in the heart of Lombardy. The policy that had been unable to prevent the war, now attempted to limit and stop it as speedily as might be, by exciting the doubts and fears of the Emperor; and assuredly such a policy found efficacious backers in the overwhelming heat of a torrid season, and the fatigues of a sovereign who, at an age past fifty, fancied himself capable of conducting great military undertakings.

In truth, the glorious and bloody battle of Solferino was but the final *coup de soleil*, which, so to say, ripened the situation. Immediately after it the Emperor received news from Paris leading him to dread the appearance of Germany on the scene. He had, moreover, been profoundly shaken by the frightful carnage he had witnessed. "I have lost 10,000 men," he said to someone, with the accent of a man absorbed by the thought of it.

His mind was variously swayed. He saw the difficulties and dangers lying in a continuation of the war, and the possible though restricted advantages of an arrangement proposed in the hour of victory; and under this impression he despatched General Fleury, on the evening of July 7, to be the bearer of a proposition of an armistice, that in his idea might lead to peace, to the Austrian camp at Verona. Three days subsequently, after an interview between Napoleon III. and the Emperor Francis Joseph, at Villafranca, on the road to Verona, the preliminaries were signed which put an end to the war. The main headings of the treaty of peace were sketched: Cession of Lombardy to the king of Sardinia; creation of an Italian confederation under the "honorary" presidency of the Pope; the ultimate return of the Grand Duke of Tuscany and the Duke of Modena to their principalities ; Venetia to remain "under the crown of the Emperor of Austria." These preliminaries were the basis of the definitive treaty signed by the plenipotentiaries in the neutral city of Zurich.

Thus, then, the French vanguard reached Turin on April 30 ; on May 20 the first battle was fought, that of Montebello ; and the Italian war terminated on July 11 at Villafranca. To conclude it Napoleon III. had been compelled, as he stated, to "cut off from his programme the territory stretching between the Mincio and the Adige. In stopping midway in the execution of plans that had been the object of the alliance of Plombières, he had likewise to renounce—temporarily, we will say—the benefits to be obtained by France on her side of the Alps ; nor did he hesitate—he asked for nothing. Plainly he believed himself to have performed a great act in the face of Europe in signing peace. But it was a perplexed and precarious peace, leaving many problems unsolved, and open to the capital charge, that it left the permanent interests of France unconsidered and disappointed the hopes of Italy. It spoke strongly of that unhappy tendency of a mind so strangely fascinated by chimæras and wanting in will. Not enough or else too much had been done.

This, however, is positive : the Emperor had con-ceived and executed his design without consulting his ally. Notwithstanding the indications of a difficult situation naturally disquieting him at times, Cavour had not foreseen so proximate a *coup de théâtre.*

Shortly previous he had been summoned to the Mincio by the King, specially to tranquillise the Emperor concerning what was passing in the Legations. He thought he had succeeded; and he had quitted the army, deeply affected by the spectacle of the field of Solferino, but without suspicion. Further, on July 6 he had written to Marquis Sauli, Sardinian ambassador at St. Petersburg, who had mentioned the possibility of a mediation : "A mediation at present could bring nothing but bad consequences. Austrian influence must entirely disappear from Italy before we can have a solid and durable peace." Still less did he consider the likelihood of a peace directly negotiated between the belligerents. He was unaware while writing this that the idea of a direct negotiation had already been accepted by the Emperor.

Two days later, on July 8, he received a despatch at Turin from General La Marmora, with news of a suspension of arms ; and La Marmora confessed that no one knew "how or by whom the armistice had been proposed." He started for the camp at once; and reaching Pozzolengo, the King's head-quarters, he knew the truth : he found himself in the presence of a peace, all but established, which frustrated his hopes and confounded his policy. The peace was visible; as yet he was ignorant of the conditions. They were communicated to him only on July 11, in a familiar and dramatic scene, when the King came from the imperial camp at Valeggio bearing the deed, which he signed with this formula or singular reserve : "As far as I am concerned."

Throwing off his uniform, with a heavy face, Victor Emmanuel seated himself in his habitual soldierly attitude, and commanded one of the four persons present to read the preliminaries aloud. Cavour at this reading fell into a violent passion. So intemperate was he that the King had some trouble in calming him, and entrusted him to La Marmora. But Cavour knew well that the King had done no more than he was obliged to do. Between the alternatives of singly carrying on an unequal war, or subscribing to a peace that rescued Lombardy while leaving many questions open, Victor Emmanuel had not or could not have hesitated. Indeed, his resolution once taken, he had shown some *finesse* even in his submission—letting his grief be seen, but no resentment.

Nor would Cavour himself, in his bitterness of spirit, have counselled other proceedings to the King. As for him, he declined to accept the responsibility of the peace, and he washed his hands of power under the weight of so cruel a deception. As soon as things were settled, he considered it due to himself, his honour, and his policy, to quit the Ministry, and after handing his resignation to the King, he left for Turin, overcome with grief, revolving all kinds of projects in his head. As he was passing through Milan, many persons, and among them the Governor, Vigliani, were at the station, impatient to see him. The weariness following stormy emotions had thrown him into a deep sleep. They did not awaken him. It was his first wink of sleep during the whole of his lamentable excursion to the camp.

XI.

Cavour, while on the Mincio, had not seen the Emperor, and the Emperor had not, for his part, been desirous of entering into explanations with him. The interview at Valeggio would have been somewhat different from that at Plombières. It was only on his passage through Turin, returning to France, some days later, that Napoleon III. expressed a wish to see him, and the interview softened the acuter pangs of his recent wounds. The two at least parted like men who may meet again. Cavour had gone to the palace in the evening with a friend, who accompanied him through the most deserted streets of the city, and on his way he said: "I have been invited to a Court dinner, but I refused. I am not in a state of mind to accept invitations. To think that I had done so much for the union of the Italians, and that to-day all may be compromised! I shall be reproached for not having consented to sign the peace. I was unable absolutely, and I cannot sign it."

Cavour's sole idea was to be out of the way, and leaving La Marmora to form a ministry with Rattazzi and General Dabormida, he hastened to depart for Switzerland.

The state of his mind is seen in a letter he wrote on July 22 to Madame de Circourt: "If," he said, "Bougival, instead of being at the gates of Paris, were in some obscure corner of France, I would eagerly accept the hospitality you offer me so cordially. You,

dear countess, would help me, I am sure, not to despair
of my country ; and I should leave you after some time
in a better condition than I am in at present to renew
the struggle for independence and liberty.   But I could
not be at the gates of Paris without entering it; it would
look as if I were sulking ; and there is nothing so ridi-
culous in the world as the sulking of a fallen minister ;
especially if he is so foolish as to pout with the city of
all others the most careless of misfortune and most
mocking.   I am bidden by my position to be as quiet as
I can.   I came trudging into Switzerland, the hospital
of the politically wounded ; but as the announcement of
a congress at Zurich might give my innocent journey a
suspicious look, I shall beat a retreat to Savoy, and I
shall take my station at the foot of Mont Blanc, there
among the marvels of nature to forget the wretchedness
of the works of men ; then, when the heats are over, I
shall return to my estates."

He added with fine irony, doubtless replying to
rather hasty compliments on his retirement : "What
you tell me of the new kindness of my former friends
entirely consoles me.   I am bound to look on my fall as
a providential event, if I may owe to it the recovery of
the esteem of the chosen circle around you, from which
my misconceived policy had in some sort shut me out."

Writing and speaking in this manner, he used the
language of a beaten man ; he thought himself vanquished, and he was less so than he supposed.   He still
retained a touch of the bitterness which had burst from
him so terribly in his first anguish.   He had need to
escape from the fiery atmosphere he had lived in for

six months, and seek the repose he was sure to find in Switzerland, in the society of his friends De la Rive. One morning at the end of July he disembarked at Hermance, on the Lake of Geneva. Finding no other means to get to Pressinge, he hired a farm-cart, and the owner of it offering to drive, Cavour talked with the honest countryman on the road of the harvests, the value of the land about, and the divers cultivations going on in those parts. At Pressinge there was no one to receive him, so he went afoot, his coat on his arm, under a tremendous heat, to another house of the De la Rives, where he was hailed as a guest as little foreseen as he was welcome. None would have said to see him that he was the man who had just stirred all Europe. He passed some days there, happy in the family life, conversing freely with his friends, fishing in the lake, and for a solitary incident coming across a huge Bernese soldier with a long moustache, who asked him if he was Cavour in person, and then passed on in silence, after squeezing his hand.

It might be called the convalescence of Cavour after the fever. A week had barely passed, and he was no longer the same man; he had recovered his prodigious elasticity of nature which saved him from the danger of those first fits of passion he could not always control in the heat of action.

He judged matters with perfect freedom of mind, without recrimination and superfluous regrets, striving above all to comprehend them as they had come to pass.

"It is useless to look back," he said, "now let us look ahead. We have been following one trail; it is cut : well then, now let us follow another. It will cost us twenty years to do what might have been done in so many months. What is there for us ? Besides, England has not yet done anything for Italy ; to-day it is her turn." And to his friend Castelli, who had remained at Turin, he did not delay to write : "I have not abandoned politics. I should if Italy were free ; then my work would be finished : but so long as the Austrians are on our side of the Alps, it is my duty to dedicate what remains to me of life and energy, to realise the hopes I have laboured to make my countrymen conceive. I have resolved to waste no time in vain and sterile agitations, but I shall not be deaf to the call of my country."

Manifestly Cavour, in yielding to a sudden fiery impulse, had by his protestations and his retirement gone rather far. All one can say is that he had been the first to feel what Italy felt almost instantaneously. In all parts of the peninsula, excepting perhaps Lombardy, where a deep sense of deliverance was foremost, the feeling was deep and poignant. The disappointment was measured by the hopes and the confidence in a war undertaken to make Italy free up to the Adriatic, according to the proclamation of Milan. Nothing was seen at first but the abandonment of Venice by a new Campo-Formio, and the threat of the restoration of their former masters to Florence and Bologna.

The peace of Villafranca caused the Italians to forget, for the moment at least, what France had done for them ; and even at Turin they were far from the enthusiasm which had welcomed the French soldiers on

April 30. "If this problem had been proposed six months ago," wrote the most moderate of men, Massimo d'Azeglio : "To enter Italy with 200,000 soldiers, spend half a million of money, gain four battles, restore the Italians one of their finest provinces, and then to return with their curses ; such a problem would have been declared insoluble. Well then, it is not ; and facts have proved it. In Central Italy, where all heads have been inflamed by the great deeds of the war, they will not accept the peace of Villafranca. For me, I abstain from judging the conduct of the Emperor. The end of it is, he has been under fire in our cause against the Austrians; and as regards the splendid soldiers of France, I could embrace their knees. Still all this does not hide the fact, that the situation of our poor Italy is terrible. To tell the truth, I lose my head. . . . ."

It was this sentiment of a terrible situation, and of an unforeseen and bitter deception, that Cavour expressed and caused to resound when he gave in his resignation, which made the vanquished minister the popular representative of a national crisis, the possible workman of new fortunes. He was in full accord with the public instinct ; if he had been guilty of hastiness he had committed this fault in common with the country ; for him, as for his country, it was a force of which he, in his temporary and voluntary retirement from office, was the always-ready champion.

XII.

Nevertheless, when the first outburst was over, people looked about them ; and herein Cavour soon found himself in accord with Italy. The impression was unmitigatedly keen, but there was a disposition to look close at the situation newly created for them, to read the meaning of events, and seek a fresh direction.

The peace of Villafranca was not without its advantages, though it had stopped military proceedings. If it allowed the foreigner to keep a footing in his last entrenchments in Venetia, it offered the prospect of new combinations, and a certain liberty that might be put to profit. The dukes might re-enter their duchies : and in what manner ? "Indispensable reforms" were to be demanded from the Pope. Supposing the Pope to refuse the granting of these reforms, and the Romagna to refuse to submit to the Pope ? France, after fighting for Italian independence against Austria, could not abjure the moral consequences of her intervention, and join Austria against Italy. Napoleon III. was bound by his deeds, his connivance, and his sentiments ; England, which, according to Cavour, had as yet done nothing, had just gone through a ministerial crisis that had overthrown the Tories and brought the Whigs to power— Lord Palmerston and Lord John Russell. England, without lending material assistance, upon which they must not count, might give good help with her sympathies and her diplomacy ; and her interests lay in doing so, if it were but to extend her influence beyond the Alps and seek her advantage in the new organisation of Italy. In reality, everything hung more than ever in suspense.

What was to come of it ? The first moment had been one of confusion, trouble, and irritation. That which neither Napoleon III., in improvising a peace that he deemed necessary, nor the Italians, in submitting to this peace, which seemed a mortal wound to them, had foreseen, was, that Villafranca, far from settling, was hardly a stage between the crisis of yesterday and that of to-morrow; it was only a truce, by favour of which an Italian campaign of a new character was preparing, and Cavour could return on the scene to gather fruits of a kind very differently unforeseen from this peace he had imprecated.

CHAPTER V.

THE ITALIAN CRISIS AFTER VILLAFRANCA—CAVOUR AND THE CESSION OF SAVOY.

I.

On the day following the campaign of 1859, when Napoleon III. gave audience at St. Cloud to senators, deputies, and councillors of state, all as eager to belaud his moderation as they would have been to acclaim his resolution and energy if he had pursued the war, the Emperor seemed to think the occasion good for explaining and specifying the nature of his work at Villafranca.

It was a singular scene. To the adulations of courtiers comparing him to Scipio, and raving of the "prodigy" of a will that could so control itself, the Emperor replied in the nervous tone of a man who had to defend himself for having in "weariness" abandoned "the noble cause he had wished to serve." He was thinking doubtless of Cavour when he confessed that it had cost him much to stop short in a work he had commenced, and to see "brave hearts robbed of their noble illusions and patriotic hopes." He appealed to the interests of France, endangered by the probable extension of a struggle that might at any moment have broken out on the Rhine as well as on the Adige. "When the destinies of my country seemed in peril, I made peace," he said; and in explaining why he had stopped, it pleased him to point to the fruits of victory, once more an exhibition of the prevailing of French arms ; Piedmont enlarged by an opulent province ; Italian nationality, recognised and organised by a federation ; the Princes restored or supported, "understanding at last the imperative necessity of salutary reforms."

This was unfortunately but a vain flourish before courtiers, barely disguising the truth of things. The peace improvised or patched together in a little village of the Mincio, between two emperors equally sick of the horrors of a battle-field, had nothing stable or settled in it. The war was terminated, but none of the problems let loose by the war were solved. France and Austria had joined hands, and Piedmont stood deceived and embarrassed; the Central Duchies were half emancipated and left to themselves ; the national sentiment of Italy was cheated and irritated ; and Europe stood astonished and suspicious, in contemplation of that enigmatic meeting of the two emperors on the Mincio.

I wish to specify the exact situation, immediately after the arrested conflict. France thought right to push the war no farther ; Austria thought right to purchase peace, at the cost of a province, that still left her Venetia and the hope of restoring the Princes to Florence and Modena. Between France and Austria laying down their arms, the Treaty of Zurich completed what had been outlined at Villafranca. The Italian questions proper — the questions of reorganisation, federation, and reform—were reserved for a European congress.

Here we have everything apparently arranged or foreseen. It was on the contrary a new beginning of the unforeseen. The settlement was but on the surface ; and side by side with Villafranca, Zurich, the congress, and official diplomacy, suddenly we behold an original and startling phase, which I may call the phase of the Italians taking the conduct of their destinies into their own hands, upsetting all calculations, and themselves venturing to give their interpretation to a peace by which their hopes were fettered. Cavour had said : " The track is cut ; let us pursue another." Napoleon III., before leaving the Mincio, had let fall these strange words to Victor Emmanuel : " Now we shall see what the Italians can do unaided." It is the secret of the period commencing on July 11, 1859, that of another and a national diplomatic drama, which, under new conditions and with new characters, is about to work itself out by unexpected ways, up to the crisis once more prepared by the great master of the Italian revolution.

II.

The terms of the peace of Villafranca had the misfortune to be fitted to a different situation, and not to be suitable to circumstances ; they were but an insufficient and a contradictory make-shift, without vitality in regard to the future.

This confederation, imagined by Napoleon III. as a means of preserving a portion of his programme, would have been a gain and a guarantee—before the war. Transpose the hypothesis : the confederation would still have been possible, even with the restored Princes, if the war had been pushed on to the Adriatic, up to an independence made complete by the total ejection of the foreigner from Italy ; and thus France would have had more right to demand the acceptation of it, the Italians less reason to refuse it. But with Austria encamped in Venice, holding formidable positions, and continuing to overshadow Italy with her power and her alliances, the confederation was rather a permanent menace than a promise of repose ; for the enemy, that is to say the foreign preponderance, was left in possession of the field.

The peace, such as it had been concluded, destroyed in advance the idea of confederation, or, in other words, the confederation thus organised compromised the peace of the two emperors from the very beginning. A further contradiction. The preliminaries of July 11 said : " The Grand Duke of Tuscany and the Duke of Modena shall return to their States." At the same time the Emperor Napoleon had prohibited the use of force to help their return; he had stipulated that the rights and the will of the populations should be consulted; so that the Italians discovered in this strange, incoherent piece of work, at once a stimulant to revolt and an easy means to evade the deceptive tangle wound about them.

For a moment undoubtedly their uncertainty was grievous and full of anguish. Cavour had disappeared, and with him apparently the last chance of a national policy and leadership. The new Piedmontese Ministry of La Marmora, Rattazzi, Dabormida, formed to execute the terms of peace, was necessarily compelled to make its official proclamation. At Florence, Modena, Parma, and Bologna, still more than at Turin and Milan, the treaty of Villafranca burst like a clap of thunder, and seemed to offer Central Italy the option of an enervating submission, or the more perilous issue of revolution in resisting it. A single hesitation, one false step, a riot, might ruin everything, and complicate events irremediably.

Resolute men were needed to hold the country in hand; masters of themselves, and capable of seeing, as by inspiration, the resources belonging to so novel a position. The Cabinet of Turin was obliged at first, that it might act in harmony with diplomacy, to disengage Piedmont from Central Italy, and abdicate the semblance of a protectorate, by the recall of its representatives— Farini at Modena, Boncompagni at Florence, Massimo d'Azeglio at Bologna; but the link officially broken was renewed morally in the elections made by the people.

Farini ceased to be the commissary of Victor Emmanuel, only to become the dictator of Modena and Parma. Baron Ricasoli was made governor of Tuscany in the place of Boncompagni. The head of the new government of Bologna was one little known till then—Colonel Leonetto Cipriani, prudently chosen on account of his close relations with the Napoleons.

There was hardly even an apparent change, and these chiefs and improvised dictators lost no time in developing what they were meditating—to win through the peace possibly more than they would have gained by the war. Before the end of August, assemblies were sitting to systematise the interregnum. A military league for the common defence was established between these States abandoned to their fate. Envoys were despatched from Bologna, Parma, and Florence—Count Linati, Marquis Lajatico, Bianchi, Ubaldini Peruzzi, Matteucci—to plead for the national cause at Turin, Paris, and London. In a word, while diplomacy, deeming itself all-powerful, sat in the thick of its more or less specious webs, Central Italy was organising and marching to its fixed aim.

This aim was indicated by circumstances and the very nature of a situation so unexampled. For seeing that Austria, shorn of a province only, remained with the overflowing resources of the empire on the Mincio and the Po, there was nothing for it but to gather together what Italian forces could be got, create what was called the "strong kingdom," and at all costs unite with Piedmont.

Annexation was the predominating thought. That which had been done to forestall greater changes, turn aside or suspend the current of fusion represented by the Piedmontese protectorate, was precisely what quickened the work of unification, and drew the small central states nearer to the subalpine kingdom. " Austria in the Quadrilateral," writes D'Azeglio, "has Italy at her mercy whenever she pleases. Italy sees nothing else ; she has but this one desire—that of constituting, never mind how, a group of States able to offer some serious opposition to a Power that has lost nothing of her strength, and is twice as evily disposed to us as she was. How are we to be thinking of our historic traditions and particular clock-tower interests ? But for this peace, they might not have been without their influence. In our actual position, we think solely of creating fresh forces. That has been marvellously well understood by the good sense of all Italy. Hence we have this unanimous movement towards Sardinia, hence the casting away of egotistical traditions, the deepest rooted of our instincts, the dearest to Italian municipalism."

Two things may be cited to account for this remarkable change in the feelings of the Italians : primarily the national necessity, and next, the ten years' long influence of Piedmontese policy ; the watchword of courage, the conception of military honour, tried patriotism, constitutional government, and an orderly and beneficial freedom. In other words—mark well— even in his eclipse, it is the policy of Cavour triumphing and bearing fruit : when seeming beaten at Turin, it reappears under another aspect at Modena as at Florence, in the person of Farini and of Ricasoli, who in their turn come to the front. And if anything proves the ripeness of a revolution it is the fortune of Italy in finding at every decisive step workmen fitted for the work of the hour.

III.

One of the chiefs of Central Italy, Farini, was a doctor of medicine, Romagnole by origin, Piedmontese by adoption, a fervent and devoted heart, of a mind both brilliant and lettered, who had written his recollections in a " History of the Roman States." Mixed up in youth with the Liberal movement of his native province, but holding aloof from factions, he had been in turn one of the Pope's ministers with the unfortunate Rossi in 1848, then deputy and minister at Turin with Cavour, whose ideas he shared, and whose policy he passionately supported. The representative of Victor Emmanuel at Modena during the war, he signalised himself by not wavering an instant. At the first rumour of negotiations between the emperors, before he knew a single word of the peace, he had telegraphed to Turin : " Do not leave me without instructions. Understand that if, owing to conventions of which I am ignorant, the Duke makes any attempt here, I shall treat him as an enemy of the King and of the country. I will not be driven from my place, though it cost me my life." Recalled by the Piedmontese Government, he remained at Modena, the elected chief of a provisional government, and raised the courage of the people to the height of his own, launching from the old ducal palace the significant words, that Italy had not " countersigned the peace of Villafranca." Before quitting Turin, Cavour had time to write to him: "The ministry is dead; your friend applauds your resolve."

In all probability things were saved by Farini's initiative. He checked a hasty restoration, that might easily have been tried by the Duke with his little army from his place of refuge in the Austrian camp, in the same way that a handful of troops left by D'Azeglio along the line of the Marches stopped the irruption of the Papal Swiss troops into the Romagna. The first danger over, Farini soon took occasion to go farther, extending his governorship from Modena to Parma, and as far as Bologna, and forming a sort of provisional state under the old Latin name of the Emilia. He had but one idea, the realisation of which he prosecuted feverishly—to hurry on, at all costs, the fusion with Piedmont. "The stroke is done," he wrote, on the day of his entry into Bologna; "there is now only one government. In the coming year, from Piacenza to the Cattolica, laws, orders, down to the very names of them, all shall be Piedmontese. I shall see to the fortifications of Bologna; good soldiers and good guns against those who are for combating the annexation—there you have my policy!" It was in fact the sole end of his policy. Farini would possibly have had to succumb, even with his reunion of the Emilia, if there had not been in one of the States of Central Italy, in Tuscany, another chief at that time who stamped his energetic and fiery originality on the movement— Baron Bettino Ricasoli.

He virtually—after Cavour, or with Cavour—was one of the great authors of the Italian transformation.

Through him Tuscany became irrevocably pledged to the path of unification; and the adhesion of Tuscany was far more decisive than those of the minor duchies. Baron Ricasoli had distinguished himself in the revolution of 1848 as one of the heads of the Moderate party. He had been of those who recalled the Grand Duke from his refuge at Gaëta, and experienced the bitterness of seeing that prince allow an Austrian escort to lead him back to Florence. He thereupon sent in all his grand-ducal decorations and retired to his beautiful estate of Brolio, near Sienna, where he gave himself up to agricultural pursuits; blending with an independent existence the duties of an all but feudal patronage, the cultivation of the mind, and a taste for the arts; nor less, though absent, the strict ally in his opinions of that patrician liberal class—the Capponi, the Ridolfi, the Corsini, the Peruzzi. He had, like many others, watched with increasing interest the Piedmontese policy; and he had been one of the first, on the approach of the conflict with Austria, to give sign to Florence. Minister of the Interior during the war, under the Piedmontese protectorate of Boncompagni, President of the Council after the peace of Villafranca, he, like his colleague at Modena, had henceforth no other thought than that of annexation; and no one, in truth, better than he could cast an air of grandeur on this abdication of Tuscan autonomy before the idea of the one Italian Land.

There was nothing in him of the common politician. He was like a portrait of Holbein's—with his erect, stiff figure, severe bearing, frigid yet courteous dignity, his fine and lofty mien, and imperious gestures. He was a

Tuscan of the old stock, preserving in his person the traditions of that Ricasoli of former days, a Guelphic captain in the wars of the Romagna, who wishing on one occasion to obtain a decree of the Council of the Twenty-four of Florence, put the councillors under lock and key, and starved them until the decree was voted. The baron of our time, without starving anyone, used the iron will of his ancestor in the service of a modern idea, a national desire, of which, when in power, he was the impassioned and haughty representative. It was he who said one night at the Palazzo Vecchio to a compatriot on the point of starting for France : " Go, tell those gentlemen that I claim an existence of twelve centuries' duration, that I am the last of my race, and that I would give my last drop of blood to maintain my political programme in its integrity." And what he said he did in his own particular manner : not with the large and pliable genius of a Cavour, but with the firmness of a man whose energy was dreaded, whose disinterestedness and patriotism were respected, and who would be obeyed. Beholding this grave and imperturbable minister, who, instead of drawing emoluments from the Treasury, gave on the contrary from his private fortune to assist it, and worked steadily from six in the morning till midnight, the people did not seek to reward him with vain acclamations, which he would have disdained : they felt they were safe under such a leader, and held him in the esteem ranked by Royer-Collard above all popularity.

The work Ricasoli was engaged in had no revolutionary taint in it. It was a work of national necessity, and he made it his business to carry it through without suffering it to deviate and be compromised by intrigues on the one hand or agitations on the other. The Florentine dictator knew well that he was encircled by every kind of danger. Above all, he knew that the first condition of well-being for the country lay in the preservation of order; he felt that an appearance of disorder, whatever tended to complicate the imminent question by revolutionary irruption from without, would weaken the national cause, and serve for a pretext to the abettors of restorations or for foreign interventions, and he would not suffer them to have a pretext. Therefore, he was inflexible in repressing any show of agitation or division. Mazzini had flattered himself that Tuscany might be made a centre of operations, of which he was to be ever the shrouded chief. Ricasoli, not without some haughty irony, gave him to understand that, if he caught him, he would hinder him from doing harm by locking him up in his castle of Brolio, till such time as the definitive constitution of Italy was proclaimed. Republicans were straightway conducted to the frontier. Guerrazzi himself, the president of the democratic ministry of 1848, found a difficulty in entering Tuscany. The brilliant Montanelli, with his dreams of the kingdom of Etruria for Prince Napoleon, was only licensed to stay because there was very little fear of him. Garibaldi, whose services had been accepted, and to whom the Tuscan contingent of the military league for the common defence had been entrusted, Garibaldi himself came under the scourge of the terrible baron. Once with his Tuscans and Romagnole volunteers, he was on the point of invading the Marches and Umbria; if he had done it, the immediate intervention of France would have been the result—this was known at Florence as well as at Turin. Ricasoli did not delay an instant to check Garibaldi's warlike propensities and cut short the earliest manifestations of a turn for military dictatorship; and Garibaldi had to submit; he fell back growling, but without attempting anything, to Caprera. The stubbornness of Ricasoli, seconded by advices from Turin, warded off a possibly mortal danger.

In a word, the redoubtable Florentine meant to be master of his domain on the Arno; he would not yield it up to soldierly dictation, nor let it be swamped by demagogues; nor would he allow it even to be joined in a fusion proposed to him with Modena, Parma, and the Legations. Vain efforts were at one time exerted to draw him into a sort of political league that should complete the existing military league; in vain Farini and Marquis Pepoli did their utmost to show him the advantages of a partial and temporary fusion, a prelude to the absolute junction with Piedmont, that they might appear before Europe with the authority of an undivided government, speaking in the name of the whole of Central Italy. Ricasoli positively refused, and he refused for a characteristic reason. He declared that it would be offering Europe the " elements ready made for a separate kingdom," and nothing would induce him to hear of a separate kingdom of Central Italy, though with the addition of the Legations to it, as little under a Napoleon or any other new prince as under a Lorraine duke.

The annexation to Piedmont was his fixed point, because annexation signified the strong kingdom, as against Austria, and meant a constituted and armed Italy : before Italy only would be put off the splendid crown of Tuscan independence. Declining a union that he considered dangerous, he did not the less move in harmony with Farini, and thus, for a space of six months, by the help of some few men, Central Italy was enabled to present the spectacle of orderly populations, bound together by the same sentiment, neither carried away by enthusiasms nor listening to provocations. There was one crime, the murder of Colonel Anviti, that afflicted Parma, and it was followed by a universal outcry of condemnation. D'Azeglio writes in homely style : "If what is now passing had been foretold to me two months back, I should have laughed in the face of the prophet. Who would have thought it possible we should see the Romagnoles gentle and wise, the Tuscans energetic, and all the grudges ages old, crumbling to pieces with so entire a concordance in every Italian city ?"

IV.

It is true that this pacific campaign of Central Italy could hardly have been carried through, even with the skilful boldness of such chiefs, and the docility of the populations they headed, had not the troubled mind of Europe on the morrow of the peace of Villafranca unexpectedly favoured it. The advantage of being animated by one firm idea was with the Italians ; they had a distinct policy in opposition to a diplomacy that knew not what it would nor what it could. Their good genius taught them to control themselves, and turn all things to profit, in the midst of one of the most curious imbroglios that have ever disturbed human affairs—a six months' confusion, during which Austria, France, England, and Piedmont played so strange a part, perpetually arranging matters for a congress—that was never to sit!

The object of Austria was clear enough. She had been compelled to relinquish one of the most brilliant provinces of the empire, and she designed to keep fast hold of the remainder of her dominions in Italy, specifically as regarded Venice, indirectly as to the restoration of the Princes to their duchies, which had been promised to her. She lent her ear to the scheme proposed by France for a confederation that Venice should form part of, but her immediate demand was for the execution of the treaties; she held tenaciously to these restorations which had been danced before her eyes, and took care to remind France, as well as Piedmont, that if the restorations were not granted, she should on her side consider herself disengaged from the terms of the peace, even in Lombardy.

It is incontestable that she was justified by Villafranca and Zurich; but morally lessened by defeat as she was, more than ever doubtfully viewed by the Italians, all but abandoned by her European allies, and shaken by internal dissensions, Austria was in fact powerless. She could do no more than vainly fret, with an impatience mingled with bitterness, at these revolutions of Central Italy where she was disabled from interfering: she dared not cross the Po. Each fresh proceeding then called forth a series of protestations

from her, which Florence could afford to deride. Europe
made no answer to her appeals, or encouraged Italy.
Austria had a sufficient task to defend herself in a situation more threatened than threatening, altogether abandoned to herself as she was. Russia left her to her
isolation. Prussia, accused of treason by the resentful
Cabinet of Vienna, was beginning to reflect on the
example set by the Italians, and maintained a particular
reserve. England went much farther. After having
been the advocate of Austria up to the eve of the war,
and stoutly defending the treaties of 1815, England
went straight over to the Italian camp after Villafranca,
showering her sympathies and encouragements on her
new allies.

English foreign policy was no longer guided by Lord
Derby and Lord Malmesbury, but by Lord Palmerston
and Lord Russell, and the England of the Whigs was
now as fervid on behalf of Italian independence as she
had previously been lukewarm. She was little inclined
to a federation that offered a less safe guarantee to her
commercial interests than the extension of Piedmont,
the country of economic freedom. Naturally she had
not a word to say to arrangements that dismembered the
temporal power of the Pope. She was the first to
uphold the liberty of the Central Italians, and their right
to dispose of themselves and to cast in their lot with
Piedmont if it pleased them. She made herself the
guardian of the principle of non-intervention, and the
patroness of the ambitions and broadest hopes of the
Italian people.

The Whigs had assuredly no intention, not a whit more

than the Tories, to pledge England to promises of armed
succour. They promised " all possible moral support,"
in the words of Lord Palmerston ; and Marquis Emmanuel d'Azeglio, Sardinian representative in London,
could write to Turin : " The English ministers, in
alluding to annexation, are always careful to add
that England looks on it as the best arrangement.
England perceives the double advantage in the annexation, that it renders us more independent, and will be
done in deference to the wishes of the populations."
The Queen's ministers appeared desirous to make up for
lost time by showing themselves more Italian in their
feelings than the French, who had just fought for Italy,
by flattering and goading the passion for nationality on
the other side of the Alps. Provided that no attack
was made on Austria in Venetia, anything might be
done at Florence as in the Papal States.

The design of the English ministers—and there was
scarce any disguise about it—was to stimulate the annexation scheme as a means of counteracting French
ascendency, in the fear of seeing France in the place
formerly usurped by Austria in Italy, either owing to her
direct influence, or through some half-vassal kingdom
under a Napoleon. They were increasingly distrustful
of the Emperor. Lord Russell, as head of the Foreign
Office, gave himself up to this propaganda with his
habitual impetuous candour, which had more than once
affrighted and perplexed his companions in power. He
did not reflect that his conduct exposed him to serious
contradictions ; for after inflaming the minds of the
Italians, he could hardly think of turning them aside

from the war for the recovery of Venice; and in favouring
the extension of Piedmont he hurried on the eventuality
he stood in fear of—that cession of Savoy which the
Emperor had renounced at Villafranca, but which the
creation of a powerful North Italian kingdom could not
but cause to be reconsidered. The Italians were not
deceived. If they were wary enough to make use of the
support of England, they were not the less aware that for
them the question lay rather in Paris than in London,
rather with the country whose army was still encamped
in the heart of Lombardy.

V.

The main point was what France wanted and meant
to do. Lord Palmerston declared that there were two
policies in Paris, and no great sagacity was required to
penetrate this mystery. These two policies had existed,
confounding and thwarting one another, all along : one
triumphed in the war and the kindling proclamations of
Milan ; the other in the premature and imperfect deed
executed at Villafranca ; and now the two policies were
wrestling again over the interpretation and execution of
the peace. Indeed, if there was a chance that the terms
of Villafranca would be realised in their fullest integrity,
it lay with the continuing in office of the French
Minister of Foreign Affairs.

Count Walewski, a gentleman of perfect loyalty, was
not only for making good the engagements contracted
with Austria ; his opinions, traditions, and instincts
were opposed to the development of the Italian revolu-

tion, favourable to the ducal restorations, and disposed to limit Piedmontese influence. He would not have the annexation at any price, and he was assiduous in making the weight of the imperial authority and French diplomacy felt at Turin, at Florence, and at Bologna. Agents upon agents had been despatched by him to propose the restoration, and Count Walewski appeared as astonished as indignant at the resistance his diplomacy encountered.

He chose to imagine that there was nothing serious in what was going on at Florence, and that it was only the conspiracy of a party in the pay of Piedmont; a revolutionary work, managed with considerable skill and boldness by Baron Ricasoli. He held the very same language as Austria! At Paris, in his audiences with the Tuscan envoys, Marquis Lajatico, Signors Ubaldino Peruzzi and Matteucci, he delivered himself sharply and very menacingly. The French Minister was not afraid to declare that the Tuscans must " bow the head; " he expressed regret that the Italians had been permitted to think that there would be no armed intervention: humiliating discussions from which the Tuscan envoys withdrew without having " bowed the head." On another day Count Walewski summoned the Sardinian minister and said to him : " I do not intend to enter into a dispute with you; I wish simply to make you acquainted with the state of things, and ask your aid in inducing your Government to come to an understanding with us upon the affairs of Central Italy. These populations must be taught that it is inevitable that the Pope should return to the Legations, the

Lorraines to Florence, Francis V. to Modena. If Piedmont helps us, compensation will be given in Parma and Piacenza; if the annexations are persisted in, fresh evils will be raised in Europe, and Piedmont will have to bear the merited punishment for them."

Such, without doubt, was the policy of Count Walewski; but there was at the same time the policy of the Emperor. Do what he would, Napoleon III. could not evade the responsibility of the Italian uprising, due to his progress in Italy and the noise of his awakening proclamations. He had bidden the Italians arise and organise, follow the banner of Victor Emmanuel, and make their own destinies : the Italians had risen ; they were shaping their own destinies; they were acting "unaided"—what reply was there for him? He believed evidently that he had accomplished much by means of the peace of Villafranca ; he thought at least that the Italians had been assured of a degree of independence and advancement compatible with the circumstances, and once pledged to the peace, he could not immediately disavow his work. He spoke the same language, to all appearance, as his Minister of Foreign Affairs. He likewise, through the medium of diplomacy, in his communications with Victor Emmanuel, and in his conversations with the Italian delegates who approached him, began by putting the obligations incurred at Villafranca beyond question. He assumed a particular ostentation of good faith, all the more from feeling himself suspected, and above all, jealously watched from all parts of Europe. He bore the burden of his reputation, according to the saying of Prince Napoleon.

Events, however, did not fail to operate on the

mind of the Emperor. This mind, which no one had ever sounded, was undergoing a singular travail; and at all events the words of the Emperor, far less downright than those of Count Walewski, lent themselves to all kinds of interpretations. Attempts to fathom his designs by inquiries whether he was not interested in seeing the dispossessed princes restored, were met by the answer, that he had "no personal interest whatever in desiring the re-establishment of the Lorraine dukes:" and he spoke with a smile of incredulity of the candidature of Prince Napoleon for one of the crowns of Central Italy. Asked if there was not a limit to the obligations to which he declared himself to be bound, he replied with some melancholy that they had doubtless a limit : "The limit of the possible." When ultimately the question was put as to how far foreign pressure was to go in favour of the restoration in the Duchies, he said unhesitatingly : "No violence shall be done to the Italians." He did more ; he informed Prince Metternich at Compiègne, that if Austria crossed the Po, it would be instant war with France.

One day, when he was subjected to a certain probation, at the instigation of Signor Peruzzi, he replied : "Signor Peruzzi seems to be a man of comprehension ; he should know that when I am asked as to my intentions concerning Tuscany, I can only answer as I have done; but let the populations vote, and when it shall be shown that the terms of Villafranca can only be executed in contempt of those principles of popular rights from which I draw my power, I may change my mind."*

* These negotiations of the Italians with the Tuileries are full of curious details; some of them are luminous at the present day. Signor Peruzzi, in one of the

It was sufficiently significant. By perpetually invoking Villafranca, the Emperor abandoned it by degrees ; he opened the door slowly to all possible combinations, even those which involved a dismemberment of the States of the Church ; and what he could not say himself, his friends said for him. Dr. Conneau occasionally served for the echo of his secret thoughts with the Tuscans. The French ambassador in London, M. de Persigny, saw no harm in disavowing the language of Count Walewski. This devoted follower and confidant of the Emperor, ambassador to one of the first Powers of Europe, went about repeating everywhere that the Emperor perceived that he had been mistaken in Italian affairs ; that he insisted no farther, and that an evasion of the obligations of Villafranca depended on the firmness and wisdom of the Italians. Before he had been very long Sardinian minister at London, Marquis Emmanuel d'Azeglio was able to write to Turin : " I have read the autograph letter of Napoleon, thanking the English Government for their protest against foreign

very interesting reports of his mission, relates a conversation that he had with Prince Napoleon. The Tuscan envoy did not forbear to say that, if they were abandoned, the Italians might be reduced to throw for all or nothing, dragging Piedmont with them, and that the Emperor would then be obliged to uphold them. Prince Napoleon replied : " *You will be in a pretty pass, when you have caused the ruin of the Emperor and the arrival of the Prussians in Paris.*" He was answered that the Emperor exposed himself to ruin more certainly by abandoning Italy, and that France, in the presence of the Prussians, would repeat the prodigies of 1792. " The Prince," says Signor Peruzzi, "then remarked, that before the war his hopes were in war, because he believed that the Emperor would prove himself to be a general, and would be at the head of capable generals ; but that now his illusions had been dispersed ; for the army knew well both that the Emperor was no general, and that he had no capable generals under him." These words were spoken in October, 1859. I confine myself to stating that then as ever, courageous and capable generals would have been found, if there had been an able chief who could plan and command.

intervention. . . . . It is thought here that the official language, so different from what is said in the letter, has no other object than to keep Austria quiet. The Emperor adds, that it will not grieve him to see events making his first provisions impracticable. All the statesmen here, including the French ambassador himself, are of opinion that we must proceed resolutely and rapidly, though with prudence, taking for rule that in reality at Paris they only want to have their hands forced."

In the depths of his mysterious policy, Napoleon III. had a double thought. He asked for nothing better than to have his hand forced, as was said, that he might extricate himself as soon as he could, and cover with the name of England, in his relations with Austria, the non-performance of the engagements undertaken at Villafranca and Zurich. Was it England or the Emperor that first had this idea? It matters little: Lord Cowley had been the useful intermediary in a negotiation by which the Queen's ministers assisted the unravelment, still obscure and slow, of the French potentate. Napoleon III. had another thought, that he did not confide to the English Cabinet. In preparing to tolerate the tacit abrogation of the treaties binding him to Austria, he was careful not to unmask, and to hold himself in reserve. With the freedom of action granted them, he wished to burden the Italians with the responsibility of their deeds—this creation of a great kingdom, not openly encouraged by him, but for which he had resolved to demand the price.

He, too, like Lord Russell and Lord Palmerston, deceived himself strangely. If, as it appeared, the English ministers did not perceive that, in pushing forward the scheme of annexation in Central Italy, they offered the Emperor an apology for renewing his pretensions to Savoy, the Emperor, for his part, did not see whither he might be led by this temptation to claim Savoy—in which, for that matter, there was nothing so very extraordinary. One and the other seemed to be at a game of weaving and unweaving the web, until the coming of the firm hand to cut it.

VI.

But Piedmont, surrounded by conflicting policies, in the thick of divers influences, attracted or held back by Italy and by Europe, was the most embarrassed. It was no mystery that Piedmont was in connivance with Italy. Piedmont encouraged her efforts, often covered her with her diplomacy, lent her officers—was for Italy, in a word, the rallying-point and the centre of action. An official distinction between them, however, was matter of necessity. Dangerous enemies were on the frontiers: a French army was in Lombardy, the treaty-makers were at Zurich, difficulties everywhere. The King was obliged to hold incessant communications with the Emperor, to whom he sent, now General Dabormida, now Count Arese, a trustworthy Milanese gentleman, always welcome at the Tuileries. And Victor Emmanuel, in giving audience to deputations that brought him offers of the crown of Italy, certainly promised to defend their rights as well as respect their wishes, but without daring or being able yet to take the title of their sovereign. Piedmont was thus reduced to shrink from the object of her desires, and appear to repulse those who besought her to do as she wished.

The Central Italians well understood that in maintaining order, accomplishing a national revolution in the least possible revolutionary manner, they would have right on their side, and that the main point for them was to hold firm and proceed. They replied to Villafranca by decreeing in their Assemblies the deposition of the princes, and a proclamation of the principle of annexation. They replied to the Treaty of Zurich by voting the regency of the Prince of Carignano; a step that diplomacy smoothed over, but it was not the less one distinctly in advance. Hostility and provocation were met by the daily exhibition of a settled calmness, an obstinate adherence to their scheme. Such was the marvel of the policy of the Ricasolis and the Farinis. A settlement became necessary at last for all concerned. The provinces of Central Italy had stood fast for six months without belying themselves for a single day; they were sick of so perilous a provisional state of things. Piedmont could go no farther, with a despotic ministry falling into unpopularity from its weakness and inability to cope with the embarrassments of the time. And Europe was approaching a congress that she dreaded while seeming to invoke it.

Circumstances were pressing all round, when the world was astonished by a double *coup de théâtre*, that speedily changed the aspect of affairs. The Emperor Napoleon emerged from the cloud of his negotiations with England to have an end to them after his own manner. In a letter of December 31, 1859, he proposed to the Pope to place the Legations under the viceregency of Victor Emmanuel: a plan that had small chance of obtaining the sanction of the Head of the Church. By the publication of a pamphlet, "The Pope and the Congress," as famous as that one of the winter of 1859, he contrived to render the congress impossible. In dismissing Count Walewski from the Ministry of Foreign Affairs, he signed the burial deed of Villafranca and the policy inimical to Italy; and it was M. Thouvenel, a man still young, and able as he was resolute, who came from his embassy at Constantinople to take in hand the new policy of France.

Cavour, too, was called back to the government in Turin, and he reappeared on the scene as the only man who could meet the crisis, and lead Piedmont and Italy on the road together. The Emperor's change of policy, and the return of Cavour to Turin, were facts indicating perhaps the beginning of the end; at any rate, the period of action had set in. M. Guizot, a sagacious judge of passing events, could then pronounce that: "Two men divide the attention of Europe at the present moment—the Emperor and M. de Cavour. The game has commenced, and I should bet on M. de Cavour."

VII.

Thus the force of circumstances brought back the first of Piedmontese, next to the King, to direct the Italian movement he had relinquished on the morrow of Villafranca. He had supposed it partly lost; he found it amplified, strengthened, penetrated as it were with his own spirit. The six months that had gone by did not, in truth, stand for lost time either with him or with Italy; they had but ripened the situation of the country, and permitted him to hold his liberty of action and natural vigour in reserve for the opportune moment.

If, during his excursion in Switzerland, the feeling of a bitter deception which had driven him from Turin in July survived, he came back to Piedmont reinvigorated, full of fire and confidence. His position was not a light one in the front of a ministry scarce able to bear its loads, about as much embarrassed by his assistance as by his passivity; and his wish was to avoid any annoyance to this ministry, sprung from an imperative necessity. He had written from Pressinge to his friend Castelli: "Greet Rattazzi from me, assure him of my goodwill in everything, and for all purposes. I have no curiosity whatever to know the secrets of his policy. My choice would rather be to remain an entire stranger to the affairs of the day. Though, should Rattazzi seek my counsel, I am always ready to give it candidly." And some days later: "I shall take my way back to Turin to go into a corner and there give advice if I am asked for it, or be silent if there is no need of me."

He was hardly the less an embarrassing presence; he felt it himself, when some weeks afterwards he wrote with a free and flowing pen to Madame de Circourt: "You will perhaps be astonished to see me in a state of incertitude, for commonly I do not hesitate. This astonishment will cease if you reflect on the position in which I find myself. My presence in Turin is of use to none, and it is a burden to many. I am well disposed to support the ministry, composed of honourable men, and animated by the best intentions; but I cannot stir without giving it a shock. And again, I should injure it if I took to hiding in my rice-fields. They would say I was pouting, and I should look absurd. I have the option of travelling, but whither? Italy is interdicted by policy, and it would not be becoming to visit France or England. I have not the heart to encounter the cold and heavy atmosphere of Germany, and I am too much a victim of sea-sickness to attempt a trans-atlantic trip. So I am compelled to cast about for what I should do, without reading the riddle. It is probable that as I can find nothing good to do I shall do nothing, and let fortune direct me." Here is a man considerably perplexed; but Cavour was of those who have an understanding with the chances of fortune, and the chances had this time decided that he should stay in Piedmont—now at Turin, now at Leri, always ready and at the disposition of events and his country.

Do what he would, Cavour could not cease to be the leader of Italy, and to interest himself in the common work. He was minister no longer, and his manner of quitting the ministry had only augmented his popularity, by identifying him with a national crisis. Italy consulted him on all sides. At Leri or at Turin he received visits from Italians and foreigners of every description: one day Lord Clanricarde, "who insisted on coming;" another day a deputation from Parma, with Verdi in the list; or else it was the Tuscan deputation, bearing the offer of the crown to Victor Emmanuel. What was passing at Florence, Bologna, and Modena had revived his ardour and his hopes. He was the centre of the general activity though not in power, cordial with all around, counselling prudence or boldness, or suggesting expedients; above all, anxious for the purely noble character of the revolution that was being accomplished. At the first bruit of the murder of Colonel Anviti at Parma, he hastened to write to Colonel Bardesono, whom Farini had made a minister: "I do not doubt that you will know how to fulfil your new duties as well as those you have fulfilled hitherto; and if the people of Modena should yield to excesses similar to what has occurred at Parma, you will stand to the death to save the Italian cause from being dishonoured by acts of savage vandalism. . . . . Tell Farini that if he does not bring more energy to bear on these Parmesan assassins, the Italian cause runs the greatest risks. . . . ." To the Tuscans he said : " Quick, get together a Liberal Government, firm to resist diplomatic pressure or armed assailants. Let Tuscany maintain the national spirit, and she may save all."

After having cursed the peace of Villafranca, he spoke of it with an exaltation that might have passed for irony, to such a degree did the commentary belie the first apprehension of that piece of work, and he did not delay writing to Prince Napoleon : "The consequences of the peace of Villafranca have developed splendidly. The military and political campaign following that treaty has done more for Italy than the military campaign preceding it. It works higher claims to gratitude in the hearts of the Italians to the Emperor Napoleon than the battles of Magenta and Solferino.

How often in the solitude of Leri have I not cried out: Blessed be the peace of Villafranca!" The more these results, so little foreseen by the author of the treaty, developed, the more did Cavour strain nerve and brain to make the most of them. He joined with increased earnestness in the fray, set himself to all kinds of business, even official business; and naturally there came an hour when occasion only was wanted to make him again the necessary minister of a new situation.

Everything led him to power; two things facilitated his accession. It is well known that at first the peace had caused delicate relations to exist between the Emperor and Count Cavour. Napoleon III. had not been unaware of the Piedmontese minister's outbursts of indignation; he had striven to soften them; at heart he entertained no malice towards his confidant of Plombières; and if the former friendship had been subjected to a trial, it had only been half eclipsed. Cavour was wary enough to avoid breaking with the Emperor, who, on his part, soon recovered his taste for this fresh and fecund genius. Napoleon III. thought so little of excluding him from power that, when it was supposed the congress was about to sit, he had asked King Victor Emmanuel to send him as plenipotentiary. Cavour had accepted it, and he wrote with his usual good-humour to a friend: " If this winter you make a journey to Paris, you will find me at the Hôtel Bristol. I have taken the apartments occupied by Count Buol in 1856, just for the sake of invading Austrian territory." The disappearance of Count Walewski, and the friendly disposition of the Emperor, lightened the difficulty for Cavour in Paris, and at Turin things conspired to recall him to the Government.

The Ministry of six months, which had certainly performed an act of devotion in accepting the mission to conduct Piedmontese policy through a crisis of graceless transition, was bending under the weight of circumstances. La Marmora continued the vigilant and active organiser of the new army, a function he had preserved for the last ten years. The Cabinet was well meaning and honest, but mediocre. It shrank from acting decisively under the pressure of Central Italy; its laws of assimilation for the Lombards wounded them without satisfying the Piedmontese. It delayed the calling together of parliament, retaining beyond time of war the full powers voted for the war, and in sheer indecision prolonging a despotism principally embarrassing to itself. Rattazzi, though eager to create a party and a policy, wanted the breadth of a directing minister, and his insufficiency, by leaving the minds of the people fluctuating, was the cause of wretched divisions. In brief, there was need of a vigorous hand. Admitted frequently to the councils of ministers, Cavour saw that an end must be put to this wavering state of things, and a dissension with the Ministry on the subject of the summoning of parliament gave the signal. Probably Cavour may be accused of a certain impetuosity that did not always smooth the way for the feelings of his former colleagues. He yielded to that "impatience to have power again in his grasp," of which one of the faithfullest and most intelligent of his followers, Signor Artom, speaks, a "joyful high excitedness," that gave him prospect of "new horizons opening before him." He felt that he was needed, and on all sides, in Italy as well as in Europe, it was felt that he was needed. Marquis Lajatico had written from London in October : " We want Cavour for minister now."   At the end of 1859, Lord Russell pointed him to the seat of power in expressing the wish for a conference with him ; and when the matter was settled in the early days of 1860, Massimo d'Azeglio wrote : " Now we shall go ahead : I have the full assurance that we shall ; a firm hand directs the Government."

VIII.

Cavour was not of those who have the passion for power, to do nothing with it.   What was it he purposed in returning thus, borne back, we may say, by the reflux of events ?   He had, it is clear, now as ever, a distinct and fixed design, a policy derived from the situation and adapted to it.

His first determination was to call parliament together as early as possible.   Vainly the difficulties in legislating with a parliament, bureaucratic formalities, and the complications that would come of telling the electoral lists in the new provinces were objected to him ; he placed above everything the necessity of associating the country with the resolutions which might have to be taken.   He saw that the country had a right to claim it, and that it would be a support and a guarantee for himself.   He was ready to undertake the responsibilities of the proceeding, and he was anxious in so urgent an hour that the national revolution should no longer be separated from free institutions. More, and principally, he wished to settle without delay the annexation of Central Italy. He knew that he would have to square accounts with Paris; and that the Emperor, fallen back into one of his impenetrable moods after his recent *coup de théâtre*, would be making stipulations and reservations; he knew his man; he was able to read his mind, and prepared to come to an understanding with him. "We must," he said to a confidant, "treat France and England with all the consideration compatible with our dignity and the definitive success of our aims; I do not expect the Emperor to pronounce in favour of annexation. I fancy he will hardly do it; and, in truth, his Villafranca engagements render it impossible for him; but I think it necessary to assure myself that his opposition will not be very positive. We have to study him, sound his mind, observe his bearing towards us at every step that we take. At all events, I mean to admit the deputies of Central Italy to our parliament." Cavour counted on the half superstitious, more or less sincere, respect entertained by Napoleon III. for popular rights and the national will. And, moreover, he had another card to play with the Emperor—Savoy—of which there had been no mention since Villafranca; and which again became a decisive element of negotiation in Italian interests. Cavour's merit was to perceive a necessity and frankly accept it; to seize, at one glance of the eye, the relationship between the fortunes of Central Italy and the cession of Savoy. "The knot of this question," he wrote to Count Pepoli, "appears to me to be no longer in the Romagna and Tuscany, but in Savoy. Although

I have not received any communication on the subject from Paris, I have seen that we were on the wrong road, and I have taken another direction." The idea of the sacrifice of Savoy had in reality been part of Cavour's programme on his resumption of power : it was soon to bear the title of " an incident of his policy."

A singular question has sometimes since been raised : Who was it that had the chief part in this negotiation— Baron de Talleyrand, the successor of Prince de la Tour d'Auvergne, at the court of King Victor Emmanuel, or M. Benedetti, at that time political director of the French Foreign Office, and who unexpectedly departed for Turin as plenipotentiary ? M. Benedetti has written : " In 1860 I suddenly received orders to proceed to Turin to hasten the union of Savoy and Nice with France, a union that met with unforeseen obstacles. Leaving Paris on March 20, I signed the Treaty of Cession on the 24th." I do not desire to lessen the value of our diplomatists. The fact is, that this time they had nothing to win, for the simple reason that the whole thing had been settled beforehand, and Cavour had in no way been taken unawares, when, even before the arrival of M. Benedetti, Baron de Talleyrand was commissioned to speak officially of Savoy. It was at Milan, during the winter fêtes of 1860, in the honeymoon of the new independence. A despatch reached Baron de Talleyrand from Paris, charging him to announce to Cavour at once the wishes of the Imperial Government in the matter of Savoy, and the recall of the French army from Lombardy. This double communication implied something as much as follows : " You are about to annex Tuscany, you will run the risks, you will assume the responsibility of it; ours we disengage by calling our army out of Lombardy. We do not counsel this annexation; but, as after all we look on it as accomplished, we ask you for the price that is due to us." Cavour was not deceived in his anticipation, he was astonished only at the hasty recall of the army, and he answered smiling : " If the English had occupied Genoa under the same conditions as your occupation of Milan, do you think they would have been in such a hurry as you are to abandon Italy ? However, all is for the best. We shall accept the Emperor's decision with greater satisfaction than we do the second half of your despatch. The Emperor seems to hold extremely to Savoy and this unhappy city of Nice ! "

Oh ! without doubt the prime minister of King Victor Emmanuel would have been glad to avoid the cession of Savoy, still more "the unhappy city of Nice;" and naturally he did not think himself obliged to anticipate the sacrifice, and opposed some of those little resistances even in the minor points of a negotiation, which are for the honour of diplomatic arms. If he could have kept everything and given nothing, he would have done it. Having escaped the dilemma a first time, on the morrow of Villafranca, be sure that he would not have failed to elude it still, had he been able. He had not made up his mind to it without chagrin, he took it as the king did, saying, with a secret pang, "that after giving the daughter, they might give the cradle." Signor Artom, a frequent assistant at these private deliberations, relates that " this act was the sole one of his political life to which he did not bring the kind of heroic serenity he displayed in the gravest situations." Although during a space of ten years he had often found Savoy hostile to his policy, he loved this land, which was like a native country to him; for it had given its old name to the dynasty whose ensign it was. He was very much at the mercy of these old recollections, even while at work upon his firm resolve to proceed, and he thought what D'Azeglio expressed, when writing to a French friend : " You know that it would be unbefitting us to show ourselves indifferent to a separation that bids us say adieu to brothers-in-arms of eight centuries. My personal sentiment—shared, I believe, by everyone—is to regret sincerely the severance from a population full of rare and eminent qualities, counterbalanced by some few insignificant defects, who have always faithfully followed us in our Italian struggles, have filled our armies, councils, and diplomacy with devoted, gifted, energetic men. Once let the Savoyards have said : ' We will be annexed to France;' we shall be like a father who lets his daughter marry according to her desire, embraces her with a painful heart, wishes her full happiness, and says adieu to her."

In common with D'Azeglio, Cavour said adieu to Savoy painfully; but it was not a matter of sentiment for him. He had come to his determination as a duty in policy, weighing what he did, resolutely cutting " the knot of the question," as he called it; and, be it said, seeing more clearly and farther than those who asked him to relinquish what liberated his hands. If the French plenipotentiaries had been tempted to rate their victory high, they might have been undeceived in the hour when the act was made irrevocable. Cavour walked up and down his cabinet thoughtfully and gravely, not on this occasion rubbing his hands, as he listened to the reading out of the treaty. His signature was affixed to the deed in silence; recovering his habitual sprightliness the moment it was done, he went up to Baron de Talleyrand, and said to him, with a significant smile: "Now we have you for accomplices!"

Foreseeing all the issues of the act he had premeditated, Cavour knew well that the question of Savoy would raise a storm, and create every kind of difficulty for him at home and abroad. He stood resigned to meet it—even the prospect of the discontent of England, which was not long in showing itself. Reassured for a term after the peace by the declarations of Count Walewski, England's distrust revived at the rumours of a fresh transaction, and she at once began to worry Cavour. Interrogations, complaints, and remarks poured in on him. Lord Russell took up his sharpest pen to write to Sir James Hudson: "In speaking to Count Cavour of the rumours relating to the cession of Savoy, you will not disguise from him that it will be a blot on the escutcheon of Savoy to cede to France the cradle of the illustrious house reigning in Sardinia." Cavour, at home as he was with his friend Sir James Hudson, was put to it a little at times; and I know not indeed if he did not make shift to slip out of the net like that Piedmontese minister of the eighteenth century, the Marquis D'Ormea, who, in a similar position, being pressed to state whether Sardinia had joined in a treaty with

France and Spain, required that the question should be submitted to him in writing. " Is it true that the King of Sardinia has contracted an alliance with France and Spain ?" The Marquis D'Ormea wrote spiritedly underneath : "*This alliance* does not exist." There was, in fact, a treaty with France only !

Cavour behaved in some such manner. To all the interrogations besetting him, he replied that the Sardinian Government had not the slightest intention to cede, exchange, or sell Savoy. He added, it is true, that "if the people of that country had any proposition to make for the bettering of their condition, the proposition would be examined in the usual parliamentary manner, and justice would be done to it as parliament might decide." Sir James Hudson understood perfectly what was meant by that.

The best means of shaking off England was to refer her to France, and here England found the efforts she was continuing more vigorously than ever on behalf of the annexation of Central Italy turned against her. She was caught in her own meshes. Lord Cowley said to M. Thouvenel that, " in the opinion of the English Government, the annexation of Savoy to France was a European question ;" and M. Thouvenel replied : " Yes, if England will accept the proposition that the annexation of Tuscany to Sardinia shall not be accomplished without the co-operation and assent of the Great Powers, we will accept the same conditions for Savoy." In vain the English Government carried its protests to all quarters. Addressing itself to Vienna, Austria replied ironically, that there was nothing more extraordinary in the annexation of Savoy than in that of Tuscany. When it turned to St. Petersburg, Russia replied, that the cession of Savoy appeared to her to be a transaction in due form. And the Emperor Napoleon seized the occasion to soothe the vexed temper—rather noisy than efficacious—of England with the rich indemnification of the commercial treaty of January 23, 1860. This simplified remarkably the diplomatic position of the Piedmontese Government in relation to England, as well as in relation to Switzerland, which was left alone to cry for a portion of Savoy neutralised by the treaties of 1815.

The inevitable internal difficulties to be encountered had been clearly foreseen by Cavour. He was well assured that the renunciation of two ancient provinces might stir some emotion in Piedmont proper, and even in other regions of Italy. In any case he knew that it would be a pretext for hostile parties—Mazzinian agitators, and every form of opposition inclined to make use of a weapon when they found one. Had it been Savoy only, passions perhaps would not have been so angrily roused; but the ultra-Italians laid particular stress on Nice, and, as it happened, Nice was the birthplace of the popular chief, Garibaldi, in whom the abandonment of his natal city provoked a deep and bitter resentment against the man who, in his own words, "made him a stranger in his country." The Italians held that Cavour had yielded a fragment of their national territory; the Piedmontese of the old school accused him of sacrificing the stoutest and solidest portion of the state; all declared that he had paid a reckless price, in an almost humiliating concession, for an equivocal alliance.

Cavour was aware of the risks he ran, but neither internal nor diplomatic complexities arrested him. He was ready to bring before parliament the responsibility of an act in which he saw a pledge of national policy, and, to begin, the union of the Central provinces of Italy with Piedmont.

IX.

It was on January 20, 1860, that Cavour took up the reins of power; and from that date he was at his work, hurrying forward the annexation of Central Italy, carrying on negotiations with London and Paris, making use of England in spite of her moodiness, appeasing France by the cession of Savoy, and triumphing over the last hesitations of Napoleon III. by means of a plebiscitum in Tuscany and the Emilia. Matters proceeded briskly. On March 11, the voting in the central provinces took place; on the 18th a decree established the result by pronouncing the annexation to be confirmed. On the 24th the treaty of the cession of Savoy was signed and sealed; on the 25th the election lists were opened for the Chambers in all the provinces of the new kingdom, so that it was no longer before the Piedmontese parliament, but before the first national Italian parliament that the question was to be laid which embodied for the moment the policy of Cavour. The head of the Cabinet hardly knew how near the truth he was when in April, 1859, after a parliamentary sitting that had voted full powers on the eve of the war, he exclaimed : " I have left the last Piedmontese Chamber, the next will be that of the kingdom of Italy ! " This forecast was a reality one year later ; nor could Count Cavour have much fear of being unsupported by an assembly owing its life to him, and of which he became more than ever the experienced and trusted guide.

The new assembly, composed of the *élite* of Italy, represented marvellously in its spirit the national Liberalism which for ten years had decided the success of Piedmontese policy ; and this made it of priceless assistance, a strong governing force under a skilful hand. The prime minister of King Victor Emmanuel had first to demand an act of patriotism and good sense of it—the sanction of the treaty ceding Savoy and Nice, and the discussion following thereon presented curious features. As a matter of course, an unrestricted liberty reigned throughout this discussion. Every form of opposition was exhibited, even the most eccentric, and Guerrazzi, the former Tuscan chief, prodigal in sarcasms, threatened Cavour with the fate of Clarendon, condemned to exile for having ceded Dunkirk to France ; but the opposition containing the greatest elements of danger centred in a man in whom Cavour found an adversary both impassioned and self-contained, all but an enemy—Rattazzi.

Here was a sort of dramatic counterstroke of the differences and dusky conflicts which had brought about the last ministerial crisis leading to the elevation of Cavour and the fall of Rattazzi. The latter had evidently been profoundly mortified, and it was said that between these two men, in spite of all parliamentary and ministerial alliances, notwithstanding an intimacy of long date, all personal intercourse had ceased. Under an appearance of moderation, with calculated art and polished shrewdness in his blows, Rattazzi delivered a speech of the nature of an impeachment, full of bitter shafts against the treaty ceding Savoy, and principally the cession of Nice. Everything had been unfortunate in this miserable business, the principle, the proceedings, the negotiations. It would have been possible to unite the Italian provinces, without prostration to a powerful ally, without thus abjectly courting the Emperor, who would undoubtedly in the end have resigned himself to consent to the annexations. With Savoy, a conservative and dynastic force, precious in a crisis of transformation, was lost. With Nice an Italian city was lost, the Italian programme was cast aside, and a policy of territorial barter supported the policy of nationality! The price of the annexation was paid without even a guarantee in exchange. Like an able tactician, Rattazzi did not indeed, like Guerrazzi, speak of Clarendon, "severe to the king, scornful of parliament, and believing in his pride that there would be no check to his authority ;" he did not adopt such angry taunts, though he alluded maliciously to Cavour's retirement in July, "an excellent method of escape from a dilemma, no doubt, but of small use in solving the difficulties." In one way and another he said sufficient to betray an implacable animosity, and compel the President of the Council to take up all those gauntlets of the Opposition, and justify his honour and the character of his policy before the Italian parliament, now for the first time assembled at Turin.

The struggle, we may remark, was unequal, for facts told weightily for Cavour, and his was a genius as prompt to seize an advantage as it was formidable to his adversaries. Clarendon was alluded to : " Signor Guerrazzi will permit me to observe to him," he said loftily, " that if Lord Clarendon, to defend his conduct from violent accusations, could have pointed to several millions of Englishmen delivered by him from a foreign yoke, several counties added to the dominions of his master, it may be that the parliament would not have been so pitiless, and perhaps Charles II. would not have been so ungrateful towards the faithfullest of his servants. Since the honourable deputy Guerrazzi has thought proper to give me an historical lesson, he should have given it complete. After telling us what Lord Clarendon did, he should have told us who were his enemies, what sort of men his accusers, who shared the spoil they had torn from him. He should have told us that these enemies formed the famous coterie of men possessed of no antecedents in common, no community of principles, no ideas, and who were actuated by nothing but the most impudent egotism ; men fallen away from every party, professing all opinions—Puritans, Presbyterians, Anglican Churchmen, and Papists, each in turn ; to-day Republicans, Royalists to-morrow ; demagogues in the street, courtiers in the palace ; Radicals in parliament, reactionists in the councils of the king ; men, in short, whose coming together produced the ministry stigmatised in history as that of the *Cabal.* So much being said," he added, "I leave it to the Chamber and to the country to consider what may be thought of the present case." Not one stroke of this magnificent fulmination escaped the electrified assembly acclaiming to the end.

X.

No, of a surety, Cavour had sold no cities, as the sarcastic Guerrazzi charged him with doing, nor had he turned aside from the national programme, as Rattazzi hinted; he had simply performed an act that he deemed necessary, an act forced upon him by everything in the state of Italy and of Europe. The real cause of the cession of Savoy he confessed before the assembly, without circumlocution, with a mind above petty considerations : "The true ground for it is that the treaty is an integral part of our policy, the logical and inevitable consequences of a past policy, and an absolute necessity for the carrying on of this policy in the future."

A consequence of the past, a condition of the future ; in this the whole case was stated. Nothing was easier than bandying words, disputing over little points. The truth was, a choice had to be made between a system of barren isolation that was barely practicable, involving perilous revolutionary measures, and the policy of the alliances that in the space of ten years had led from Novara to the Crimean war, from the Congress of Paris to the war in Italy and the new kingdom, whereof the parliament was the living image. The choice could not be doubtful. In the path followed up to that time, and which had led to success, the thing to do was to advance without deviating, or even stopping ; and admitting alliances to be part of the policy, where was the useful and helpful ally to be found if not in France ? Cavour was perfectly clear-sighted. He knew the posture of French affairs, and with unfailing penetration he traced out the game of parties, the troubles, doubts, and antagonisms of opinions in France regarding Italy; he felt, moreover, that sympathetic though the Emperor was, omnipotent though he appeared to be, he had also difficulties at home to manage. The object of Cavour, an interested one, as we need not say, and cleverly conducted, was to hold the Emperor engaged up to a certain point, without alienating the general opinion of the country, but to keep the bond of sympathy fast between the French and the Italian nations. His most devoted friends in Paris wrote to him : " For the love of Heaven, for the love of Italy, sign, sign ! if you wish to have the French alliance; for if you hesitate your country will lose all sympathy in France." Hence the treaty, the moral nature of which raised it above the acrimonious and ribald commentaries running along with it.

Such was the feeling with which he signed it, and he now did his utmost to impart it to the Italian parliament with an increasing vehemence of argument and emotion : " I tell you, under a profound conviction of the truth, that the cession of Savoy and Nice was indispensable to keep the French people friendly towards Italy. Right or wrong, I will not debate on it. They believe that these provinces belong naturally to France. It may be an error, but whoever is acquainted with France must acknowledge frankly that it is a fixed idea. Now, this cession being once demanded of us, if we had replied with a refusal, the minds of Frenchmen would not have taken into consideration the difficulties that a matter of the kind would encounter in Italy. We should have been charged with ingratitude and injustice; we should have been told that we declined to apply on one side of the Alps principles which we invoked on the other, and for which France spent her blood and treasure. In presence of these facts, was not the ministry bound to accede to the Emperor's demand? a demand made—yes, I can say it—not solely in the name of French interests, but in the name of the alliance of France with Italy. For my part, I hold it a great honour to have yielded to it, for it behoved us to consolidate the French alliance necessary to us. The true, the only advantage for us, is the consolidation of the alliance, not so much of two Governments as of two peoples. You then, who are the Italian people, forbear to put yourselves in opposition to French interests. If there must be chafings and disputes, let them all be borne by the Government. If there is something odious in it, I counsel that it should fall upon us. We are as fond of popularity as others are, and often have my colleagues and I drunk of that intoxicating cup; but we know how to waive it away at the bidding of duty. When signing, we were aware what unpopularity awaited us; but we knew likewise that we laboured for Italy, for that Italy which is not the sound body a certain member has spoken of; Italy still has big wounds in her body. Look towards the Mincio, look on the other side of Tuscany, and say whether Italy is out of danger." And speaking thus he carried the assembly with him; he obtained the abandonment of an order of the day that a distinguished deputy from Vintimiglia, since President of the Chamber, Signor Biancheri, had proposed on a question of frontiers, and which, at the request of the President of the Council, he withdrew. Cavour gained the vote for the treaty by a majority of 229, while 33 protested against it, and 23 members obeyed the signal to abstain from voting given by Rattazzi.

XI.

One year previously the Marquis Costa de Beauregard, foreseeing the separation that already seemed inevitable, had exclaimed in the Piedmontese parliament: "So long as we are united, you will see Savoy in the front rank fighting the enemies of Piedmont. If one day our soldiers are in line with the powerful armies of France, like us they will be too proud to express a regret." Shortly after the annexation Victor Emmanuel reviewed with emotion the old brigade of Savoy departing for France. The work whereby the chief of the Piedmontese Cabinet proposed to give scope to his policy was accomplished.

Preoccupied as he was, before the meeting of parliament, and in the interval of these exciting discussions, Cavour had found time to visit some of the provinces recently united. He had accompanied the king to Milan during the winter fêtes, in the midst of ovations of all kinds. He had seen the venerable Manzoni, who reminded him of the conversation that had taken

s

place one day in 1850 in the house of Rosmini at Bolongaro. He had desired to see some of the cities of Lombardy—Cremona, Brescia, Bergamo, and everywhere on his road he had received a welcome that bore witness to his popularity. Shortly after the annexation, still accompanying the king, he had also gone to Tuscany and the Romagna, and strange to say he beheld those provinces for the first time; he knew neither Florence nor any of those delightful Tuscan countrysides.

One morning at Pisa, wakening at break of day, in the silence of the still sleeping city, he had with Signor Artom betaken himself to the Campo Santo. He remained speechless a moment, then the words escaped him : " How pleasant it would be to repose here ! " Signor Artom observed laughingly that he would find himself on holy ground, for that this earth they trod upon had been brought from Palestine in the period of the Crusades, and he answered gaily : " Are you sure they will not one day canonise me ? " He had marvelled greatly at all that he had seen at Pisa and Florence—the profusion of the works of human genius there ; and he declared on his return that he had discovered in himself a sense he had not imagined he possessed, that of art. This expedition was like a happy interlude for him, which he appeared to enjoy.

Already, however, even before the annexation of Savoy, strange rumours began to rise in Italy, " on the other side of Tuscany," according to the expression of the Piedmontese minister. Scarcely had they come upon a term of tranquillity when a new campaign was preparing across the Mediterranean; and with a man every one of whose words had a bearing, notice might have been taken of a phrase and a declaration that Cavour had let fall lightly: "And now we have you for our accomplices," he had said to the French plenipotentiaries when signing the Treaty of Savoy. On the other hand, on being asked whether he had at least obtained a guarantee from France for the annexation of Central Italy, he had replied: "Not only the union of the Emilia and Tuscany to the ancient provinces of the kingdom has not been guaranteed by France in return for Savoy and Nice, but I will affirm that if this guarantee had been offered us, we should have declined it; a guarantee would have implied a control." With this in his mind, Cavour was capable of leading those who thought they held him; and of this complicity without control, as it pleased him to put it, he was one to win prodigious fruits, still richer than those he had been gathering. Already his eyes were on Sicilian and Neapolitan waters.

CHAPTER VI.

CAVOUR AND THE UNITY OF ITALY—ROME AND NAPLES.

The Idea of Unity in the Mind of Cavour—Insurrection of Sicily and the Expedition of Garibaldi—Attitude of Cavour at Turin—Relations with Naples and with Rome—Negotiations with Europe—Cavour and the Dictatorship of Garibaldi in Sicily—Matters touching his Policy—Advance of the Insurrection in the South—The Revolution in Naples—Projects of Garibaldi—Threats of an Attempt on Rome and on Venice—Private Dissensions between Cavour and Garibaldi—Necessity for a Resolution—The Chambéry Mission—Words of Napoleon III.—Invasion of Umbria and the Marches—The Piedmontese Army in the Kingdom of Naples—Assembly of the Chambers in Turin—The Policy of Cavour before Parliament—Triumph of that Policy—Annexation of Sicily and Naples—Programme of Cavour as to Venice and Rome—Letters and Speeches—Rome the Capital—The Free Church in the Free State—Views of Cavour concerning the Papacy.

I.

A QUESTION naturally arises from this labour of a daring head beset by a developing national revolution. Count Cavour, the scion of an old Piedmontese house, prime minister of the King of Sardinia, standard-bearer of the House of Savoy, had he originally the idea of the unity of Italy? If he had stood predetermined a fanatic for unity, and had based his proceedings on that idea, there would have been only one Mazzinian the more across the Alps, and Italy would probably still be seeking her way. The secret of his strength and his success lay, on the contrary, precisely in his having a mind exempt from prejudice and extravagance, in his reckoning always with the reality of things, mixing his policy, according to the saying of Napoleon, with " the calculation of combination and chances." He held but to one fixed point, the restoration of Italy to her national independence and powers through the absolute departure of the foreigner, that is to say, the Austrian lordship or ascendency ; he left the rest to circumstances, fortune, the changes of the times, never refusing an advantage, however small and partial it might be, when it was offered ; as also he never shrank from broader visions when the horizon opened out before him.

In the "fair days" of Plombières, his calculations did not extend beyond the kingdom of Upper Italy, and he did not reject the idea of a confederation in which he would naturally have maintained the headship of " eleven millions of Italians," gathered together under the flag of Savoy. For lack of better, the morning after Villafranca, he would have been satisfied with the semi-independence of Tuscany, provided that there were to be no more Lorraine princes in Florence. Even after the annexations, he would have agreed to go no farther for the moment, that he might devote himself to organise and consolidate the kingdom just issuing from six months of laborious negotiations.

The question of unity burst forth imperiously in reality only on that day of May 5, 1860, when, while the parliament in Turin was discussing the cession of Savoy and Nice, Garibaldi, followed by his companions-in-arms, the "Thousand," quitted the villa Quarto, near Genoa, to cross the Mediterranean, with the intention of raising

Sicily, Naples, and still more perhaps, to the echoing cry of "Italy and Victor Emmanuel!" It was, if you like, another result of Villafranca, a fatality of the situation, a fresh extension of the national movement which had already absorbed Florence and Bologna; but it was at the same time most certainly a strange complication, a crisis graver than all those that had been passed.

Up to that period, in fact, things had come about without a conflict, by a sort of pacific victory, in harmony with national rights. Tuscany had not been conquered, she had given herself freely. Even France regarded the Romagna as virtually detached from the Holy See. These provinces belonged to the territorial system of Upper Italy, and the annexation up to the Cattolica had nothing in it that was not in the nature of things. But beyond it, in the South, the unknown reigned full of doubts and perils. The work of unification could only be carried out by revolution or by war; it assailed the independence of a kingdom having friends in Europe, it touched another portion of the States of the Church—that Roman question which agitated the Roman Catholic world—and the inviolability of Austria, which could not but feel herself defied and menaced by such a concentration of Italian power.

All these problems burst forth at once in the risky enterprise Cavour was suddenly called to face, by the terrible logic that swept Garibaldi over Sicilian waters. Danger was everywhere, in every form; and here, in this supreme and decisive conflict, the fertility of genius and supple vigour of the man waxed in the fire of action; quick in expedients, knowing how to remain a Liberal and a Conservative still in a revolutionary chaos, determined above all not to be subordinate to events, even when they seemed pressing to force his hand.

II.

"The unexpected leads us and leads all Europe," it was said, in this spring of 1860. It is the key-note of the fresh crisis, that begins with a heroic adventure; unfolding, for a term of five months in the thick of our European commonplace, as a very drama of revolution, diplomacy, and war, to conclude with the fiery junction of the South and the North of Italy, the consummation of the unity.

It is like a fabulous history, this of Garibaldi: speeding secretly on a night of May from the gulf of Genoa, sweeping in his pair of vessels, the *Piemonte* and the *Lombardo*, through the Neapolitan cruisers, landing at Marsala, and conquering kingdoms at a gallop—it reads like a legend. Cavour at Turin was the spirit of policy working his combinations amidst every form of change. Without the first, the drama would not have opened; without the second, the end would have been lost in disorderly tumults: and for a further singularity between these two men, bound at one and the same time to the same campaign, holding the future of Italy in their hands, there was neither an understanding nor a pre-arranged plot. Garibaldi had gone with an angry heart, easily won over to the Sicilian insurrection by resentment at the cession of Nice; and on starting he had let fly a barbed arrow at Cavour in a letter, in which he said to

the king : "I know that I embark on a perilous enterprise. If we fail, I trust that Italy and Liberal Europe
will not forget that it was undertaken from motives pure
of all egotism and entirely patriotic. If we achieve it,
I shall be proud to add to your Majesty's crown a new
and perhaps more brilliant jewel, *always on the condition
that your Majesty will stand opposed to councillors who
would cede this province to the foreigner, as has been
done with the city of my birth.*" Cavour, for his part,
had not encouraged the epedition. Without doubting
the sincerity of Garibaldi, he dreaded his rashness, and
he mistrusted in a higher degree those who surrounded
and bore him on, hoping to turn his popularity to their
own account. But when once the enterprise was on foot,
he had only one idea—to hold himself ready for the up-
shot, and play as he best could the terrible game, in
which the business he had led up to Bologna might be
completed at one blow beyond expectation—or else might
founder suddenly.

It would be childish simplicity at the present time
to ask whether Cavour was a minister of irreproachable
orthodoxy, and did or did not violate public law. He
played his game like a man who did not mean to lose
if he could help it. He had in truth done nothing to
hasten the explosion of this question of Southern Italy ;
he had not even desired it. He would have wished
rather to connect the "two great kingdoms of the
peninsula," as he called them, in an alliance, to bind the
federative bundle of Italian forces of North and South in
common interests for a national future. A year previously, on the death of King Ferdinand and the acces-

sion of the young Francis II., son of a princess of Savoy,
Cavour had seized the occasion to send Count Salmour
on a mission of peace to Naples. It was an offer of
amity and support to a reign in its infancy. Early in
1860 the Cabinet of Turin had renewed the attempt by
sending Count Villamarina, formerly ambassador at Paris,
to Naples, charged to bring about an understanding if
possible. Both with Rome and Naples Cavour would
gladly have had dealings and arrangements. Unhappily
those governments of the South were purblind in their
prejudices and passions.

At Naples, the unfortunate Francis II., deaf to the
appeals of "revolutionary Piedmont," as well as to the
counsels of France and England, in a mesh of court
intrigues and Austrian and absolutist influences, bent
under the weight of a crown already within a few
months jeopardised by a reactionary policy, puerile as it
was violent. At Rome all the vapouring fire-eaters were
for reconquering the Romagna. An army was to be
formed to take the place of the French garrison, whose
departure seemed close at hand, though it was indefinitely adjourned by events. Nothing was talked of
but the recruiting of soldiers, Zouaves of the Roman
Catholic and French legitimists' aristocracy, Belgians,
disguised Austrians, turbulent Irish ; and a thankless fate
destined the command of the army of the Holy Keys for
one of the most brilliant of French captains, condemned
by the *coup d'état* of December 2 to a premature retirement, and impatiently thirsting for action, a man of
perfect sincerity and not less imprudence—General
Lamoricière. The impetuous Lamoricière had signalised

his entry into office as " gonfalonier " of the banner of the Church by an order of the day resembling a challenge, in which the Italian revolution was likened to " Islamism," and the cause of the Pope was identified with that of Europe and civilisation. In a word, Rome and Naples were nests of hostility, and had become centres of a coalition, of which Austria was the soul, and whose dream it was to head Europe in a crusade for the restoration of order. These unfortunate Southern Courts imagined that they had to defend themselves—and be it so. But in their perplexity they did not see that, instead of warding off, they attracted the danger, and after their own way of doing it, made ready the unity they shrank from : by their persistence in clinging to an illusion they turned all liberal instincts and the passion for nationality into auxiliaries of Piedmont, and accomplices of the first indications of a movement. The Sicilian insurrection was a symptom and a prelude.

Cavour knew there was a plan that might result at any given moment in placing Northern Italy between the Austrians encamped on the Mincio, commanding the Po, and Lamoricière leading an army from the south. He had seen his offers of conciliation declined ; he heard of the march of a Neapolitan corps in the Abruzzi, and that is how it came that, without having advised it, and in no degree misapprehending the peril it involved, Cavour allowed Garibaldi to go forth and bear the spark to the fiery elements of the South. Not only did Cavour abstain from preventing the expedition of Garibaldi, it is notorious that he covered it with a protection that expanded and grew in the ratio with its success. The

President of the Council, who had been careful at the same time to make himself Minister of Marine, was served in the Mediterranean by him whom we now know as the luckless Persano; and Persano knew how to play his part, by aiding in the furnishing of supplies, and covering the passage of new convoys of volunteers under Medici and Cozenz. Cavour did what he could to keep on terms with the popular chief, beloved of Italy, and ardently watched by all eyes; on the other hand, he would not surrender everything to an adventurer, nor compromise his position before Europe by too open a support. Hence came a policy mixed up of audacity and stratagem, perfectly unfathomable, the natural issue of a complicated and desperate situation. The difficulties were enormous; and all the more critical that, immediately surrounding him, Cavour had to deal both with those who accused him of not doing enough, and with those who were alarmed at his rashness, even when, like D'Azeglio, they said of him that "he only could save the ship."

III.

No sooner was the landing of Garibaldi at Marsala noised abroad, than a tempest of protestation broke loose on Turin. Austria did not fail to seize the occasion to renew her pleadings against Sardinia in Paris and London, representing Sardinia as more than ever the disturber of Europe, and asking nothing better than the privilege of bringing her to her senses. A step farther was taken at Berlin, where nothing less was talked of than the revival of the alliance of the Northern

Courts, to protect public rights and laws against "Piedmontese ambition." At St. Petersburg, Prince Gortchakoff delivered himself sharply to the Sardinian envoy to the effect that, "if the Cabinet of Turin was so far carried away by the revolutionary spirit as to be unable to pay due respect to international duties, the European Governments would be bound to take such a state of things into consideration, and regulate accordingly their relations with Piedmont. If the geographical position of Russia permitted it, the Emperor assuredly would intervene with arms to defend the Neapolitan Bourbons, without allowing the proclamation of non-intervention of the Western Powers to stop him." France had a word to say; and even England was anxious—less, it is true, concerning the deeds of Garibaldi, than as to what might be the consequence of them. As to the Governments of Naples and Rome, they filled the Courts of Europe with their outcries and recriminations. Cavour preserved his usual serenity in the thick of the storm.

His first act was to reject every interpellation in parliament upon the affairs of the South. Diplomacy, of course, demanded speech, and with diplomacy he had recourse to subterfuges, gaining time by disavowals that disavowed nothing. He replied to those who accused him of abetting revolutionists, in the words he addressed to his friend Sir James Hudson: "On what ground is Sardinia charged with the crime of not having hindered the landing of this hardy adventurer in Sicily, when the whole Neapolitan fleet was incapable of doing it? The Austrians and Irish embark at their ease to go to the assistance of the Pope; how then can the Sardinian

Government, supposing it cognizant of the expedition, stay the Sicilian exiles from running to succour their brethren in a struggle with their tyrants? The flower of the youth of all Italy flies to the banner of Garibaldi. Were the Sardinian Government to attempt to check this national movement, the monarchy of Savoy would destroy its own prestige, and therewith its own future, and we should soon have anarchy in the peninsula and new troubles in Europe. To stem the tide of revolutionary ideas, the Italian constitutional monarchy must preserve the moral power it has won by its resolution to make the country independent. This is a beneficent treasure which would be lost if the Government of the King stood against the enterprise by Garibaldi. The Government of the King deplores the enterprise, but cannot stop it; does not aid, but is unable to use force to put it down."

Meanwhile he, whom they called a "flibustier," pursued his prodigious undertaking, becoming in a few days master of Sicily, and causing the Neapolitan Government to fall upon a course of Liberal concessions which might, six months previously, have been of some effect, but were now useless, and significant simply of a cause more than half lost.

The art of Cavour was shown in the skill with which he turned Garibaldi's successes to use before Europe, and kept the Courts of the North from passing to more decisive acts than protestations. The fact is that Russia and Prussia soon ceased to speak of interfering in Italian affairs; they showered their offerings of sympathy on the King of Naples, but confined themselves to promises of "moral support."   Cavour hung mainly upon what would be done or would be permitted in London and in Paris.   English ministers might entertain good wishes for the independence of Naples, but nothing would be done by them to ensure or defend it.   England was pledged up to a certain point by what she had done in promoting the annexation of Tuscany and the Romagna. On the very day of Garibaldi's departure from Genoa, May 5, Lord Russell charged Lord Loftus at Vienna to communicate particular views and ideas that indicated the course likely to be taken by England : " If tyranny and injustice are the characteristic features of the government of Southern Italy, liberty and justice are the features of the government of Northern Italy. This being so, sooner or later the people of South Italy will come to a political union with their northern brethren, and will insist on being governed by the same sovereign."   Cavour could not have said more.

The anxiety of England, in reality, was lest Piedmont should be led to "acts of aggression" against Austria, and she feared still more that Cavour, beset by so many perplexities, should be tempted to purchase the aid of France by new cessions of territory, the sacrifice of the island of Sardinia or even Genoa.   When a note of six lines was presented to him, demanding his guarantees upon these two points, Cavour naturally hastened to reassure Lord Russell.   He signed an engagement readily not to attack Austria, and " not to cede to France any portion of territory beyond and in addition to that which had been ceded by the treaty of Turin of March 24." Seeing acutely what it was that Lord Russell had most at heart, the dexterous Piedmontese had been careful to put in the first line the article of cession, which had been made secondary in the English note. Satisfied on this head, England felt herself at liberty to encourage all proceedings or hinder none.

What in her turn was to be expected of France? Cavour was not ignorant that there was the grave and delicate question for him : more depended on France than on England in this new phase. He counted on the "complicity," of which he had spoken the day when he signed the cession of Savoy and Nice, which had only become an accomplished fact at the moment when Garibaldi was already at Palermo. He counted also on the force of circumstances, the secret leanings and the interests of the Emperor, the thousand ties by which Napoleon III. and the destinies of the Empire were linked with the success or failure of the Italian cause. With profound sagacity he discerned, in short, that the Napoleonic policy could not push very far the protection of decaying legitimacy. Nor was he much in error in his calculations.

France, it was true, had been one of the first of the Powers to protest against the expedition of Garibaldi, and against the enrolment of volunteers day by day being shipped for Sicily. Evidently Napoleon III. did not look with a favourable eye on this revolutionary enterprise ; he had no wish to see the Southern Kingdom disappear, or the annexation pushed to the uttermost. What he thought of it was, however, sufficiently placable or sufficiently obscure. To those who spoke to him of Southern Italy, the Emperor replied sadly :

" What is to be done with a Government like that of
Naples, which refuses to listen to advice of any kind ? "
Napoleon III. chose to go into retirement for a time.
" The Emperor is absent," wrote Marquis Antonini,
" and the Minister of Foreign Affairs (Thouvenel) is not
of the best mind towards us. He has told me that
nothing can be done here for the King's Government.
It would appear that this government believes a revolution inevitable, even in Naples." The Tuileries declined
all responsibility, could not, whatever happened, do anything without acting in accord with its allies !

When at last the King of Naples, reduced in his
extremity to submit to the infliction of a Liberal Ministry,
a constitution and alliance with Piedmont, solicited the
mediation of France, Napoleon III. said to the Neapolitan
envoys : " It is too late ; a month back, all might have
been arranged ; to-day it is too late. The position of
France is very difficult ; a revolution is not to be stopped
by words. The Italians know what they are about ;
they understand perfectly that after having given the
blood of my soldiers for the independence of their
country, I shall never let a shot be fired against that
independence. This conviction has led them to annex
Tuscany contrary to my interests, and now it pushes
them on Naples. I am not strong enough to save the
king. I must have the aid of my allies." " What ! "
said the Neapolitan envoys, " can France consent to the
success of an enterprise so opposed to her interests, so
advantageous to England, so radically revolutionary ? "
" All that may be true," said the Emperor, " but we have
to do with facts ; the force of opinion is irresistible ; in

one way or another the national idea in Italy must triumph." And the last piece of counsel was : " Go to work quickly, furnish the means of backing you up ; Turin is the place for you. It is not to me, it is to King Victor Emmanuel that you should appeal. Sardinia alone can stop the course of the revolution ; I will support you at Turin."

At Turin Cavour was too adroit not to offer the Emperor and Europe the semblance of a negotiation with Naples. He felt himself under the necessity of managing the Powers, who, without being of one mind, were yet assailing him with remonstrances and recommendations. One day, indeed, to quiet them and shake himself loose, he allowed the king to try personally what could be done with Garibaldi—to check the "hero" in mid career if he could, or at least turn him from carrying the war over to the mainland.

In reality, Cavour used extreme dexterity in opening the doors which he appeared to be wishing to close. He practised evasions, and manœuvred with the Neapolitan messengers who were sent to him ; appeared to lean on England as regarded France, and on France and England when it concerned Russia and Prussia. Pressed a little too urgently to do something for the King of Naples, he replied promptly : "The Neapolitan Government is in a singular position. After several times refusing our alliance, after letting slip the favourable moment for seating its authority on a broad basis of national policy, now surrounded by dangers of its own making, it suddenly shifts its tactics and claims our friendship. Under what circumstances is this claim

made ?   Francis II. has lost the half of his kingdom ; in
the other half, the people, rendered suspicious by the
former proceedings of the Government, have no longer
even a belief in Liberal ministers, and dread that they
may hear the cannon of the reaction in the streets at
any moment.   In order to destroy that incurable feeling
of suspicion, and to fill up the abyss which exists
between the king and the people, Victor Emmanuel is
asked to become surety for the Neapolitan Government !
to invite Francis II. to share with him the halo of popularity which a sound and liberal policy, and blood spilt
on the battle-field, have obtained for the house of Savoy !
. . . . . The true enemy of the Neapolitan Government
is the discredit into which it has fallen ! . . . ." Cavour
might be unable always to convince, but he knew how
to interest some while he encouraged others, leaving
with all a deep impression of his ascendency ; and by
dint of suppleness he contrived to steer clear of Europe
while still keeping her in suspense, and preparing fresh
facts for her to swallow.

IV.

It was not only with European Governments, whose
divisions and indecisions might serve him, that Cavour
had to do.   He had at the same time to measure his
policy hour by hour with what was taking place in
Sicily, with the progress of the revolution, which he
screened in every possible way without recognising it,
and fully intended to make the most of.   He had to
deal with Garibaldi, and this was anything but diplo-

matic work : it was a strange, complex, and feverish interchange between Turin and Palermo—between political genius and ungoverned instinct in the form of a revolutionary chief in South Italy. Garibaldi was quite sincere in selecting for his pass-word, "Italy and Victor Emmanuel!" He was not one of those whom D'Azeglio anxiously accused of the cry *Viva Vittorio!* to which they added in a whisper : *Re provisorio,* while promising themselves to raise the republic out of a convulsion. He sincerely liked the king, but he liked him in his own way, just as he had his own way of working for Italian unity, dashingly and defiantly ; and he carried into this new enterprise his passions, his intemperateness, his indefinite aspirations, his tenderness towards the revolutionists, his misgivings, and his personal animosities. It will perhaps be said that but for all these he would not have been Garibaldi ; and had he not been Garibaldi, he would not have landed at Marsala, nor been to Calatafimi, Palermo, Milazzo, Messina, and ultimately Naples ; and so it may be. Cavour was under no illusion about the "hero ;" he understood him thoroughly, knew his weakness as well as his strength ; and his ability consisted in manipulating the powerful nature of the popular chief by leaving him the utmost liberty of action, saving the liberty to ruin or compromise the common cause.

The watchful and daring Piedmontese marked with unwavering eyes the man disembarking at Marsala, and rapidly becoming dictator of Sicily, as a prelude to the mastership of the whole of the Southern Kingdom. He neither grudged him the help which Persano and his ships were ordered copiously to supply him with, nor did he withhold manifestations of sympathy. He sent him word that "the King and his Government placed entire confidence in him." He congratulated him, almost officially, after the battle of Milazzo, in July. "I am happy," he wrote to Persano, "to hear of the victory at Milazzo, which does honour to Italian arms, and will prove to Europe that the Italians are henceforth determined to sacrifice their lives to recover liberty and their country. I beg you to take my sincere and warmest congratulations to General Garibaldi. After this brilliant victory, I do not see how he can be hindered from passing over to the continent. . . . . The national standard once hoisted in Sicily, should traverse the kingdom, and float along the coasts of the Adriatic. . . . ."

So spake Cavour, and no doubt he believed what he said ; but at the same time the victor was made aware of a sting ; Cavour did not shrink from imperiously demanding of the dictator the arrest of Mazzini, should the latter set foot on Sicilian soil ; nor would he allow Bertani, well known for his republican opinions, to be left at Genoa as the representative of the new Sicilian Government. This Mazzinian intervention, the influence of the rasher spirits of revolution over Garibaldi, and the growing anarchy in Sicily, were causes of deep anxiety to Cavour. "The King's Government has no intention of being trifled with," he wrote ; . . . . "the course which General Garibaldi is following is fraught with danger. His idea of governing, and the consequences ensuing from it, reflect discredit upon us in the eyes of Europe. If the disturbances in Sicily are repeated at Naples, the cause of Italy will run the risk of being misrepresented before public opinion, and condemned by a verdict that the greater Powers might hasten to put into execution." Cavour was not always successful in averting the evil; he saw his confidential envoys, such as La Farina, sent back by the dictator, who took a pleasure in spiting the ministry at Turin. He, who so well knew how to evade others, felt Garibaldi slipping from his grasp, to be led away by sinister counsels.

The relations between the head of the Government at Turin and the dictator of Sicily could not indeed be other than delicate; they were both conspiring for the same object, and were allied by the force of circumstances, but divided by numberless diversities of opinion, character, and instinct. There was, however, between them a difference that the roving chief did not perceive. The chief of the Piedmontese Cabinet had one great advantage over his formidable ally: he knew him and could judge him; he had a hold upon him in the protection afforded him, and without which nothing would have been possible, from the landing at Marsala to the passage of the Straits of Messina. The minister mastered the dictator by the ascendency of his policy, by an inexhaustible spirit of resource, and the incessant and occult activity which he exercised in every direction—at Naples as in Sicily. He did not desire a rupture; on the contrary, he did all in his power to avoid one; but while willingly granting Garibaldi the popular title of conqueror of kingdoms, Cavour felt that sooner or later there must be a struggle, unless he consented to be carried away with the rest of Italy, by the burning zeal of passion or of imagination, which the bold soldier no longer disguised.   At what moment and under what form this conflict, not to be anticipated without some degree of anxiety, would take place, he could not foresee ; everything depended upon the march of events, and the manner in which the now inevitable downfall of Neapolitan monarchy was brought about.

Cavour at heart would have preferred that the revolution, already victorious in Sicily through Garibaldi, should take place, as it were, spontaneously at Naples, without Garibaldi, or at least before the dictator crossed over to the continent.   He had prepared everything for that object by divers communications with the navy and army, extending even to the Government of King Francis II., not omitting members of the royal family. He considered it the best chance of his being able to govern the crisis, that he should keep the power to limit it, and so hold Europe to her attitude of observation.   "The problem we have to solve," he writes, "is this : to further the revolution, while we contrive that before Europe it should appear to be spontaneous.   In that case we shall have France and England with us ; otherwise I do not know what they will do."   In default of this more or less spontaneous revolution, if it should not declare itself, in the event of the arrival or decisive intervention of Garibaldi, and of the disorder and threatening agitation that might result from it, Cavour took the measures and precautions he deemed requisite.   Like a general engaged in vast and delicate operations all pointing to the same end, his eye and hand were alert and ready, issuing orders that were always the expression of a clear and resolute thought. He wrote to Persano : " The real object is to cause the national principle to triumph at Naples, clear of the Mazzinians. Italy must be saved from foreigners, evil principles, and madmen. . . . If the revolution is not accomplished before the arrival of Garibaldi, our condition will be very serious, but that must not trouble us. You will, if you are able, take possession of the forts, you will gather together the Neapolitan and Sicilian navy, give every officer a commission, make them swear fealty to the king and to the "statuto"—and then we shall see ! The king, the country, and the ministry have full confidence in you. Follow the instructions I give you as closely as possible. If any unforeseen case should occur, do your best to further the great object we have in view, which is to build up Italy without letting the revolution overwhelm us." At the same time he despatched additional naval forces and *bersaglieri*, that were only to be used in the last extremity. He took every measure to prevent being outstripped on the eventful day ; and thus, in protecting the most perilous of enterprises, for a great national cause, he resolved to keep it from deviating and lapsing into excesses ; while, on the other hand, he exercised all his diplomatic craft in masking it before Europe.

v.

In the midst of these ever-increasing complications, he found time to write the following to Madame de Circourt : " If I get out of the scrape this time, I shall try not to be caught again. I am like the sailor, who, finding himself surrounded by tempestuous waves, swears never more to expose himself to the perils of the sea. . . . ." He was, for the time being, in the midst of tempestuous seas, and at every turn he had a false move to correct, a new resolution to take, or a peril to avoid. I do not pretend to say that violence and intrigue had no place in the dramatic affairs of South Italy in August, 1860. In reality, the struggle in which Cavour was engaged, and which he was determined to carry on to the end, far exceeded the limits of vulgar intrigue, or even those of personal antagonism between two men brought face to face with one another by the irony of fortune.

In this conflict of policies, schemes, and passions, the fortunes of new Italy were at stake; but even in a labyrinth from which he seemed scarcely able to extricate himself, Cavour never swerved. He remained the representative of a ten years' policy, sanctioned by success; a consummate politician, making Piedmont, as it were, the solid centre point of all assimilations, and the monarchy an instrument of every national and liberal transformation, while it was the guarantee of conservative interests; knowing how to press forward, as well as to combine prudence with boldness, diplomacy with war; always taking into consideration the necessity for alliances, and the situation of Europe, especially that of France. What was the policy opposed to him? It was a policy of rashness and defiance, that aimed at disturbing the centre of action, adjourning the union of the South with the North, prolonging the state of revolution while it made use of the king's name, making Naples the first stage of a series of conspiracies against Rome, Austria, and the peace of the whole of Europe.

So long as the revolution, triumphant in Sicily, had not crossed the Straits, the collision of the two policies was avoidable, or not of moment; an island in the Mediterranean circumscribed the problem. With the development of events, however, on the day when Garibaldi touched the continent, and finding nothing before him but a king and an army in flight, entered Naples, and, in the midst of an intoxicated people, suddenly became dictator of the two Sicilies and master of a kingdom, things underwent an extraordinary change. The question narrowed and showed its features; it was the more serious that, with a victor's confidence in himself, Garibaldi appeared less than ever disposed to listen to advice; and indeed it seemed as though nothing now could stop him.

Carried away by his own instinct, urged on by those about him, living in the exciting atmosphere of revolution and war, giving little heed to the anarchy he allowed to spread under his name at Naples and in the provinces, Garibaldi resembled a lunatic ready to burst forth. He did not conceal either his audacious projects or his animosity towards Cavour; and at that very time, in a conversation he held with Sir Henry Elliot, the English minister, who had gone to moderate and influence him, and endeavour in the name of England to dissuade him from pushing his enterprises farther, he showed his real colours. "I will," he said, "speak to you frankly, without hiding from you my intentions, which are just and clear. I purpose going as far as Rome. When we have become masters of that city, I will offer the crown of united Italy to Victor Emmanuel. It will be his business to set Venice free ; and in that war I will be no more than his lieutenant. . . . . In the present condition of Italy, the king cannot refuse to do this . without losing his popularity and his high position. Permit me to say, I am certain that in advising that Venice be left to her fate, Lord Russell does not faithfully render the opinion of the English people. . . . ." In vain Sir Henry Elliot endeavoured to dispel his illusions, by declaring to him that the English people, however much they might sympathise with Italy, would not forgive provocation to a European war : Garibaldi did not stick at such a trifle. " But," said Sir Henry Elliot, " have you made a fair reckoning, general, of all the contingencies likely to ensue from a collision between Italian arms and the French garrison at Rome ? If this takes place, it will immediately result in the intervention of France. It is the interest of your country to avoid that." At these words Garibaldi lost his equanimity, and exclaimed : " Well, then ! is not Rome an Italian city ? Napoleon has no sort of right to interfere with our possession of it. By the cession of Nice and Savoy, Cavour has dragged Sardinia through the mire, and thrown her at the Emperor's feet. I have no fear of France, and I would never have consented to so profound a humiliation. Whatever the obstacles— even if I should be in danger of losing all that I have gained—nothing shall stop me. There is no other road for me than the one to Rome ; nor do I believe the undertaking to be so very difficult : the unity of Italy must be accomplished !" And, as it were, drunken with his mad project, not content with speaking abusively of Cavour in a conversation with Sir Henry Elliot, Garibaldi wrote a flaming letter to one of his friends at Genoa, in which he declared that he could never be reconciled to those who had heaped humiliation on national dignity and sold an Italian province. He went further ; he sent one of his confidential friends to Turin to demand of Victor Emmanuel the dismissal of the ministers. He wrote to the king with an easy assurance : "Sire, send away Cavour and Farini ; give me the command of one brigade of your troops ; send me Pallavicino with full powers, and I will answer for everything." Another moment, and war would be declared in the midst of a tremendous anarchy ; this was the climax of the crisis.

The situation was fraught with every sort of danger. A march of the Southern volunteers upon Rome would lead fatally to French intervention, as Sir Henry Elliot had said ; and the intervention of France, in existing conditions, would change everything, even at Naples, where Francis II. still had forces enough to defend himself on the Volturno and at Gaeta, perhaps also in the recently-annexed provinces. Not only did Cavour perceive all the political consequences likely to follow upon so rank a piece of folly, but his very soul revolted against an antagonistic encounter between the Italians and the French ; for though not disposed to "abase the national dignity" to France, he had a profound belief in an alliance in the blood of the two countries; and more

—a strong feeling of all that Italy owed to the Emperor. Threats on the subject of Venice afforded too plausible a pretext to Austria, herself impatient to seize her opportunity, and occupied at the time in trying to win the support of Russia and Prussia. To put back the settlement of Neapolitan affairs, in order to press the claims of Venice and Rome; to adjourn the annexation of the Southern provinces, as Garibaldi proposed to do, was to throw the gates open to every passion, and superinduce a term of revolution and anarchy likely to threaten the safety of the Northern Kingdom itself. To yield to Garibaldi's orders, demanding the dismissal of ministers, or even one of them, was to degrade king, parliament, liberal institutions, and public authority beneath a military dictatorship. To do nothing was no longer possible.

VI.

What was to be done? Cavour was not beating about to comprehend the nature of the crisis, or to find a way out of it. For some days past he had written incessantly to his agents: "The critical moment has arrived! We are nearing the end; it must come up to our hopes, and answer the true interests of Italy!" Then it was that Cavour's hardy spirit had recourse to one of those resolutions by which a man who has reached the last extremity stakes all for all. He saw but one way of cutting the knot: boldly to take the initiative, and resume the direction of this movement about to go astray, by accepting the unity as far as it was realisable, treading down the revolution to stop it in its murderous follies, and so prevent it from compromising the national cause, perhaps irreparably. But to get the mastership in Naples, and to unite the North to the South, a way must be cut through Umbria and the Marches, and the Pontifical State enclosed; in its last hold, and in order to have the whip-hand of Garibaldi, strength of arms would not suffice—the moral strength of liberal institutions must be tellingly opposed to soldierly extravagance. Cavour determined upon two ways: the intervention and the convocation of parliament. He, too, whispered to himself the famous saying, *Andremo al fondo!* but in the meantime he laid his plans so that the independence of a fortified Italy should be plucked from this new crisis, and the monarchy of Savoy established more firmly than ever.

To accept the unity in full activity, as it were, in mid-career of conquest, and to act as though the revolution of Naples were a fact requiring only to be recorded, before Francis II. had fought his last battle; and, moreover, to cross the Marches up to the Neapolitan frontier, for the sake of holding Garibaldi from a move back to the North, or a mad dash on Rome, was an extraordinary proceeding. Cavour knew that well enough; regular methods were not to be thought of; and he bowed to international right, only to demand of it, with his peculiar air of self-possession, permission to outstep it. He felt absolved in doing so, only by the national necessity impelling him and by the transparently imminent danger. He required, besides, a mask for his undertakings; and it was here that the danger of these unreserved manifestations of hostility, and the armaments which the Roman Government had been preparing since the beginning of 1860, burst forth.

This fact had been lost sight of: that with the creation of an army comes the temptation to make use of it, especially with a chief burning to fight the enemy. It had been overlooked that the strength of the Papacy lay, as it has often been said, in its material weakness, and all that was being done was too little for serious military work, and too much for the part befitting the Holy See. Pius IX., with his profoundly religious instinct, felt it to be so. He had but a weak belief in the armaments. He sometimes looked on ironically, asking whether the lost provinces were to be reconquered by such means. Cardinal Antonelli, more affected by human considerations, felt it less. The warlike prelate and Minister of War, M. de Merode, had no such feeling. The compromising defenders of the temporal power had taken a pleasure in turning Rome into the camp of a militant Catholicism, and the meeting-place of that cosmopolitan army which roused the irritation of the Italians, and of which the leader of the Piedmontese Cabinet had foreseen the danger, six years previously. This was precisely the pretext he now availed himself of, by sending, as early as September 7, a summons to Cardinal Antonelli, bidding him "disarm those corps, the existence of which is a continual menace to Italian tranquillity."* He found another pretext in certain

* Human events sometimes reproduce themselves, after an interval of half a century, with startling analogies. Cavour had no idea how greatly his summary proceedings resembled those of Napoleon, in 1808, when he endeavoured to make General Miollis suddenly enter Rome. Napoleon wrote to his Minister of Foreign Affairs, M. de Champagny: "You must inform Alquier

deputations from Umbria and the Marches, who had hastened to Turin to ask the king's protection.

Cavour had no time to lose if he wished to outstrip Garibaldi, who had already reached Naples. He put everything to account, and in enforcing his summons with the threat of immediate military execution, he promptly furnished Europe with the word for what he was doing.

Piedmontese intervention thus became a guarantee against revolutionary excesses. The Venetian question, the settling of which time alone could bring about, was kept back, and every mark of respect bestowed on the Pope, who was reassured as to the integrity of the patrimony of St. Peter's. The organiser of the invasion of the Marches concluded by expressing, as he called it, " the conviction that the spectacle of the unanimity of the patriotic sentiments now bursting forth in the whole of Italy will remind the Sovereign Pontiff that he was, a few years ago, the sublime inspirer of this great national movement." He needed all his resources to emerge successfully from this new campaign.

In spite of all his explanation and assurances, Europe

that General Miollis, who commands my troops, and who appears to be directing his steps upon Naples, will stop at Rome; that he will assume the title of commander of the division of observation of the Adriatic. . . . . " Alquier, hearing of the arrival of the troops at the gates of Rome, was to hand to the Cardinal Secretary of State a note, ultimatum, or "summons," containing chiefly this order : ". . . . . That the assembling together of Neapolitan subjects which had taken place at Rome, be dispersed. . . . . " Napoleon went on to say : " As soon as this note has been delivered, Alquier will be careful to see that all is prepared for the reception of the army. . . . . The Emperor does not desire an extension of territory for his Italian States. . . . .; but he insists that the Pope shall be in his scheme. . . . . " Of course there was this difference in the two instances : Napoleon entered Rome, to convert it shortly into a French department ; Cavour entered Umbria and the Marches, Italian territory, to convert them into provinces of Italy.

could not but be stirred by such a *coup de théâtre*, and Austria might be tempted to find the occasion she sought. Cavour was prepared for it : he was prepared for everything. But before engaging himself he had taken the precaution of confiding his plans to France, and, at least apparently, consulting the Emperor. He had despatched Farini, the Minister of the Interior, and General Cialdini to meet the Emperor, who was passing by Chambéry. Napoleon III. did not utter the words so often attributed to him : *Fate presto!* He had listened in silence with a brooding look, perfectly understanding what was being done, recognising the sagacity of Cavour, but refusing to make promises or any engagement, and on the morrow of the interview at Chambéry he said once more : "If Piedmont thinks this absolutely necessary to save herself and Italy from an abyss of evil, be it so ; but it must be at her own risk and peril ; let her bear in mind that should she be attacked by Austria, France cannot support her. . . . ." He who had often dealt with the Emperor, and had often heard this language, and who was used to the reserves and indecisions of that complicated mind, found this enough. Cavour knew Napoleon III. well. He knew what had taken place at Rome on the subject of the formation of that very army which he was now about to disperse. He well knew the imprudence of all these semi-political, semi-religious manifestations which for some time had been taking place at the Vatican, whose aim was directed quite as much against the Empire as against Italy.*

* This was the period when, according to official diplomatic reports, visitors to the Vatican were questioned at the doors as to whether they were Bretons, and when it was triumphantly stated : "The Pope is receiving the homage of

Finally, he knew, having read it in the pamphlet called "The Pope and the Congress," that Napoleon III., by protecting the temporal power at Rome, and in the "Comarca," relinquished the Marches and the Romagna.

From that moment he knew beforehand to what extent French policy would consent to move; and with regard to the attack from Austria, of which the Emperor had spoken, he had foreseen the chance of it. He understood how much danger there would be in an Austrian attack at the time when Piedmontese divisions existed in the South. He was not asleep: he and certain Hungarians had already come to an understanding. He did his utmost to gather together the forces in Lombardy, and he wrote to La Marmora : "In the serious position of the country I am sure you will not think it strange in me to turn to you with the confidence I have always shown you since the days when we were colleagues and friends. . . . . I flatter myself that you will not refuse to lend your help to save the country from the dangers that may be menacing her. The invasion of the Marches, rendered necessary by the entry of Garibaldi into Naples, gives Austria a pretext for attacking us. France is aware of it, but she seems little inclined to oppose it with arms. We must rely only on ourselves. I admit that an aggressive movement on the part of Austria is not likely, it is true, for the internal condition of the empire would make it perilous

Brittany !" A citizen of Lyons who, though a fervent Catholic, did not think fit to repudiate his nationality, was told : "Sir, you must be the Pope's subject before being the subject of your king; if these be not the doctrines you profess, why are you here?" I recall the matter in order to show that Cavour, thoroughly alive to all that was going on, had some reason to think the Emperor's tone at Rome would necessarily be somewhat cool.

for her ; nevertheless it is not impossible." He calculated in his mind that France would not so easily detach herself from solid co-operation with Italy, and that in any case she would still have an interest in holding back Austria. He had at all events done what he could, and while he kept a watchful eye upon the Mincio, whence an attack might spring, he continued to negotiate with the Tuileries ; and he felt sure of England, for England at that very time was backing the intervention of Piedmont at Vienna, with singular vivacity. It is thus that he pressed forward.

VII.

"*Fate presto !*" Cavour did not need such a recommendation from the Emperor, which indeed would have been a strange one from him who gave it and to him who received it. The hardy politician was the first to know that promptitude, dexterity, and definiteness of aim could alone secure success. Even before the signal was given he had everything in readiness—he had temporarily assumed the management of the War Department, the Naval and Foreign Affairs. On the one hand he was hurrying the march of the relatively considerable, and intentionally considerable, army towards the frontier, to open the campaign under Generals Fanti and Cialdini. On the other hand he wrote to Persano as follows : " General Cialdini will enter the Marches, and direct his steps rapidly upon Ancona, but he cannot hope to make himself master of that place unless he is energetically seconded by our squadron. . . . . . Tell me what you think necessary for the success of this enterprise, and in what way you intend to carry it out. . . . ." This enterprise, skilfully prepared and promptly put into execution as early as September 11, was carried through in a startling manner, in a few brief days, by the joint efforts of the army and the fleet.

Protests instantly burst forth on all sides from Russia, Prussia, and France, each in turn recalling her ambassador. Cavour had a perfect escort of protests: he listened; he did not allow himself to be discomposed. He replied to Prussia's admonitions, conveyed to him by Count Brasier de Saint-Simon : "I am sorry that the Cabinet of Berlin should think fit so severely to judge the king's conduct and that of his Government. I am conscious of acting in accordance with the interests of my king and of my country. I could with advantage reply to all that M. de Schleinitz says, but, in any case, *on this occasion I console myself with the belief that I am setting an example which, probably some little time hence, Prussia may be very happy to follow.*" He scarce made any reply to France, not being anxious at the desire exhibited by the Cabinet of the Tuileries to get away from him. He had guessed what the Court of Rome at this moment either did not or affected not to perceive, which was that France might protest by the recall of her minister, but would go no farther; the Emperor would confine himself to protecting the Pope, and the patrimony of St. Peter in a strictly military arc. He left Cardinal Antonelli and French diplomacy to contend at Rome as to whether or no the Emperor had said that he would see himself "compelled to oppose

Piedmontese aggression," or whether he had said that he would "oppose it by force"—a grave question, which Cavour proposed to settle by success.

During this time, in fact, the Piedmontese army was cutting the knotty point. It is true that it was for a moment about to encounter a handful of men, joined together by honourable convictions, and headed by a chief who deserved a better fate; but what could Lamoricière do in the false position in which he was placed? He had no longer even his illusions left, for he had had a close view of the incurable disorders of Roman administration. He knew that he had no army fit to be brought face to face with a positive army. If he had believed for a moment or so what was told him about the intervention of France, he had soon been undeceived. His honour being engaged, he could still say with his soldierly vivacity and dash: "If we stand alone, God will fight for us; we will cry to him in the name of our right and our steel—to our trusty sword!" He could but gild with one last ray a defence broken by the shock of Castelfidardo. It expired in the square of Ancona, harassed by the army of Cialdini and the fleet of Persano; it was soon compelled by stress of arms to capitulate.

This done, the question of the Marches was settled. The Piedmontese army, reaching the Neapolitan frontier, remained mistress of the situation, and, strange to say, the unfortunate Francis II., no longer able to help himself, had just done Cavour a singular service without intending it, or even without knowing it. He had stopped Garibaldi on the Volturno; and it was fortunate ; for the terrible fellow, more obstinate than ever, might, had he not been prevented, have pushed on to Rome, and reached it before the arrival of the Piedmontese. This was no longer possible. Cavour saw Fortune smiling on his audacity in every direction, by the rapid conquest of the Marches, and by the resistance offered by the Neapolitan royalists.

The blow had been cleverly dealt, it is quite certain. If the military game was won, the political one was still more triumphantly so ; and I venture to say that if, in this matter of the invasion of the Marches, there is a character of violence and subterfuge from which bold men, struggling against the difficulties of a hazardous situation, do not always shrink, the political and parliamentary side of it showed loftiness of mind and liberal confidence in this powerful and subtle nature. In the thick of this tangle of troubles and conflicts, Cavour was urged on every side to assume the dictatorship, or at least to demand full power in parliament. He was deaf to all suggestions of the sort : and as one day, during his deepest embarrassment, Madame de Circourt communicated to him the contents of a letter, from a personage of high position, who proposed a similar expedient, he replied :

" I am greatly flattered by the opinion your illustrious friend entertains about me, but I cannot share it. He too greatly mistrusts the influence of liberty, and he relies far too much on the influence I possess. For my part I have no confidence in dictatorships, especially civil ones. I believe that many things can be done with a parliament which are impossible with an absolute power.

Thirteen years' experience has convinced me that an honest and energetic minister, who has nothing to fear from revelations of the tribune, and who is not in a humour to allow himself to be intimidated by the violence of extreme parties, can only gain by parliamentary struggles. I never felt so weak as when the Chambers were closed. Besides, I must be true to my nature; I cannot be false to the principles I have held all my life. I am a son of liberty, and it is to her that I owe all that makes me what I am. If a veil had to be put on her statue, it is not I who would consent to do it. If the Italians could be persuaded that they need a dictator, they would choose Garibaldi, and not me, and they would be right! The parliamentary road is the longest, but it is also the surest. . . . ."

The idea of Cavour, in political life, was that of a great liberal—of the greatest of liberals—knowing how to invent expedients if necessary; but giving the chief place to that policy which was the secret of his strength, and which, with a sort of audacity, he practised to the end. What he said to Madame de Circourt, in the form of a friendly and homely confidence, he repeated with greater energy and deeper intent, more keenly defining the situation, and giving a sharper outline to the nature and conditions of the Italian movement, of which he had to be the leader. It was to Salvagnoli, of Florence, that he wrote: ". . . . . You remember how greatly the English papers blamed the Italians for suspending constitutional guarantees during the last war. To renew this measure now, in a moment of apparent peace, would have a fatal effect on public opinion in England, and on all the liberal papers of the Continent. It would not bring concord to the national party in the interior. The best way of showing how far the country is from sharing Mazzini's ideas, and the animosities of certain others, is to leave parliament full liberty of censure and control. The favourable vote of the great majority of deputies will give the ministry far greater power and authority than any form of dictatorship. Your advice would only carry out Garibaldi's idea, which tends to establish a great revolutionary dictatorship, to be exercised in the name of the king, without the control of a free press, and without individual or parliamentary guarantees. On the contrary, I am convinced that it will not be Italy's smallest title to glory that she has known how to constitute herself into a nation without sacrificing liberty to independence, and without passing through the dictatorial hands of a Cromwell, keeping aloof from monarchical absolutism without falling into revolutionary despotism. Now there is no other means of attaining this end than by asking parliament for the only moral force capable of overcoming factions and preserving the sympathies of liberal Europe for us. A return to committees of public safety, or what comes to the same, to one or more revolutionary dictatorships, would be to smother legal liberty at her birth; and it is legal liberty that we want, as being the inseparable companion of national independence."

Thus he spoke both in public and in private, aiming, through liberty, and legal powers in the bosom of liberty, to solve the most complex as well as the simplest questions, and making the parliamentary *régime* the most persuasive instrument of moderation or the fullest means of action. It was with this view that from the beginning of his conflict with Garibaldi he had decided on the convocation of the Chambers; and on the day that parliament met at Turin, early in October, while the crisis in the South was still proceeding, he used no subterfuge, nor did he consent to envenom or cloak the conflict. He defined the whole situation : the necessity of calling on the Southern provinces to declare their wishes as to annexation, and to close the revolutionary state of things by the definitive creation of a kingdom of twenty-two millions of Italians; and he dwelt on the seriousness of this new fact, of the intervention of "a man justly precious to his country" exhibiting a lack of confidence in the Cabinet. "A profound breach," he says, " exists between us and General Garibaldi : we did not provoke it. . . . . What could the ministers do ? Pass on without even knowing whether or no parliament shared Garibaldi's ideas on the subject of his policy ? If we had done that, we should with reason have been blamed for not taking parliament into consultation on so critical a matter. . . . . Resign ? If the crown had come to changing her councillors at the demand of a citizen, however illustrious and meritorious he might be, it would deal a death-blow to our constitutional system. . . . . We could not but call parliament together, and we did so. . . . . It was for parliament to decide. . . . . If your vote is against us, the ministerial crisis will take place, but in conformity with great constitutional principles. If it is in our favour, it will act on the generous soul of Garibaldi.

We are convinced that he will have faith in the representatives of the nation rather than in bad citizens, whose miserable work it is to put division between men that have long and persistently struggled for the national cause. . . . ." The discussion ended with an almost unanimous vote of confidence in the Government, accompanied by a not less unanimous one of admiration of Garibaldi, which the minister was very careful not to oppose.

The victory, therefore, both moral and political, was Cavour's, leaning on parliament; and Garibaldi himself, it must be admitted, did not assume the air of a rebel. He no longer contested the immediate annexation sanctioned by vote; he hastened to go to meet the king, who entered Naples with him. And if, in starting suddenly, almost covertly, to return to Caprera, he concealed a secret wound; if he did not lay aside his ill-feeling, and mentally resolve to reappear some day, his momentary retirement at least testified both to his disinterestedness and his simplicity of character. What followed—the final resistance of Francis II. at Gaeta, and the troubles immediately following upon a revolution—was but the epilogue of the drama. The Neapolitan question was settled, and Piedmontese intervention had gained its point.

VIII.

On the day when new parliamentary elections had just taken place in all the provinces, and when the new parliament met at Turin to inaugurate the existence of the kingdom of Italy, a curious scene was taking place on the Piazza di Castello. Old Manzoni, notwithstanding his advanced age and enfeebled condition, had insisted upon making the journey from Milan to Turin in order to be present at what he called the coronation of Italy. An excited crowd surrounded the palazzo Madama where the parliamentary debates were taking place, when suddenly Manzoni appeared leaning on the arm of Cavour. Applause immediately burst from the crowd, while the minister turned to the poet, saying : " This is intended for you ! " The old poet quickly withdrew his arm in order to clap his hands, pointing to Cavour. The enthusiastic acclamations of the crowd became greater, and Manzoni exclaimed with pride : " Well, Signor Conte, do you see now for whom this applause is intended ? " Both minister and poet may have at that moment called to mind the first meeting between them, ten years previously, at the house of Rosmini, the villa Bolongaro, when Cavour said, while he rubbed his hands ; " We will do something ! " He had assuredly turned time to account in those ten years, for representatives of Naples, Turin, Milan, Palermo, Brescia, Florence, Bologna, and Genoa were that day assembled in parliament. " Something " had indeed been done, and that " something " exhibited itself in an outburst of popular enthusiasm for one man. Yet, even with the prodigious annexation just accomplished, much remained to do. Not only had Cavour laboriously to pursue the work of pacification in the Southern provinces, and maintain before Europe a position always difficult and perilous, he had also to shape and direct his policy under the very eyes of foreign diplomacy, and place himself, as it were, on a solid footing with regard to two questions constantly in agitation, and which henceforth stood out like two formidable problems, before united but incomplete Italy : Venice and Rome ! One of these questions, the Venetian question, was still the sorest wound, owing to the Austrian dominion left beyond the Mincio; the other was a great moral question, and more than a territorial one. Both were in reality as difficult to settle as to evade, and Cavour only emerged from one crisis to find himself face to face with tasks more than ever thorny and delicate. With the help of a little revolution and a little fighting, Naples and the Marches had been carried ; to go to Venice and Rome with an army of red-shirted volunteers and noisy manifestations was not possible. Garibaldi alone thought it so; and the situation became the more serious that it was no longer a time to stake all for all, or risk in new adventures the existence of a kingdom of twenty-two millions of Italians, and Italian unity, scarcely as yet more than nominally acquired—still unfinished.

Cavour, we may well believe, had the freedom of Venice at heart as warmly as Garibaldi ; he could not forget Venice, for it was in her behalf that he so violently burst out after Villafranca, almost causing a rupture with the Emperor ; nor could he lose sight of the dangers which an act of imprudence might at any moment provoke on the Mincio, and he was resolved not to commit it or allow it to be committed. To him it was henceforth a matter of leadership, an opportunity in which he sought, as he always did, to have the mind of the country with him, and not to deceive it. " However strong may be our love for Venice—that great martyr," he said, " we must admit that war with Austria at this moment would be impossible ; impossible because Europe will not suffer it. I know that there are men who think little of the opposition of Cabinets. I do not. I would remind them that to run counter to the wishes of the Powers has ever been fatal to princes and people. Great catastrophes have resulted from too great a contempt for the feelings of other nations." When asked how, then, he meant to solve the Venetian question, he would reply that Europe must be brought round; opposition springing from Governments only must be disarmed ; this last illusion of a possible reconciliation between the Venetians and Austria must be dispelled ; and, finally, it must be shown that the Italians, after constituting themselves into a nation, were capable of being organised and formed into a solid State based on the will of the people. " Then," he exclaimed, " the opinion of Europe will change. . . . . When the truth can no longer be seriously contested, the fate of Venice will awaken immense sympathy, not only in generous France and in just-minded England, but in noble Germany. I believe a time is not far distant when the greater part of Germany will no longer consent to be an accomplice in heaping misfortunes on Venice. When this occurs we shall be on the eve of deliverance. Will this deliverance take place through the agency of arms or negotiations ? Providence alone can decide upon that."

We see that Cavour gave himself time to take counsel with circumstances, though he well knew that at any moment the Viennese Cabinet might be tempted to bring matters to a sudden termination, and he held himself in readiness for what might happen. The Venetian question was as yet relatively simple. The Roman question was far more complex : it affected everything, from the very constitution of Italian unity by the choice of a capital, to the beliefs, interests, and traditions of the Catholic world through the Temporal Power ; and by the prolonged presence of a French garrison at Rome it affected the most intimate relations with France. It was at once a national and universal, a religious and diplomatic question : and it is here that Cavour displayed indeed the powers of a mind marvellously penetrating and clear, showing himself a master in the art of contriving and combining, absolutely free from vulgar prejudice, and pursuing, by the aid of Liberalism, the solution of an apparently insoluble problem.

IX.

This Roman question, which he had so often met with for the last twenty years, and could not fully face when he was only the representative of little Piedmont, he again encountered as minister of united Italy ; and the business he had to settle was in reality nothing less than a complete transformation of the political conditions of the Papacy. He had one advantage which belonged to his liberal and open mind, and it had often come to his assistance in all these delicate religious affairs. He had no animosity or prejudice of any sort as regards the Church : it is true that he looked upon the Temporal Power as lost; he thought it as incompatible with Italian nationality as it was little favourable to religion; he spoke of it openly and temperately, like one with a great problem to solve, no sectarian passions to appease; and precisely because he looked abroad from the height of a lofty policy, he was able to accept whatever was in harmony with his object in view, and eager to offer the Church the fullest compensation in liberty and independence for her lost Temporal Power. One day, about this period, he wrote to a confidential friend: "There are to my mind two methods; the one above board, the other secret. The first would be resolutely to submit the matter to the public judgment: for instance, if I or another member of the Cabinet, or the king himself, were officially to declare, either in public speech or before parliament, the views of the Government in relation to religious affairs. The second would be to despatch a secret agent to Rome, whose presence would be unknown to our adversaries, and Antonelli among them: this agent to have the fullest confidence of the Government, in a manner to impress the belief that he is the bearer, and may be the receiver of serious proposals." Cavour made use of both these methods alternately, sometimes simultaneously, as a man who joined to a purely logical mind the rarest flexibility in practical issues.

It should be understood that even in the sharpest of these struggles and crises Cavour was not long without having secret dealings with Rome. Early in 1860 the king's private chaplain, Abbate Stellardi, had been sent to the Pope, with the mission to propose a Vicariat stretching to Umbria and the Marches, as well as over the Legations. Pius IX. listened suavely, and with some show of emotion; he went so far as to discuss certain points, and ended by refusing his consent. When the Marches were being overrun, or shortly afterwards, Cavour, instead of envenoming the breach, did his utmost to moderate the wrath of Rome. He gave orders for the unconditional release of the prisoners, and wrote, towards the end of October, to Dr. Pantaleoní, a friend of his established in Rome : " I send a person to Rome deputed to yield up the captured gendarmes. The same person is commissioned to inquire whether the Holy Father begins to perceive the necessity of coming to an understanding with us, which the Roman Court will do well to do, and by which its spiritual independence will be far better assured than by foreign arms." The same idea had struck Dr. Pantaleoni, and of this came a secret negotiation, continuing up to the close of 1860 and the first weeks of 1861, Father Passaglia speedily becoming associated with it.

Other negotiations were concurrent; the one conducted by Dr. Pantaleoni was the main one. Cavour concealed nothing from the Emperor, who had his own projects, but ended by joining the mysterious business in hand. What was the aim of it? The Temporal Power was quietly to be swept away. The Pope remained sovereign with all sovereign prerogatives, rights, inviolability, and honours; with a large patrimony in real estate in the kingdom, and absolute ownership of the Vatican and other palaces and residences. The Church became completely free and independent in its spiritual ministry.

The State renounced all rights of intervention in the affairs of the Church. It was the notable treaty of peace long dreamed of by Cavour, and summed up in his famous phrase : " A free Church in a free State."

How far was the Court of Rome serious in this negotiation ? At all events it seemed at one time to lend an ear to it. Father Passaglia was the most active intermediary between Rome and Turin ; Cardinal Santucci accepted the office of negotiator. One and the other had interviews with the Pope, who listened to them, insomuch that Cavour one day received the following despatch at Turin : " Cardinal Santucci has thought fit to tell the Pope everything ; he has spoken to him of the certain loss of the Temporal Power, and the friendly propositions that have been made. The Holy Father has shown himself resigned. Antonelli has been summoned ; he began with a lively opposition, then became equally resigned, and requested the Pope to absolve him and Santucci from the oath, that they might treat of the possible surrender of the Temporal possessions. They are to see Passaglia, and the latter asks me on their behalf for someone to be indicated here or sent from Turin to negotiate. It is desired that the person selected be not a lawyer." The telegraph was immediately at work to carry the news to the Emperor, who, to tell truth, while anxious for success, seemed to have little hope of it. Cavour, of course, could scarcely flatter himself that he was so near his ends ; still, he thought he perceived a door open ; he redoubled his efforts ; he designated the negotiators that had been asked of him, and wrote to Father Passaglia : " I entertain the belief that before next Easter you will be able to send me the olive branch, symbol of peace between the Church and the State—between the Papacy and the Italians. . . . ." And what occurred ?   At the moment when the first step to a negotiation seemed to be made, the whole aspect of things changed.   Either it was that Cardinal Antonelli had only appeared to yield in order the better to master the designs of his enemies and find the means of combating them, or else that his hope of evading the necessity had revived, and he believed he saw symptoms of coming events in Europe, signs of a possible intervention of the Catholic Powers.

A final attempt had evidently been risked to hold back the Pope, half inclining to reconciliation.   In any case, Cardinal Antonelli lost no time in cutting the threads of the projected arrangement; and he went so far as to give orders to Dr. Pantaleoni to quit the Roman States within four-and-twenty hours !   The intrigues of the foes of peace triumphed for the time : everything was in suspense.   Cavour had not succeeded by the " secret means ;" he had the " public means " to try—the parliament; and he found occasion in due course in an interpellation addressed to him on the affairs of Rome, in March, 1861.   This opportune interpellation was for him but another manner of taking up and continuing the negotiation in the light of day, in the face of Italian and universal opinion, and frankly avowing to its full extent— I might add, in its grandeur—the policy whose realisation he had never ceased to prosecute.

He had said in parliament : " The star now directing us is this, that the Eternal City, upon which twenty centuries have cast glory of all kinds, should become the capital of the kingdom of Italy." What he had already said he confirmed, with more precision and breadth, in the month of March, 1861. Cavour certainly was not one to be led astray by imagination and artistic enthusiasm. He confesses, with some humorous modesty, that for his part he preferred the plain straight streets of his native town to all the monuments of Rome. He loved Turin; it was not without regret that he thought of sacrificing it; and he was led to exclaim: "Ah! if only Italy could have two capital cities: one for Sundays, the other for the days of the week!" His resolution was taken entirely on political grounds, because the name and majesty of Rome alone could dominate the rivalries of Italian cities, and so put the definitive stamp on unity; and he considered it was of prime necessity to let Europe know that Rome was looked on by the whole nation as vitally the capital of the country. "No city but Rome," he cried, "can be the capital of Italy; but here we come upon the perplexities of the problem. We must go to Rome, but on two conditions: that we are acting in concert with France, and that the great body of Catholics in Italy and elsewhere do not see in the reunion of Rome with Italy the source of the subjection of the Church. In other words, we go to Rome, but not to restrict the independence of the Sovereign Pontiff—not to bring spiritual things under the yoke of civil authority. . . . . ."

X.

Unquestionably the task was not a light one; neither was it an impossible one as regarded France. He said plainly: "It would be madness, in the present state of Europe, to think of going to Rome in spite of France. . . . . . We owe France a great debt of gratitude; but there is a graver motive for being in harmony with her. When, in 1859, we called France to our aid, the Emperor did not conceal from us the engagements by which he was bound to the Court of Rome. We accepted his assistance without protesting against the particular obligations he had imposed on himself; and now that we have won so much from this alliance, we cannot protest against the engagements to which, up to a certain point, we have consented." There was but one way of disengaging France, and quieting with her the whole Catholic world; and it was by giving the Church what a pretended Temporal Power—painfully sustained for twenty years by foreign arms, incapable of supporting itself or regenerating itself by reforms— could not give it: this was by establishing the dignity with the independence of the Sovereign Pontiff and of the Church by the separation of the two powers, a large application of the principle of liberty in relation to civil and to religious society. "It is clear," he pursued, "that if this separation were distinctly and irrevocably accomplished, if the independence of the Church were thus established, the independence of the Pope would be much more securely based than it is to-day. His authority would be more efficacious, being no longer bound by concordats, and all those bonds and treaties which have been and must remain indispensable so long as the Pope is a temporal sovereign. The authority of the Pope, far from diminishing, will be greatly extended in the spiritual sphere which is his own." If it was but a mighty hope, and if they were not to succeed at the first stroke, let there be no discouragement, and let it not fail to be reiterated : "Whether or not an understanding with the Pope precedes our entrance into the Eternal City, Italy will no sooner have declared the fall of the Temporal Power than she will separate Church and State, and establish the liberty of the Church on the broadest foundations."

Cavour sincerely believed what he said, and he believed what he asked was in the interests of the Church as well as in the interests of Italy. One day, when his intimate friend, Signor Artom, was expressing his doubts and fears, he exclaimed with his kindling vivacity : " I have more faith than you in the effects of liberty. Do you not see that the time has come to settle the question of the Temporal Power, which has ever been the stumbling-block in the way of Italian nationality, and that the only way of settling it is to reassure the Catholic world as to what Italy will do with the Papacy ? Injustice is done to Catholicism, when it is urged that it is incompatible with liberty. On the contrary, my conviction is, that as soon as the Church shall have tasted liberty, she will feel herself renewed in youth by that wholesome and fortifying regimen. When Europe shall have been convinced that we are not striving against Catholicism, she will find it natural and fitting that the

Italian rather than any other flag should float over Rome. The enterprise is not easy, but it is worth being attempted." More than any other, Cavour was made to attempt it. He had not yet succeeded, it is true; but after disentangling a revived Italy from her disorders and divisions, he had marked on the horizon a final aim, while shaping the road to reach it. He himself had touched the supreme point in human destiny, when a man made powerful by freedom, begirt by a solid popularity, though still with struggles before him, can only be stopped by death surprising him in harness, and in the hour of victory.

CHAPTER VII.

THE FINAL VICTORY OF A POLICY—DEATH AND LEGACY OF CAVOUR.

I.

To have shaped a reality out of a dream ; to have succeeded in leading the revolution of a partly-enslaved
people almost to the farthest limit, without suffering it
to run to wreck in convulsions, by covering it before
Europe with the mantle of a traditional monarchy—such
was the fortune of Cavour early in 1861.

What the bold Piedmontese had accomplished up to
that time, he had not done unaided. Had he not met
with many favourable circumstances on his way ; many
propitious conditions—a European situation lending
itself singularly to adventurous daring ; a small country
forming a firm and vigorous instrument of action ; a
soldierly and patriotic king ; concurrence of opinion and

national sentiment; auxiliaries of every kind seconding his designs, either skilfully or audaciously—had he not met with all this, he could not have succeeded. His genius was shown in his power of combining these many elements, and in handling them with a profound knowledge of the secret springs of policy; and if he was successful to the end, it was because he knew how to lay out his work ahead. In fact, that which had lately occurred—this last act of the drama enacted at Ancona and at Naples—was after all but the crowning event, itself perhaps somewhat precipitate and unexpected, of the scheme which for twelve years had been developing itself in successive widening circles from Novara to the Crimean war; from the congress at Paris, to the war of 1859; from the peace of Villafranca, to the annexation and final unification. The unity of Italy, springing to life ultimately in a whirlwind—it might almost be said, a victory over revolutionary passions as well as over Bourbons and the Pope—had become now and henceforward a living fact. It comprised Italy, from the Alps to the Adriatic, except Venice and Rome, the two immovable points before which it must halt for a time. Italy had her king, her army, her parliament, and her chancellor. The thing was done, and though, like many others, elated by so prodigious a transformation, Cavour himself could not be ignorant of the fact, that all was not as yet accomplished. He knew that, following the romance and adventure, the entire political business remained to be taken up and settled, and it was a thorny and complicated business : thus, amid the victor's cares, never doubting of the future, but putting away illusions, he wrote : " My task is even more laborious and painful than it used to be. To build up Italy, to blend the divers elements of which she is composed, and harmonise the North with the South, presents as many difficulties as does a war with Austria and the struggle with Rome. . . . ."

II.

The question was in fact exceedingly serious. Knowing what others did not know, and with an eye fixed on Europe as well as on Italy, Cavour could not be deceived, and he lost not a moment in fitting himself either to overcome or evade the difficulties of every kind surrounding him.

The first of these was the probable collision with Austria openly defied. The situation of Italy relative to Austria was perilous when the annexation of Tuscany or Romagna was at stake ; it became very much more so when the whole of Italy united under the influence of an ardent passion of nationality, and Venice became the watchword. Morally speaking, war had begun through the violation of all treaties, and by the very nature of that Italian revolution of which every step threatened the imperial power on the Mincio and on the Adige. Hostilities might commence at any moment ; Austria might take advantage of the Southern crisis, and more than once in those cruel moments of suspense Cavour had feared that she would. Towards the end of 1860 he wrote, not without some emotion, to Madame de Circourt : " We may perhaps be severely tried. It seems as if Austria meant to take advantage of the absence of the king and of all our divisions to attack us. We are preparing to oppose her to the uttermost. Cialdini and Fanti are at Naples, but we have here La Marmora and Sonnaz, and they are not men to be intimidated. We are ready to stake all for all. The country is as calm as though the sky were cloudless; it knows the danger but does not fear it, for it also knows the cause to be great enough to warrant any sacrifice. . . . ."

Austria, it is true, had remained motionless; she had been unable to obtain either from Russia or Prussia the support and encouragement she had hoped to gather from an interview then famous—the interview of Warsaw; and on the other hand she was made dubious by the enigmatical attitude of the Cabinet of the Tuileries, as well as by the protection France was in any case bound to extend over Lombardy. She stood to her arms, nevertheless, ready to enter on a campaign, resolved not to fail in her steps forward if the fault of an attack on her were committed: in reality, perhaps anxious for a pretext, if it were only some rashness on the part of the Italian volunteers, which she might have made good use of before Europe. Cavour warily avoided furnishing the pretext; he was, on the contrary, especially vigilant in preventing anything that might have worn a semblance of an armed aggression. After having feared that he himself would be attacked, he was not long in detecting the Austrian game. "It is evident," he wrote in March, 1861, to Count Vimercati, at Paris, "that Austria seeks a provocation: we will not do her the particular service."

At this critical moment Cavour was chiefly solicitous to keep Austria in good humour without yielding to her, while leaving the Venetian question in some sort open, without wildly and prematurely rushing to meet a contest that might prove mortal for Italy. In order to succeed, Cavour had not only to make use of the wariest prudence towards Austria, he had to clear away all the suspicions and prejudices that were roused in Europe by recent events : in a word, to reconcile all policies to the idea of Italian unity and the existence of a new Power. With England this was not difficult. The English Cabinet was the protector and backer of Italy, so long as Italy engaged not to attack Austria on the Mincio, thus giving the signal for a European war. Russia and Prussia had evinced their displeasure by an open rupture, and by the recalling of their ministers from Turin : with them the task was not so easy. Notwithstanding all this, Cavour did not relinquish the hope of calming the two Northern Powers, at least Prussia, whose secret ambition he always contrived to flatter, trusting sooner or later to win her over to his cause. He had been wise enough not to attach too great an importance to the rupture ; he only looked for a good opportunity to renew an amicable understanding with Prussia ; and accordingly in the early part of 1861, when the Prince Regent—the future Emperor William—was about to assume the Crown, Cavour despatched La Marmora with a special mission to Berlin.

This act of royal courtesy from Victor Emmanuel towards the Prussian sovereign was really only a cloak for the renewal, after the war and annexations, of Marquis

Pepoli's mission before the war of 1859. Cavour sought to reassure Prussia as to his pacific intentions, persuading her that this Venetian question, which troubled her, had nothing of the importance regarding German frontier defences that artful Austria sought to attach to it. La Marmora was especially charged to reiterate, in all his conversations at Berlin, that the two Governments had common interests, that they both drew their strength from the national idea they had in view; that a united Italy could never be other than a natural and useful ally to Prussia, destined to create and support the hegemony of Germany.

King William had not yet had time to become accustomed to the views that another bold hand was about to open to him "with fire and sword." He received La Marmora with courtesy, but said not a word of the events which had recently taken place beyond the Alps. Baron Von Schleinitz, the Minister of Foreign Affairs, complacently pursued the conversation, in a tone half sympathetic and half reserved, expressive of the undecided attitude of Prussia. "No doubt," he said, "there is between Piedmont and Prussia a striking analogy; but we cannot approve everything that you have done. I admit that in the critical situation in which you were placed, you could scarcely do otherwise. We, for our part, have thwarted you as little as possible. As to Venice, and her unfortunate condition, rest assured that we have no intention of throwing oil on the fire, should Austria sooner or later show herself disposed to relinquish it; but in that case we must come to an understanding how best to secure the interests of Germany on the

Adriatic. . . . . I understand your wish that Prussia should acknowledge the kingdom of Italy ; do not put a knife to our throats, and we will do all in our power to keep on good terms with the Government of Turin. We leave it to Count Cavour's keen-sighted wisdom to afford us the opportunity for doing more." It was all that Cavour wanted ; in leaving to the future what the future was actually to bring forth, he had for the moment succeeded, since he perceived at once Prussia less hostile and Austria more isolated.

III.

Another element in this still uncertain and always perilous situation, and another source of perplexity, was Rome : a question affecting everything ; affecting Italy in the definite construction of her unity ; France in the protection with which she covered the Papacy ; and Europe and the Catholic world as to the independence of the Pontiff. Cavour felt the weight and measured the difficulties of all these things. " I do not conceal from you," he wrote about this time, " that even in my moments of busiest occupation, my thoughts are always centred on the Roman question. . . . ."

At the point reached by Italian affairs, Cavour could not put aside that problem of " Rome for the capital," and the Temporal Power of the Pope, imposed upon him by the irresistible logic of events, and which the re-volutionary passions, heated by Garibaldi's call, might turn into a formidable weapon and a plan of action. At the same time, he well knew that he dared not deal with what remained of the Temporal Power, with Rome and the patrimony of St. Peter as he had done with the Romagna, Umbria, or the Marches —he knew that he must not attempt or sanction any surprise *vi et armis* in the presence of Catholic Europe disquieted and France encamped in the Eternal City. Cavour had a profound consciousness of these difficulties, which might prove a stumbling-block to the unity he sought; and to make head against a situation so entangled, he became doubly energetic and wary, not excluding any transaction compatible with the national integrity. Scarcely emerged from the great Southern crisis, he was tentatively pushing at Rome, about the person of the Pope, those mysterious advances which he did not despair of bringing to a good issue. While diplomatising with the cardinals, he took advantage of the full light of parliamentary debates, to lay his schemes of liberal policy before Italian and European opinion, nor did he limit himself to this. He was at the same moment giving his whole attention to a private negotiation with France, in order to obtain from the Emperor the recognition of the kingdom of Italy, and, by a new application of the principle of non-intervention, the recall of the French garrison at Rome.

It would have been a decided success for Cavour, and a step towards the realisation of that portion of his programme by which he declared that nothing should be done but what was in agreement with France at Rome, and to this end he did not refuse the guarantees claimed of him. Here was one more phase in the everlasting diplomacy between Turin and Paris. Prince Napoleon was the agent in this secret negotiation. In the earlier days of April, 1861, he communicated to Cavour the Emperor's views on the subject of Roman affairs as follows: "The Emperor, who has occupied Rome for twelve years, will not consent that the withdrawal of his troops should be interpreted as a giving of the lie to his policy; and as the beating a retreat before this unity of Italy, effected independently of his wishes; but he desires to withdraw his soldiers from Rome to be free of a false position. It is of the greatest importance to the Italian Government that this act should take place; it behoves it, therefore, to overlook all secondary and temporary difficulties in the matter. The policy of non-intervention applied to Rome and the patrimony of St. Peter might serve as the basis of a common accord. The Pope being considered as an independent sovereign, France could withdraw her garrison from Rome without affording Austria the opportunity of taking her place; the Italian Government, on its part, would enter into an engagement with France, not only to abstain from hostilities with the Pontifical Government, but also to prevent any armed attack either from Garibaldi's volunteers or other Italians. . . . . Without recognising the Pope's right to have recourse to foreign intervention, the Emperor will probably require that the Italian Government should grant the Pontifical Government the right to organise a Catholic army of foreigners, on the condition of that army being a defensive force, and deprived of the power of becoming a means of offence against Italy. To you the immense advantage of this understanding is that it will give you an immediate opportunity of renewing your diplomatic relations with France, considering that Austria may recommence hostilities at any instant, and you will see Rome liberated of a foreign garrison. . . . ."

Cavour, on his part, hastened to reply: "I confess that in the first instance I was alarmed at the difficulties and dangers presented by the execution of the plan to which the Emperor might consent, that we may come to a provisional solution of the Roman question. The promises we should have to make, and the probable condition of Rome after the departure of the French troops, place us in a most equivocal position before the country, parliament, the Romans, and especially before Garibaldi; but when only two courses are open to us, we must choose the least dangerous, whatever the precipices lying in our way. I have not been long in convincing myself that we ought to accept the proposals made to us; alliance with France being the basis of our policy, there is no sacrifice I would not be disposed to make, that the alliance should not be questioned. . . . ." The two confederates of Plombières, though they had one momentary rupture, more apparent than it was serious, always felt attracted towards one another; they found themselves in harmony again as to the new condition of Rome, and the remains of the Temporal Papacy in the midst of a united Italy. This was virtually the origin, as it were the first sketch, of a combination that did not become an act of official diplomacy until three years later, but which was being arranged by Cavour and Napoleon III. in the months of excitement and alarm beginning 1861.

IV.

But this was only a part of the difficulties brought about by the new situation. The more serious and immediate complication was in the interior—at Naples, in those southern provinces suddenly annexed to the North. I am not even alluding to the defence of Francis II. at Gaeta, the final resistance of a young and unfortunate sovereign, prolonging the struggle for nearly four months, as if to afford to Europe time to come forward to his assistance. The Bourbon standard, fixed on the rock of Gaeta until February 13, 1861, represented but a vanquished cause.

There was less difficulty in this military protest, without response or hope as it was, than in the moral condition of this southern country, suddenly given up to a kind of stormy transition, and the disorganisation of a revolutionary interregnum. As long as the annexation extended only to such regions as Lombardy, Tuscany, the Romagna, or Parma, it was easy. But representing, as it then did, an entire kingdom, separated from the North by manners, customs, and traditions—the passionate, clever, mobile, and exuberant Neapolitans formed at the extremity of Italy an ungovernable mass, rebellious to any assimilation. Every element of anarchy accumulated under a demoralising system was bursting out. In the bosom of unbounded liberty, each party naturally took advantage of the fanaticism, the passions, and disorderly instincts of an impressionable population, easily set against laws, taxes, and the whole new order of things. A veritable system of brigandage was organised, with a political cloak to it, by the defenders of the fallen *régime.* Mazziniism, on the other hand, took up the name of Garibaldi; to make the southern provinces the centre of its agitations. In vain the Cabinet of Turin tried to govern this chaos by sending a succession of lieutenants—first Farini, then the Prince of Carignano, with Cavaliere Nigra; next Signor Ponza di San Marttino; these excited, turbulent, and undisciplined rather than hostile southern provinces continued an anarchical riddle to the Piedmontese who succeeded one another at Naples. The South threatened to become another Ireland in a scarcely constituted kingdom, so that Cavour was brought face to face with every external and internal complication of an unfinished work.

He might well say that he had not yet the right to rest on his oars, or be satisfied with his conquest. He had simultaneously to negotiate the accession of a new Italy with Europe, to fix his policy in Venice and Rome, to continue to quiet the southern provinces, assimilate the legislation and administration of all these different provinces, reorganise the army of the new kingdom, and unite six or seven budgets into one, which from the very first presented a deficit of 500 millions of francs!

Sometimes, notwithstanding his natural vitality and vigour, he fell into indescribable apprehensions, asking himself whether he could carry out this absorbing work on which he was bestowing his activity and his life; but he soon took courage again. He braced himself against the difficulties which assailed him, and which proceeded from divisions, personal resentments, things, and men, in turn—often from men in the highest position ; and from those many questions of organisation which he directed and settled in the midst of absolute liberty, for he would consent neither to a dictatorship, to simplify the work of unification, nor a state of siege to pacify Naples.   It was through discussion that he hoped to succeed, though the trials in store for him should be heavy. His strength was in the parliament and in the confidence of the country, in his immense influence on the popular mind, and the gatherings of the elect of the nation, the liberals who rallied to his views. His weakness consisted in a situation still unsettled and undecided, where all might be wrecked by some ill-regulated outburst, or the daring of some popular leader ; a condition of things in which incandescent passions, especially in the South, might rush headlong into some adventure in the direction of Rome or Venice, and ruin in a mad enterprise schemes of the most far-sighted policy.

What was wanted to revive a struggle such as that which Cavour had sustained with Garibaldi, in October, 1860 ?   Perhaps only a pretext, any unforeseen incident ; and neither pretexts nor incidents were wanting in the spring of 1861—one of those stormy springs of that period which, to use Lord Palmerston's expression, " came in like lions." The pretext of the moment was the dissolution or reorganisation of the army of the South, that is to say of those volunteers who had gone through the campaigns of Sicily and Naples with Garibaldi.   So irregular a force evidently could not be allowed to subsist, good as it was at best either for an adventure like the Sicilian expedition, or any such time of high national enthusiasm. General Fanti, the Minister of War, would not have it, in the interests of the army ; and in the interests of diplomacy, Cavour could not consent to retain it. Great consideration was shown. Generals, who proved worthy of their rank, were made of officers like Nino Bixio, Cozenz, and Medici. Many of the officers were offered rank in the national army ; in short, the principle of volunteer service was maintained. Nevertheless, the southern army, such as it had existed, existed no longer ; and perhaps the Minister of War may have been guilty of some slight want of judgment in the execution of these delicate matters.

No more was needed to awaken the wrath of Garibaldi, and this was precisely the kind of conflict Cavour was far from seeking ; he was troubled by it, but he accepted it with as little animosity as weakness. It was felt that the quarrel of the previous October was but inefficiently settled, and that it might at any moment kindle again with all its fury, with all its dangers likewise.

v.

It was Garibaldi's misfortune not to content himself with being a man of mark ; he mistook his warlike or revolutionary fancies for a policy, and flattered himself with the belief that nothing would be denied to him.

Stopped in his plans with regard to Rome and Venice, after the annexation of Naples, Garibaldi had carried with him to his island of Caprera a soured and irritated mind, full of an undying resentment against Cavour. He had retired, leaving to his companions an

Y 2

order of the day, in which he appointed to meet them the following spring. In the meantime, from the depth of his retreat, which he had not even left to go to the meeting of parliament at Turin, he was spreading fire and flame. He gave utterance to declamations which were a signal for disturbance. Had he rested content to be the defender of the southern army and of the volunteers, or had he even agitated for a general arming of the people, he would have been keeping to his part; and his impetuous patriotism, although it might have been thought imprudent, would only have met with sympathy; but he would not rest content with that. With the intemperateness of the soldier and popular idol he attacked everything, abusing the Government and all who upheld it. He pointed to the Moderates and Liberals, to those parliamentary members who recognised in Cavour their first representative and their guide, as being all but conspirators in treason. To a deputation of Milanese workmen, who presented an address to him at Caprera, he said, among other things: "For the holy redemption of this land, I rely on the rough hands of men of my stamp, rather than on the *lying promises of false politicians.* Notwithstanding the sad effects of *a vassal policy unworthy of the country, and notwithstanding all that the crowd of lackeys upholding this monstrous and anti-national policy may say,* Italy must stand: she must live. . . . ." Shortly afterwards, in accepting the presidency of the Association of Italian Unity, he used the same violent expressions, arousing the same excitement. He recommended to his fellow-countrymen to fortify themselves against "that cowardly fear which those seek to inspire who have dragged Italian honour in the dust."

It was with such declamations as these that the Cincinnatus of Caprera called for a general arming! He strangely outstepped the limits of his popularity, and of his prestige as conqueror of the Two Sicilies. He did not see that he was subjecting Italian unity, only just created, to a still greater risk than any that it had yet known; that with one blow he struck king, army, and the parliament of which he was himself a member; and that if a man, whoever he might be, could speak thus, nothing was left but the dictatorship of an ungoverned will and an implacable resentment. Garibaldi certainly had not calculated the effect of these intemperate and dangerous words, which, no doubt, stirred up the passions of the country, and might find an echo in the South, but reverberated in a very different manner at Turin and in the Chambers, where they excited the liveliest susceptibilities. Not only was the Government offended, but the deputies expressed a firm resolution not to allow such an outrage to pass unnoticed; and thus this singular conflict began to assume serious proportions. It was loudly said that it was time to have done with it; and that even for the honour of liberal institutions parliament was bound to set a watch over its dignity, though it should strike the popular hero, and show him that he could not have impunity in abuse.

But who was to take the initiative? If the Government, it would seem too official; besides, the President of the Council would not appear to accept offensive words which were, more than at any other, aimed at him; if a deputy, notorious for particular views, or obscure, the parliamentary demonstration might be led astray or fail of its object. There happened to be a man in parliament exactly fitted for the part, <u>Baron Bettino Ricasoli</u>. By his energetic and decisive activity in the events which had brought about the unity, by his relations with Garibaldi during the interregnum in Central Italy, and by his independence both of station and character, he fulfilled all the required conditions, and he was fashioned to measure himself with any one.

The former dictator of Florence had just arrived at Turin; and on his first appearance in the Chamber, his proud and grave aspect, the natural dignity and severity of his manner and person, made a strong impression. His presence inspired a mixture of curiosity and respect. Like many others, the Florentine baron had been wounded by Garibaldi's violent language. He spontaneously undertook to meet the defiant attack, and protest on behalf of institutions; and in Ricasoli a parliamentary manifestation necessarily assumed the most serious character. He proposed to ask the Government for explanations on the measures it had taken, or was about to take, with regard to the southern army, and the development of the military forces of the nation. But, previous to this, he had another account to settle: he wished to put an end to the anxieties for some days past troubling every mind; and it was on April 10, in the midst of an excited assembly, that he rose to his feet, all being hushed about him instantly.

He was known as the dictator at Florence; it was

not yet known what sort of a speaker he might be, nor what he was going to say, when with a clear vibrating voice, and an imperious tone, which gathered fire as it went, he uttered the following overwhelming words : " A calumny has been circulated abroad concerning one of the members of the Assembly. Expressions hostile to the majority in parliament have been attributed to General Garibaldi. They cannot have been uttered by him. I know him, and I shook his hand when he was about to take command of the central army : we were then animated by the same sentiments—we were both equally devoted to the king. We both swore that we would do our duty ; I have done mine ! . . . . Who is it, then, that could proudly claim for himself the exclusive privilege of devotion and patriotism, and exalt himself above his fellows ? One head only has the right to be higher than any other among us—that of the king. Before him we must all bend, and any other attitude would be that of a rebel ! . . . . Victor Emmanuel has made our nation. . . . . Italy's liberator being the king, and all Italians having marched to liberty under the command of a chief so magnanimous, one citizen is not above another. He who has had the good fortune to do his duty more generously, in a wider sphere of action, or in a manner more profitable to his country, and who has perfectly fulfilled it, a greater duty still lies before him, and it is to thank God for allowing him the inestimable privilege, which is granted to so few, of being able to say : ' I have served my country well, I have absolutely done my duty ! ' "

These words, emphasised by his bearing and a

vibrating delivery, as it were with the inflexible judgment of conscience and patriotism, shot a thrill through the whole of the Assembly, which burst forth in acclamations. . Cavour had never heard his austere Florentine ally and rival speak, and had not always found it easy to deal with him in the affairs of Central Italy, and he had listened rather curiously at first; but he soon began to share the universal excitement, and in leaving the House, he said to a friend: "To-day I have understood and felt the nature of true eloquence." Others have declared that he said: "Were I to die to-morrow my successor is found!" In any case, royalty, parliament, institutions, and the dignity of an entire policy, had just received satisfaction by this harangue, replete with a noble severity, which singularly changed the parts, and transformed Garibaldi into one accused, and put him at the bar before his judges.

Garibaldi, under pain of being considered a rebel— and notwithstanding the violence of his language he was not one—evidently could not decline the challenge. On first arriving at Turin, and as though he had felt the importance of Baron Ricasoli's words, he hastened to publish a letter, wherein he disavowed—and not without some spirit of dignity—all intention of censure either towards the king or the national representatives; this, however, was but a beginning.

VI.

Shortly after came the decisive collision in parliament, now unavoidable, for which rendezvous had been given, and the presence of Garibaldi made it dramatic. For the last week Turin had filled with volunteers, hurrying thither to escort and support their leader. The sturdy Piedmontese city, faithful to its king, looked upon this uproar with no favourable eye; it had little enthusiasm for the conqueror of Naples ; it saw with no little impatience and apprehension a conflict in which its firmness would have to be the mainstay of the Government.

On the day fixed—the 18th of April—the sitting was opened with a particular solemnity. The diplomatic corps had wished to be present at it; the tribunes bent under the weight of an excited crowd. A few moments elapsed, and then Garibaldi appeared in his singular costume—the legendary red shirt and South American poncho. As he entered, the galleries burst forth in shouts of welcome, but the Chamber remained immovable and cold. When the first moment was over, Baron Ricasoli, taking up the thread of his former subject, questioned the Government as to the southern army and the military reorganisation of the nation.

The Minister of War, General Fanti, replied in his turn in a detailed statement of the measures he had adopted, and had found necessary. Without either weakness or diplomacy, he did his best to prove that he had done all he could do for the volunteers and the Garibaldian officers—for an institution born of the circumstances of the time—without running the risk of introducing into the regular army a disastrous spirit of rivalry, or wounding military feelings and interests. It was the speech of a minister defending his acts on good grounds. Garibaldi then rose, and the scene became animated.

At first Garibaldi felt a little strange on this new stage; he entangled himself in laborious phrases embarrassing to his friends; but speedily setting circumlocution aside, he went straight to the point in question, and to the antagonism of which he had been accused by Baron Ricasoli—to the personal question in short—he replied: "I have not given any occasion for *dualism.* It is true that plans of reconciliation have been proposed to me; but these have only been in words. Italy knows me to be a man of deeds, and deeds have always been in opposition to words. . . . . Whenever *dualism* could have damaged the cause of my country I have bowed, and shall always bow. . . . . But I leave it to the conscience of the Italian representatives here present to state whether I can give my hand to one who has made me a stranger in Italy!"

The agitation was beginning to manifest itself in loud interruptions, when Garibaldi, returning to the subject of the southern army, which he stated was "the principal object of his presence in the Chamber," added, with growing excitement: "Having to speak of this army, I should above all relate its glorious deeds. The wonders it achieved have been darkened only when the cold and inimical hand of the Ministry has made its evil influence felt. When, through love of peace and horror of a fratricidal war, provoked by that same Ministry. . . . ." At these words, before the sentence was complete, the tempest burst out, and protestations were shouted on every side; the real struggle had come at last ! Cavour, full of indignation, scarcely able to keep seated among the ministers, called upon the President of the Chamber, saying : " Such insults as these are not permitted ; we cannot suffer them ; see that proper respect is paid to the Government and representatives of the nation. We demand a call to order !" Rattazzi, the President, sadly perplexed, and almost extinguished in this storm, could think of no better way than to request Garibaldi to clothe his opinions in a less gene-- rally offensive form. Cavour exclaimed : " He has said that we provoked a fratricidal war ; this is far more than an expression of an opinion." " Yes, a fratricidal war !" replied Garibaldi with vehemence. An extraordinary agitation convulsed the assembly. Loud shouts on the part of the deputies for a call to order, mixed with frantic. applause from the galleries crowded with Garibaldians ; abusive challenges, and violent invectives crossed each other in rapid succession, causing an indescribable confusion. The President was reduced to break up the sitting.

This scene in reality, by awakening the irritation of the majority in the Chamber, had confounded the most sincere among Garibaldi's friends, and when, after some minutes the debate was resumed, one among them, Nino Bixio—himself one of the band of heroes of Sicily and the Volturno—made himself the spokesman of the general sentiment of affliction. Bixio endeavoured to palliate the violent language of his ancient chief by invoking a patriotic return to reconciliation. " Count Cavour," he hastened to say, " has undoubtedly a generous heart. The earlier part of this day's session should be forgotten. It is a misfortune that it has happened : let us banish it from our minds. . . . . ."

In spite of the wound he had received, and the emotion he had been unable to repress, Cavour controlled himself sufficiently to reply to Bixio's request that the insult should be overlooked, and to enter into an explanation. "It is not," he replied immediately, "that I flatter myself with the hope of seeing the friendly feeling spring up again, which the honourable member Bixio has just entreated us to entertain. I know there is one deed which has put a gulf between General Garibaldi and me. I thought to accomplish a painful duty—the most painful I have ever known—in urging upon the king and parliament the approval of the cession of Nice and Savoy to France. Through the pain it caused me, I can realise that which General Garibaldi must now feel on the subject, and if he is unable to forgive me for that deed, I cannot hold it to be a reproach to him. . . . . ."

Garibaldi in his turn became more calm, expressing a desire that, according to him, would tend to moderate their dissensions ; he said : "Although my sentiments towards Count Cavour are those of an adversary, I have never doubted that he also is the friend of Italy. My wish would be that the honourable Count should make use of his powerful influence to cause the law which I propose for the national armament to be adopted ; namely, to despatch the forces remaining of the southern army to a point wherein they might serve Italy, by combating a reaction daily growing more threatening : this is my desire !" It was always this question of the volunteers and the southern army, which reappeared in the shape of a desire, after showing itself under the form of an injunction.

Cavour was ready to do all he could to relax a situation of extreme tension, promote reconciliation, and strive to bring Garibaldi to reason. Quick to recover his coolness, after the first moment of just indignation, he was not long in reflecting that all these rashly kindled conflicts descending from parliament to the country, might become civil war, to the destruction of the dawning unity; therefore no effort was too strong for him, no sacrifice too great—neither the forgetting of personal injuries, nor concessions in particulars. There was but one thing—the essential one, it is true—that he positively refused, because in it he saw another danger, the external danger. He would at no price, in appearing to submit to Garibaldi's desire, accept a sort of active organisation of volunteers, which would have the appearance of preparation for an offensive war, and might ruin all his labour of diplomacy, of which he alone had the secret. "We will not," he said resolutely, "have an active volunteer corps, in the positive acceptation of the word. We decline to do what would be a real provocation, because we do not think ourselves bound to follow a provocative policy."

This was the question at issue, and for the space of three days he fought with consummate skill, not exactly in order to win over a Chamber already convinced and devoted to his schemes, but to prevent an equivocal state of things from sliding, under pretext of conciliation, into a not carefully weighed vote. He wished, since they were in for the struggle, that the result of it should be clear and decisive.

"You know the policy of the Ministry," he said, rising high above the sense of a personal conflict. " We have proclaimed it before the country, as well as to the whole of Europe. . . . . More than once we have repeated, in various ways, that, in our opinion, the Italian question will remain unsettled as long as the independence of the peninsula is not thoroughly established ; as long as the important questions of Rome and Venice have not been satisfactorily arranged ; but at the same time we have declared that the Roman question should be settled peaceably, without hostility or discord with France. We do not look upon the French troops at Rome as enemies. In the same way with regard to Venice, we have stated moderately and firmly that the present state of Venetia is incompatible with a durable peace ; we have also avowed that, in the present state of Europe, we should not have the right to kindle a general war. In other terms, we have declared that, with regard to Rome, our policy relies entirely on an alliance with France ; and that, in the case of Venice, we must take European interests into consideration, and the counsels of friendly Governments and Powers which at critical times have lent us willing and efficient help. Such is our policy. No doubt there is another. Declaration may be made that Italy is in a state of war, tempered by a kind of tacit truce, a truce at Rome and a truce at Venice ; and that, as a natural result of this condition of things, it is not only desirable, but also indispensable, that we should take measures necessary for an immediate war. These are the two alternatives in juxtaposition. We frankly tell you that the first policy is the only one suited to the nation. . . . . The other is practicable too ; it is a very dangerous one, fraught with difficulties, obstacles, and snares, but it may be adopted. That which, however, would be fatal, and which would lead to inevitable ruin, would be to adopt one policy one day and another the next, and neglecting to follow before the eyes of the country, and still more before those of Europe, a definite, frank, and honest line. England would more easily overlook a piece of folly than she would forgive us for misleading her." It was under the influence of these words that the vote for an order of the day, proposed by Baron Ricasoli, and accepted by the Government, put an end to the conflict.

That which had begun in a wild tumult and uproar, and might have turned to a dangerous crisis, finished quietly enough ; the drama had an epilogue, due to the diplomacy of the king, who used all his influence to bring about, if not a personal reconciliation—a task of some difficulty—at least a meeting between the President of the Council and Garibaldi in one of the private apartments of the Palace. A few days later, on April 27, Cavour wrote as follows to Count Vimercati at Paris : " My interview with Garibaldi was courteous though not warm ; we both kept within the limits of reserve. I acquainted him, however, with the line of conduct which the Government intends to follow, as regards Austria as well as France, assuring him that, on those points, no compromise is possible. He declared his readiness to accept the programme and to be willing to engage himself not to act contrary to the views of Government. He only asked me to do something for the army of the South. I gave him no promise ; but I told him I would seek a means to provide, as well as might be done, for the future of his officers. We parted, if not good friends, at least without any irritation."

Once more Garibaldi disappeared to return to his Mediterranean island, and out of an ordeal that for a moment seemed to be so full of danger Cavour's policy emerged more than ever whole and free, sanctioned by the vote of parliament, and by the defeat and eclipse of his terrible adversary.

VII.

At the time when Cavour was winning his last and decisive victory of reason and foresight over the disorderly instincts of an empty-headed popular hero, he was still in full vigour. He had even appeared with a sort of new brilliancy, as though in the fulness of a generous maturity.

The greater and more complicated the work, the more inexhaustible seemed to be his resources of vigour and activity. He needed his robust constitution and strength of mind to suffice to all this. At one and the same moment he was engaged in establishing the relations of Italy with Sweden, Denmark, and Portugal ; he was in the heat of negotiations with the Emperor of the French on the subject of Rome ; he was minutely observing the troubled affairs of Naples ; he was regulating the finances, and attending to the navy of the new kingdom ; and every day he was in parliament, taking his part in every discussion. No doubt he was not called upon to struggle for a majority—that was not wanting to him; but he had to direct it, to guard its inexperience from surprises and imprudent measures which he alone could counteract.

In reality it was a trying life, enough to break the strongest constitution. The contest with Garibaldi especially had given Cavour a heavy blow. The effort he had made to master himself in the thick of the storm, and the constraint he had put on himself, told seriously upon him. Excess of work of every kind could hardly be other than murderous to his health. On May 29 he was still in parliament animatedly discussing a project that was to be turned into a sort of manifestation in favour of the republicans fighting at Rome in 1849, and on that day, still more than on preceding ones, he exhibited a certain over-excitement and an impatience under contradiction causing some surprise. That evening, on returning home, he seemed weary and gloomy: " I am exhausted," said he, " but I must go on working, for the country needs me; perhaps this summer I may be able to take some rest in Switzerland. . . . .". That same night he was seized with violent indisposition; the athlete was already beaten !

His illness indeed began to show grave symptoms. For a moment it seemed to be conquered by early care and bleeding—the habitual remedy at Turin—and even Cavour thought himself all right. On May 31 he was again able to assemble about him his colleagues of the Ministry. He worked with Nigra and Artom; but this was only the illusion of a man fretting himself with the idea that he had not time to be ill. From June 1 the remedies ceased to take effect, and all hope was vanishing hourly. Cavour fell into the last struggle between life and death for some days, passing from fits of delirium to lucid moments, during which all that had been occupying him came to his mind. With his niece, the Marchioness Alfieri, always attentive at his pillow, and with his friends Farini and Castelli, he spoke of all he had yet to do : of the loan of 500 millions which was impending, of the recognition of the kingdom of Italy by France, a letter expected from Count Vimercati in Paris, and of the navy it was necessary to create. He was anxious about Naples, and spoke of it urgently.

"Northern Italy is established," he said. "There are no longer Lombards nor Piedmontese, Tuscans nor Romans. We are all Italians ; but there are still Neapolitans. Oh ! there is much corruption in their country. Poor people ! it is not their fault, they have been so ill-governed ! . . . . We must impress the country morally, but it is not by abusing the Neapolitans that they will be brought to reason. . . . . Above all, there must be no state of siege, none of the measures of absolutist Governments. Anyone can govern with a state of siege. I will govern them with liberty, and I will show what ten years of liberty can do for these fine countries. Twenty years hence they will be the richest provinces in Italy. No, have no state of siege ; that is my advice to you. . . . ." Victor Emmanuel wished to visit his illustrious minister, and Cavour, recognising the king, exclaimed : "Oh ! your majesty, I have many things to communicate to you, many papers to lay before you; but I am too ill, it will be impossible for me to come and see you, but I will send you Farini to-morrow, he will give you all particulars. Has your majesty received no letter from Paris? The Emperor is friendly to us now. . . . ." Sometimes Cavour complained of confusion in his brain, imagining that his illness lay there: he felt that the power of thinking was fast leaving him.

To the end, however, he remained what he had been —what he wished to be. He requested that the priest of the Madonna dei Angeli, the Fra Giacomo, with whom he had seven years previously made every arrangement, should be in readiness to come to him; and accordingly, at the summons of the Marchioness Alfieri, Fra Giacomo hastened to the deathbed of the great man. Cavour spent half an hour alone with the priest; and when the latter left him, he called for Farini and said to him: "My niece has summoned Fra Giacomo; I must prepare for the great passage into eternity; I have confessed and been absolved. I desire that it be known—that the good people of Turin should know—that I died the death of a good Christian. I am without anxiety; I know that I have injured no man." That same day, the "good people of Turin," who were anxiously watching the course of the illness, tearfully followed the priest carrying the viaticum to the most illustrious citizen of the Piedmontese capital. The worthy priest himself, it is said, comforted a relative of the Count by reminding her that "no man in this world had known better how to succour and pardon than that one." Among the last words uttered by Cavour to Fra

Giacomo, who was reciting at his bedside the prayer for the dying, were these : *"Frate, frate,"* he said, in pressing the priest's hand, *"libera chiesa in libero stato !"* It was almost in pronouncing these words that, at a quarter before seven o'clock on the morning of June 6, 1861, Count Camillo Cavour rendered to his God one of the noblest souls that ever animated a mortal being.

He seemed to have been struck down in the heat of action, as on a field of battle, on the morning after a victory that he owed to the moderation as well as the greatness of his intelligence. Massari states that : " He who did not see Turin that day, knows not what is meant by the grief of a people." The town was filled with mourning. The tribunes of the Chambers and the standard on the palace were veiled with crape. The whole of Italy responded to the feeling in Turin. The startling rapidity of the catastrophe, as well as the immense void left by the sudden disappearance of one particular man, spread consternation everywhere, and the news of this death resounded over Europe as well as in Italy.

Friends and enemies alike felt that the world had to sustain the loss of one of its forces and one of its great lights. In the English House of Commons, Palmerston, following Brougham in the Lords, and Milnes, said : " The name of Count Cavour will live for ever, embalmed as it were with gratitude and admiration in the memory of the human race. And when I speak of Count Cavour I do not mean simply to praise him for those administrative acts which have most astonished the world, that is to say, for the unity of his country.

He has done many other things that make him no less
great. The foundation of the constitutional Government
in which Italy now rejoices was laid by him ; it is he
who managed all the affairs of the peninsula, and secured
inestimable benefits to those who are living, and to all
who will live after us. Of Count Cavour it may truly
be said that he taught a moral, and ornamented a
history. The moral is this : that a man of eminent
genius and indomitable energy, as well as of inex-
tinguishable patriotism, thanks to the impulse he knew
how to give to his fellow-citizens, may by devoting
himself to a just cause, seizing favourable opportunities,
overcoming difficulties which seemed insurmountable—
I say that such a man may endow his country with inestimable advantages. The history he ornaments is an
amazing one ; the most romantic in the annals of the
world. Under his influence and his directing authority
we have seen a people awakened from a sleep of centuries. . . . . These are events which history will
record, and he whose name will pass on with them
to posterity, however premature his end, will not have
died too soon for his glory and his renown. . . . ."

Thus they spoke of Cavour in London. France, for
her part, felt an emotion deep as it was sincere, and
Cavour's sudden end had, as a first result, the hastening,
in one degree at least, of the negotiations which had
secretly been carried on for two months past by the
great minister with Paris ; it caused an immediate
recognition of the new kingdom of Italy by the French
Government, and thus, even in death, Cavour triumphed
in doing one more service to his country.

Many a time, especially at first, and even since June 5, 1861, when the creator of a new Italy suddenly disappeared, a singular question has been raised: it has been suggested that perhaps Fortune favoured Cavour to the end in causing him to die before experiencing possible deceptions. Up to that time he had been successful; everything, it is urged, had turned out well with him; he might have failed in the work he had in hand, and which he had not as yet completed; and D'Azeglio himself, who confessed to having been "stunned by the death of poor Cavour," whom "he mourned for as a brother," even D'Azeglio said, three days after: "For him it may be well; to disappear without having fallen is not given to everyone. For us it is a terrible trial; but if it be the will of God to save Italy, will he be at a loss to do so without Cavour?" This, of course, was only a touching sentiment, or else the wild impression of a shaken imagination. If Cavour did not die too soon for his glory, according to Lord Palmerston, a prolonged career would not have exposed him to a "fall," as D'Azeglio seemed to fear; he was not of those who have to rely on the mysterious poetry of a premature and opportune end, in order to leave a famous reputation behind.

No, he who for the space of twelve years had passed through every difficulty and every snare, displaying new resources at every step, and acquiring greatness in the fire of strife; bringing his country from the depth of defeat to the summit of fortune even beyond the limit of hope; such an one had no cause to dread to live on or to shrink from a few more trials before reaching the point distinguishable to him. Had he been capable of falling he would not have been himself. He would have finished what he had begun, and he was in full working order. He would have continued his negotiations and his combinations, more and more uniting Italy, who had confidence in his directing power, and daily winning for her the interest of Europe, already accustomed to his clear and inventive diplomacy. If more struggles had been in store for him he would have sustained them with a growing authority. Never had he shown more activity or more security than when disease came and crushed him in the midst of his unfinished task; and I do not know on what was founded the statement so often repeated after D'Azeglio, that Cavour had disappeared "just in time for his glory."

There is no doubt that his death was a dangerous crisis, a "terrible trial" for Italy; but that which in the first moment of excitement was hardly discernible, and which has given a fresh testimony to Cavour's greatness, is, that although he was prematurely snatched away, he had done enough for his work to survive him. Had he lived, he would have continued to be the most powerful athlete of the new kingdom he had founded; and dying, he left it, as an inheritance—together with the unity almost complete—his idea, his traditions, his whole policy, one which had been the instrument of his schemes, the secret of his success, and which, after him, remained the guarantee and strength of new Italy—the inspiration of the liberal *élite* who continued his work.

Let there be no misunderstanding about it. It is with this idea, and these traditions, it is by following Cavour's directions, often by adopting his plans and realising his schemes, that Italy has managed to exist and to consolidate and complete herself during the past fifteen years; and so true is this that a strange phenomenon of a significant eloquence may be observed: whenever difficulties have presented themselves, or questions arisen which Cavour had not in some degree at least prepared the answer for, or enlightened with the luminous rays of his reason, perplexity has been the consequence; and this the honest minds which, for fifteen years, have had to conduct the affairs of the peninsula at the most critical times, do not conceal; they never felt more reliance in themselves than when able still to follow out the designs of that guide in great struggles. Each time that a deviation from the path he had traced has been made, doubt, disquietude, and threatened crises have resulted. A living testimony to the influence of a great brain.

VIII.

Italy a nation is the legacy of Cavour. The fruit of a policy starting from an idea of independence and patriotism, and embracing internal order, economical interests, religious affairs, and diplomacy, developing and enlarging itself daily, by the help of the most astonishing mixture of dexterity and daring, justice and high-mindedness, practical good sense and unbaffled energy in contrivance.

Others in good numbers, no doubt, before him and about him, have been devoted to the cause of national liberation. Cavour outstepped them from the moment that he was able to make use of that idea seriously ; he knew how to bring it into the sphere of possibilities, that might be realised ; he made it pure of any factious spirit, led it away from barren Utopias, kept it clear of reckless conspiracies, steered straight between revolution and reaction, and gave it an organised force, a flag, a government, and foreign allies. This difficult task, laborious as we have seen, he pursued by a process as simple as it was grand ; for it was in the large understanding of liberty practised in all its forms. He had the passion and the science of liberty, for which he felt himself shaped ; and none more than he has repudiated anarchical agitations and dark plottings on the one hand, and dictatorships, arbitrary combinations, and the convenient measures of a state of siege, on the other. As parliamentary leader of a small country, devoted, temperate, and firm, he knew how to make this Piedmontese land a centre of attraction for Italy ; as minister to the King of Sardinia, he worked for the moral ascendency of the House of Savoy, before he put his hand to its material aggrandisement.

He was at heart a Liberal Conservative, a Constitutional Monarchist, in the broadest interpretation of the word. He often repeated that : " No republic is able to grant so true and fruitful an amount of liberty as that which a constitutional monarchy affords, provided it be on a solid basis. The form of republic best adapted to the customs and needs of modern Europe has still to be discovered. It presupposes, in any case, the accomplishment already of that great task of popular education which will be the work of our century." Cavour was in favour of constitutional monarchy, as being the necessary regulator of consecutive and effectual action, in the whirlwind of parties; but he held the interests of royalty to be inseparable from those of the nation; he believed that " far from languidly following the thoughts and necessities of the people, it should, on the contrary, take the initiative with regard to generous and practicable measures, that it might be able to make head with a capable authority against popular passions, when dangerous impulses misled the mob."

His ideal, which a patriotic dynasty helped him to realise, was that the Government should be a guide and an ever active adviser; and it was thus that he worked out his problem. He used liberty as a means of extension and conquest, on behalf of monarchy, at the same time that he converted monarchy into the regulating force of a victorious revolution, and made it the guarantee of unity. He so fully identified the two causes that, on the day when the House of Savoy became, almost without an effort, the Italian House, the Republicans, altering a famous saying, have been able to say, subsequently: " It is Royalty that causes the least division among us." There is the originality, the novelty of the policy of Cavour: he has bequeathed a monarchy to Italy, which cannot be touched without endangering national existence itself.

One of the most characteristic manifestations of the Liberalism of Cavour was undoubtedly that part of his policy touching religious matters, which never ceased to develop itself through every event, until it was summarised in the prophetic words he uttered with his last breath :

" *Libera chiesa in libero stato.*" He had encountered
these formidable and delicate questions at the outset of
his career, even before he became minister, in the narrow
circle of Piedmontese affairs ; he had seen them grow and
become more complicated in proportion as the Italian
movement broadened, to the extent of questioning, at
Rome, the Temporal Power of the Pope ; these were a
part of the elements of the national problem. He could
not avoid them. Nothing, however, less resembles
despotic or revolutionary traditions, than the bold and
independent mind with which he broached these
religious difficulties. Without doubt he had a grand
aim in view, and he never lost sight of it—it was the
complete emancipation of national and civil society ; he
consented neither to inflict persecutions nor to impose
shackles, nor indeed to run counter to opinion or national
habits and customs. He was especially careful to avoid
rough dealings, and angry provocations, and intemperate
language in discussions, and in deeds from which he did
not shrink.

To his essentially politic nature, the passionate contests were repugnant in which religious excitement might
tend to weaken the national cause. His faith as a
reformer made him indifferent to what he considered
useless precautions with regard to the Church regula-
tions and the interference of the State in sacerdotal
matters ; he did not even claim the right to a very
close supervision of ecclesiastical teaching. He did not
behave as an enemy to the Church. He intended to
make the abolition of the Temporal Power a means of
freedom for the spiritual power of the Pope. In exchange

for the complete liberty he claimed for the State, he was ready to grant every liberty; and if it was observed to him that perhaps it could not be done without risk, and that in certain provinces it was necessary that civil authority should hold a firm hand over a fanatical, hostile, or rebellious clergy, he did not allow himself to be deterred by such reasons as these; he never doubted the beneficent effects of a liberal system.

He wished to ennoble the revival of Italy by some memorable act, and to Signor Artom, who expressed his doubts to him, he replied, with a certain enthusiasm: " To us belongs the privilege of putting an end to the great combat now going on between the Church and civilisation. . . . . Whatever you may say, I have a good hope of gradually bringing the more enlightened of the clergy, the good Catholics, to accept this view. May be I shall be able to sign, from the top of the Capitol, another religious peace, a treaty which will have consequences much more important to the future of human societies than the peace of Westphalia!"

In this confident and generous intrepidity lay the strength of Cavour. Two things were in his favour: there was this liberal conception, which has clung to the Italian revival; and until the realisation of this fair dream —if it was ever to be other than a dream—there was at least the option of living on quietly, preparing the means for the end. Cavour's practical mind neglected nothing; even up to the moment of his death he had made every combination, leaving the solution ready for his successors. The settlement he was negotiating at Paris, which was awaiting the signature delayed only by his death, became

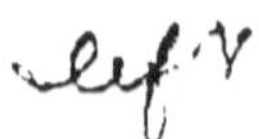

the convention of September 15, 1864 ! The object of
the secret negotiation with the Pope and Cardinal
Antonelli, early in 1861, shaped itself later into the law
of guarantees ! All was linked together in that policy,
to which perhaps Italy owed the fortune of entering
Rome without breaking up the religious world ; and
assuredly she will not find her advantage in straying
from it.

IX.

What finally I wish to point out is the idea of
Cavour in that labour of diplomacy which, from the first
day of his entrance into the Ministry, was one of the
most essential features of his policy. The force of the
national sentiment, that liberal propaganda of Piedmont
and of the constitutional government, created Italy. Be
it so : but in reality it became possible only through the
most far-sighted and watchful diplomacy, pursuing its
task now with commercial treaties, now with a military
alliance and co-operation in the Crimean war, now with
the interview at Plombières, and the many combinations
preceding or following the arrival of French troops at
the decisive moment. If in his impetuosity and the
nature of some of his acts Cavour sometimes resembled
a revolutionist, every art of a negotiator was known
to him. He had not the futile infatuation to believe
that Europe was made for Italy ; on the contrary,
he held that Italy should adapt herself to Europe ;
he knew how to estimate European interests, and
measure circumstances ; and with his indefatigable
activity in acquiring alliances, retaining them, or

adding to their number, his whole ability consisted in constantly indicating that the liberation of a people, for which he was indefatigably working, was the best guarantee of peace. The revolutionist became a Conservative in order to reassure or win over Cabinets, while proving to them, if necessary, that in the most audacious of his resolves, and in the accomplishment of Italian unity, he was still the defender of order. In playing this part he had the immense advantage of leaning on one of the oldest monarchies of Europe, long since admitted into the circle of recognised Powers. He had his place in the Courts of Europe, his credit among Governments, and the new force he represented to prompt his dealings with the various policies.

Fronting Europe, whose friendliness he had to win, or to disarm her suspicions, Cavour was perfectly free from any prepossessions of mind; and as events developed he left no stone unturned to extend his diplomacy. He had especially, at an early date, turned his attention to Germany and Prussia. He was anxious to reassure Germany and Prussia, and take away from them every pretext for joining arms with Austria on the Adige. It was to his mind a necessity of the hour as well as of the future : he was unremittingly busied with it.

" Prussia," he said, "is one of the Powers having a direct and immediate interest in changing the actual state of Europe. Prussia cannot have forgotten Olmutz; she cannot look malevolently on the efforts we are making to bring down her fortunate rival. We do not ask her to draw the sword for our good pleasure, but I think when Austria is weakened Prussia will find the benefit. She would therefore be committing a grave error should she espouse the cause of Austria against us. We do not ask the Cabinet of Berlin to help us in the struggle, we only claim to be let alone." On another occasion, after a fresh attempt to get hold of Prussia, he said : " What cannot be done now, shall be done later on. Prussia must inevitably be carried away with the current of a national idea. The alliance of Prussia with an enlarged Piedmont is written in the book of the history of the future." Cavour was clear-sighted, and in this respect, as in many others, he opened a way for those who came after him ; but at bottom, great as was the importance he attached to bringing about future relations with Germany and Prussia, his intelligence and instinct were all with the two great Western Powers—France and England.

It was through them that he had been able to take part in the affairs of the world in the glorious days of the Crimean war. The aid of French arms had enabled him to engage in the struggle against Austria. His dream was ever the intimate relations of Italy with the two Powers in his eyes representing the greatest forces of civilisation.

Gratitude towards France was no burden to him ; he was glad to express it, as a man who stood naturally above the perfidies and puerilities of party spirit, who knew how to remain an ally ; independent, doubtless, but an ally.

If sometimes he was not insensible to the animosities levelled against him in a certain Parisian circle, his more sober judgment, and I venture to say his sentiments, were not affected by them. He took his revenge without bitterness. " I have no desire to speak ill of French society; I am too greatly indebted to it. I resign myself to the fact of the regeneration of Italy, in spite of the salons of Paris." Cavour loved our nation, which he only reproached on the score of so little knowing how to use or to retain liberty. He made the French alliance an important basis of his policy, a permanent condition for both countries; and what may most assuredly be said is, that if he had lived he would, by his counsels perhaps, and a daily increasing influence, have succeeded in giving a different direction to events that have resulted in a disaster for France.

In this passage of an age in which so many things vanish, and so many others are doubtful, the last Empire, it has been said, has produced two great novelties and two great ministers: unity in Italy and unity in Germany; Count Cavour and Prince Bismarck. I will attempt no comparison where there would be more contrasts than analogies. Prince Bismarck is still living, and the future belongs to us all. It is now fifteen years since Cavour disappeared from the scene, and for his part he has had the good fortune to realise the freedom of his country through liberty; he did not make his great work a menace to Europe. And in this reconstruction of a people, which is now the triumph of his policy, and the legacy of a cordial and powerful genius, he did not deem it necessary to mutilate another nation.